UNLEASH
LONDON VAMPIRES BOOK 6

FELICITY HEATON

Copyright © 2013 Felicity Heaton

All rights reserved. No part of this publication may be reproduced, stored in a retrieval system, or transmitted, in any form or by any means mechanical, electronic, photocopying, recording or otherwise without the prior written consent of the publisher, nor be otherwise circulated in any form of binding or cover other than that in which it is published and without a similar condition being imposed on the subsequent purchaser.

The right of Felicity Heaton to be identified as the Author of the Work has been asserted by her in accordance with the Copyright, Designs and Patents Act 1988.

First printed August 2019

Second Edition

Layout and design by Felicity Heaton

All characters in this publication are purely fictitious and any resemblance to real persons, living or dead, is purely coincidental.

THE LONDON VAMPIRES SERIES

Book 1: Covet

Book 2: Crave

Book 3: Seduce

Book 4: Enslave

Book 5: Bewitch

Book 6: Unleash

**Discover more available paranormal romance books at:
http://www.felicityheaton.com**

Or sign up to my mailing list to receive a FREE vampire romance ebook, learn about new titles, be eligible for special subscriber-only giveaways, and read exclusive content including short stories:
http://ml.felicityheaton.com/mailinglist

CHAPTER 1

"Snow."

The gentle feminine voice curled around him, warming him in spite of the frigid cold that bit at his fingers and nose. A sense of joy spread through him as he tried to run through the deep snow, his small legs and arms pumping hard, his focus locked with determination on his prey.

The owl's wings were bright even though no moon shone tonight. The crisp white blanket spread across the landscape highlighted everything as though his night vision was already as acute as it would be when he matured.

"Snow." The voice called to him again, tender with affection and laced with amusement, but also a note of concern.

Mama.

Snow ran harder, giggling and arms reaching, stretching towards the bird in flight above him. Colours danced across the inky starlit sky beyond, ribbons fluttering on an unknown breeze in the heavens. He had never seen anything as beautiful as this night.

The snow began to shallow, the incline leading him deep into the valley basin. Mountains rose around him, pure white ragged canvases that reflected the luminescent turquoise, pink and blue shimmering above them.

Breathing hard, he slowed to a walk and scanned his surroundings, searching for the owl. His hearing sharpened and he caught the quiet flutter of wings and the whisper of a branch shifting as the owl landed in a nearby copse.

His mother's voice was distant as she called to him. He knew he should return now before he made her frantic again, but he wanted to capture the owl and show his papa that he had grown since last winter and was able to hunt now. Papa would be proud if he killed the owl.

Snow hunkered low, his pale furs and white hair allowing him to blend into his stark environment. He stalked towards the trees, his eyes fixed on the owl, keeping as close to the ground as he could and moving silently through the icy snow that reached his knees.

Mama called again.

He stilled and slowly looked back over his shoulder, following the trail of his footprints through the snow, torn between returning to her and continuing.

"Snow!" The usual softness in her voice was gone, replaced by fear.

Snow stood swiftly and frowned.

His hands were warm.

Wet.

He looked down at them and stumbled backwards, eyes wide and heart thumping wildly. Blood.

His gaze darted from his drenched arms to the snow around him. Blood slashed across the snow too, stark crimson against pristine white.

Snow panicked and bolted for the trail that would take him back to his mother, his heart thundering hard against his chest and limbs shaking so badly he could barely keep himself from falling to the ground.

"Snow." His mother's voice was frantic now, terrified.

Mama.

Hot tears burned his eyes and he ran harder. His foot snagged on a tree limb hidden beneath the snow and he slammed into the cold embrace of the earth. His arms shook as he pushed himself up and his heart missed several beats when he saw that the landscape around him had changed.

The mountains were different.

He looked back over his shoulder. The moon was full and a lake nestled amongst the mountains, glittering under its silvery light.

His mother called again and he found the strength to shove to his feet and run, faster this time, using all of his speed and his limited senses to scour the strange land for her.

A beautiful chateau loomed ahead, warm golden light glowing in several of the windows of the grand stone building. Conical towers speared the dark sky in places, the deep brown tiles obscured by snow, giving the place a gothic appearance suited to this nightmare unfolding before him.

A bloody trail led towards it, cutting across the white landscape, black in the moonlight.

Snow followed the wretched trail, knowing it would lead him to his mother, fearful that he was already too late to save her.

The steps became easier as he sprinted, his legs longer now, his body more powerful and senses more acute.

He vaulted a wooden fence with ease and shoved through the pine trees on the other side. The thin branches whipped at him, scratching his muscular arms through his loose white shirt and his face, snagging in his overlong white hair, but he refused to slow down. His mother needed him.

Snow broke through the trees and skidded to a halt on the icy ground, barely keeping upright. He stared at the dark patch on the wide path just metres ahead of him and steadied himself as his gaze followed it to a low stone wall. Booted feet rested in the blood, splattered with it. Snow's heart lurched as he tracked up the man's black trousers and had his worst fears confirmed.

His father.

Snow rushed forwards and then sharply turned away as the full horror of what had happened struck him.

His father's broken lifeless body bent backwards over the wall, his blood pooling around him, still dripping from the violent gashes across his neck and chest that had sliced clean through his black waistcoat and torn open his pale cravat, and had stained his white shirt crimson.

Snow barely recognised him.

Whatever had done this to him had ripped his flesh to shreds. It was as though a wild animal had savaged him brutally and without mercy. But what beast in this world was strong enough to bring down his father?

Snow bent over and retched, his hands grasping his knees to steady himself, fingertips tugging at the material of his own black trousers. He shook uncontrollably, the stench of his father's blood and the sight of his corpse causing his head to spin. No. It couldn't be. He looked back across at the dead male, unable to bring himself to believe he had seen things right, desperate that he had been mistaken.

Nothing had changed.

How had this happened?

His father was old and powerful, far more so than any vampire in this area. His father was strong.

"Snow!"

Mama.

He pushed off, running at full speed, nothing more than a blur in the night as he raced towards her voice. He spotted her near the mansion, her arms wrapped around her slender body and her dark elegant dress making her stand out in the snow. Her long pale hair was bright in the moonlight but dark in places. Bloodied.

"Mama." Snow crashed through a large rose bed, thorns tearing and grabbing at his clothes, slowing him down.

He reached for her, just as he had reached for the beautiful bird before.

She turned wild pale eyes on him and began shaking her head and backing away from him, heading towards the arched double doors of the stone building. Blood covered her trembling body and saturated her hair.

What had she done?

Snow's stomach rebelled as an image of his father's battered body flashed across his eyes and he ground to a halt before her. She hadn't.

Tears cut down her face, glistening in the moonlight, and she continued to shake her head, a wild look in her eyes. Her breaths came in short gasps and she pressed her bloodstained hands to her chest, clutching it. A sob broke past her pale lips.

Snow moved forwards and reached out to comfort her.

His hands closed around her neck and his thumbs pressed hard against the front of her throat. She choked and he tightened his grip until her windpipe collapsed under the pressure and she could no longer cry out.

Blood covered his arms, streaked across his skin and his white shirt.

His bones ached from the blows he had taken.

His flesh burned from the lacerations. The futile attempts to stop him.

His heart pumped wildly, so fast he couldn't think above the noise and the dizzying rush.

Snow squeezed harder, pressing sharp claws into her flesh, tearing before he realised what he was doing and powerless to stop it from happening. Fresh blood spilled over his fingers and trailed like a morbid waterfall down her shoulders to her chest where it soaked into the boned corset of her dark dress.

Her wide eyes locked with his, no longer showing fear. Pity filled their pale irises, together with affection and acceptance that lashed at him, but still he couldn't control himself, couldn't tame the dark need to maim and destroy, to bloody his hands and drink until the burning thirst receded. He had to feed. He had to kill.

Tears streamed down his cheeks as the flicker of light in her eyes began to fade.

No longer would laughter leave her lips to delight his ears. No longer would she smile at him with pride and love. No longer would her arms hold him close and comfort him. No longer would he hear her voice calling his name.

He tore his hands away from her throat and she slumped to the ground.

Gone.

"Mama."

What had he done?

Snow collapsed to his knees. Blood soaked into his trousers. He tilted his head back and stared up at the starlit sky, chilled to his marrow and adrift in the darkness.

Colourful ribbons danced across it once more, bright against their velvet backdrop, beautiful and soothing his pain. His bones throbbed, the pain threatening to pull him into a black abyss, but he clung to consciousness. The snow was cold beneath him, stealing more of his strength.

"Snow?" The soft feminine voice curled around him, chasing the chill from his body as it warmed his heart.

She rounded him and crouched in the snow before him, her beautiful face full of affection and concern, her smile renewing his strength.

Dark furs covered her body, her long pale hair spilling across the soft fibres. She stood much taller than he was even though they both knelt in the snow, and he looked up at her, into her ice-blue eyes that looked almost white in the low light.

Her warm hand swept the strands of his white hair out of his face and she stilled when he flinched in pain.

"What happened?" She leaned down and licked his cheek, sealing the cut there.

"I made a friend, Mama… but the man made her go." Snow's head turned and he wavered. His mother caught his arms and white-hot pain seared his bones. He cried out and squeezed his eyes shut, tears leaking from their corners and freezing against his skin.

"Darling!" his mother called and Snow managed to shake his head.

He didn't want his father to come to them. He didn't want his father to see him like this, weak and useless. He had to be strong. His father would be proud of him then.

Snow tried to push up onto his feet. He clutched his mother's shoulders and pulled himself up, but his left leg screamed in pain, the shattered bone grinding together beneath his flesh. He collapsed onto her lap, breathing hard as he fought a vicious wave of pain that threatened to render him unconscious. She gathered him closer to her and looked down at him, fear in her eyes as she gently stroked his brow to soothe him.

She raised her hand to her lips and didn't take her eyes from his as she sank a single fang into her wrist. The strong scent of her blood filled the night and she lowered her wrist to him. Snow took the offered blood, his small mouth working furiously to draw enough from the wound. He wasn't big enough to cover a full bite.

His mother had tried once when he had fallen from a tree and he had spilled her blood everywhere.

He swallowed a mouthful and his pain began to ebb, his body swift to ingest the blood and use it to kick start the process of healing his broken bones. The darkness faded with it, the dizziness passing. He took another mouthful from his mother and then she drew her arm away and licked the cut, sealing it. Snow licked his lips.

His father called from the distance, drawing closer, and Snow willed his body to heal faster so his father wouldn't see him as weak. Papa prided himself on the strength of their bloodline and their breeding. Snow wanted his father to be proud of him too.

His mother gathered her furs around them both and rocked him gently in her arms. She leaned over him and pressed soft kisses to his brow, and Snow closed his eyes, savouring the feel of her embrace and feeling safe and warm. Loved.

He loved his Mama more than anything. He would love her forever and would make sure nothing bad ever happened to her.

"What was your friend's name?" she whispered between kisses, stealing his thoughts away from the pain of his injuries.

Snow's brow crinkled. The little girl hadn't said what it was. He would give her a name.

"Aurora."

CHAPTER 2

The vampire raged in his sleep.

His bare torso bowed off the mattress and his powerful muscles strained as he pulled at the heavy cuffs chaining him to the steel posts of the large bed.

When they didn't give, he thrashed his long muscular legs, pulling the black covers down and revealing more of him to her eyes, including the start of a colourful tattoo on his right hip. The lower half of it disappeared beneath his black underwear. She couldn't make out the design from this distance and refused to give in to the temptation to move closer.

She shouldn't be here.

Her master would be angry with her if he discovered she had left her post to be here, unable to keep away.

Snow snarled and twisted his arms in the thick steel and leather restraints, reopening the ragged marks around his wrists and spilling fresh blood. He had been lost to his bloodlust for many weeks now and a few days ago, things had taken a sharp downwards turn, plunging him into the darkest throes of his curse, far worse than any she had witnessed before.

What did he dream to make him turn so violent and wild?

She could see others' dreams but never his.

Her master believed they would prove to be too much for her, and she felt he might have been right to take that ability from her where this vampire was concerned.

She moved a step closer but kept her distance, standing several feet from the end of the bed in his grim black-walled apartment. He had been doing so well recently, gaining ground against his addiction and learning to master it. Now he seemed worse than ever. Lost.

He growled again, the sound pained and feral, like an animal caught in a vicious snare with no hope for escape. His claws scratched at the heavy steel chains of his restraints, blunted by the sheer number of times he had attempted to grasp them.

He thrashed his head and bared his fangs, his face twisting into a dark visage that was so different to his normal appearance. It had startled her the first time he had changed and revealed his darker nature all those countless centuries ago. Part of her had known then that Snow's future would hold more pain than one man could bear, and she had wished she had spared him such a life when she'd had the chance.

Snow twisted and bucked, the ferocity of his thrashing causing the steel posts of his bed to groan against the large bolts that secured them to the floor and ceiling of his room.

She had the oddest urge to go to him and stroke his brow. Why?

Did she hope it would soothe him?

She wanted to soothe him somehow. She knew that. It was why she had come to this dangerous place, cloaked from the eyes of those who resided in the London theatre, Vampirerotique.

She had visited him often over the past few weeks, always remaining in the shadows, shrouded and invisible to those she observed. She had watched the way everyone interacted with Snow, even though he was unconscious most of the time or maddened by rage at the rest.

She knew what this place meant to him and these people, and what he meant to them.

Over the past century, she had witnessed how each event that had occurred at the theatre had changed him. He had been wary at first, watchful, keeping to himself and keeping his distance from all but his brother, but then he had begun to grow closer to the other males who ran Vampirerotique, and then he had taken the first step towards a brighter future without even knowing it.

He had started to consider those at the theatre as his family.

It had surprised her at first and she had been convinced that she was mistaken for many long months, but then she had begun to hope that the new family he had constructed for himself would become his salvation.

She only wished he were lucid enough to hear those who visited him and know their heartfelt wishes, because she was sure he would battle his bloodlust if he knew they all desired him to be well again.

There were new additions to the theatre she felt he would want to meet too.

Babies.

Unleash

Callum, the black-haired elite male with the striking green eyes, had come to Snow's room one day with a baby cradled in each arm. He had spoken to Snow, who had been unconscious at the time, peaceful, and had shown the babes to him. He had told Snow that he wanted him to get better because he had to meet the twins, and even his wife, the werewolf Kristina, desired it.

It had been difficult to keep her emotions in check that day, watching as Callum talked to Snow, sensing his hope that the male would wake. He had wanted to give Snow a reason to fight and had wanted him to come around in order to ease everyone's minds and lift the burden from their hearts.

She had found a new level of respect for the green-eyed male.

She had also discovered a deep affection for the young female vampire, Lilah. The brunette regularly visited Snow to sit in the wooden chair near the four-poster bed and read to him, keeping vigil at his side whether he was unconscious or raging with bloodlust. Her mate, the sandy-haired elite vampire Javier, often came with her and she knew it was because he feared for his mate and wanted to protect her from Snow if something bad happened.

There were others at the theatre who visited too. A mixed blood male with fair hair and intriguing markings came from time to time, and always apologised. Payne felt responsible for Snow's current state. He wasn't alone in that feeling.

The succubus who was bonded to Javier's younger brother, Andreu, shared Payne's sense of guilt. She had been the one to kiss Snow, stealing his energy and rendering him unconscious.

"Aurora." Snow bucked and growled, his tone dark yet pleading.

She frowned at him. She knew not why he said that word so often but it had drawn her to him that night on the stage of the theatre all those weeks ago, and it drew her again each time he spoke it, as though he was calling out to her. He always spoke that word in a voice edged with pain and she ached to do something to ease his suffering.

She ached to bring him back to the world. He had never suffered like this and she didn't like it. She felt as though he was fading from this world and she could do nothing to stop it from happening. She felt as lost as those who loved him, who spent hours at his side, hoping for him to return to them.

Antoine burst through the mahogany panelled door to her left, his expression revealing his panic as his pale blue eyes sought his older brother. He shoved his long fingers through his wild brown hair and stalked across the room to the bed where it stood against one of the shorter sides of the apartment, opposite the bathroom at her back.

"Snow?" he whispered, fear mixed with hope in his voice.

Snow failed to respond. He lay still on the bed, but not unconscious.

Antoine neatened the black bedclothes, covering his brother's legs and drawing them over his waist to hide his black boxer shorts and give him some shred of dignity. He heaved a sigh and went to the ebony nightstand beside the bed, retrieving the wad of cotton wool and tearing a piece from it.

He wetted it with something from a glass bottle and then rounded the bed to Snow's feet. She watched on as he cleaned the dried blood from Snow's ankles and feet, his actions careful and speaking of the deep affection that he held for his brother.

She felt sorry for him. Sympathy. An emotion well within her grasp. She had felt it for Snow too once and it had changed the course of her life, and she was no longer sure it had been for the better. Perhaps she had thought it a long time ago.

Antoine finished cleaning Snow's ankles and wearily tossed the soiled cotton wool into the overflowing waste bin near the black nightstand. She hated the colour of Snow's room. Everything in it was morbid, funerary, and left her feeling it was a tomb for the living dead.

A grave for a man who was waiting to die.

Antoine tunnelled his fingers through his hair again, shoving it out of his face, and sat on the edge of the mattress on Snow's right. Only he was brave enough to sit so close to him, and she admired him for it and the faith he had in his brother, especially after everything that had happened between them.

Snow's younger brother sighed again, the sound as weary as his appearance made him look. He was normally a neat and elegant man, dressing in fine tailored shirts, polished Italian leather shoes, and perfectly pressed slacks. Now he wore crumpled black trousers and had fastened only the middle three buttons of his charcoal shirt, the tails of it left to hang outside his trousers. His feet were bare.

"Snow?" Antoine leaned forwards, planted his right hand against the mattress and stroked his brother's brow with his left hand, clearing the ribbons of white hair from it.

Again the urge came, the strange need to mimic that action he did so often when he visited his brother.

Another urge joined it as she sensed Antoine's pain and knew his secret fear. He feared that Snow wasn't strong enough to pull through this time. His brother had been seeking his death for centuries and Antoine was afraid that Snow would take this as his chance to escape the pain of his life and find eternal peace.

The sympathy she felt for Antoine grew stronger, consuming her, and she wanted to reveal herself to him and ease his suffering by reassuring him that his brother would not leave him and he would wake soon.

She would see to it.

The door opened again and Sera entered, blinking sleep from her forest green eyes and struggling to tie her long blonde hair into a knot at the back of her head. She rubbed her eyes and then fastened her dark red silk robe around her waist, covering her black slip.

"Antoine," she said softly and her mate turned and looked over his shoulder at her, his pale blue eyes flooded with fatigue and pain. She opened her arms to him, crossed the room and wrapped them around his shoulders. He settled his head against her chest and she ran her fingers through his hair. "You need to rest."

"I cannot… not while…" He turned and buried his face against her, and she tightened her grip on him, holding him close and dipping her head to press a kiss to his hair.

"He will be well," she whispered and continued to stroke the shorter hair at the back of his head. "Give him time. You need to rest too… this has all been too much for you and I don't want—"

Sera cut herself off.

She knew what the female vampire wanted to say but couldn't. She feared that Antoine would follow his brother and lose himself to the bloodlust he fought to keep at bay if he didn't keep his strength up, both physically and spiritually.

Sera stepped back and took hold of Antoine's hands. He looked up at her and nodded, and she released him. He rose to his feet and then pressed one knee into the mattress and leaned over Snow. He pressed a kiss to his brother's forehead.

"Don't you dare give up." His voice cracked and tears filled his eyes.

Antoine straightened, turned, and walked swiftly out of the room. Sera stroked Snow's cheek and sighed.

"You'd better be listening to him, big guy. You know he can't live without you. None of us can." She brushed her knuckles along his straight jaw and then turned and followed her mate from the room, closing the door behind her.

Another door closed and she was alone with Snow again. His breathing quickened and she knew what was coming. He had been still for long enough, had regained some of his strength, and was now going to use it in an attempt to break free of his bonds.

It was always the same.

He would go in circles, a pattern she had learned by heart over the past few weeks. He would fight, and then rest, and then fight again, and then take a shorter rest as his frustration mounted, and then he would fight harder than ever, and fail to free himself.

The end result was always the same too. Exhaustion, leading to unconsciousness. Sometimes he was out for days. Other times it was only minutes before he began the cycle again.

Snow turned savage, the change between placid and violent swift and startling. The chains rattled and then groaned under the pressure of his harsh movements on the bed. He tugged at them, powerful body bowing off the mattress and his muscles bunching and tightening as he fought the restraints that kept him flat on his back. Helpless.

The cuffs bit into his ankles and wrists, and his flesh seeped droplets of blood that the thick restraints then smeared across his skin, renewing the stains. He snarled and fought, lashing out with his fists and feet, shaking the whole bed. The metal sliced deeper into his wrists, until rivulets spilled down his bloodied arms and soaked into the black sheets. Crimson tainted the overlong strands of his white hair and stained his shoulders and neck too. His eyes rolled open and then back again, a flash of scarlet irises and thin black vertical slits for pupils.

They had been red since the night he had first stirred after the incident on the stage, a sign that his bloodlust still had a strong hold over him.

They were red even when he was unconscious.

His lips parted, revealing enormous fangs.

She pitied him even as she despised him.

Her feelings had never been as muddled as they were now.

He sniffed and suddenly stilled, and a prickle of awareness ran down her spine. He had sensed her. How?

He bellowed in fury and thrashed violently against his restraints, causing the metal post that secured his left ankle to bend slightly. Fresh blood ran over his ankles, coating the steel cuffs. He fought harder and it pained her because she knew that after this time he would fall unconscious.

She should leave.

Her place wasn't here.

She knew that in her heart, but that same heart had urged her to come to him when she had felt his pain and his distress. Now that she had seen how fiercely the bloodlust gripped him, she couldn't turn her back on him. She needed to do something to help him.

She could calm him, but if anyone discovered what she had done, she would have damned herself.

She edged closer to him, her heart thumping crazily in her breast, her gaze locked on him and watching for an attack even though she knew he couldn't break his bonds and reach her. He tried to lunge for her, his blunt claws scratching at the air. His red eyes shot to her, focused and sharp, locked on her like lasers.

Her stomach fluttered but her step didn't falter.

She swallowed her trembling heart and reached out to him, afraid that he would somehow manage to injure her but strengthened by the knowledge that she might be able to do something to crack the hold his bloodlust had on him and guide him back to his loved ones.

She stopped at his side and dared to lift her cloak so he could see her, hoping it would calm him and he would see she wasn't a threat to him. She gently lowered her hand, intending to touch his face as the female, Sera, and his brother had.

Snow snapped at her fingers and tried to bite her, his sharp fangs gleaming in the low light from the lamps around the black room.

She changed course and settled her hand on his bare chest instead. His powerful heart thundered hard against her palm. A heavy tribal beat.

It accelerated as she stood over him and then she shifted her eyes to meet his and it began to slow to a more gentle sedate rhythm.

He blinked slowly, long dark lashes shuttering his crimson eyes before lifting again to reveal them to her.

She whispered to him, soft words in a tongue that was probably foreign to him now.

A song to soothe him.

She sung of soaring in a midnight sky, dancing over mountains, and reaching towards the horizon, beyond the snowy valley and the frozen waterfall.

Snow stilled, his expression turning docile, and she bravely moved her hand to his face, stroking his stubbly cheek as she softly sung to him of a prince and his love, his kingdom on earth while hers was in heaven.

Two worlds too far apart.

Two hearts too close to part.

Snow blinked languidly again and then his eyelids drooped and he settled heavily into the bed, his arms lax and hands hanging limply from the cuffs. She focused on his wrists, on the red lines that slashed across them, and willed them to heal.

She brushed her fingertips across his cheek and whispered, "Sleep… dream… remember who you were."

Voices sounded in the hall and she tore herself away from him, stroking his cool cheek one last time and leaving a streak of beautiful colours on his skin.

She stepped back and spread her wings, her eyes still locked on him.

The vampire slumbered peacefully, and it warmed her heart and gave her hope.

"Take more care of yourself. I will be watching."

The door behind her opened, throwing golden light across her and Snow, though she cast no shadow upon him.

She was already gone from this world.

She stood at the edge of a white battlement, staring down at the world far below her, distant and indistinct.

It was done.

Now she had to leave him alone or her master would discover that she had sinned again because of Snow.

He would never forgive her this time.

CHAPTER 3

Pain. Blinding. Debilitating. Sickening. Pain.

It rocked every inch of him. Throbbed deep in his marrow. Lived inside him and refused to die, no matter how hard he struggled to contain and obliterate it.

There was peace too though, a strange sense of calm and warmth that felt as though it was trying to subdue the pain and drive it away. There was also a weird notion that he hadn't been alone.

Snow's head thumped the hardest, fiery lightning splintering across his skull and causing his eyes to ache. He opened them a sliver but the light pierced them, increasing his agony, and he screwed them shut again. He tried to rub the salt and grit from his eyes and grimaced when steel cuffs bit into his wrists, causing sharp lances to jab across them.

His ankles blazed too.

He managed to crack his eyes open enough that he could see his wrists. Shackled and scarred. Multiple lacerations. Dried and fresh blood.

Snow focused on them and his body, taking mental note of any injuries and how weak he felt, trying to gauge how long he had been chained to his bed. Possibly a few days. His senses came fully back online.

He wasn't alone.

His gaze slid painfully down to the male sitting in the wooden chair beside him to his right.

Snow spoke but it came out as a gravelly rumble. He cleared his throat, realised it was sore, figured he had been screaming his head off as usual, and tried again.

"How long have you been in the room?" It took a lot of effort to get that many words out. He drew in a deep breath and it wheezed past his throat and rattled in his lungs. Snow changed his previous calculation to over a week without leaving his bed. He didn't normally feel this refreshed after an extended period lost to his insanity though.

Perhaps he was wrong about how long he had been lost to his bloodlust. He might have screamed more than usual this time.

It would help if he could remember what had triggered his latest round of crazy.

"Not five minutes," Antoine said, his voice a low steady rumble that spoke of fatigue. His brother looked like hell too, dishevelled and weary, and that made Snow look away.

Guilt gnawed at his heart. He had worried Antoine again. Hurt him.

"I sensed you calming and came to check on you, and found you sleeping soundly so I thought I would stay a while to keep you company." Antoine raked his fingers through his thick brown hair. It was longer than usual. Definitely more than a week. More than two? "I did not mean to wake you."

Snow frowned at his brother's odd words.

"You did not wake me. I wasn't sleeping... I mean... I was at least conscious." Snow looked himself over, the pain in his eyes fading as they adjusted to him using them again. Clearly, he had missed something. He didn't remember sleeping. He remembered the rage, the dark hunger for blood and violence, the insane craving to kill everyone who came near him but being unable to get free and satisfy that desire. He remembered feeling trapped in his body, caged by his bloodlust, unable to break its hold over him. He recalled coming around from bouts of unconsciousness to rage all over again too. He had been doing neither of those things prior to this moment. "I was asleep."

Antoine nodded, a glimmer of hope and curiosity in his blue eyes, and rose to his feet. "And you are awake now. Very awake."

Snow understood why he looked curious and what he was implying. His bloodlust had receded. Receded but not gone. Snow could feel it lurking within him. Something had driven it back but it was waiting to seize hold of him again. Something that had made him sleep too. He never slept before coming around from one of his attacks. He was always unconscious or came out of it while awake.

Antoine took some items from the ebony nightstand to Snow's right. Cotton wool and antiseptic by the looks of things. His brother doused a wad of the white padding and moved to Snow's feet, and began cleaning the blood from his ankles.

He looked at his younger brother and frowned, unable to shake the feeling that he hadn't been alone, and it hadn't been Antoine's presence he had felt.

"No one was in here with you?" he said and Antoine shook his head, came up beside him and began cleaning his neck and shoulders. "You did not hear anyone singing?"

"No." Antoine's expression darkened, as though the thought of someone being in here with him disturbed him. Had he been that far gone that Antoine had wanted to keep everyone away from him? Someone must have come regardless. He sniffed and smelled Antoine and Sera, and lily of the valley mixed with snow. No one at the theatre smelled that way. "Perhaps you were dreaming?"

Snow hoped his brother was right, but the sense that someone had been here with him plagued him, together with the song. It had been familiar. His brow crinkled as he struggled to remember it, the tune and lyrics drifting towards the surface of his mind only to slip through his grasp and disappear again, teasing him.

He growled. "Someone was singing… I swear it, Brother."

Antoine moved to sit on the bed beside him and gave him a sympathetic smile. "Do not push yourself. Will you take a little blood?"

Snow forced himself to nod. He wasn't hungry but it would ease Antoine's mind and help Snow maintain his current mental state. It would also take his mind off the feelings he couldn't shake. Maybe Antoine was right and he had been dreaming. He had long ago made it a habit to forget his dreams upon waking, because he never saw anything good in them. His dreams were where the past waited to punish him.

Seeing his brother every night and knowing what he had done to him all those years ago was punishment enough for his sins.

Antoine left the bed and walked around the foot of it to the cluttered black dressing table on the left side of the room, opposite the door, his bare feet silent on the wooden floor. He picked up the small metal canister there, unscrewed the cap and brought it to his nose. He sniffed, smiled, and picked up a glass and returned to Snow, settling on the bed beside him again.

Antoine poured some blood into the glass and held it out to Snow.

Snow reluctantly nodded, closed his eyes and opened his mouth. He hated cold blood, but it was all he had known for centuries now. He could no longer remember what fresh blood straight from the vein tasted like.

Antoine carefully brought the glass to his lips and tipped it, allowing a steady flow of it to enter Snow's mouth. He swallowed it down and grimaced, suppressing a shudder as it chilled his throat. Disgusting.

It did what he needed it to though. The moment it reached his stomach, his body began to absorb it, using it to restore some of his strength. With his returning strength came memories that had eluded him. The black empty stage of Vampirerotique bathed in blood and entrails. An unfamiliar female and a child. Payne defending them. Males attacking his brother.

His brother's blood spilling.

Snow growled and bucked against the restraints, the image of Antoine bleeding from wounds across his chest driving his bloodlust back to the surface. He ground his teeth as his fangs elongated, filling his mouth, and threw his head back and roared.

"Snow!" Antoine pressed his palm against Snow's forehead and pushed his head down onto the black pillows, effectively restraining him. "Look at me, Brother."

Snow rolled his eyes open and sought Antoine. Antoine knelt over him, concern shining in his pale blue eyes.

"I am well. See for yourself."

Snow dropped his eyes to his brother's chest. No blood marred the dark material of his shirt. No wounds. Antoine had already healed. Snow breathed slowly to calm himself and kept his eyes locked on his brother. He was well. Not bleeding. Not hurt.

Not dying because of him.

"Brother," Snow said and Antoine frowned at him. He ached to be free of his bonds so he could take Antoine into his arms and hold him. He needed to reassure himself that his brother was unharmed, alive and with him. He longed to feel that he did have the power to break the hold of his bloodlust even when he feared that he didn't. All he could do was ask though. "Your injuries are healed?"

Antoine's dark eyebrows knitted into a confused line.

"It is a simple question. How are you feeling?" Snow tried again, needing an answer this time, afraid that if Antoine didn't reassure him, he would lose his mind again and the bloodlust would claim him.

Antoine released his forehead only to stroke it. "Are you feeling alright?"

Snow frowned at that. He had asked the same damn thing and Antoine hadn't answered. Was Antoine still injured? Had he not healed?

"I am fine… but your injuries… tell me you have healed, Brother." Snow tried to touch him and the cuffs sliced into his wrists again. He winced at the fleeting stab of pain. Antoine took some more cotton wool from the black nightstand and cleaned the blood off his wrists for him, and then cast him a worried glance. "What is it?"

Antoine sat back on the bed and Snow could sense his concern and frustration. He lobbed the bloodied cotton wool into the bin near the nightstand, drawing Snow's attention to how full it was. Some had fallen out, littering his wooden floor. How long had he been lost to bloodlust?

"Antoine. Answer me."

His younger brother's expression grew even more concerned. "I do not understand a word you are saying, Snow, and you are beginning to scare me."

Snow frowned now and thought about the words that had left his lips. They had seemed normal to him.

"I never learned the language of our family's homeland." Antoine refilled the glass with blood and rested it on his knee.

Snow stared at him, struggling to take in what he had said. He had been speaking the old language?

His eyes shot wide and he tried to sit up, only to have the cuffs around his wrists jerk him back against the pillows. Antoine hastily set the glass down on the nightstand and grabbed his shoulders, his fear flowing over Snow. Evidently, he thought Snow was having a relapse.

For once, it wasn't the case.

"The prince and... homeland. Prince." Snow knew he wasn't making any sense and it wasn't because he was speaking the old language this time. He was speaking English. The look in his brother's eyes as they darted between his and the glass of blood said he definitely thought the blood had had a negative effect on him, driving him back to insanity.

"Are you okay, Snow?" Antoine moved his hands to Snow's face, cupping both of his cheeks.

"Not crazy for a change," he snarled and instantly regretted it when Antoine released him and picked up the glass. "Prince. The song. Winter skies. Snow."

Antoine lifted the glass to Snow's lips. "Drink a little more. You need to sleep. Do you feel you can sleep?"

What he wanted to do was slap his brother into the next century and get him to listen, but any act of violence right now would have Antoine calling in Javier and restraining him until he forced blood down his throat and possibly stuck him with a lion-sized dose of sedative.

Snow didn't have good memories of the last time they had tried that one. He had hallucinated for days about all manner of weird creatures and demons jumbled in with flashbacks of his past, hadn't slept at all, and had come out of it worse than before they had tried to tranquilize him.

"I will try," Snow said and allowed Antoine to pour a little more blood into his mouth. It was cold on his tongue and he swallowed it quickly. A sense of calm returned as it flowed into him, making him sleepy. "Prince. Snow. Winter skies."

It swam around his head, the melody haunting him and chasing sleep away.

"I am sure it will come to you, Brother." Antoine set the glass down again and sat beside him, his closeness comforting Snow and easing him. "Do not push yourself."

"Stay a while," Snow mumbled, struggling to keep his eyes open. He didn't want to be alone. "Will you?"

"Of course," Antoine said.

Sleep tried to overcome Snow but he fought it, not wanting to waste this precious time with his brother. He didn't know when the bloodlust would win and grip him again, and right now he feared next time it wouldn't let go. Right now, he wanted to be normal again.

"How long was I out?" he whispered and blinked rapidly, trying to keep sleep at bay a little longer. He should have refused the blood. It always made him sleepy when he was recovering. "You look like shit."

Antoine smiled but it didn't lift the darkness from under his eyes. "It was over three weeks ago that Chica took you down."

Twenty-one days. It scared the hell out of Snow.

Antoine's voice was hoarse, strained as he spoke. "I thought I had lost you this time."

Tears rose into Snow's eyes, mirrored in Antoine's, and he fought to stop them from falling. He didn't know what to tell his brother. He wanted to tell him that if he had known that he had been scaring him, he would have battled his bloodlust and overcome it to take away his fear and his pain, but it would be a lie. How many times had he lied to his brother?

Too many times, and always about the same thing.

He had promised Antoine that he would fight and he would live, and he would never succumb to the temptation death presented.

It was becoming impossible to keep that promise.

"I am back now," Snow said, voice thick with emotions that felt more like a burden each day longer that he lived.

Snow wished he could offer his brother more comfort. He wasn't sure if he would come back from the next bout of bloodlust. He was surprised he had come back from this one. He glanced at his wrists again. The blood on them had been fresh when he had woken, no more than an hour old, yet all the cuts had been nothing but scars.

Snow fell quiet, allowing Antoine to talk to him, his mind elsewhere. The healed cuts and the sleep. The sanity. Someone had been with him and whoever they were, they knew how to calm him.

They had sung to him in the old language.

That was why he had spoken it to Antoine.

Snow couldn't recall the last time he had spoken it before today. It had been centuries or possibly more. Had he spoken it since Antoine was born? He didn't think he had.

It hadn't been a dream.

Someone had been here in this room with him.

A female who smelled of lily of the valley and snow.

A woman who had sung in the language of his homeland.

A song for a prince and an angel.

He sung fragments of it in his head, trying to recall it all. The more he tried to remember, the harder it became to keep his eyes open. His eyelids dropped once, twice, his vision swimming whenever he managed to get them open again, and then fell and darkness claimed him.

CHAPTER 4

Snow wasn't sure how long he slept. When he came around, Antoine was gone and Lilah was there in the wooden chair to the right of his four-poster bed, her greeting smile bright and cheerful. His gaze flickered to the mahogany panelled door beyond her.

"He hasn't been gone long," she said as though reading his thoughts and leaned to her left, towards the ebony nightstand. The action caused the loose lower half of her black empire-line camisole top to sway with her, brushing the waist of her dark blue jeans. She picked up the tattered book from on top of the small cupboard and settled back in her chair. "Would you like me to read to you?"

Snow shook his head and she set the book back down but made no move to leave. "I do not require a babysitter, Lilah."

Her pretty face darkened into a frown, turning her golden eyes the colour of rich amber, and he silently apologised for his harsh words. He normally enjoyed Lilah's company, even when chained to his bed as he was now, a situation that would have embarrassed him once but no longer bothered him.

At least Antoine had pulled the covers up over his chest, giving him some dignity, and had cleaned the blood from his arms and torso. Or perhaps Lilah had.

She had taken to him shortly after her turning and it had been nice to have someone else to talk to and spend time with in his room, but he wasn't in the mood for company tonight.

He was tired, cranky, and hungry.

If he requested blood, Antoine would come running, fretting that he needed more. He would have to admit that he had been thirsting again, drinking more than a normal vampire should, let alone one affected by a vicious affliction like the one that constantly rode him.

Antoine would be disappointed.

Snow didn't want to be something like that to his brother.

Lilah bounced back with a smile and a flick of her long chestnut hair over her shoulder. "I know who does need a babysitter."

Snow raised a single eyebrow, intrigued by her statement. "Who?"

"Callum and Kristina."

Both eyebrows shot up now. "The babies came?"

God damn it. He had wanted to be sane when they had arrived so he could celebrate the births with everyone. Had they celebrated the arrival of the twins without him?

Snow paused and derailed that thought. No good would come of it. He was already too attached to those at the theatre and had come to depend upon them. Part of him actually wanted to recover and defeat his bloodlust, hoping he would then be able to spend more time with them and become a more active member of the theatre staff. He wasn't even sure when he had begun to desire such a thing.

It had come on slowly, sneaking up on him, and then Javier had got himself into trouble with Lord Ashville, a vicious bastard of an aristocrat vampire, over Lilah and Snow had instinctively come to their defence.

He had even tried to take Javier's punishment on his own shoulders, but had come away from the meeting with their elders unscathed.

Snow had often wondered since then whether the elders knew of his affliction and that it would be extremely dangerous for them to attempt to execute him. Getting him chained up for it would likely end in a bloodbath, let alone carrying out the decapitation. Whenever he felt threatened, he had a tendency to lose control and turn on everyone near him.

"We were waiting for you to wake up before we had a big celebration." Those words snapped him back to Lilah and he stared at her, his dark silver eyebrows pinned high up his forehead.

"You were?" He couldn't believe that, but her wide smile and the warm affection in her eyes told him that she wasn't lying, and that Antoine hadn't been the only one spending time with him while he had been in the throes of his bloodlust. "Javier didn't let you come here to see me when I was... tell me that he didn't."

Her expression turned sheepish and her honey-coloured eyes sparkled with something akin to mischief. He had. Her mate and sire had actually allowed her to come and see him while he had been lost to his demon, crazed and dangerous.

"What the hell was he thinking?" Snow barked at her and had half a mind to shout for Javier and ask him too. If he hadn't been cuffed to the bed, he would have been out of the door, down the hall to Javier's room, and shaking the elite vampire male by his throat until Javier cursed him in his native Catalan tongue.

Lilah raised an eyebrow at him this time. "He didn't have a choice, but he didn't let me come here alone. I was perfectly safe. I know you would never hurt me, Snow."

Snow scoffed at that. Hurt was putting it mildly. If he had escaped his restraints, he would have killed her, and Javier would have just been a warm up for the bloody main attraction.

The door opened before he could reprimand her and Javier entered with Antoine, deep in discussion. Next year's shows seemed to be the topic of conversation for the two tall slender males and both were dressed for business in sharp black tailored shirts and crisp pressed trousers. Was it the closed season already?

Antoine smiled at Snow and relief coursed through him when he saw that some of the fatigue had lifted from his face and he looked more refreshed and rested. He must have taken the opportunity to sleep while Snow had.

Javier crossed the room in a handful of long-legged strides and dropped a kiss on Lilah's dark hair. She smiled up at him and took his hand, clutching it tightly. Matching gold bands encircled one finger on their left hands and Snow regretted missing something else too.

While they had married at Vampirerotique so Javier's younger brother, Andreu, could attend the ceremony, they had celebrated the wedding at the family estate in northern Spain. Andreu had remained at the theatre to stay with Chica, his mate, who had been trapped within its boundaries at the time, and Antoine had decided to stay in London too. Callum hadn't been able to travel because of Kristina's pregnancy.

It had meant that none of Javier's friends here at the theatre had attended the endless parties they must have held in Spain. Snow would have liked to have been there.

He had a feeling that Lilah and Javier would have liked it too.

Lilah had asked him to give her away after all.

Antoine had baulked at the request. Javier had been more than a little wary too.

Snow had been proud. He had walked her down the middle aisle of the theatre towards the stage with her arm draped over his and all eyes on them, and he hadn't made one mistake or suffered even a momentary flicker of bloodlust.

Of course, Antoine hadn't shut up then. He had spent the night saying how Snow was recovering and would be free of his bloodlust before long. The bloodlust already drove him mad. He didn't need his brother's repetitive nonsense relentlessly shoving him towards insanity too.

Lilah rose, led Javier across the room and whispered something to Antoine as though a two thousand year old vampire such as himself wouldn't be able to hear it. She wanted Callum to come with the babies.

Snow wasn't sure how he felt about meeting squalling babes while chained to a bed, but he had helped raise Antoine around a thousand years ago. He wasn't averse to small people. They were often amusing. Antoine had always been doing something ridiculously stupid.

Snow smiled at that.

Everyone looked at him as though he had gone insane again and he noted with a frown that they were all holding their breath. He scowled at them.

"I was recalling the time Antoine wet—" Snow flinched when Antoine's hand slammed over his mouth and his fangs cut into his lower lip.

"Play nice." Antoine glared at him, looking for all the world as though he wished Snow was mad with bloodlust again and unable to resume his normal duty of driving him crazy or embarrassing him.

Antoine slowly removed his hand, giving him a pointed look that warned he would have him gagged again in a millisecond if he attempted to mention all the times he had wet the bed as a child.

Snow grinned, flashing fangs. Antoine's face fell.

"I did not mean to hurt you," Antoine said.

Snow shrugged it off and licked his fangs clean. It wasn't the first time his fangs had ended up a little bloodied because of Antoine, and it probably wouldn't be the last.

Javier led Lilah from the room and Snow tracked them with his senses. They were heading towards the end of the black and gold corridor at his back. A knock sounded. A door opened. A baby wailed.

"You used to sound like that." Snow smiled at Antoine when he looked displeased. "You would cry like a wild thing all day long. I used to have to bring you to my room and into my bed if I wanted to get any sleep."

"You are certainly talkative tonight." Antoine smiled at last and Snow nodded. He was feeling brighter. The sleep and blood had done him good, but the darkness was still pushing inside him, trying to break free and consume him again.

And the scent of lily of the valley and snow still haunted him.

"You are certain no one else visited me?" Snow couldn't shake the feeling that a stranger had been with him, singing to him in his native language, soothing him out of his bloodlust and into sleep.

Antoine nodded and a flicker of concern lit his blue eyes. He opened his mouth and an almighty wail cut him off. It seemed the twins had voices and wanted to make themselves known.

Callum appeared in the doorway, wearing a rumpled black t-shirt, creased black trousers and no shoes.

Fatigue dulled Callum's green eyes, the dark crescents beneath them making Antoine look as though he had been catching twelve hours sleep a day, and his short black hair was wild on top, as though he had shoved his fingers through it every second of the night. His lips compressed into a thin line and he struggled with the writhing babies. Both of them sported a head of dark hair and matching deep crimson romper suits that covered them from toe to wrist.

Snow flinched when one of them hit a high note, screaming it at the top of their little lungs, driving the noise like a spear through his ears and into his brain.

Delightful.

He couldn't stop himself from smiling at the twin bundles of fury though, and the fact that Callum had to battle to keep them both in his arms. Little demons. They needed a pointed tail on those red suits and a pair of horns each.

Callum made a beeline for the chair near Snow and sat on it swiftly, a degree of his tension leaving him the moment his backside hit the wood. Snow agreed with his move. The way the babes were wriggling, there was a likelihood that Callum would drop one at some point. A fall from chair height was better than a fall from over five foot. At their tender age, they were vulnerable and weak, and could break bones as easily as a mortal babe could.

"They seem… rambunctious." Snow grinned at Callum, feeling genuinely amused by the tiny terrors and their father's dire efforts to contain and calm them, until Callum moved them so Snow could see them fully.

His smile lost all feeling then. He couldn't feel anything positive about what he was seeing before him.

Life. Very small and vulnerable. New to this world. Untainted and pure.

It made him feel the full weight of his sins, and for a glimmer of a moment, he felt his death would be acceptable now because there was new life in this world to replace him.

Antoine's gaze bore into him. "They will be trouble. Always getting into scrapes. I think they will need all of us here to keep an eye on them and keep them safe."

Snow smiled sadly at his brother's coded words. Antoine wanted him to know that he was still needed in this world and not to think about leaving it. It was all Antoine had wanted and strived to make him see for centuries now, and Snow wished with every part of his blackened soul that he could grant Antoine's request and find a reason to live amongst the many reasons to die.

Lilah and Javier reappeared, the Spaniard leaning with his back against the doorframe and his mate wrapped in his arms with her back pressed against his front, both of them watching Callum as he struggled with the babies.

Callum tried to pass one of the babies to Antoine, who grumbled about it and eventually reluctantly took the squalling bundle. Snow found a real smile again at the sight of his brother holding the baby away from him with both hands as though it was a bomb that would go off if he moved a single muscle.

It triggered a strange warmth in the centre of Snow's chest.

Antoine had spent months complaining about the impending babies but Snow knew that his brother was softening towards them and the unlikely couple. He hadn't cursed about Kristina being a werewolf for many weeks now.

Snow thought it was Sera's influence. She had changed Antoine for the better and it pleased him that his brother was no longer alone in the world, afraid to trust another with his heart and move forwards in life.

"This one is Abby." Callum held the little girl so Snow could see her face, clutching her under her arms. She stopped wailing, blinked big blue eyes at him, and then broke out into giggles and reached for him, her tiny fingers clutching the air in his direction. Callum and Antoine exchanged a surprised glance before Callum looked back at Snow.

"What?" Snow had the feeling he had done something either very wrong or very right, and he hadn't done anything at all. He had only looked at the baby.

Abby continued to reach for him, shoving forwards in Callum's arms, almost breaking free. Her delicate features crumpled in frustration when she failed. Snow knew that feeling well. It was a bitch when you found yourself unable to break free of something, whether physically or emotionally.

Callum shook himself. "Nothing... she's just never laughed before."

Snow wasn't sure why the sight of him was a reason to laugh, but he wouldn't hold it against the kid. If she wanted to laugh around him, he was game for that.

"Kristina!" Callum shouted in the way only a hysterically pleased parent could and the brunette werewolf came rushing into the room with a wild look on her face, her clothes dishevelled as if she had thrown them on in a hurry, and her claws and fangs bared, ready to attack. Her hazel eyes darted from Snow to the babies, and then Callum, a calculating look in them. When it appeared no one was harmed or in danger, she relaxed and then slapped Callum hard on the shoulder.

"You nearly gave me a heart attack. Dumb male." She scowled at him for good measure and hastily buttoned her loose black jeans and tugged the hem of her dark grey t-shirt down over the waist. "What the hell are you screaming my name for?"

"It's wonderful. Look." Callum grinned, ignoring her tirade and glares that spoke of staking the moment they were alone, and held a now-crying Abby out in Snow's direction.

"Are you sure that's wise..." Kristina trailed off, her fear forgotten as Abby burst into giggles again and reached for Snow, hands pumping the air in a desperate attempt to reach him.

Snow wriggled his fingers in a wave and the little girl kicked her legs, bouncing in her father's hands.

Kristina gave him that same awed look that Callum had. Snow shrugged, uncomfortable with the scrutiny.

"Try the other one." Kristina grabbed the other baby from Antoine and held it out to Snow. It continued crying. Kristina turned it towards her and gave it a look that spoke of confusion and disappointment, and a vague sense that either the baby or Snow was broken. "How does he work on the werewolf and not the vampire?"

Antoine had told Snow months ago that one of Kristina's babies would be born fully vampire and the other fully werewolf. Snow had figured that the female, Abby, would be the vampire since she seemed to like him. The little tyke was a werewolf though, and still laughing as she stared at him with huge blue eyes.

They grew fast at her age. A few weeks was more like a couple of months to a human child. Her aging would slow when she neared three months old, looking around one year old to human eyes. After that, she would age like all werewolves and vampires, taking years to physically age a single one.

"It's because he's a boy," Sera said from the doorway and Antoine moved out of Snow's line of sight. She smiled at him, as bright as Lilah had been, her dark green eyes warm with tenderness. "Who here doesn't know that women have a way with Snow when he's suffering with his bloodlust? I think it works both ways. Snow's a charmer."

Snow wouldn't go that far. Lilah, Sera and Chica teased him mercilessly about his tendency to calm in the presence of a female whenever he was in the midst of his bloodlust. He would never live this down if they were right and Abby was the only one affected by him.

"Try again with the boy." Snow jerked his chin, hoping to convince Kristina to bring him closer and do as he asked. "I charmed the hell out of Antoine when he was a baby. I was the only one who could get him to sleep. Maybe I just charm babies?"

Antoine didn't look pleased that Snow had put that titbit about him out into the world but he didn't care. He wanted to prove that it was babies in general he could soothe and not just the females. He couldn't remember the last time he had charmed a female in any way. He didn't want to remember because he would realise how long he had gone without what so many of his friends here at Vampirerotique had found.

Love.

Had he ever truly felt it for anyone?

He didn't think he had. He had experienced lust and infatuation, and thought there was a slim chance he might have loved one of the females he had romanced.

Very slim.

Maybe not a chance at all.

He had never allowed anyone to get that close to him, not before he had realised he had a terrible affliction and certainly not afterwards. Once he had experienced his first uncontrollable rage and the dark hungers that hounded him whenever he lost all sense because of his bloodlust, he had cut all ties with females and kept his distance.

It was safer that way.

Kristina looked wary about placing her baby nearer to him and he couldn't blame her. If he were in her place, he wouldn't want to place his child close to a savage beast either.

"What is his name?" Snow said, aiming to deflect the conversation away from his apparent charm if he couldn't erase it by proving himself able to cause the boy to laugh as easily as the girl.

"Alistair." Callum handed Abby over to Sera, and Abby immediately began pulling at the shoulder ties of her short blue dress, causing Sera to smile. Callum took the boy from his mother and approached Snow with him. It seemed Callum was willing to tread where angels daren't.

Angel. Prince. Snow. Winter skies. Frozen waterfall. Mountains. More of it came to him each time.

A song of impossible love.

Callum turned Alistair in his hands, causing the boy to squirm and kick, stretching the material of his dark red romper suit. Red was a good colour for baby vampires. Black was better. Practical.

Snow noticed the fresh scars on Callum's wrist as he held the boy out to him. Callum was probably feeding him from the vein several times a day. Abby was lucky. Werewolves didn't have to feed on blood when young. They could ingest milk and soft foods.

Snow's father had fed Antoine for the first few months of his life, before he'd had to return to his business and running the family, and he hadn't been around as much. Snow had taken over feeding him then whenever he had been at the chateau. If he had realised back then how tainted his blood was, he never would have agreed to it.

Bloodlust was genetic, and Antoine had it regardless, but the thought of his blood flowing into his innocent young brother turned his stomach and ruined what was once a happy memory for him.

Alistair quieted, drawing Snow back to him. He shoved his darker memories away and focused on the present and the young boy in front of him. Elite blood at best ran in his veins. He would never know the horror that Snow had experienced for the past several centuries, and Snow was glad of it. He would never wish his terrible affliction upon anyone.

His eyes slid to Antoine where he stood near the foot of the bed, his arm around the slender shoulders of his mate, Sera, gazing at her with affection as she held Abby in her arms.

Snow hated that Antoine might one day suffer as he had, losing himself to bloodlust, becoming a mindless animal that would have to be chained to his bed, rendered helpless and vulnerable in order to protect others. Antoine looked across at him, his smile fading and expression turning serious as he caught Snow's gaze.

"Perhaps we should allow Snow some rest," Antoine said just as Alistair proved Snow's theory and broke into a fit of giggles.

"I would like that." More than his brother could know. The calm he had felt upon waking was gradually fading and, little by little, he was losing the battle to keep his hunger subdued and his bloodlust in check. Too many memories were surfacing, dragged up by the presence of the babies and thoughts of Antoine at that tender age.

Callum drew Alistair close to him, cradling him against his shoulder. "We are having a party this evening. Antoine thought you might be well enough to attend and we waited until you were recovering before deciding to celebrate the births. Do you think you will come down, even if it's just for a few minutes?"

Snow nodded. "I would like that too. I just need more sleep."

A few millennia more.

Kristina took Abby from Sera and led the way. Callum filed out of the room behind her, followed by Javier and Lilah, and finally Sera. She paused at the door and looked back at Antoine.

"Don't keep him up too long." She turned her forest green gaze on Snow. "Try to get some sleep."

"I will," he said and she left the room, closing the door behind her.

The babies began crying again and he could hear Callum arguing with Kristina about him. Snow could understand Kristina's reluctance to have him babysit their twins but he appreciated Callum's faith in him, even if it was born of the desire to have a quiet night for the first time in weeks and Snow seemed to be the only one in the theatre able to calm their twins.

"Here." Antoine unlocked the cuff around Snow's left ankle. He opened his mouth to protest and Antoine cut him off as he freed his other ankle. "Save it. You have been lucid for a day now and Sera says you need a shower."

Snow could well imagine that he did. Three weeks chained to his bed. He hadn't tasted blood in most of that time but that was never a guarantee that his bodily functions weren't in normal working order.

And here he had considered pointing out that Antoine had wet the bed as a toddler.

Antoine undid the cuffs holding his wrists and helped Snow into a sitting position. Thank whatever power watched over his dark soul. It appeared that this time he hadn't given himself cause to feel embarrassed around everyone. The only thing soiling his black sheets was a disturbing amount of dried blood.

He rubbed his wrists, the muscles in his arms aching. His legs shook when he tried to move them. Antoine darted forwards to help him.

"I can take care of myself, Antoine." Snow really didn't want his brother around to witness what three weeks with only insane thrashing to keep his muscles active did to his ability to walk. It would only cause him to worry, and he had already given him reasons enough to do that over the past three weeks.

Or the past several centuries.

Antoine sat beside him on the bed.

The babies continued wailing down the hall. He could hear Callum trying to shush them, and Kristina singing a lullaby. Javier and Lilah were laughing about something across the hall from them. Sera was fidgeting in her apartment nearer to him.

Below him, the performers moved around their rooms, talking and passing time. Even farther below, he could sense the succubus and Andreu. Payne was there too, and the young incubus boy that the witch had brought with her.

Snow cringed. "I did try to kill the witch, didn't I?"

Antoine nodded. "And Payne too… he was going to leave with her."

"You stopped him?" Snow managed to shuffle to the edge of the bed, draped his bare legs over it, and looked across at Antoine. His brother nodded again. "I am glad. I would like to apologise to them, and meet the female and the young one."

"Later. They will be at the party." Antoine wrapped his arm around Snow's shoulders and fell silent.

It was peaceful. Snow felt it right to his marrow as he sat beside his brother in his black apartment, listening to the activity in the theatre, the laughter and happiness that filled it now, but it didn't ease the restlessness in his heart.

"Take a shower and get some sleep." Antoine stood and Snow looked up at him. He leaned over, settled his hands on Snow's bare shoulders, and pressed his forehead against his. "Keep fighting because there are people in this world who love you and who need you here with them."

Snow closed his eyes. His brother wasn't talking just about himself. He was telling him that he was a part of everyone's lives regardless of what he thought or wanted to believe, and a sliver of his heart couldn't deny it because they were a part of his life too. He wanted to keep fighting but he was exhausted and the bloodlust was riding him harder than ever, never giving him a moment's peace.

Snow lifted his hands, cupped Antoine's cheeks, and pressed their foreheads harder together. There was so much that he wanted to say but he couldn't find a voice for it. He settled for saying the only thing he could and, for once, it wasn't a lie.

"I will."

CHAPTER 5

~~~~

Snow ducked his head under the hot spray of water and closed his eyes as it soaked through his hair, washing away the shampoo.

He braced his hands against the black tiles in front of him in the double-width shower stall and hung his head forwards, letting the water hit his nape and cascade over his back. The heat soothed the last remnants of tightness from his muscles.

He had worked out in his apartment after Antoine had gone, putting his body through its paces to try to bring himself back to full strength, and had needed this shower. It completed the therapeutic and almost ritualistic process of putting the past three weeks out of his mind by erasing the evidence stamped on his body—the weakness, the bloodstains, and the fatigue. He always felt better afterwards. Almost normal.

Snow opened his pale blue eyes and stared at his feet. Rivulets streamed from the tips of his white hair and his chin and nose, catching the light and sparkling as they fell to the tray far below.

His lips parted and he sighed. Working out had felt good but a shower was always the best medicine after an extended period of captivity. It revitalised him, leaving him feeling alive and awake, and at peace.

He had already scrubbed himself from head to toe twice over, paying close attention to his wrists and ankles.

Snow straightened, the water beating on his broad bare chest, and removed one hand from the wall. He turned his palm upwards and stared down at his scarred wrist.

The marks would fade in time, his preternatural healing taking care of them and leaving smooth skin behind. They were always chafed though, permanent evidence that he had to spend his days wearing leather-lined steel cuffs attached to inch-thick chains that were secured to the industrial grade steel posts at the corners of his bed.

When they had first moved to the theatre, he had forced Antoine to purchase the strongest, thickest metal posts he could find and make a bed out of them for him. Antoine had protested but had done as he had asked in the end, arranging for the restraints at the same time.

His younger brother had told him countless times that he didn't need to chain himself each day, and Snow had always countered that it was necessary and he did not mind it.

He did. He hated it.

That was beside the point though.

It was necessary, and ever since that fateful night centuries ago, he had always done whatever was necessary to protect others from himself.

Snow heaved a sigh, his chest expanding with it, powerful muscles straining, and ran his hand down his face.

It would have been so much easier if Antoine had agreed to do as Snow had asked that same night and destroyed him.

He deserved to be put down like the rabid beast he was.

Antoine was nothing if not stubborn though. He had been bleeding profusely from the savage wounds Snow had inflicted upon him, carving up his chest and arms so badly that Antoine had scarred rather than healed completely. Snow had thought he would seek revenge for himself and their family, or perhaps take his head as an act of mercy. He had dared to hope his brother would do what was right.

Antoine had refused to kill him and had even pressed him to promise that he would never kill himself either. Snow had agreed and regretted it the moment it had left his lips.

The past few centuries had been hell. Seeing Antoine every night and knowing what he had done to him, the fact he had almost killed the brother he loved with all of his black heart. Seeing Antoine and knowing that he had stolen everything from his brother in one night of madness. Seeing his brother and knowing that he had butchered their entire family.

Seeing Antoine's face and seeing their mother's pale blue eyes and their father's dark brown hair.

It was enough to drive a man insane.

It was a good job he was already crazy.

Snow switched off the shower, ran his hands over his hair to squeeze the water out, and slid the glass cubicle door open. He stepped out onto the black tiles and grabbed a thick white towel. A very impractical colour, but he liked the touch of purity and lightness it brought into his dark world.

He scrubbed the towel over his hair and then dried himself off with one hand. He swiped his free palm across the clouded mirror, clearing enough to reveal his reflection and the main room of his apartment through the open door behind him.

He never liked to look at himself, normally hated seeing his reflection and seeing his mother's eyes and hair, knowing what he had done to her, but he sometimes felt the need to look and remind himself of what he had done.

A twisted form of punishment.

He dropped the damp towel, pressed both palms against the edge of the black counter, and leaned forwards over the sink, staring hard at his reflection.

A face his mother had often called angelic.

The face of a cold-blooded murderer.

Snow growled and slammed his right fist into his face in the mirror, splintering the glass. Fire seared his knuckles and blood instantly ran down the shards of mirror. He pulled his fist back and plucked a sliver of glass from the soft flesh between his index and middle finger, and dropped it into the sink.

The scent of blood compelled him to taste it, stirring the darkness that constantly lurked within him, stalking just beneath the surface, barely restrained.

He rinsed his bloodied knuckles off in the black oval sink and then inspected them. Two of the cuts were deep. He lifted his hand to his face and sucked those two, drawing more blood to the surface. It tasted foul.

His stomach cramped and he spat the blood into the sink and then swiped his tongue across his knuckles to seal the wounds. The bleeding was already slowing. Within a few minutes, his flesh would begin to knit itself back together and heal.

He took a small towel and wrapped it around his hand, and then strolled naked into his bedroom. The bed loomed directly in front of him. He had promised Antoine that he would sleep and he meant to keep that promise.

He wanted to be sane enough to head down to the party even if it was only for a few minutes. Everyone was depending on him and he didn't want to let all of them down. They had held off on celebrating the arrival of the twins so he could share in the joy of the event. He needed to be there.

He veered right, heading for the ebony chest of drawers that lined the black wall there next to his elegant wardrobe. He pulled out one of the smaller drawers at the top, fished a fresh pair of black boxers out, and shut it again. Someone spoke in the hall. Snow paused and listened. Callum was talking to

Payne as they walked along the hall towards Callum's apartment beyond Snow's one. Discussing children.

Payne had taken responsibility for the witch's youngling? Snow had never pictured the young vampire as a father. He had always imagined him to be more of a bachelor forever type because of his incubus blood.

Was everyone going to settle down and produce offspring now?

Snow tugged his boxer shorts on. They were all going to leave him behind. Everyone had a female now, something warm and tender in their lives. They were complete.

Where did that leave Snow?

With a frustrated growl, he pulled his wardrobe doors open, grabbed fresh bed linen from the stack he kept at the bottom, and slammed them shut again. What did he care about females? No female in her right mind would want him, and he certainly did not want a female.

He could never trust himself with something so weak and breakable.

He lumbered across his room, bare feet thumping against the wooden floor, and dumped the black linen beside his bed. He stripped the soiled covers off and focused on replacing them with fresh ones to keep his mind off a topic that had often angered him.

He had warred with himself many times about finding a female, debating the pros and cons of such a mission, and all the possible outcomes. It was highly likely that a female would leave him the moment she discovered the ugly truth about him, his bloodlust, and his horrific past.

He would probably react to her betrayal by losing his head to bloodlust and killing her.

He had a tendency to react violently whenever someone sought to hurt him.

Breaking his heart would cause him the ultimate pain.

Snow shook that thought away and smoothed the edges of his black covers down, neatening them. He grabbed his black robe and slung it on, but didn't bother to fasten the belt.

Darkness swirled inside him like a rising tide that he was powerless to hold back. He breathed slowly, trying to work past the tightening knot in his breast, hoping to calm down before he lost himself again.

He sat on the bed and lay with his back against the pillows and his head against the steel bars of the headboard. He cast a glance at the restraints that rested on the pillows on either side of him. They were there if he needed them and that gave him back a fraction of his control, but didn't quell his rising bloodlust.

His heart galloped, refusing to heed his attempts to slow it, and he closed his eyes and focused on positive things. The battle between his darker hungers and his desire to remain sane intensified and he breathed harder, drawing deep and filling his lungs with cool air. The soft scent of lilies and snow lingered in that air and his mind drifted to the lyrics of the song.

Calm swept through him, driving back the darkness for a brief second before it surged forwards again, obliterating the sense of peace.

A breeze washed over his bare flesh.

Snow frowned. There were no windows in his room. The breeze carried the unmistakable scent of snow yet it felt warm, and familiar.

Someone was in his apartment. He felt their presence as a soft caress that reached right down to his tainted soul and chased the black shadows from it.

Snow drew in a deeper breath of lily of the valley and snow, the pure feminine scent stirring his body and soothing the tension from it. He held it in his lungs and slowly opened his eyes, settling them directly on the dark beauty standing at the foot of his bed.

She was stunning, with a fall of glossy raven hair that playfully curled around slender shoulders and contrasted against her milky skin, heart-shaped rosy lips, a button nose, and the most incredible yet familiar eyes. They were turquoise around the outside but faded to a brilliant blue at their centres, around the dark mesmerising chasms of her pupils.

A pure white dress clung to dangerous curves and full breasts that would make any man's eyes linger on her, evoking images in his head that he shouldn't entertain but couldn't keep at bay. He had never seen a female like her.

The white layers of her dress criss-crossed over her torso, forming a zigzagging line downwards from between the swell of her creamy breasts to the point above her navel. They flowed from there, free and untamed, drifting down to caress her ankles and her small bare feet.

Beautiful.

It was the large black wings furled against her back that eventually stole his attention away from the sublime innocence of her face and the wickedness of her body.

An angel.

"I never thought I would see one of your kind." Snow had meant it to come out strong and forceful, but the words left his lips as an awed whisper.

She moved a step closer and the scent of her grew stronger, and while that pleased him, his senses screamed of danger and his bloodlust reacted violently to her proximity. A seething, vicious hunger to launch himself from the bed, capture her head in his hands and smash it hard against the unyielding wooden floor of his room bolted through him and he struggled to resist complying with it and satisfying his need to render her unconscious in order to make himself safe once more.

He ground his teeth and shot her a glare when she appeared to consider moving another step closer.

"What do you want?" It came out snappish this time, as dark and menacing as the twisted desires that taunted him.

The angel moved back a step and surveyed his room in silence. Ignoring his question was not the wisest move she could have made. Until he understood why she was in his room, he would feel threatened, and he would eventually lose his fight to retain control of himself.

Her striking eyes settled on his bed.

"Your bed is strange." Her voice was melodic and light, a sound that curled around him and soothed his ears but not his bloodlust. That worsened, as though it despised her presence. She played havoc with it, and with him, and he was haemorrhaging patience. She pointed to the thick steel bars at the corners of his bed and the cuffs attached to them. "You have strange tastes. Why?"

Her gaze lit upon him, bright and curious, and Snow had the feeling that she was testing him for some infernal reason.

He could ignore questions too. "What do you want?"

She walked in a shallow circle, those curious eyes flickering around everything, cataloguing it and then coming back to take every inch of him in.

"I want nothing," she said and drifted across the room to his dressing table.

Her fingertips danced over everything on it, from the lamp to the candles, to the stack of books. She leaned forwards, cocked her head to one side, and ran her fingers down the spines. The action shifted her black wings, causing the longest feathers of the right one to graze the floor.

She straightened and turned back to face him. "I felt you suffering again and was unable to ignore it, even though I know I should have this time."

Snow frowned. "You were here with me… before. It was you."

She nodded and walked towards him, her steps so light even he couldn't hear them. She twirled her black hair around the fingers of her left hand and smiled at him. It hit him square in the chest and knocked the wind out of him.

"If you were here… then you know why my bed is the way that it is, and why I must chain myself. So why did you ask?" He growled the question, growing tired of her cryptic behaviour.

"I was curious to know what you would tell me." She wrapped her small hands around one of the steel posts at the end of his bed and leaned her shoulder against it.

Snow didn't like that she had seen him in the throes of his bloodlust, but he was beginning to share her sense of curiosity. "Why are you here... and why did you sing to me?"

A pretty blush coloured her flawless pale cheeks. "You remember?"

Wasn't he supposed to have remembered? Evidently, she hadn't expected him to recall that someone had been in his room, singing him to sleep, speaking to him in a language that hadn't left his lips in close to one thousand years before he had awoken to find Antoine watching over him.

Snow nodded.

She didn't tell him why she was here. She pushed away from the post and twirled so her back was to him, the white layers of her dress spinning outwards to reveal the outline of her shapely legs beneath. Snow barely bit back the growl that rumbled up his throat at the sight of her long slender legs.

Her black wings shifted and stretched, almost spanning his room before settling against her back again.

"I do not enjoy your choice of decor," she said in a bright tone and looked over her shoulder, past her black wing to him. "It is morbid. Mortals would call it depressing."

Snow folded his arms across his chest. "You know that I am not mortal, and I feel this decor suits me and this place."

He smiled slowly. Desire to make her blush again so he could see it shot through him.

"You must know the sort of business I run with the others here, and the sort of creature I am."

"I do not care." She twirled to face him, affording him another glimpse of long legs that would have made him blush if he hadn't been in perfect control of himself.

"Again, female, why are you here?" If she didn't answer this time, he might leave the bed, grab her shoulders and shake the answer out of her.

She was petite, delicate in appearance, but his senses warned that she was powerful and more than able to put him on his arse if he tried to harm her.

"I said... I was watching over you." Her black eyebrows pinched in a frown. "Do you not listen?"

Snow scowled back at her and scoffed at her words. "My own guardian angel? I have done nothing to deserve an angel watching over me. Your kind should be put to better use, given to those who deserve you."

Her frown hardened. "You do not deserve compassion?"

There was an edge to her expression and the hint of her emotions that he could detect that told him she didn't believe him worthy of compassion either and that she hated being here. Confusing female.

He wanted to pick her up on her feelings towards him and ask her why she was here when she harboured such dark, un-angel-like emotions. Did she despise all of his kind or just him? Had he done something to gain her scorn?

It bothered him but he pushed it to the back of his mind, unwilling to contemplate the notion that she may hate all vampires because it would inevitably lead to him deciding that she was a danger to everyone at the theatre and then his bloodlust would break free of the tattered threads that restrained it.

She had been in the room before, and he didn't know how many other times she had visited him over the twenty-one days he had been out of his mind. If she were a threat, she would have attacked before now.

No. Attacking the theatre or killing him were not the reasons she was here. There was another one, one she was unwilling to share with him right now.

The angel meandered around his room again, the longest feathers of her black wings almost grazing the wooden floor with each silent step.

She delighted in the strangest things, such as looking through his drawers and pulling out items of clothing and holding them up for inspection. She rummaged through his wardrobe too, and held more than one shirt against her small, wickedly sensual body.

Those shirts would smell like her, and he had the stupidest urge to wear one of them tonight and carry her sweet scent with him to the party. It was almost as pathetic as the pleasing image of her dressed in only one of his shirts, curled up asleep and sated on his bed, that leaped into his mind.

She hummed as she poked at everything on top of his dressing table again and thumbed through several of his books. The same melody she had sung to him. The sound of it soothed his bloodlust and relaxed him, and he found himself enjoying her company.

She turned on the spot again and looked from his black-tiled bathroom and the broken mirror to him, her dark eyebrows rising as her gaze fell to his injured hand.

"Why did you taste your blood only to spit it into the sink?" That question leaving her lips caught him off guard and almost knocked the wind from him.

"You saw?"

"Of course," she said in a matter of fact tone, as though it shouldn't surprise him that he hadn't been as alone as he had thought.

"From here?" He didn't like the thought of her being in his room, invisible to his senses, watching him. It stirred his bloodlust, reawakening the sense that she was a threat to him.

She shook her head.

"No. From my home." Another pretty blush stained her cheeks. "I did not watch when I should not have. I only saw you strike the mirror and what came afterwards, and then I turned my gaze away from you again."

Snow raised a single eyebrow at her. He hadn't even considered that she could have been watching him in the shower. The thought of this beauty secretly watching him bathe had something other than his bloodlust rising and he cleared his throat and shifted his leg so she wouldn't notice.

"Why did you spit out your blood?"

Snow averted his gaze, settling it on the black covers beside his left hip. Why indeed. He would sound stupid if he told her the truth, but the thought of lying to her didn't sit well in his stomach, causing it to squirm worse than his hunger did.

He sighed. "Because it tastes foul."

Snow lifted his head again, locking his eyes on her, monitoring her for a sign that might tell him what she thought of that. Her expression remained placid but the pink tint on her cheeks darkened as he stared at her and a flicker of curiosity reignited in her striking eyes.

"Why ask me about my blood and not about why I struck the mirror?" He couldn't hold that one inside any longer. If she had watched him strike the mirror and then suck blood from the wound only to spit it out, shouldn't her first question have been about his reason for smashing the glass? He was sure most people would have chosen that as their starting point.

Her gaze held his, unwavering and unreadable, emotionless. "Because I already know the reason why, Snow. I know what haunts your soul."

Snow swallowed hard, the action forcing his galloping heart back down into his chest. The way she stared at him, her cool impassive eyes looking deep into his, as if she could see beyond his physical form, down to the soul she claimed to know, set him on edge and made him believe that she spoke the truth.

She knew all about him and the wretched acts in his past that he couldn't escape.

This angel knew his pain and he had the feeling that she had been watching over him for longer than these past few days.

She turned away again and the instant the link between their eyes broke, he sagged against the pillows and his mind raced with the possibility that this angel had been watching over him for centuries or longer. His gaze followed her, tracking her as she resumed her perusal of his room.

Her eyes leaped from one thing to another in his apartment, but never fell on him. In fact, she seemed to be avoiding him now, as though she feared gazing upon him for some reason.

He doubted it was because she had noticed the effect of her earlier words on him and how quickly his body had reacted to the thought of her watching him shower. He even doubted it was because she knew his dark past and that it still tormented him now.

Was it because he wasn't decent? He refused to close his robe for her sake. She had come to his room, an intruder not an invited guest. She would have to take him as she found him or leave.

When she turned in his direction to study the cuffs attached to the posts at the foot of his bed, her beauty arrested him again, claiming all of his attention. Her strange eyes darkened as she opened and closed one of the cuffs, and even went as far as shutting it around her delicate wrist. Her nose wrinkled in a frown when her hand easily slid free of the closed cuff.

Even the ones for his hands would produce the same result. They were designed for his thicker wrists and larger hands, not the slender ones of a female.

Her eyes finally lifted and met his, and the longer he stared into their mesmerising depths, the calmer he felt. He wasn't sure why.

She curled her hand around the post at the foot of his bed to his right and swung around it until her knees hit the edge of the mattress. Closer than ever. She was within five feet of him now and not a trace of fear flickered in her eyes. Even Antoine was afraid of him at times and with good reason too.

His stomach twisted and rumbled, his hunger rearing its ugly head. He needed to chain himself and sleep, not give in to his urge to feed. Taking more blood tonight would be a grave mistake. He had to wean himself off it again, dropping to the smaller doses that had proved effective at keeping his bloodlust under better control before he had fallen off the wagon in dramatic style by draining three canisters in a row a few months ago.

"Leave, before it is too late," Snow growled in warning and sat forwards with the intention of securing his ankles.

His gut clenched violently and his hands shook from the pain that ripped through him, shattering his fragile control over his bloodlust. He glanced at the angel, afraid he would harm her if he didn't shackle his wrists this second. He trembled as he lay back, his stomach churning again, twisting in on itself until he couldn't draw breath. Blood. He needed blood.

Unleash

His eyes fixed darkly on the female.
Her blood.
He would drink her dry.

CHAPTER 6

No. He needed to resist.

Blinded by the pain, Snow fumbled for the wrist restraint and slammed his arm into it. The cuff whipped shut and locked automatically. After the incident with Anya and the party, Snow had asked Antoine to custom order him new restraints for his wrists, ones he would be able to close himself without any need for assistance, and therefore no need to risk the lives of those he cared about by asking them to help him.

He flopped onto his back and brought his other arm down hard. It hit only mattress. He tried again and missed the cuff for a second time.

The female foolishly moved forwards as though she wanted to assist him, and he snarled and lashed out at her with his free hand, his blunt claws swiping the air just millimetres from her stomach.

She gasped, flapped her black wings, and shot away from him, towards the mahogany panelled entrance door of his apartment. She didn't leave. Her wide luminous eyes locked on him.

Snow smacked his arm down again and hit the cuff this time, causing it to snap shut around his wrist. He breathed hard, fighting the hunger for blood and death, and swallowed. His insides burned with the need for blood, setting him aflame and pushing him to the edge of oblivion. Couldn't lose it. Not again. Not when everyone was expecting him to come down later and be around the babies.

Not when the angel was perilously close to him.

She had moved to the foot of the bed again and was staring at him with pity in her eyes.

He cursed her in the language of his homeland for that and she flinched away, her jet-black hair falling down to mask her face. Her fear reached out and curled around him, tempting him into breaking free and slaking his thirst for violence on her.

No. Couldn't.

"Feet." He forced the word out from between clenched teeth and his fangs cut into his gums, flooding his mouth with the taste of his wretched blood.

She didn't move.

Snow snarled and lashed out with his legs, hoping to show her what might happen if she was foolish enough to ignore his request.

"I presume angels can die?" he growled the words at her, throwing them like barbs in a black deadly tone.

She visibly shook, her wide eyes darting to his before they shot to his ankles and then the cuffs attached to the heavy steel bedposts. Her nerves washed over him but she moved this time, bravely inching forwards. He tried to control himself but her proximity to him wreaked havoc and he kicked out again, trying to injure her to satisfy his dark needs even when he didn't want to hurt her.

She grabbed the cuff in one hand and tried to capture his ankle with the other. He snarled, planted his left foot onto the mattress and used it as leverage to thrust his other leg as close as he could get it to her. The cuffs around his wrists bit into his flesh and almost jerked his arms out of their sockets, but the pain didn't stop him from kicking out at her with his right foot.

She skilfully evaded the blow, snagged his ankle with a lightning fast strike, and had the cuff around it before he could catch up.

Her face set in grim lines of determination, she tackled his other ankle and easily captured it.

Snow hated feeling completely vulnerable and weak, he always had, and the feel of the cuff locking around his ankle sent him off the deep end. He thrashed wildly, bucking and snarling, pulling against his restraints until his bones blazed and his skin shredded.

Still it wasn't enough to stop him from thirsting for blood and fearing he would escape and make a meal out of the angel.

"Come." He jerked his chin, trying to entice her. He had broken restraints before when lost to his bloodlust and although these new ones had held him firm for three weeks, he wasn't about to trust they wouldn't give out if he used all of his strength on them.

She held her ground, refusing to budge, her eyes on his fangs. "No."

Snow roared. "Come here or die! I will not harm you."

Perhaps threatening her wasn't his best move given the situation and his current condition. She shook her head.

"Collar." He pushed the word out before another surge in his hunger overpowered his ability to speak and left him snarling in agony and bowing off the mattress. He dug the back of his head into the black pillows and growled through the blistering wave of fire that rushed through his veins.

When a glimmer of sanity returned, the angel was standing at the head of the bed on his right, pity back in her eyes again. He snapped at her with his fangs and cursed her. She glared at him and struck him hard, the slap burning his left cheek.

"You dare speak to me that way again and I will leave."

Good. He wanted her to leave. Snow cursed her again, blacker and fouler this time, calling her names that would have shamed his mother if she had heard them. The foolish wench had tried to raise him to be a placid, gentle man. Snow chuckled darkly. Placid. Gentle. Stupid bitch. He was vicious. Evil. Twisted.

The angel struck him again, hard enough this time that pain splintered across his skull like a spider web, driving him towards darkness. God damn it. Snow wanted another one of those blows. He wanted oblivion and unconsciousness.

Her eyes flicked to the thick steel chain attached to his headboard and the collar at the end of it.

"I will not put that on you." She sounded resolute but the fear in her eyes said he could probably convince her to go through with it.

He tried to grab her, twisting his body towards hers, and she moved back a step.

"Collar," he snarled.

"No," she whispered, shaking her head, her beautiful eyes imploring him not to ask her again. "It feels wrong to do such a thing to a man."

Snow snapped at her. "I am not a man. Collar me."

He threw his head back and snarled again as a fresh wave of fire burned through him and his stomach cramped harder than ever, his insides feeling as though they were trying to tie themselves into knots.

Snow lurched forwards and in that moment, cold steel brushed the back of his neck and then closed over the front. Mercy. She had done it, and while he had been lost to his dark urges too. Foolish female.

He collapsed onto the bed and breathed hard, trying to edge himself through a coming episode without it hitting him fully.

Her soft warm fingers brushed a line across his throat, the action soothing him even as it stoked his hunger to a dangerous new level. She smelled so good this close. He could scent her blood flowing beneath her creamy skin. Saliva pooled in his mouth. His fangs itched for a taste of her.

Snow managed to turn his face away from her.

"You have marks that say you wear this collar often." There was pity in her voice. "Why is it so necessary?"

Snow looked up at her and smirked. "I have a little drinking problem."

As if prompted by his words, the thirst attacked him. He gasped and bucked, straining against the cuffs that barely gave him room to move a few inches. They ground into his wrists and ankles, digging into bone and blood vessels, making his hands and feet throb in pain.

Snow panted hard, fighting a losing battle against the consuming tide of his bloodlust, desperate to retain a shred of his sanity and fearing that if he didn't, he would somehow harm the angel.

He screwed his eyes shut, not wanting to see her pitying look as he struggled like a snared beast against the bonds, fighting them with every shred of his immense power but failing to break them. He spat curses at them, foul words that a sliver of him hoped that the angel didn't take as an insult to her. He wanted the bonds off him. He ached to be free.

Couldn't.

He would rip the angel to shreds if he were free.

A blistering wave of fire burned up his blood, setting every molecule in his body aflame, and he rolled his eyes open and arched off the bed, his mouth opening in a silent scream. Couldn't roar. If he did, Antoine would come. Antoine would see the angel. Antoine would harm her.

Snow growled low in his throat at that thought.

He would kill any who touched her.

His claws extended at the same time as his fangs, and the apartment brightened as his eyes changed, burning red around his cat-like pupils.

Snow fought harder than ever to break the restraints, driven by a mindless need to free himself so he could protect the female and by a dark hunger to drain her dry at the same time.

She rushed forwards as the collar sliced into his throat, spilling a thick stream of his blood down his neck.

"You must calm yourself," she whispered softly, those words laced with emotions that were beyond his grasp as the bloodlust seized hold of him again and her proximity drove him mad with a need to taste her. "You are hurting yourself."

The note in her melodic voice told him more than she was willing to say. She couldn't bear the sight of him hurting himself. The scent of blood filled his room and, even though it was his own tainted life force, it sent him back over the edge.

"I am unsure how to help you." She hovered close to him and he managed to get his eyes to focus on her for a brief second, long enough to see the frustration that darkened her innocent features.

Snow growled, rolled his eyes back and snarled as he pulled harder on the chains. The steel bedposts creaked under the pressure. Agony shredded his insides, liquefying his bones and stealing his strength away, leaving him helpless. He still fought like a wild thing, ferocious and vicious as he battled his restraints, hungry to escape and taste the female.

"So much pain and suffering," she whispered and he cursed at her again, telling her in the old language to leave him alone, hoping she would listen this time.

The need for blood became too much and he sank his fangs into his own lower lip and sucked furiously on it, ravenous and unable to stop himself.

The angel left his side and he couldn't track her. The bloodlust dulled his senses. He opened his eyes again and followed her as she paced around the room, studying her every move.

If she came close enough, he would bite her. He sucked harder on his own foul blood, imagining it was the sweet nectar that flowed in her veins. He ached for her blood even as he ached to leave her unspoiled.

She searched his room, her air desperate, small hands clenching and unclenching in front of her stomach. "You must have some blood here somewhere. Where do you keep it?"

Snow released his lip and wheezed, "No use… like ashes… empty of life."

She gave him another pitying look and then her dark eyebrows rose high on her forehead, something dawning in her incredible eyes, and she approached him.

She stood beside his bed with a calm and decided expression on her face and held her arm out to him.

Snow stared at her in shock and then turned his face away. "Do not touch me… I will taint you. You are pure… I am not."

She huffed. "I am not as pure as you believe."

She leaned over him and brought her wrist right up to his lips.

Snow swallowed hard and his gaze slid to the soft flesh on the underside of her forearm. He told himself to resist even as another part of him demanded he take what she offered so freely. No. It wouldn't help him. It wouldn't free him of his bloodlust. It would only make it worse. He had to abstain from blood until he was weak and then begin again with smaller quantities.

Unleash

He had to drink.

He couldn't deny that dark urge.

Snow struck hard, burying his fangs deep into her soft body. She cried out and slapped her free hand over her mouth to stifle the rest of it, the sound distant to his ears as her blood rushed into him.

It was warm and tasted incredible, like nothing he had ever taken before, sweet and bitter at the same time, imbued with power that shot through his system like a drug, giving him what should be an illegal high.

He drank greedily, powerless to stop himself from taking all that he could, desperate for more of her. His cock hardened painfully, his body coming alive with sensation that left him dizzy and hazy, lost on a warm sea of bliss.

"Enough!" She tore her arm away from him and stumbled backwards. She blindly grabbed the metal post at the foot of his bed for support and slid down it to land on the floor with a harsh thud.

Snow opened his eyes, craned his neck as much as he could and stared down at her, shocked by what she had done and how she had tasted. Tears streaked her cheeks and there were red marks on them where she had pressed her fingers into them when covering her mouth to stop herself from crying out in pain. She held her wrist to her chest, clutching it tightly, her knuckles blazing white. Blood already spotted her pristine pale dress, marring the pure fabric.

He had hurt her.

He cursed himself this time, guilt riding him hard and chasing him down from his high. He had tainted her and harmed her. He had made her cry with his vicious attack on her and his greed.

He should have eased his fangs in gently and sipped from her with the reverence she deserved. He should have made it pleasurable for her.

"Do you often starve yourself to the point of insanity?" She snapped the words at him like a whip, her innocence evaporating as she scowled, her eyes dark with the pain and fury she emanated.

Snow was quiet for a few long seconds, unsure what to say in response to that or how to make things better. Would she accept an apology? He had told her not to offer her wrist. She had seen him at his worst. She should have known he would hurt her.

"I had blood a short while ago," he confessed, "but it tastes like death to me these days. But you… you taste like life. How?"

He hadn't missed the little fact that drinking her blood had driven him right through the other side of his bloodlust and into the clear too. The way he felt right now, he knew he wouldn't suffer another attack for at least a day, if not more. He had never felt this normal, not since before his bloodlust had first emerged.

"Do you suffer like this every night?" Her expression softened to reveal the innocence that he was coming to like about her. Her wide luminous eyes still sparkled with the tears that were drying on her pale cheeks, but they no longer held anger and darkness. They were soft and bright, inquisitive again. He nodded. Her fine black eyebrows puckered into a small frown. "There is no cure?"

"Only death." Something he had long desired but had always been denied.

She swallowed and closed her eyes, her frown hardening. She released her wrist and pressed her bloodied hand to her head, smudging red across it.

"You are unwell?" he said, his guilt returning with a vengeance.

"I feel dizzy... and a little weak." Her eyes opened and fixed on him, the brightness in them gone.

Snow frowned. How much had he taken from her? She was slender and delicate. He had drunk greedily. He had taken too much. If she had been a normal weak human, he probably would have killed her. The black wings curling around her shoulders were a constant reminder that she was anything but weak. An angel.

And she had given him blood.

That couldn't be a good thing for her to have done.

"Come to me. Let me seal the wound." He jerked his chin, trying to coax her into doing as he asked.

She grasped the bedpost and slowly pulled herself up off the floor, and then stumbled forwards and collapsed onto the mattress beside him, her breathing rapid and shallow. She shook as she bravely offered her right wrist to him.

Snow gently licked it, cleaning away the blood. His tongue on her flesh felt so good and he liked the way she stared at him, watching him intently.

Her skin was hot, her taste delectable.

He ached to feel her body against his, soft against hard, warm against cool. He hadn't touched a female in centuries, hadn't wanted to either, but he longed to lay his hands on her and learn her curves, her fragrance, and her sweetest spots.

It was wrong of him to desire her, an angel, one pure and untainted while he was wretched, but she brought out the devil in him. She made him want to taint her and ruin her.

Possess her.

He shifted his focus back to her wrist, taking care to ensure that the bleeding had stopped before he leaned his head back on the black pillows.

His gentleness seemed to please her and she offered him a small smile as she drew her arm back to her.

"I had feared you would begin drinking again," she whispered and ran her thumb over the marks on her wrist, her gaze on them now. "They tell our kind that vampires are foul."

Her gaze flickered over his face to settle on his hair and she reached out and lifted one of the long strands, drawing it out of his eyes.

"Snow," she murmured and his vivid scarlet eyes shifted to meet hers and narrowed. "Your hair is like snow. It is pure and beautiful."

Snow turned his face away. "You of all people should know how impure I am."

She sighed and even that sounded melodic and soothing to him. Her hand left his hair and she shifted on the bed. When he realised what she intended, he snapped his head around to face her, catching her reaching for the cuff that secured his right wrist.

"Don't!" he barked and she ignored him.

"You are safe now, satisfied. You will not hurt me." She sounded so positive that he almost smiled and couldn't resist pointing out something that would contradict her belief and most likely have her blushing again.

"I am not so sure," he said and she paused to look at him. "My bloodlust is under control, but you are still not safe from me. I am not sure you ever will be."

She looked confused at first and then her cheeks darkened to the deepest shade of red so far and her eyes widened, and he knew she had understood him and was now aware of the danger she was in. His bloodlust was sated, but he still felt an undeniable and consuming lust for her.

Snow smiled at the way her eyes edged downwards, towards his hips, as though she was unaware of what she was doing before it was too late and her gaze settled on his groin. Her cheeks darkened another shade. She swallowed and her heart fluttered wildly. Why?

Were her thoughts running along the same line as his were? He wanted to feel her hands on his flesh, touching and stroking him, pleasuring him and bringing him to climax. Did she desire the feel of his hands on her, using his strength and dominating her as they made love?

The angel hid her nerves well but she left the bed and he was sure that she would keep her distance now, afraid that he might pounce on her and ruin her.

She surprised him by locating the key to his restraints on the dressing table and coming back to him. She unlocked his ankles first, frowning and muttering soothing things about his wounds, things that left him feeling she truly did care about his wellbeing.

She tackled his collar next and she sighed, reached down and grazed her fingers over his throat as the cold metal fell away. Her eyebrows furrowed and her touch stole his pain away, leaving warmth behind and an incredible soothing sensation.

Could she heal with a touch?

She had somehow healed his wrists when she had been singing to him while he was lost in bloodlust before. It had to have been her. His natural healing ability couldn't fix a wound that quickly.

Her actions were gentle, careful as she unlocked the cuff around his right wrist and then moved around the foot of the bed to his left. She unlocked the final cuff and he brought his hands down and flexed his fingers. He wiped the sleeve of his robe across his face to clear the blood from it.

Someone knocked on his door and she gasped, her wide eyes shooting to it.

"Are you all right?" A male voice sounded through the thick wood.

"I am fine, and I am busy," Snow replied gruffly.

Antoine remained silent for a few seconds during which time the angel stood frozen beside the bed, as though that action could make her disappear from his brother's senses.

"You are not alone in the room. Who else is there?" Antoine said, a darker edge to his tone now.

Snow knew his brother. If he didn't like Snow's answer and if he felt Snow was in danger, he would burst into the room and attempt to take the angel down. He also respected Snow's strength and desire for privacy most of the time. Snow hoped that was the case today.

"It is not your concern. I am safe. I am fine. I will explain later."

Silence stretched into infinity before Antoine spoke again. "I will come back later. Be careful."

Snow sensed his brother cross the hall to his apartment and looked back at the angel. She was scowling at the door.

"Does your brother feel I am going to hurt you?" The sharp edge to her tone backed up the hint of her emotions that he could detect, confirming that Antoine had offended her. "Or does he fear that you will hurt me?"

Snow licked the cuts across his wrists, stemming the flow of blood and sealing the thin lines while he debated the answer to her questions. What was the best answer? She probably wouldn't like either and both were true.

He was tired of lying to people though, and she struck him as the sort of female who preferred honesty to sugar-coated half-truths.

"Both." He drew his black robe closed and tied the belt, and then shuffled off the bed. His muscles ached as he stood and he stretched, trying to crack bones back into place and ease the pain. He still felt marvellous. Would any fresh blood from the vein make him feel this way or was it because she was an angel?

He looked over his shoulder at her where she stood on the other side of the bed. Her cheeks were still too pale, her lips ashen. She needed to rest in order to recover her strength. If he bid her to sleep a while, she would probably react in a negative way, possibly even throwing his concern in his face. She was a strong female, liable to take his desire to see her rekindle her strength as an attempt to belittle her.

"Sit a while." He casually gestured to the bed and distanced himself by crossing the room, removing himself from the outcomes she was no doubt running through her mind after he had revealed he desired her. It worked.

The angel clambered onto his bed and settled herself with her back against his black pillows, taking a lot of care to place her black wings and lie in such a way that they weren't ruffled.

His whole bed would smell like her now.

Even if he lost himself to his bloodlust and had to be chained to his bed for a week, he would refuse to replace the sheets and wash her scent away. He liked the way she smelled—soft and female, delicate.

Snow opened his ebony wardrobe and scanned the contents, trying to decide what to wear tonight. He hadn't slept as he had promised he would, but he no longer felt the need. He was wide awake, buzzing from her blood in his system, and he wanted to talk to Antoine to ease his brother's mind.

The angel shuffled but he paid her no heed and selected one of the black shirts she had pressed against her delicious body. He lifted it to his nose and secretly inhaled her sweet fragrance. Warmth spread through him. He glanced across at her and frowned.

She had moved to lie on her side with her head on the pillows, the waves of her black hair spilling across them and blending into the midnight material, and had tucked her legs up against her stomach. Her wings were gone too. Had she made them disappear? She probably needed to in order to sleep comfortably.

And she was asleep.

Snow walked silently back to the bed and stood on the left side of the room, looking down at her. Her face was soft with slumber, more innocent than it had ever appeared, and it stirred a foreign feeling in the place behind his sternum that normally felt empty.

He felt dangerously protective of her and possessive.

She had her hands held close to her face and her soft lips were parted, her breath skating over her fingers. Her little feet were bare and dirty, poking out of the end of her dress. The layers of white fabric remained tight against her torso and flowed over her hips, a stark contrast against the black of his covers.

Light against darkness.

The sheer strips had parted here and there to reveal patches of smooth pale skin on her calves and thighs.

He wanted to lean over her to breathe in her scent and assure himself that he wasn't dreaming. There was an angel slumbering in his bed as though it was the most natural thing in the world for a pure being to nestle into sheets belonging to a beast who was as likely to destroy her as he was protect her.

His pale blue eyes fell to her wrist and the twin ragged marks on her arm. Her blood was delicious. He had never tasted such ambrosia. It had even made his blood taste good. Why?

Blood had been like ashes in his mouth for over a century now and these past few decades his fits had worsened. His thirst had become relentless and there were too many times when he couldn't remember things he had done.

One sip of her blood had left him feeling satisfied and he was sure he wouldn't need to feed tomorrow.

Snow tore himself away from her side before he succumbed to his desires and did something he might regret, and loped across the room to his wardrobe. He dressed in a pair of black jeans and the black shirt, tucking it into his jeans before fastening them, and then jammed his feet into his army boots. He went into the bathroom and washed the blood off his neck, wrists, and any remnants from his face.

He strayed back to the female and stared down at her. He didn't want to leave her in his room, felt a dark need to stay with her and protect her, but he needed to speak with Antoine and join in the celebrations. They had waited for him to wake before holding them after all.

He forced himself to turn away from her and walked out of the room, closing and locking the door behind him. He wasn't sure that a simple locked door could contain an angel. In fact, he was certain it couldn't. He wasn't locking the door to keep her in. He was locking it to keep others out.

He strode down the hall, swiftly took the flights of steps that led down to the floor below and then continued down to the ground level. The large double-height black room was empty. His gaze flicked to the door of Antoine's office across the room from the staircase. His brother wouldn't be there. Already he had picked up the sound of merriment coming from a room at the back of the theatre.

Snow turned right and strolled along the black-walled corridor that led backstage. One of the double doors at the end of the hall were open, allowing light to spill out together with the chatter of the performers and owners of Vampirerotique, and the gurgling wail of babies.

He slowed his approach and spotted Sera leading Antoine across the cream brightly lit room, her long deep red evening dress swaying around her legs with each step, and a smartly dressed Callum coming forward with the boy, Alistair, in his arms.

Crimson-soaked flagstones and his brother covered in blood flashed across Snow's eyes and he reached out and slammed his left hand against the black wall of the corridor for support as he flinched away from the dark painful memory.

"Snow?" Antoine's voice was loud and close, and he managed to get his eyes open and look at his brother. Antoine took his other arm, supporting him as Snow's knees threatened to give out, a look of concern in his pale eyes.

Snow could never understand how his brother could still look at him with love in his eyes after everything he had done.

"Are you feeling unwell?" Antoine said and Snow shook his head. It was passing, the pain fading. "Are you all right? You look different. Who was in your room?"

Snow leaned his back against the wall, trying to process all the questions while the last tremors of pain wracked him. He did feel different. Perhaps his brother could see the effect the angel's blood had on him.

"What do you know about angels?" Snow whispered and his brother frowned, his dark eyebrows knitting tightly together. Snow knew he sounded crazy. Before tonight, he hadn't believed angels existed either, even though he had seen creatures who claimed to be the fallen variety of that species.

"Why?" Antoine said cautiously and Snow realised that if he talked about angels without offering Antoine visible proof of one, his brother would think he truly had gone insane.

He took Antoine's arm, clutching it tightly through the fine black material of his suit jacket, and ignored his questions as he led him up the stairs and to his apartment door. He released his brother, slid the key into the lock, twisted it and opened the door. He stepped inside and held the door for Antoine.

Antoine looked as though he was about to ask another infernal question and then his eyes fell on the bed and widened.

His brother silently entered the room, his movements slow and wary, his eyes fixed on the female. Snow didn't like the way he stared at her. His possessive streak came back full force and he considered that it might have been unwise to bring Antoine up and show him the female. He didn't want anyone seeing his woman.

Snow cocked a single eyebrow. His woman?

Disappointment tinged Antoine's expression when he glanced over his shoulder at Snow. "She has no wings. Are you sure she is an angel?"

Snow nodded. "I have seen her wings… and this is not the first time she has visited me. She came to me before when I was lost to my bloodlust."

Antoine's look darkened. "Tell me you have not slept with her."

Snow's gut tightened at the thought and it rekindled his hunger, igniting the urge to possess the woman sleeping so innocently on his bed, vulnerable and at his mercy.

He managed to shake his head. "No… but she did give me blood."

Antoine's head whipped around and he pinned him with an incredulous stare. "You are thirsting again?"

Snow grimaced and mentally cursed himself. He hadn't expected his brother to figure that one out and he wasn't sure what to say in response.

"You lied to me?" Antoine's look turned to one of worry and then hurt.

Snow tried to shut him out by staring at the angel. The things he had done to his brother in the distant past made him feel bad enough, he didn't need to add new ones to the growing list of reasons he had to feel as though all he ever did was hurt Antoine.

He had never wanted to hurt his brother. He had wanted to spare Antoine the pain of watching him spiral down into bloodlust again after everything Antoine had done to bring him back from the brink so many times before.

"Her blood revitalised me." Snow kept his gaze locked on the angel.

He could sense Antoine's disquiet and irritation, and knew it was because he had again ignored a question.

"At what cost to her?" Antoine said and a chill crept down Snow's spine. He turned slowly to face his brother, a frown working its way onto his brow.

"What?"

Antoine nodded towards her. "If she is an angel, then surely giving life to you via her blood is a sin? Vampires are close to demons. I am sure angels would classify us amongst that breed."

"I hurt her when I bit her." Snow looked back at her, his gut twisting at the memory of hearing her cry out and seeing the tears on her cheeks after he had released her.

"No doubt allowing you to take from her vein pained her greatly and will forever be a black mark against her, and we both know forever is a long time to bear a sin."

He didn't need the reminder. It was constantly there at the back of his mind, awaiting him in his nightmares. He knew the danger of forever.

But he was troubled by what his brother had said. Not just because he had hurt her, but because he needed to taste her again. Now that she had committed an unforgivable act, would it hurt her if he drank from her vein again?

Snow shook that thought away, the remaining fragment of good in his wretched soul telling him not to consider it. He didn't want to damn her.

He stepped backwards towards the door and Antoine took the hint and turned away from her, walked to the door and headed out into the hall. Snow lingered, his eyes on the female. She needed to rest and recover her strength.

When she was well again, he would ask her why she had come to him and why she had allowed him to violate her by biting her, and he would demand an answer this time.

He left the room and locked the door behind him, and tried to get his mind off her as he followed Antoine back down to the party.

It was impossible.

Everything in him screamed to return to her and watch over her, protecting her as she slumbered.

His senses had been right about her.

She was dangerous.

But she didn't pose a threat to him physically.

She posed it emotionally.

He had to keep his distance from her.

For the first time in endless centuries, he had to guard his heart against a female.

A female he knew with startling certainty would be his undoing.

CHAPTER 7

She woke alone. The vampire was gone. While alertness had slowly dawned, she had thought that perhaps he had gone into the bathroom or was watching her silently and still enough that she had failed to detect him while the last vestiges of sleep held onto her.

That opinion had altered dramatically when she had finally pushed herself up in the centre of his dark four-poster bed to see that she was completely alone in his grim black apartment.

She couldn't even feel any others of his kind on this floor with her. Unusual. Normally when she visited Snow, there was at least one person on this level. There wasn't even anyone on the floor below tonight. Where had they gone?

She focused, trying to detect whether they had all vacated the theatre or were somewhere else within its environs.

There was a large gathering far below her and it was hard to place how many were there. There was too much interference from the levels of the building between her and them, but she could still feel Snow there.

She shuffled to the edge of the bed, slipped off it to land on her feet and raised her arms above her head, clasping her hands together. She stretched and yawned, and her wings grew from her back until the tips of her longest feathers grazed her ankles.

Lifting her right arm, she moved her wing forwards and extended it to its full span. She bent her head and looked at the feathers beyond the space below her arm. A solitary white feather remained, downy and small, tucked in a place that wasn't normally visible to others.

She lowered her arm and stared at the dark marks on her forearm.

They throbbed and it was difficult to ignore the pain. Giving blood to a vampire was a sacrilegious act but she had committed the sin without remorse, and she refused to succumb to that emotion now.

Snow had needed blood to soothe the terrible rage that had come upon him and she had known that her blood would give him the vitality he needed to regain control of himself and vanquish the evil that lurked within him.

She furled her black wings against her back and walked to the door, grabbed the brass handle and twisted it. Locked.

Why?

Had he sought to contain her and keep her captive? His behaviour dictated that it was the most likely reason he had locked the door on her. He probably desired her as a blood slave of sorts now. She crushed that cruel thought and listened to what her heart had to say on the matter, trusting it to guide her when her clouded emotions could not.

Perhaps he had desired to protect her from others here at the theatre.

She smiled at that, preferring it as his reason.

It took minimal effort with her powers to transport her from inside his apartment to the corridor beyond. She walked along the black hallway, admiring the accents of gold that lent it a decadent air that suited the naughty theatre.

Snow needed such accents in his room.

They took away the morbid air black could have and made it appear chic and designer. She wished she could decorate her small rooms in such a modern and interesting manner. She had tired of the stark white of them a long time ago. Everything in her realm was pristine white. She had once told her master that white was boring.

He had scolded her.

She didn't bother to cloak herself as she headed down the stairs and instead enjoyed a moment of freedom in the theatre. She preferred to move around as much as possible without shrouding herself or teleporting to places. It made her feel tangible and real, a part of this world even when she didn't really belong here.

The sound of merriment drifted up the dim staircase to her and she waited until the last possible moment, when she had reached the black-walled double-height room at the side of the stage, before she finally shadowed herself from prying eyes. She followed the noise around to her right, along another black corridor to a large warmly lit room at the back of the theatre and slipped inside, keeping close to the pale walls.

She had never realised how many vampires resided in the theatre. Not just vampires, she reminded herself as her eyes darted over familiar faces amongst the crowd.

The male who had fae blood muddled in with his vampire genes was here, and he was keeping amusingly close to a very pretty woman wearing a long black slinky dress with silver stars stitched in a sweeping arc over one breast and down in a diagonal over her opposite hip. Her dark chestnut hair had thick threads of silver streaking through it that matched her eyes.

She might have thought the elegantly dressed woman was human if she didn't already know she was a witch called Elissa, and she was part of the reason Snow had experienced his worst bout of bloodlust in centuries.

The woman bent her head and smiled at the small sandy-haired boy tucked between her and Payne, her silvery eyes twinkling with affection as she spoke to him. Another incubus, although this one was a full-blooded member of that species, and she suspected he was related to Payne in some way because they shared the same deep grey eyes and hair colour.

They also seemed to share the same taste in clothing, both males wearing pinstriped charcoal shirts with the sleeves rolled up to their elbows, paired with dark blue jeans and biker boots. The outfit looked far cuter on the young boy, and she had the feeling that he was trying to be like Payne. He even wore his sandy hair tufted in soft spikes tonight.

The boy grinned at Elissa and went to bound off into the crowd but Payne's large hand caught his shoulder and steered him back into the fold, keeping him close.

Why?

Did he not trust the vampires with the child? Would they harm him?

The thought that they might seek to injure an innocent filled her with a desire to lift her shroud and threaten retribution upon any who tried. She tamped down that desire, and this time issued herself a reminder of what had happened the only other time she had sought to protect an innocent.

The female with a wild black bob that she knew as the only succubus at the theatre bounded up to the group, squatted and rubbed the young incubus's cheek, earning a giggle from him. She rose to her feet and her vampire mate joined her.

Andreu looked much like his older brother, Javier, with the exception that his short hair was dark chocolate brown and his eyes were rich blue. Both of them preferred to dress in impeccable black designer suits though. He spoke to Payne as the witch spoke to his mate, and the young incubus tugged at the hem of the succubus's short ruffled purple skirt, trying to get her attention.

Unleash

Gathered together like this, it looked as though Payne and the succubus were better suited for each other, their casual and slightly offbeat attire making them a sharp contrast against the neat and elegant clothing of their true mates.

Her eyes moved on, scanning the room for Snow.

They paused on the sharply dressed couple at the centre of everyone's attention.

The black-haired vampire male with dazzling green eyes and his brunette werewolf shimmered with happiness and affection. The shapely female's hazel eyes shone as she bounced a baby in her arms, the girl's pink romper suit clashing with her burgundy dress. The little girl reached up and twined her fingers in Kristina's long wavy hair, pulling on it and causing her mother to wince.

Callum, her partner, bent over and tickled the baby under her chin. Her innocent face scrunched into a frown and then she wailed. Callum grimaced and Kristina's expression shifted towards desperate as she scoured the room for someone.

"Snow?" Callum called out and she watched on, filled with curiosity as she caught sight of him across the room.

He peered over the heads of everyone, formidable in his stature and build, and the crowd parted to allow him through.

Her breathing slowed.

He looked more handsome than ever in his black shirt and jeans, a twinkle in his blue eyes that she hadn't seen in a very long time.

He was enjoying himself and it showed, and she was glad. He needed this moment of normalcy after everything he had endured these past few weeks. It would help him shake off the last threads of darkness that clung to his heart and mind, restoring his faith that he could be in the company of others without the need for his restraints.

His brother followed with his beautiful mate, the blonde elite female Sera. Antoine looked much brighter tonight than he had the last time she had seen him. Dressed in a tailored black suit and his favoured Italian leather shoes, he cut an imposing figure of authority, but Snow still outshone him.

Antoine lacked the wild, hellion edge that Snow had always had. They were complete opposites in that regard. Antoine was the sensible one. Snow was the rebel.

Sera carried the male child of Callum and Kristina's twins, and he was leaning forwards in her arms, small hands grasping the air in Snow's direction. She struggled to keep hold of him and keep upright in the tall heels she wore with her elegant deep crimson evening gown.

Why did Callum want Snow?

Her eyes widened when Snow reached the fretting couple, hunkered down and pinched the baby girl's rosy cheek. She quieted and then burst into a fit of giggles.

Surprising.

She hadn't expected or even considered it possible that Snow would hold any sense of tenderness towards the tiny babes, and she definitely hadn't seen his ability to soothe them coming. It hit her hard in her chest, warming her heart and melting some of her hatred towards him.

The baby girl bounced in her mother's arms, vying with her brother for Snow's attention as he tried to entertain both of them.

It was strange seeing him smiling at the babies, teasing them and talking to them. It didn't fit the image she had of him, or the man she knew him to be, no matter how long she watched him interacting with them. He looked so much more like the man he used to be and the hold of the dark feelings in her heart grew weaker.

Sera handed the boy back to his father, who held him in the crook of his arm. Antoine said something to Snow and left with Sera. Snow looked uncertain at last when the baby boy grasped his index finger, his tiny fingers clutching it.

Kristina laughed, as though amused by Snow's discomfort. The baby girl began to settle, her eyes drifting closed as her mother gently rocked her.

The baby boy opened his little mouth to reveal small fangs and tried to draw Snow's hand up to him so he could bite it. Callum uttered something that looked as though it might have been an apology as Snow hastily removed his hand from the baby's reach. Snow laughed and rubbed the back of his neck, his actions speaking of nerves that she failed to notice because she was transfixed.

She couldn't remember the last time Snow had laughed.

It soothed her, stirring hopes long forgotten, and took her back countless centuries to a night that had changed her life forever.

Snow said something and moved away from the couple, leaving Callum to offer his wrist to his child.

Her gaze tracked Snow through the room. He settled himself into a corner, leaning against the wall there with one boot planted on the wooden floor and his other knee bent and that foot resting against the cream wall.

She wanted to go to him and wondered if he could sense her presence. He had sensed her in his room when she had been shrouded. She took a step forwards with the intent of crossing the room and mirroring him by leaning against the wall near to him, but paused when a female approached him.

Lilah.

She looked radiant in her dark green slinky dress with her long chestnut hair sleek and straight.

Snow's lips curled into a smile when he spotted Lilah.

She didn't like that look. It was one thing for him to smile and laugh with babies, and completely another for him to smile at beautiful women. She checked herself. It was none of her business who he smiled or laughed around, and she would do well to remember it.

Even if it did irk her for some reason.

She skirted the edges of the room, moving closer. She wanted to hear their conversation. She had to avoid several vampires, ducking around them and feeling them turn as they felt the air shift as she passed. None of them sensed her. Her heart pounded and she edged closer to Snow and Lilah.

She paused and leaned against the pale wall just a few metres from them.

They were deep in conversation and if Snow could sense her, he didn't show it.

"I am sorry you felt you needed to return to the theatre early," Snow said, genuine regret in his tone.

Lilah touched his arm and smiled. "Don't be. As soon as we heard what had happened, we decided to come back and be here for you. We couldn't celebrate while we knew that you were unwell, and we knew Antoine would need us. We knew you would need us."

Snow smiled at her. "I am sure Javier was not so thrilled about having to return. I am sure he resents me for ending what should have been a long joyous celebration."

"It was a good celebration." Lilah leaned closer to him and dropped her voice to a whisper. "I'm not going to complain about having to end it early. Believe me, a few weeks with my in-laws is more than enough. Don't tell Javier, but they were beginning to drive me crazy. I was longing to come back to Vampirerotique after the first week."

Lilah giggled, eliciting another, broader smile from Snow.

"It will be our secret," he whispered.

She didn't like that the two of them shared secrets with each other, or the way Lilah kept touching Snow's arm, as though they were very close. Dark claws curled around her heart, gently holding it but ready to squeeze any positive feeling from her.

Snow's pale eyebrows met in a frown and his ice-blue eyes scanned the room.

Had he sensed her?

She moved back a step, trying to elude his keen senses. His frown hardened and then he went back to speaking to Lilah. She wished he hadn't.

"You look beautiful tonight. Javier is crazy to let you out of his sight."

The claws holding her heart tightened their grip and she glared at Lilah. She was pretty, she supposed. The only thing stopping her from revealing herself and trying to steal Snow's attention for some ridiculous reason was the fact that he wasn't looking at Lilah with desire.

Not as he had looked at her.

She had seen the fire in his eyes whenever he had glanced at her and had witnessed the evidence of his arousal. He desired her.

Why did that please her?

She cursed her feelings, hating the way they flip-flopped when it came to Snow. Part of her despised him and she felt certain she would always hate him. The rest of her felt softer feelings for him and was drawn to him in a way she had never experienced before.

Her eyes moved back to him, studying his lethal beauty.

He was large compared with Lilah, powerful and like a warrior, his broad thickly muscled build making her appear tiny.

His crisp black shirt stretched across his chest, the cut emphasising the breadth of it and how narrow his waist was in comparison. He had left the top few buttons undone, revealing his collarbones and a hint of his defined pectorals. Black jeans encased his long legs, almost as tight as a second skin, and his black leather boots wrinkled their bottoms, adding a twist to his appearance.

Only Snow would pair scruffy army boots with an expensive shirt, and keep them sticking out of his jeans too. Even Payne hadn't gone that far.

Her gaze delighted in roaming back up his powerful legs and over his torso to his face. He shoved his fingers through his white hair, dragging the long strands out of his eyes. He was handsome but radiated darkness and danger. Alluring.

Enticing.

She blushed as she recalled how aroused he had been after taking her blood, his body hard and primed, because of her.

When he had bitten her, she had experienced an incredible surge in feelings from deep within her, heat that she didn't understand and urges so wicked and dark that they had shocked her.

They still shocked her now.

So had her reaction when he had subtly pointed out that he lusted after her.

Images of him naked and hard had sprung into her mind, immoral fantasies about him stripping before her and then removing all of her clothes and touching her. Her throat dried out and she swallowed, trying to wet it.

Her body quivered as those images invaded her mind again, hotter this time, a vision of them naked and entwined, his powerful body braced above hers as he made love to her, kissing her and devouring all of her, body and soul.

Snow frowned again and scanned his surroundings, and she gasped. His gaze shot towards where she stood shrouded by her powers, invisible to his eyes. He inhaled deeply, his pale blue eyes darkened with desire, and he pushed away from the wall, coming to face her.

"Snow?" Antoine's voice coming from behind her caused her to press herself flush against the wall to allow him to pass without brushing her and snapped Snow's attention away from her.

Her heart pounded, legs like jelly and threatening to give out. She pressed her palms against the wall, clutching it for support. Her stomach fluttered, hot with forbidden foreign feelings. Arousal. Her master would be more than furious if he discovered she harboured desire for the vampire.

Antoine stopped in front of Snow. Lilah greeted him and then looked over the crowd to the happy couple. Javier was there with Callum and Kristina. Lilah beamed at him across the room, as radiant as Snow had said she was, and then weaved through the crowd to take the outstretched hand of her male.

Javier pulled her into his arms, bent his head and pressed a tender kiss to Lilah's lips.

Wicked thoughts popped into her mind and she shoved them straight back out again, fearing where thinking about how Snow would kiss would lead her.

Into temptation no doubt.

She moved her focus back to Snow and Antoine. She had never been able to grasp how two brothers could look so incredibly similar in their facial features and their striking pale blue eyes, yet be so very different. Not just in personality either. Antoine's dark chocolate hair was a complete contrast to Snow's silvery-white, and Snow was taller than Antoine by at least two inches too, and more powerful in build.

Both of them looked like ancient warriors though, their years on earth gifting them with experience many never came to have, and there was a keen glint of intelligence in their eyes as they talked.

She focused on them so she could hear what had them looking as though they were ready to slay a dragon.

"Guard against her, Brother," Antoine said in a low voice and she frowned at his profile.

They were talking about her. She edged closer, eager to hear what they had to say and desiring a better answer to the question she had posed to Snow earlier.

Did Antoine perceive her as a threat to Snow, or Snow a threat to her?

Snow had said it was both but she didn't believe him. Snow felt he was a threat to her. Antoine felt she was a threat to Snow. She was sure of it.

Snow didn't respond.

Antoine wasn't going to allow his brother to ignore him though. He placed his hand on Snow's left shoulder and squeezed it.

"I have read many books, and met many people, and some of them spoke of angels. It is said they can be deceitful."

That hurt her because it was true. Angels were more than capable of deceit, especially to gain the trust of those they targeted, immoral humans and demons in particular. They were taught to charade as creatures familiar to their targets in order to get close to them, judge them, and then eliminate them.

A weight settled in her stomach. There was no need for her to feel guilt about her actions. She hadn't come to Snow in order to win his trust and harm him, not as his brother suspected. She had come to help him.

She ached to reveal herself to them and make Antoine see that she meant his older brother no harm, but there were too many powerful vampires in the room. If she stepped out of the shadows, they would probably attack her, although she didn't fear for herself.

She feared that Snow would attack them if they sought to hurt her.

She had seen his noble streak in action many times. He was often quick to defend females or those weaker than he was. The vampire was a contradiction, a walking paradox. The embodiment of war and peace in one being.

"Guard against her, Brother," Antoine repeated, his tone harder this time, a warning to Snow to heed his words. "Do not trust her."

Snow knocked his brother's hand off his shoulder and red ringed his irises. "She will not harm me. She has helped me twice now. I will not listen to your words about her. Do not judge her until you have spoken to her yourself. I accept responsibility for her and anything that may happen while she is in my care."

Her heart leaped into her throat and fluttered there. Snow had defended her. A blush climbed her cheeks. He had no reason to believe in her, and to not believe or do as his brother had asked. Antoine had looked out for Snow for centuries now, always having his brother's best interests at heart. She had expected Snow to choose his brother over her.

Snow huffed like a beast and pushed past Antoine, who caught his arm and stopped him.

"I am sorry. I did not mean to anger you," Antoine whispered in a voice laden with shame and concern. "I will meet with her if you wish me to and I will see if she is worthy of the trust you have in her."

Snow shirked his grip, the red around his irises more prominent now. "I will be in my room if anyone needs me. I just need a few minutes alone. Relay my apology to Callum and Kristina."

Antoine nodded and Snow left, heading through the crowd.

She wanted to follow him but she knew that she was already pushing it. She didn't want Snow to find her gone from his room, but she had to return to her home before her master found her gone too.

She closed her eyes and focused, and when she opened them again, she stood on the white battlements. The clouds were thick below her today, concealing the world from her eyes. A tinge of sorrow touched her heart, born of a longing to return to Snow and tell him she had to leave rather than just disappearing from his life again. He would be upset with her.

But so would her master if he discovered her gone and realised where she had been and what she had done.

She turned away, intent on returning to her quarters, and came face to face with a tall, beautiful dark-haired male.

Her master.

His pure white wings furled against his back, blending into the white armour that covered him from neck to toe. He held his helmet under his left arm and snatched her wrist with his right hand. She winced as he twisted it around, revealing the scabs that marked her pale skin.

His amethyst eyes darkened and locked with hers, and shame made her lower her gaze and turn her face away from him.

Her eyes widened when she saw her final white feather turning black and she tried to break free of his grip, her heart beating wildly. No. She shook her head, causing her long black hair to sway against her shoulders, and tears filled her eyes. No.

She struggled against her master, spreading her right wing at the same time, hoping she had been mistaken and it was a trick of the light. She couldn't lose her final feather.

Her master tightened his grip on her wrist and her bones burned from the pressure, sending pain shooting along her arm and to the tips of her fingers. She cried out and many angels stopped to stare at her, disgust in their eyes.

None held more disgust and darkness than her master's eyes though.

She couldn't bring herself to look at him and see his feelings when she could already sense them. They tore at her, bringing more tears and a desire to beg for his forgiveness and another chance.

Doing so would only make him more ashamed of her.

He had given her a thousand sins, one for each feather in her wings. She had committed the first sin and the final, and borne the shame of the rest. She had doomed herself.

"Your punishment has been decided. You will judge the vampire for his sins," her master said, his tone as dark as his eyes and his wild long black hair.

His grip loosened and his voice lightened, gaining a touch of sympathy and what she might have believed was affection once, before she had come to know her master better. There were none like him in her realm. None so vicious and just, or revered.

A judge, a jury, and an executioner in one.

Everything she had just become for Snow.

"It is the only way to save your soul now."

CHAPTER 8

Snow's head whipped around as the owl hooted, capturing his attention.

It flew overhead and he grinned, released his mother's hand, and ran after it. She called to him but he kept running, small legs and arms pumping, struggling as he hit deeper snow that reached his knees.

The owl began to drift away from him and he ran harder, pounding through the snow as quickly as he could manage, intent on keeping up with it and catching his prey. Papa would be so proud of him if he caught the owl, proving he was growing now, able to fend for himself already even though he was only fifty years old.

The ragged white mountains of the valley loomed around him, their cragged faces bright despite the moonless night. Stars blanketed the inky sky above him, and multi-coloured ribbons streaked across the dark canvas. Mama had taken him out on a walk so he could see the lights dancing in the sky more clearly, without the glow from the fires around their homestead drowning them out.

He breathed hard, wading through the snow, managing to keep up with the owl that lazily flapped its broad pale wings and glided onwards, deeper into the valley.

Snow laughed and reached for the bird, fingers grasping the air. If he were bigger, he could use the power in his legs to leap from the ground to capture it. He wasn't big enough to jump very high, although he had vaulted from the rickety staircase in the castle and landed on the grey stone floor below without injuring himself. He was getting stronger every day.

Mama had fretted and scolded him for leaping from such a height. She had made Papa scold him too, but Snow had seen the secret pride in his father's eyes.

Hues of blue, green and pink blazed across the sky above him, dancing on an unknown breeze, recapturing his attention. He almost fell into the snow but managed to keep his footing and focused back on the owl, determined not to allow the beautiful aurora to distract him again.

"Snow… do not run too far!" Mama. She was fretting again but he didn't heed her. With a mischievous smile, he kept tracking the bird. He would be alright. He always played in the valley at night and he would catch the bird before the castle was out of sight. He wasn't allowed to go out of sight of the castle. Papa had once put him over his knee because of that and Snow's backside had smarted for days. Lesson learned.

The owl veered right and Snow turned on a pinhead, his eyes locked on his prey. The cold bit at his fingers and face, the only parts of him that his pale furs didn't cover. The bottom of his thick coat, and his trousers and boots were already sodden from his running through the snow and growing cold.

He had to hurry and catch the bird before he ended up wet through. Mama would certainly scold him if that happened. She fussed over everything.

He smiled at that.

Papa told him she fussed because she loved him very much.

He loved her very much too, and he had decided that he would keep her safe and protect her as his father did. Nothing bad would ever happen to his mother.

The owl drifted down and landed on one of the branches in a dense copse.

Snow hunkered low and crept towards it, his pale furs allowing him to blend into his environment. His mother called again. He continued to sneak through the snow, edging closer to the bird. He had to catch it. He wanted Papa to be proud of him.

Could he climb the tree unnoticed to seize the bird?

It took flight and Snow huffed, annoyed that it had sensed him. He would do better next time.

The owl flew out over a flat stretch of ground and he followed it without thinking, running through the shallower snow with ease.

The ground creaked, a dark terrifying sound that echoed around the mountains.

He stopped and looked down at his feet. The snow dropped away and he plunged into black icy water. It invaded his lungs and soaked his furs, freezing his skin. He flailed, kicking his legs and trying to reach the surface of the lake. His furs weighed him down and it took all of his strength to break the surface.

He scrabbled for purchase at the edge of the hole, his short claws unable to dig into the diamond hard ice. His throat burned and he coughed up the water and tried to keep struggling, but the cold stole his strength and he couldn't claw his way out with his furs so heavy.

He went under again and feebly kicked twice before drifting down into the darkness.

Blue light burst into life above him and grew brighter as the world around him grew dimmer.

A pale shape formed amidst the light. As it drew closer, he saw it was a girl, more beautiful than even his mother. She reached for him and so he reached for her.

When she caught his hands, they both shot from the water and landed hard on the ground. The force of the impact sent him tumbling into darkness.

Snow could hear someone singing.

A song of ice and fire in the sky. A prince and an angel who were destined to love but forever be apart.

The female voice was sweet, warming the chill in his heart and his body, chasing his pain away. He tried to breathe and choked up water. It spilled from his mouth and she continued to sing, her fingers softly combing his wet hair. He shivered and trembled, weak and frozen stiff, unable to feel anything. Numb.

It took most of his remaining strength but he finally managed to open his eyes.

The dark world was foggy at first and then gradually cleared to reveal the girl he had seen in the lake. She knelt beside him, her white dress saturated and her black hair hanging in tangled threads around her shoulders. She smiled when she saw him and continued singing, although her lips didn't move.

He heard the song in his head and his heart.

She stared at him and he at her, her fingers still gently stroking his hair, and her song slowly chasing the numbness from his body, returning warmth to his chest first. It spread from there, easing down his arms and towards his legs.

"Hello," Snow said, his voice hoarse from his sore throat. He hoped she knew his language. He could understand her song. She had to know his language. He wanted to speak with her.

She didn't answer but she did stop singing. Her soft features turned sorrowful.

"What is wrong?" He sat up and she looked away from him, towards her shoulders. She had small wings, as beautiful as the owl's had been. There were darker feathers threaded into the pure white. "What do they mean?"

Even as he said it, one turned jet-black, far darker than the others were.

She wrote in the shallow snow beside her.

Bad.

Snow frowned. "Why?"

She pointed to the frozen lake to his right and then to him. He gasped, his eyes shooting wide.

"Because you saved me?" He didn't like that he had gotten her in trouble. A pure black feather. He had got his cousins in trouble a few times, his mischief normally landing them in some sort of dire situation that had the adults searching for them or having to come to their aid. His cousins were boys though. He had never gotten a girl in trouble.

She wrote another two words.

Vampire. Evil.

Snow snarled and slashed his hand through that second word and jolted to his feet, angry now.

"I am not evil," he barked and she remained sitting, serenely staring up at him, sorrow in her eyes, as though she had seen his future and knew what was to come for him. Snow cursed her and she flinched away. He panicked, ashamed that he had frightened her when she had been the one to save him from the lake. "I am sorry."

She looked back at him and shrugged.

"Are all of them because I am bad?" he crouched in front of her, shivering in his pale wet furs, his throat still burning from inhaling the icy water.

Her dark eyebrows furrowed, the sadness in her eyes increasing, and she shook her head. She pointed to the word 'bad' and then to herself. Snow frowned.

"You are bad too?" he said.

She nodded. Snow held his hand out to her and smiled.

His mother called for him.

"Do not be sad. You can run away from the mean angels who said you were bad and live with me."

The pretty girl smiled at last and went to place her hand into his.

Light blinded him.

When it receded, a black-haired male in white armour towered over him, his pure white wings spread wide. His amethyst eyes pinned Snow with a dark look of disgust.

Snow sprang to his feet, determined to stand up to the mean angel.

The man backhanded him before he could move and pain ricocheted through every bone in his body as he flew through the air, crashed hard into the ground and tumbled across it. Snow gasped for air, fire burning every inch of him, so intense that he couldn't breathe or even think. His vision swam, blurring and distorting.

He heard someone running towards him. Saw the girl and the fear in her eyes. Snow growled through his agony and tried to push himself onto his knees, determined to protect her from the nasty man.

The male grabbed her arm and hauled her back to him, holding her in spite of her violent struggling.

Snow cried out when he tried to use his arms. One was broken. One of his legs had suffered a similar fate. He could taste blood too. He spat two teeth out onto the pristine snow. His head spun but he tried to get to his feet again.

"Come." The male's voice boomed around the mountains. "I warned you to leave the wretch to die. Now you must take all of the sins he will commit unto yourself. For every sin, you will suffer, and you will have them as black marks on your soul."

The light blinded Snow again and he collapsed into the cold embrace of the earth. He struggled to remain conscious, concerned that he had got the angel into more trouble.

"Snow!" Mama.

He rolled onto his front and managed to get onto his knees this time, using his good arm to push himself up. Colourful ribbons danced above him, bright against their velvet backdrop, beautiful and soothing his pain. His bones throbbed, the pain threatening to pull him into darkness, but he clung to consciousness.

The snow was cold beneath him, stealing more of his strength, luring him into surrendering to the darkness.

"Snow?" His mother's soft feminine voice curled around him, chasing the chill from his body as it warmed his heart.

She rounded him and crouched in the snow before him, her beautiful face full of affection and concern, her smile renewing his strength. Dark furs covered her body, her pale hair spilling across the long soft fibres. She stood much taller than he was even though they both knelt in the snow, and he looked up at her, into her ice-blue eyes that looked almost white in the low light.

Her warm hand swept the strands of his white hair out of his face and she stilled when he flinched in pain.

"What happened?" She leaned down and licked his cheek, sealing the cut there.

"I made a friend, Mama... but the man made her go." Snow's head turned and he wavered. His mother caught his arms and white-hot pain seared his bones. He cried out and squeezed his eyes shut, tears leaking from their corners.

"Darling!" his mother called and Snow managed to shake his head.

He didn't want his father to come to them. He didn't want his father to see him like this, weak and useless. He had to be strong. His father would be proud of him then.

Snow tried to push up onto his feet. He clutched his mother's shoulders and pulled himself up, but his left leg screamed in pain, the shattered bone grinding together beneath his flesh. He collapsed onto her lap. She gathered her to him, fear in her eyes as she gently stroked his brow.

She raised her hand to her lips and didn't take her eyes from his as she sank a single fang into her wrist.

The strong scent of her blood filled the night and she lowered her wrist to him. Snow took the offered blood, his small mouth working furiously to draw enough from the wound.

He wasn't big enough to cover a full bite. His mother had tried once when he had fallen from a tree and he had spilled her blood everywhere.

He swallowed a mouthful and his pain began to ebb, his body swift to ingest the blood and use it to kick start the process of healing his broken bones. The darkness faded with it, the dizziness passing. He took another mouthful from his mother and then she drew her arm away and licked the cut, sealing it. Snow licked his lips.

His father called from the distance, drawing closer, and Snow willed his body to heal faster so his father wouldn't see him as weak. Papa prided himself on the strength of their bloodline and their breeding. Snow wanted his father to be proud of him too.

His mother gathered her furs around them both and rocked him gently in her arms. She leaned over him and pressed soft kisses to his brow, and Snow closed his eyes, savouring the feel of her embrace and feeling safe and warm, loved. He loved his Mama more than anything. He would love her forever, and would make sure nothing bad ever happened to her.

"What was your friend's name?" she whispered between kisses.

Snow's brow crinkled. The little girl hadn't said what it was. He would give her a name.

"Aurora."

Something stroked his brow and Snow frowned as that gentle touch drew him out of his dream long enough that he hazily saw the angel above him. She sung and he drifted back to sleep, finding himself lying in a bed with his mother beside him, his body swathed in bandages.

"Try to rest, Snow." Mama stroked his forehead, her caress soothing him. He had been stuck in bed for weeks already, his body slow to heal the broken bones, even when he frequently took blood from his mother.

The world shifted and he was sitting beside the fire outside the castle, staring beyond it to the snowy mountains and the stars hanging above them in the velvet darkness. His cousins muttered about him behind his back, complaining that he was no longer any fun. He ached to play with them but he couldn't.

Every time he came close to giving in to the urge, he thought of the angel, Aurora, and remembered that if he was bad, she would grow more black feathers and the man would be angry with her again. He wanted to stay out of trouble for her.

He would never do anything that would result in her gaining another black feather.

He would protect both her and his Mama.

CHAPTER 9

She refused to judge Snow as guilty immediately in order to save herself, earning the anger of her master, and instead returned to the vampire. Somehow, she would redeem him, because the thought of sentencing him to death hurt her.

How many times had she wished he no longer existed and now she couldn't bring herself to give him the death that he eagerly sought?

When she had returned to her home that night two thousand years ago, she had cried until she had convinced herself that her master was not cruel enough to inflict upon her the punishment he had detailed.

For one hundred years, her life had gone on as it had before she had saved Snow from the lake and death, granting him a second chance, and she had grown sure that she had been right and her master had only threatened to punish her in order to scare her into never straying from his orders again.

And then Snow had committed a sin and she had gained another black feather.

She had cried again that night, scared and alone, afraid of what her future would hold.

She had realised that Snow had forgotten her, and that had only made her cry harder because she couldn't forget him and her master had stipulated that she couldn't reveal herself to him to remind him of what would happen to her should he sin.

All she could do was follow him, hidden from the world, watching him. She had grown to hate him because he had sinned without remorse and she had suffered greatly each time, punished for his actions.

She had even suffered in the four centuries he had served in an army of his kind and had spent many years gone from this world, ventured into Hell, a place where her vision couldn't see him. She had grown more black feathers in those years than she had in all the others combined and had only been able to wonder what sins Snow had committed to cause them.

Whenever he had returned to this world, appearing in her vision again, he had changed by degrees. She had seen it in him when he had spent time with a baby Antoine. A cold, bleak aura had begun to surround him, and then she had witnessed the beginnings of his bloodlust. Whatever he had done in those years in Hell, it had affected him deeply.

The more black feathers she grew, the more the other angels had viewed her as tainted. She had become despised amongst her own kind, an outcast because of the vampire. Only her master had dared to take her under his wing and teach her how to do her duties, and she still didn't believe he had done it out of kindness. He had cursed her to bear all of Snow's sins after all.

He had bound her to Snow and only he could set her free.

No. She could set herself free. Her master had given her a way out. If she judged Snow as guilty and a danger to the world, and condemned him to death, she would have her freedom.

Tears lined her eyes because she knew in her heart that she would never be able to do such a thing to him, not without good reason.

She would never be able to save herself.

Her master had told her two thousand years ago to watch Snow die and she hadn't been able to follow his command.

She had thought him beautiful when she had seen him running through the snow chasing the owl. She had never witnessed a boy so excited and full of life, joy and curiosity.

His white hair, pale eyes, and the thick furs he wore had made him look as though the frigid land had birthed a child so linked to it that they resembled each other. She had reacted on instinct when he had fallen through the ice and plunged into the lake.

She hadn't seen something evil that the world would be better off without.

She had only seen a child like herself about to die.

A beautiful boy that she had wanted to live.

She looked upon him now as he slumbered under the black covers of his grim steel bed, his ankles and wrists restrained, and his handsome face twitching as he dreamed.

When he had killed his family, her master had made her watch it all unfold, forcing her to see that she had unleashed a monster upon the world the night she had saved him as a boy.

She had never believed him capable of such evil and it had shocked her to see him butchering those he adored, but she still hadn't been able to bring herself to admit that he deserved to die.

He had been an innocent two thousand years ago and he still was.

It wasn't Snow who committed atrocious acts. It was the terrible affliction he had been born with.

She had seen him suffer in the aftermath of every incident, loathing himself, and even begging Antoine to kill him. Antoine had seen the good in Snow too and had refused to give up on him, and that had given her the strength to do the same.

There was still a part of her that hated him though, both for everything he had done and the fact that he had forgotten her.

When he had recovered from his latest bout of bloodlust and she had revealed herself to him, she had expected him to remember her. He hadn't. It had bitterly disappointed her.

Now, in order to save her soul, she had to judge his. She refused to say outright that he was beyond salvation. She would do her best to view him and his actions independently of her feelings, with open eyes and an unclouded heart.

Snow's breathing turned heavy and he muttered in his sleep, tossing his head side to side, his hands and legs twitching, rattling the inch-thick chains.

She gazed upon him, seeing a powerful male stripped of his strength by a debilitating curse.

Whenever she saw him like this, falling into his bloodlust, she ached for him and had done for centuries. She felt responsible for everything he had suffered. If she hadn't intervened that night, he never would have fallen victim of his affliction.

But he never would have lived either.

He had been so young, just like her.

He bucked and snarled, his immense body bowing off the four-poster bed and pulling the chains tight.

A nightmare haunted him. It would send him back down into the darkness if she didn't intervene.

She crossed the room, clambered onto the black covers on the bed and curled up next to him with her knees against his side and his right arm beneath her ribs. She gazed down at him and touched his cheek. What did he dream? She wished she could see them. She would know how to ease his suffering if she could and perhaps it would help her judge him.

Unleash

He growled, baring his fangs, and the muscles in his jaw popped. She stroked the backs of her knuckles across his cheek and he snapped his teeth at her. It didn't stop her this time.

She withdrew her hand only enough that he couldn't reach it, waited for him to return to fighting his bonds, and then caressed his cheek again. It was cool and surprisingly soft now that his stubble was gone.

His face twisted in a grimace. Not a grimace, she realised as a tear slipped from the corner of his eyes and his pain echoed into her through the point where they touched. Fathomless pain. Did he dream of his family and that dreadful night?

Her eyebrows furrowed, sorrow filling her heart and making it ache for him. He had suffered enough in life. Did he have to suffer in his dreams too? She wished he could dream beautiful things, not such horror, but she knew that it haunted him, a torture he felt he had to endure in exchange for his sins.

If she could have gone to him that night, she would have.

Not so she could spare herself the weight of his sins, but so she could have spared him this eternal torment and suffering.

She wrapped her arms around his head so the back of it rested upon her left forearm, his soft white hair caressing her skin, and held him, trying not to squash his arm beneath her, hoping to give him some comfort amidst his pain. Her body tingled where his touched it, aware of him and how close to each other they were.

Snow stirred, sleepy and dazed, tears in his soulful blue eyes.

She hushed him when he frowned and looked as though he might protest about what she was doing.

"Go back to sleep," she whispered and his eyes slipped shut again.

She softly sung to him as she stroked his silver-white hair, hoping the sound of the melody would bring him good dreams, and looked down at his peaceful handsome face. She had never held a man like this before. It moved her. Stirred her. She felt dangerously attracted to him, hyper-aware of his powerful body and masculine scent.

She felt curious about things.

Her eyes drifted down to his profanely sensual mouth.

How would his lips feel against hers?

Soft. Hard. Rough. Warm. Cool?

It was difficult to resist finding out the answer.

She focused on singing to him, monitoring his emotions at the same time, her hand moving in a constant motion against his snowy hair.

He had grown into a beautiful male. Many women had known his lips and his touch. She had hated them all. None of them had been good women. None of them had deserved the affection he had bestowed upon them during their time together.

They had all led Snow to sin in some way, whether it was convincing him to join a war he didn't truly believe in or kill another male for their sake. They had all used his immense power and his standing within vampire society as a means of getting something they wanted and had used his heart to make him do as they bid.

He hadn't been with a woman in a very long time.

She was the only female to lie in his bed in many centuries. The first female to be this close to him since his bloodlust had emerged.

It thrilled her.

It shouldn't, but it did.

She watched him sleeping, losing track of time as he peacefully slumbered, his breathing steady and heart beating at a relaxed rhythm. She liked that she could steal his pain away and give him peace. It gave her hope that he could redeem himself and was worthy of saving.

He stirred again, his eyelids slowly lifting to reveal pale blue eyes that had intrigued her the night they had met. A frown creased his brow and he tilted his head back to stare up at her.

He stared at her in silence for so long that she began to feel self-conscious and was about to ask what was wrong when he spoke.

"Aurora?"

That word again. She frowned now.

His eyes softened and a smile tugged at the corners of his lips. "You could not speak then… I never knew your name."

A hot shiver spread outwards from her heart and through her limbs, lightening her insides. He remembered her.

"I couldn't speak because it was a punishment for being late to my classes and speaking back to my master." She took her hand away from his hair and settled it on his chest, feeling his heart pumping against his ribs.

He smiled at her. "We met under the most beautiful aurora borealis I had ever seen. When my… I decided to give you a name. Aurora."

Aurora.

Whenever he said that word in his sleep, he was dreaming of the night they had met? He was calling out for her?

He had called out that word over three weeks ago too, on the stage of Vampirerotique when the bloodlust and his memories had conspired to drive him out of his mind. He had shouted for her and asked her to take him home with her.

He had said she was prettier than the heavens.

A fierce blush crept onto her cheeks.

"What is it?" Snow whispered and moved his left arm as though he wanted to touch her cheeks. The cuff stopped him, the chain tightening and jerking his hand back. The curiosity and concern in his pale eyes faded, replaced by regret that she could sense in him. "I feel terrible that I forgot you… I am sorry."

He looked at her wings and the guilt she could feel in him worsened, and then he closed his eyes, as though he couldn't bear to see all of the black feathers now that he knew he had caused them.

"Everything you must have suffered," he said in a low pained voice. "It is all my fault."

She shook her head and he opened his eyes and looked up at her again, remorse still colouring his expression.

"You couldn't help it." She believed that. He had been led astray many times in his life, following his heart, and then his bloodlust had awoken and had made him do other terrible things.

"What is your real name?" Snow's pale grey eyebrows knitted together and she was glad when some of the pain in his eyes lifted, curiosity beginning to fill them again.

"Angels do not have names."

"That is sad, in a way."

It was just the way things were. Her kind didn't have names. His kind didn't have wings. This was the way of it.

"I have never thought about it before now… but perhaps I could have a name." It was a dangerous thought to entertain. She liked the idea of having a name. There were so many of them in this world that the possibilities were endless. Everyone at the theatre had a different one and many of them suited the person. Such as Snow.

What name would she have if she could?

She looked back down at Snow, into his ice-blue eyes, and tilted her head until it was at the same angle as his and she was looking at him straight on. "Could I have the name you gave to me?"

He smiled. "I would like that, Aurora."

She smiled too, enjoying the lyrical way that word sounded whenever he said it and hearing her name for the first time.

Would she get into trouble for having a name? It would make her stand out from the other angels, an individual amongst a collective. Would her master punish her for desiring such a thing?

She found she didn't care.

She was Aurora now.

CHAPTER 10

∞

Aurora paced her quarters in her master's home, her gaze turned inwards, giving her the ability to watch over Snow. He interacted with the others at Vampirerotique, moving around the theatre, dressed as handsomely as he had been at the celebration.

It had been two days since she had last visited him and she was beginning to find it impossible to ignore her desire to return to him. She needed to maintain her distance though. Whenever she was around him, she found herself entertaining thoughts that shocked her.

Such as kissing him.

She still longed to know the feel of his lips and his taste. Her master would punish her if he knew she had imagined kissing Snow many times over the past two nights while she had been watching him.

Snow had shown no sign of his bloodlust emerging.

He conversed with his fellow vampires, entertained the twins, and had even made a rather heartfelt apology to Payne and his female witch, Elissa. It had touched Aurora and strengthened her belief that Snow was capable of turning his life around, saving himself from death, if his terrible affliction would only leave him in peace.

The young incubus boy she knew as Luca had interrupted them in the end, demanding that Snow play with him as he did with the babes. Snow had spent almost an hour amusing the boy, kneeling on the wooden floor of Payne's grey room and playing with a toy train set.

That still made her smile and warmed her heart.

If only her master could see him as she did, she was sure he would change his mind about Snow and her mission to judge him. Snow had committed terrible acts but he also did good. Somewhere deep within him was the youth he had once been, before the world had conspired against him to turn him evil.

Antoine entered Snow's black room and settled himself on the edge of the double bed while Snow poured him a glass of blood. This was progress she hadn't expected. Snow had always avoided blood in an open container such as a glass if he wasn't restrained. Did he feel confident enough about his control over his bloodlust now to drink from a glass when unfettered?

She smiled at that.

The sound of a door opening below her drew her attention away from Snow for a second. Her master was home. She wanted to make him watch Snow and force him to see the other side of the vampire he believed was pure evil and incapable of good. Her master would refuse though. He always had. As far as he was concerned, Snow deserved to die.

Snow sat on his bed beside his brother, discussing business matters and new ideas Antoine wanted to try out in the next season at Vampirerotique. Snow tipped his head back and glanced up at the ceiling. His beautiful blue eyes remained locked on it for a few seconds before he dropped his chin and continued talking to Antoine.

He had done that often over the past forty-eight hours.

Was he thinking about her?

Did he want her to come back?

She pretended that thought didn't please her and she didn't desire to do as he silently bid because she ached to return to him too.

She longed to touch him again.

Ever since he had bitten her, new feelings had bombarded her, as though the act had unleashed a dormant ability to experience emotions that as far as she knew were ones beyond an angel's grasp.

Such as desire.

Whenever she gazed into Snow's eyes or caressed his hair or skin, her belly heated and quivered, and her body shook, her temperature rose, her palms sweated and she blushed.

She also had a wicked urge to strip him bare and run her hands over him.

No good would come of succumbing to those desires.

If her master discovered that she harboured such feelings for Snow, he would believe her compromised and would judge Snow in her stead. He would kill him without a fair trial or hesitation.

Her master entered her small white room and she severed her connection to Snow, bringing her vision back to her realm. He stood in the doorway, his pure wings tucked against the back of his casual white robes. He had tied his black hair into a ponytail and his amethyst eyes had an edge that she didn't like.

"It has been many hours since you were last in the mortal realm. Have you already made your decision?" He remained standing ramrod straight, as she expected of him. He had always been stiff and formal, and many angels wondered why he had taken her under his wing. Even as a child, she had been considered a hellion and beyond salvation.

Just like Snow.

"No," she said and turned to face him with resolve in her heart. "I am watching him from here. He interacts daily with the other residents of the theatre, especially the twin babies and the young boy, all without incident or danger. When I have seen enough to make an informed decision, I will give you my judgement."

His expression remained emotionless but the edge to his purple eyes sharpened. "Do you believe you will be able to make that decision before the deadline?"

"Deadline?" Her heart skipped a beat. He had never mentioned a deadline.

"You have only three days left out of the seven I gave to you."

Aurora wanted to spit out a vile curse directed at him but held her tongue. He would punish her if she let her anger show and he would no doubt choose to have her held in her room, under watch at all times, until she had thought on her sin and apologised. Even then, he probably wouldn't release her from custody until it was too late and her time with Snow was up.

Three days.

Heat prickled over her arms and down her back, an uncomfortable sensation that she had felt often since she had started visiting Snow when he had been lost to his bloodlust. Panic.

How could her master expect her to judge Snow in only three days? She had watched him for two, and that gave her a good start, but there was still so much she needed to see.

She needed to see if he could be trusted outside the reach of his brother, in the open world. She needed to see if he would relapse once her blood had left his system. She wouldn't be able to live with herself if she made a wrong judgement and he went on to lose himself to his demons again and harmed mortals.

She wouldn't need to live with herself.

Her master would make her see what she had done and then she would pay the ultimate price for her mistake.

She would lose her soul and be cast into darkness, into Hell.

"Three days," her master said in a cold voice that sent a shiver down her spine. He turned to leave. "Aurora."

She gasped and her eyes widened. He knew. He knew and was angry with her, and that was why she had such a short period of time in which to judge Snow. He had lied to her, pretending he had given her seven days from the time when he had handed her the mission. He closed the door behind him and she did curse him now, muttering the words under her breath.

She had to return to Snow.

Aurora closed her eyes and when she opened them again, she stood in Snow's room, shrouded in shadows. Antoine was gone. Snow lay on his bed, reading a book, still wearing far too much clothing even though only a black shirt and jeans encased his powerful body.

Aurora checked herself.

Angels were naturally curious but she was woman enough to admit that it wasn't curiosity driving her.

It was desire.

She couldn't succumb to it though. Her master already believed her compromised because she had a name now, given to her by the vampire she was supposed to judge. It didn't exactly make her appear impartial. Neither did her lying with him while he slept, ensuring he had good dreams. She was influencing him.

"I know you are there, Aurora."

She shivered at the way her name sounded in his deep baritone. Delicious. Erotic.

His blue gaze lifted from the pages of his book to settle on her where she stood in the middle of his room, between the foot of his double bed and his bathroom.

He must have trained his senses to detect her even when she was invisible to his eyes.

"You left without a word again. Why?" There was a note of anger in his tone, a sharp edge that reminded her of her master and demanded that she answer him.

Aurora lifted her shroud and revealed herself to him. His eyes immediately raked over her, burning her through the layers of her white dress, making her achy and hot.

"You were sleeping and I had to return." She tried to sound casual, not wanting him to know how shaken she was by what her master had announced. Three days. She didn't want to think about it. In three days, she may have saved this beautiful man that was such an intrinsic part of her life or condemned him to death.

"You were gone for a long time. I was beginning to think you would never return." He placed his book down on his ebony nightstand and sat up on the bed, arranging himself against the pillows. His gaze bore into her, darker now, and not with desire. Displeasure. He radiated it together with hurt.

What did he want her to say? That she had fought herself countless times in order to stop herself from giving in to her deepest desire and coming to him?

That she had ached to be with him every second she had watched him, wanting to be the object of his focus and on the receiving end of his smiles?

That she had dreamed of lying with him, and not in an innocent way?

She couldn't admit to those things, not even to ease his pain and reassure him that she desired his company as much as he craved hers.

It was killing her.

She stood in the middle of his morbid apartment, staring at him, battling her desire to admit why she had come to him again after thousands of years in the shadows and why she was here now. She couldn't, and she hated herself for it.

She hated to lie to him and pretend that everything was normal when her whole world was tilting on its axis and starting to crumble.

As if he knew her thoughts, he cocked his head to one side, and said, "Why did you come back now, when it has been two thousand years since the night you saved me? Why didn't you return to me when I forgot you and make me remember you again?"

Two very good questions, one she would have to skirt around because she couldn't tell him the whole reason she was here now and the other she could answer truthfully.

She moved forwards across the wooden floor, wrapped her hands around the thick steel post at the bottom left corner of his bed, and lowered her gaze to the black sheets.

"I wanted to see you again. I was drawn by your suffering… and I have always been with you when you have been in this world, even when you could not see me. I was not supposed to allow anyone in this world to see me, not even you, not even to remind you that I was there in the shadows, watching your life play out."

She lifted her eyes to settle on him but he looked away, casting his down to his knees. A frown hardened his expression and she could see his self-reproach and guilt as it flickered in his pale eyes and the grim line of his mouth.

"I am sorry that I forgot you, Aurora," he whispered, soft and tender, voice thick with emotion. "I shouldn't have. It was wrong of me… and you suffered because of it."

Aurora pushed away from the bedpost, his gruff but sweet apology melting her and making her desire to go to him. She wanted to be near to him, but she feared what would happen if she closed the short distance between them. It was already hard enough to resist her need to touch him again.

If she drew any closer to him, it would become impossible.

"It is done now." She trailed her fingers down the cold dark metal, searching her mind for something else to say to get him off a topic that evidently plagued him. She couldn't think of anything. "It is daylight. You should be resting."

Had she just talked about the weather with him?

It was something she had witnessed mortals do whenever they were lost for a topic of conversation. She had never thought she would rely on it herself.

Snow sighed. "I do not want to sleep."

"Why not?" She could spot the signs of fatigue in his eyes and the tight lines of his face.

Snow's beautiful blue eyes locked on her and he frowned, his silvery eyebrows drawing tight above them. "Because you will disappear again if I go to sleep, and… I… enjoy your company."

Aurora smiled at that, heart lifting and warming at the same time. Snow liked her being around. The feeling went both ways.

"I do not want to wake to find you gone again, not knowing when you will come back to me." His words were gruff, hard, but she felt the softness and sentiment behind them, and they touched her.

"I promise I will remain here while you sleep then." Because she honestly couldn't bring herself to leave him. If she only had three days, then she wanted to spend each minute of them with him, and not only so she could judge him properly. The hatred she had held in her heart had all melted away, thawed by his smiles and the touch of affection that shone in his eyes whenever he spoke to her, together with the heat of his desire. Desire she felt beating within her too, impossible to ignore or deny.

"And what will you be doing while I sleep?" He looked suspicious and a corona of red ringed his ice-blue irises. What scenarios was he running through his mind? She didn't intend to harm him or leave the room, if that was the root of his concern.

"I will stay here and rest too." Part lie, because she didn't intend to sleep at all. She had to think of a plan.

"Then you must sleep with me then." He looked beautifully startled when her eyes widened and then flustered. His cheeks darkened to a pale shade of pink. "I meant only that we should share the bed."

"Why?" If she shared the bed with him, she was likely to find herself tempted to carry out any one of the thousand wicked scenarios that had crossed her mind in the split second after he had talked about sleeping with him.

Sleeping with him.

Mercy, she desired that above everything, even when she knew it was sinful and wrong of her.

"Because I want to be sure that you don't disappear." He was back to gruff again, and folded his arms over his chest, the action causing the sleeves of his black shirt to pull tight across his muscles and making her feel that he wasn't going to allow any negotiation in this matter.

She was aware that if she lay close to him, he would sense it if she tried to leave, and it would wake him. He was taking no chances. He truly wanted her to stay with him and not go home again. She was willing to do as he asked, but she wouldn't be sleeping. She had to devise her plan, a way of testing Snow so she could make an informed decision.

She would lay with him so he would rest though. It had become essential to him since his bloodlust had emerged. The more rested he was, the better able he was to fight his demons.

Demons. There was something she desired to know about him, and she couldn't hold her tongue now that she could finally speak with him about it. Curiosity drove her to ask.

"Fine," she said and then paused before she blurted out, "Tell me why you went to Hell."

Snow's pale eyebrows drew together and his blue eyes darkened. "Why do you ask about those years?"

She didn't want to cause him pain, or risk the memories of his time in Hell awakening another bout of bloodlust, but she had to know. "I cannot see into Hell, so I could not watch over you when you were there. Why did you go to that realm?"

Snow's gaze dropped to his knees and his frown hardened. "I was drafted into the Preux Chevaliers after my father left the corps. It is tradition for the sons of the Aristocrats to spend some years in the corps, and often we enter them when another family member leaves."

"Preux Chevaliers?" She wasn't familiar with that term, and her grasp of the languages of this world was limited as she had only ever watched Snow.

He had learned French in order to speak with Antoine and his family when they had lived in Switzerland, near the border with France. It sounded French.

"It means valiant knights."

Even though he wore darkness like a second skin, the term suited Snow somehow. He was gallant at heart, a noble male. His mother had raised him well, teaching him to take care of those weaker than he was and to protect them. A true knight.

"You served for many centuries, and there were hundreds of years in which I could not see you because you were in Hell."

Snow lifted his gaze to meet hers and a hint of a smile touched his lips. "You almost sound as if you missed me."

And it almost seemed that it would please him if she admitted that she had in a way. She kept that to herself though.

"I'm merely curious about that world and what you did when there. Whenever you returned, you wore a haunted look, even when you played with Antoine." She paused and frowned, her mind turning over what she had just said, and then stared deep into Snow's eyes. "You mentioned that family members always join to take the place of one of their own within the ranks of this army. Antoine never joined the Preux Chevaliers."

Snow's eyes darkened a full shade again, his pupils narrowing in their centres and beginning to stretch into vertical slits. "No."

That word came out hard and clipped, and Aurora sensed that he didn't want her to push the subject. Unfortunately, curiosity told her to ignore his silent request and warning, and go ahead and voice the observation that lingered on the tip of her tongue.

"You wouldn't let him. You refused to allow Antoine to enter the army to take your place, and everything I saw leaves me feeling that it was because whatever you witnessed… whatever you did in that wretched place… it sped the awakening of your bloodlust."

Snow swallowed hard and cast his gaze away from her, the edges of his irises blazing red now. The tips of his fangs showed between his lips when he spoke, his voice dark and gravelly, rough with raw emotion that made her want to go to him and stroke his cheek to soothe him.

"I wanted to protect him."

He closed his eyes and lowered his head, tendrils of his white hair falling down to mask one side of his handsome face. The muscle in his jaw tensed and he frowned again, silvery eyebrows knitting tightly together and his nostrils flaring.

She could feel his unease, his pain, from where she stood.

The emotions flowed across the room, wrapped around her, and pulled her to him. She edged a step closer, unsure what to say to take this new pain away.

She hated that she had been right.

Snow had done and seen terrible things in Hell, and it had awakened his bloodlust. He had refused to allow Antoine to enter the Preux Chevaliers because he had known it would do the same to him, quickening the development of his bloodlust. He had wanted to protect his younger brother from the horror of serving in that army and becoming a slave to a dark affliction because of it.

"Snow," Aurora started but faltered, still unsure what to say. She clenched and unclenched her hands, her fingers trembling. She ached to soothe him but she feared he wouldn't accept it, and she didn't think she could bear the pain of him rejecting her. "It was a noble thing you did."

"He doesn't know." Snow scrubbed a hand over his face, tipped his head back and sighed. He slowly lowered his eyes to her again. "I never told him. He was so young at the time. I was over nine hundred when I joined because my… father left to spend more time and raise a second child with my…"

"You don't need to… please, don't push yourself, Snow." Because she would hate herself if he relapsed all because she had forced him to talk about his family and his past. He had experienced difficulty when mentioning his mother and father by name ever since that terrible night and she knew in her heart that each time he spoke the words it pained him, lashing at him and cutting him deep.

He shook his head. "No… it is no problem. I was over nine hundred when I became a Preux Chevalier. For those four hundred long years, I saw things that made my skin crawl and did things that I am not proud of, and you are right… it changed me. When Antoine was born, I had already served for a century. I knew the moment I held him in my arms that I could never allow him to take my place. I could never let him go through what I had. A vampire only has to serve four centuries. When it came time for me to leave that hellish legion, I made it painfully clear to those in command that Antoine would never become what I had."

Aurora cast her mind back to that time and recalled that around then many of her feathers had turned black at once, and she knew with chilling certainty that Snow had bloodied his hands in order to keep his brother safe.

"You killed your own kind." She needed to hear him admit it before she would believe it.

Snow nodded solemnly. "They left me no choice. They refused to heed my warning and told me Antoine would take my place. He was only three hundred. Little more than a youth. I had to kill them, Aurora. You have to see that… I had to kill them."

"I know," Aurora whispered and ventured another step closer to him. She swallowed and raised her hand, and then lowered it again, cursing herself for not having the courage to reach out and lay her hand on his cheek or his knee to show him that she didn't think ill of him because of what he had done that day. He had done it to protect Antoine. He had given those vampires a choice, and they had chosen death.

Snow glanced up into her eyes and lingered, the red around the edges of his irises fading and the darkness lifting. Sorrow replaced it, but mixed in with that sombre emotion were others. Warmer ones that gained ground the longer he looked up at her, obliterating the pain until it was gone and only they remained, filling his beautiful eyes with a look that verged on tender.

Aurora breathed slowly, fighting to steady herself, battling to resist the urges that look in Snow's eyes awakened in her. It would be all too easy to surrender to the pressing need to touch him and feel the coolness of his skin beneath her fingertips. From there it would be but a step to lean down and bring her lips to his.

And then she would be lost forever.

Snow would claim all of her with that one simple kiss. She would lose her objectivity, and most likely her heart, and it would become impossible to bring herself to judge him with clear eyes.

It took all of her strength, but Aurora managed to take a step backwards, placing a small distance between them. That distance felt like an ocean and she longed to cross it to him, to fall into his arms and discover the reality of her darkest desires.

Aurora lowered her eyes to the black bedclothes, focusing on them to steady herself.

"You should sleep," she said and her voice had never sounded so hollow to her ears. It wasn't what she wanted to say to him, but it was what she had to say. She had to get things back on track. She had to resist her forbidden urges.

Snow slipped off the bed and walked past her, so close that she could sense his power as a hot shiver down her spine and she ached for him to brush against her.

She looked over her shoulder, gaze following him. He reached his wardrobe and began to strip off. Slowly.

Aurora had the distinct impression that he was doing it on purpose, drawing out his undressing because he liked the feel of her gaze on him, watching as he slowly unbuttoned his black shirt and revealed inch after inch of delicious pale skin stretched tight over powerful defined muscles.

The ache started again, hot and fierce, making her belly flutter.

He tossed his shirt onto the laundry basket in the corner and then tackled his jeans. Aurora told herself to look away but failed to follow the order when he pushed his jeans down, revealing his black underwear and long toned legs.

A blush heated her cheeks.

Snow glanced over at her and she swore a wicked smile tilted his lips before he turned his face away. He was enjoying tempting her. Perhaps her master was right and he was evil after all, but it was a strange sort of evil, a sinful and sexy sort.

He finally dropped his jeans on top of his shirt in the basket and crossed the room, slowly stalking towards her, his gait that of a predator hunting prey.

She had no chance to stifle the blush that covered the full length of her body this time, burning through her blood. She wet her lips, trembling all over, stomach fluttering as she stared into his eyes, caught by them and unable to escape.

It took all of her willpower, but she tore her gaze away, only for it to fall on the top of the tattoo that poked out above the waistband of his black boxer shorts. She wanted to know what the rest of it looked like.

"Your tattoo intrigues me," she whispered, unable to find the courage to voice those words any louder.

Snow cocked an eyebrow, grabbed her shoulders so quickly that she gasped and jolted, and made her sit on the end of the bed. Her backside hit the mattress hard enough to make the springs creak. She didn't notice. Her focus was wholly on Snow as he stood before her, his lean hips eyelevel to her, the pronounced muscles of his abdomen on tempting display. So close that her breath was probably skating over them.

Aurora told herself to look up. Her willpower failed her this time. She stared at the sexy dip of his navel and all that sensual hard-packed muscle. Her heart thundered, pumping wildfire through her veins. What would he do if she leaned forwards and swept her tongue around his navel?

She wanted to find out.

Snow derailed her thought by catching the waistband of his black boxer shorts above his right hip and shoving the garment down enough that she could see the full design of his tattoo. It was hard to focus on it when the action had also revealed a thatch of crisp dark silver curls. Was it wrong of her to want to ask him to shed the underwear completely?

She had seen him in many ways over his lifetime but never completely naked. She had always closed the connection when there was a danger of seeing him fully nude, not wanting to witness the majesty of his body, a body she could never know intimately, even when she had secretly desired it.

Aurora's eyes widened as that dawned on her. How long had she desired Snow? She had never liked to watch him interacting with females. It had always left a dark feeling in her heart that she had thought was hatred towards him because he kept sinning. She had always blushed whenever he had stripped off or she had turned her gaze upon him just as he was stepping into the shower or bath, or sometimes skinny-dipping in a lake.

She had thought the flush of heat had been because she had felt it was wrong to see him in such a manner, not because she had desired to watch him but had been too afraid.

Except for the skinny-dipping times.

She had watched then, fascinated and wondering how cold the water was, or whether fish bothered him, and whether he thought about that night when she had saved his life.

"Aurora," Snow husked and brought her back to him.

Her gaze focused on the tattoo.

"I drew the design many years ago but constantly refined it, until I decided I wanted… needed… to make it part of myself."

She studied the design. It was a stylised purple cross with a tribal style black cross curling around it, forming the stem of a rose bloom that sat in the centre. Two drops of blood dripped from the bloom, and she knew what they symbolised. His parents and what he had done to them.

Aurora reached out without thinking and lightly stroked the twin stylised white-blue wings that flared outwards from the top of the cross to complete the design.

Snow inhaled sharply and his focus on her intensified.

Aurora slowly lifted her head, her eyes trailing over every taut muscle on his powerful torso. Delicious. She met his gaze. His pale irises were dark with desire again, locked intently on her. Her fingers trembled against his cool skin.

"Why did you incorporate wings into the design?" she whispered.

"It was a last minute decision when the artist was here. I wasn't sure at the time why I added them. Now, I know." His voice was gruff and thick again, deep and dark with hunger that thrilled her. "Some part of me… buried deep… must have remembered you all this time and perhaps it wanted to remind me."

She gasped when his hand gently caught hers and he brought it away from his hip. He lingered, holding her hand, and she didn't want him to let her go.

Unleash

She wanted him to hold onto her forever, even when she knew it was an impossible dream, and she was only making things harder for herself.

His large hand was cool against hers and she could sense his strength more clearly, his incredible power, but he was careful with her, applying barely any pressure to her fingers. She could take her hand away if she wanted. He was giving her the option and letting her be the one in control.

Aurora swallowed, lost in his eyes and aware of the fact that she was sitting on his bed, alone in his room with him, and the energy that crackled between them, sparks of fire that burned through her blood and made her body yearn to know his.

Snow hesitated and then took a laboured step back, as if he had struggled to convince himself to place that small distance between them, just as she had fought to do the same a few minutes ago. His fingers slipped from hers and he cast a nervous look around his room, his strong heart beating as wildly as hers was.

"I should probably sleep." His words were hollow and forced, and the look he flicked at her, the darkness that lingered in his eyes, spoke different ones to her. He wanted her but he was being chivalrous, respectful of what she was and aware of what he was. "It is still a few hours until nightfall."

He was growing hard. It was impossible to miss when she was eyelevel with his groin. Her gaze fell there, fulfilling a wicked irresistible desire. His penis already pushed at the black material of his shorts, semi-hard and rising before her eyes.

Not only that, but she had noticed the points of his fangs when he had spoken. He hungered for her in more than just a physical way. He hungered for her blood too, and the force of the need to feel his fangs in her again that swept through her in response shocked her.

Snow swiftly turned away and her eyes followed him, catching the blush that coloured his cheeks as he rounded the bed to the left side. He yanked the black covers back, lay down and tugged them over himself, up to his chest.

He paused, the air around him heavy with tension.

"I can chain myself if it would make you feel safer around me."

Aurora's heart broke for him. He wasn't a threat to her but he clearly felt he was, or that she believed he was. He expected her to want him chained, unable to sleep comfortably, unable to sleep close to her.

"I feel safe around you. I trust you not to hurt me, Snow." She looked over her shoulder at him and he looked pleased by her answer, a spark of warmth lighting his blue eyes that she hadn't seen since he had been a young man.

He was happy.

And she was the cause of it.

Aurora focused on hiding her wings and his expression turned to one of fascination as they shrank into her back.

"Sleeping without them is more comfortable, but they don't like to be gone for long. I will likely wake before you." It was a reasonable excuse. If he stirred and found her awake, he wouldn't think anything was wrong.

Snow closed his eyes and Aurora rose from the bed, switched off the lamps in the room, and then joined him on the bed.

She lay on top of the black covers beside him, on her side with her arm tucked under her head on the pillow that smelled like him. Her perfect night vision allowed her to see him clearly in the dark and she studied his noble profile, trailing her gaze over the line of his brow, down the straight slope of his nose, to his sensual lips and strong jaw.

It wasn't long before sleep claimed him.

Aurora watched him slumber, indulging herself and losing track of time. Only minutes seemed to pass but it must have been closer to hours because when she focused, the sun was edging lower in the sky. It would set within the hour and she still hadn't formulated her plan.

Her gut twisted and turned, and she closed her eyes, unable to look at Snow while guilt rode her.

She despised herself for lying to him. Unlike those she worked with, her master included, she hated to deceive any creature, even the wicked ones. The fact that she deceived Snow in order to gain his trust made her feel like one of the wicked, but she needed to remain close to him if she were to judge him correctly.

Aurora sighed, lifted her eyelids and stared at him. Her master's words rang in her ears, ones he had spoken often over the past twenty centuries.

The creature was a threat to humankind.

Aurora didn't believe that.

He was only a threat to himself.

She had never met such a trouble soul in all her long existence. He was so lost and broken, so void of hope. It pained her to see it in his eyes and feel it beating in his heart. He believed himself wretched and tainted, evil, and deserving of death.

She had seen thousands of mortals who had taken countless lives each, and none of them had shown the deep remorse for their actions that Snow did. None of them believed they deserved to perish or face execution for their sins.

They justified their cruel and often barbaric actions, blaming society or others, or their duties. They revelled in killing. Taking lives thrilled them and too many of them drew sick satisfaction from bathing their hands in blood.

Snow despised himself for the things he had done. He never blamed his bloodlust for his actions. He never sought a way of justifying them in order to alleviate his guilt and deflect the scorn of others. He hated that he had destroyed lives or ended them, and took no satisfaction from their deaths. He took only pain that stayed with him forever.

Here was one who had long ago given up and whose spirit had died but whose body had lived on, an empty husk, a pitiful existence that he longed to leave behind.

It pained her greatly.

Aurora tried to focus on her mission. Her thoughts swam, flickering over the things she had seen Snow do, both the good and the bad, and the pain she knew he carried within him as a constant reminder of his terrible deeds.

She grew aware of Snow beside her, only a black sheet separating her body and his.

The sun was close to setting.

Aurora leaned over him and studied each strand of snow-white hair that caressed his brow, his sculpted cheek, and even drifted down to softly stroke his wicked mouth.

His lips called to her, slightly parted in sleep, his lower one fuller than the top.

She wanted to kiss him and it was hard to resist that urge.

Instead, she peered closer and saw his canines. They were blunt but they had been sharp when he had bitten her. A tingling began in her wrist and spread up her arm, heat following in its wake. She licked her lips, told herself not to, and then lightly stroked the seam of his mouth with the tip of her left index finger.

His lips parted further and his cool breath caressed her finger, causing hers to hitch.

Vivid colours followed the path of her caress, bright in the darkness, a sign that she was experiencing strong emotions.

Strong was the understatement of the century.

They consumed and overwhelmed her.

How could one so rough, so fallen and lost, feel so soft and warm, so very alluring?

It fascinated her.

She wanted him.

She wanted to feel his lips on hers at last.

Aurora leaned forwards to press her lips to his and then cursed internally and stopped herself. She couldn't do it.

For his sake, she had to resist.

Snow's eyes flicked open.

CHAPTER 11

Aurora scooted away from him and off the bed. Snow sat up and tried to catch her arm before she could distance herself any further, wanting to finish what she had started even when he knew he shouldn't.

She stared at him, her eyes wild with the panic he could feel in her emotions and the frantic beat of her heart, overshadowing the lingering trace of her desire, and then bolted for the door. She was out of it before he could get the covers off him.

Snow growled, hit the floor running, and gave chase. The lights were on in the black-walled corridor. His gaze sought her, his head whipping to his left. She had already reached the end of the hallway. Rather than heading down the staircase, she went up another one further back in the corridor. The roof. She intended to fly away from him.

He damned well wouldn't let her.

He refused to let her run from her feelings any longer.

He sprinted after her, bare feet landing heavily with each long stride, and took the stairs two at a time, following them upwards.

"Aurora," he called out but she didn't slow. She kept running into the darkness ahead of him, her small feet making no sound on the steps. Her wings hadn't made an appearance yet. Was that a good sign?

Snow couldn't take comfort from it. She was still running from him after all. She intended to leave him again and he feared he would never see her again if he let her get away.

She hit the storage level at the very top of the theatre and kept going.

"Aurora." Snow tried again, hoping she would listen to him this time. "Do not run from me."

Not only because he wanted her to stay.

If she kept running, he was going to lose his temper and then his head. His bloodlust was liable to make a poorly timed appearance because the thought of her leaving was cleaving his heart into two.

"I have to go." She didn't look back. The scent of panic and fear swamped her feminine smell of lilies and snow, turning it acrid. "It was wrong of me to come to you. I should have stayed away."

Because she was an angel? Guilt lanced him again, running his chest through. He had forgotten her and committed so many sins that her wings had turned entirely black. He hated that she had seen him all those times, and had probably seen him with women, witnessed the debauched things he had done and the destruction he had caused, ending countless lives.

She had seen him at his worst and he wasn't sure that he had a best to show her to prove there was good in him, something to make him worthy of her notice.

Aurora broke out onto the flat roof of Vampirerotique and slowed to a halt, breathing hard.

Snow felt confusion breaking through her other emotions. Her feelings were clearer than ever now that he had become more attuned to her.

The desire he could sense and smell on her was the reason he bravely edged towards the door and the evening beyond.

She had been close to kissing him. Her touch had awoken him and he had remained still, feigning sleep in order to see what she would do. Her breath had been hot and moist against his lips, and he had come close to taking the lead and kissing her.

If he kissed her, would he taint her?

He stared at her where she stood on the rooftop with her back to him, a breeze tousling her fall of black hair and the layers of her pristine white dress.

He wasn't worthy of this beautiful creature. Not after everything he had put her through and everything he had done. He was wretched.

Clouds hung heavily in the sky, blocking out the final light of the sun that was now below the horizon.

Snow cautiously edged out onto the roof, not because of the danger sunlight posed to him, but because of the fact he was stepping beyond the walls of Vampirerotique for the first time in over a century.

He blinked hard, unaccustomed to even the dim light, and braced himself as a million scents assaulted him and his senses sharpened. He tensed as the breeze caressed his bare flesh, unused to the feel of it now.

Unfamiliar sounds buzzed in his ears, making him twitchy and cranking up his tension until he feared the slightest thing would trigger his bloodlust.

Unleash

A shrill noise came from overhead and Snow hunkered down, glaring up at the sky. A jet. He had seen pictures. Antoine took great pleasure in keeping him up to date about the world. Snow saw it as a sign of his brother's unwavering faith in him and his need to cling to the hope that Snow would recover and gain enough control over his bloodlust to be allowed out into the world again.

Snow did not like aircraft. He decided it as he watched it lazily move into the distance. They didn't seem to move quickly enough to maintain flight and the noise they made ground in his ears.

He glanced behind him at the dark stairwell, tempted to go back inside where the walls blocked out most of the noise and he didn't feel so on edge.

He couldn't. If he did, Aurora would leave.

He steeled himself and took another step forwards. The black tar was warm beneath his bare feet. He hadn't felt the lingering heat of the sun in a very long time, even before his incarceration at Vampirerotique.

Aurora whirled to face him, fear in her eyes. "Go back!"

She was scared of him.

Snow halted, her words cutting him to his bones and lashing at his heart.

She hesitated, looking as though she was going to run again. Perhaps not. He had the craziest notion that she wasn't intending to run, but was rather torn between standing still and stepping towards him.

Her eyes swam with panic, their striking green-to-blue colour bright in the evening. "I don't want the sun to harm you. Please, Snow... go back."

Not fear of him. She feared for him. He was glad that she was speaking to him again and concerned about him too. It was more than he could have hoped for and gave him the courage to take another step in her direction.

"I am old enough to withstand it." He continued slowly moving towards her so he didn't startle her into running again.

He drew in a deep breath and paused, savouring it. He hadn't breathed fresh air in long decades, and although he could hardly call the grimy London air fresh, it was certainly better than the air inside the theatre.

Snow ran his hand over his hair when another aircraft cut across the sky directly above. He hoped that they couldn't see him from that height, standing on a roof in only his underwear. It wasn't how he had pictured himself dressed in his first foray into the world in over a century.

The light began to fade, the clouds darkening, and the scent of rain drifted on the breeze. The weather was about to turn abysmal.

He hadn't missed that.

"Aurora," he started and then wasn't sure what to say. He had to do something to make her stay. The thought of her leaving hurt him, making his chest ache, and he would rather lay his heart on the line than let her go without a fight. "Do not leave me... I know I do not deserve you... and you probably think me a wretched monster that deserves only death."

She tensed at that, her shoulders going rigid, but said nothing.

"Please, Aurora." When was the last time he had pleaded with a woman? Probably around the time he had decided to give up desiring females too. Aurora had changed all that.

He thought of her constantly, never able to get her out of his head, even in sleep. His dreams always went back to the night she had saved him, and then forwards to her arrival at Vampirerotique. He couldn't think straight around her and couldn't picture his life without her in it now.

His hands shook so he curled them into fists, clenching them. He had never felt weak and vulnerable like this, uncertain, not in all his centuries of life, not even when faced with his bloodlust or chained to his bed.

"Do not leave, Aurora. Come back to my room... stay with me... and I will find a way to show you that I am... I do not know what I am... but I know I don't want you to leave."

"I am in trouble with my master again," she whispered in a low voice laced with hurt and a touch of fear.

"Because of me?" His shoulders sagged and his hands fell open, his hope draining away.

She nodded and her eyes filled with sorrow. "Because of you."

He knew what she wouldn't say. Her master, the man who had broken almost every bone in his body the night he had first met Aurora, despised him and thought him unworthy of her.

Snow looked at her, forcing himself to recognise that she was an angel, and he was a devil.

Her whole life had been ruined because she had chosen to save him.

"You should have let me die," he muttered and wished she would leave now. He wanted this over with already. She was going to leave him in the end, driven away by the darkness within him, and he would taint her if he touched her. It was pointless.

Aurora's eyes blazed. "You were an innocent! You didn't deserve to die like that."

She still believed that?

Snow heaved a sigh. "If I had died, my parents would be alive... Antoine wouldn't bear physical and emotional scars that haunt him, and countless other souls would not have suffered at my hands or my fangs."

She moved a step closer, her anger washing over him, far more intense than he had anticipated. Her beautiful eyes were dark with it, her lips compressing into a mulish line. She squared her shoulders and narrowed her gaze.

"And what of you?" she snapped. "Have you not suffered because of *my* actions? I saved you that night and set in motion a series of terrible events. I condemned you to a life of pain and misery... you have suffered endless agony because of me. By your reasoning, I should die for the things I have done."

Snow stepped back, unable to stop himself as the force of her words struck him like physical blows.

"You never deserved to suffer because you took pity on a child." He kept his voice soft, hoping to calm her. "It was an angelic thing to do."

She glared at him. "Even if my master had wanted me to watch you die that night?"

He had? Snow didn't like that. The bastard had tried to make her watch a little boy die. Why?

Before he could say anything, she continued. "He desired to test me. I failed. I couldn't stand by and watch as an innocent boy, a child like me, drowned in an icy lake. I saw only a child without a blemish on his soul."

"You couldn't have known what you would unleash on the world," Snow countered, wanting to alleviate the guilt he could feel in her. He drew in another deep breath to steady himself and the scent of rain grew stronger. In the distance, thunder growled through the clouds.

"No. I didn't. I saved you and then you asked me to stay with you, and I foolishly wanted that so much because I knew my master would punish me for what I had done... and this time it would be more severe than any I had endured before." Tears lined her eyes and she dashed them away, her actions speaking of irritation that he sensed in her. She hated revealing any sign of weakness to him. She wanted him to see her as strong.

It was there in the upward tilt of her chin and her battle to hide her emotions. All he could see was a woman who was breaking inside, the weight of all his sins crushing her soul to ashes.

A female torn between duty and desire.

"I accepted my punishment... and I dared to hope you would remember what had happened and what my master had said... and you would remember me."

"I am sorry, Aurora." Snow stepped towards her and the first drops of rain fell, dark spots on the black tar roof. Aurora stared at him, fighting to hold back her tears, and he ached to comfort her.

She wrapped her arms around herself and turned her face away from him.

"I should not have forgotten you..." He curled his fingers into fists to stop himself from reaching out, smoothing his palm across her cheek, and lifting her head so she was looking at him again. She would bolt if he touched her. Tainted her. "I had truly wanted you to live with me too, away from the mean angels who had upset you. You are here now. You do not have to leave. You could stay with me."

He didn't dare hope that she would.

God knew he deserved to have her throw everything in his face, his feelings included, and leave him forever.

She shook her head.

His heart broke. He actually felt the snap and the rip.

"I cannot." She lowered her head further, causing her long black hair to cover her face.

"Why not?" Snow couldn't hold the growl of frustration and hurt from his voice when his feelings were colliding within him, despair battling hope, cowardice fighting courage.

He frowned and ground his molars, unsure what to do. His head said to give up and let her go. His heart said to reach out and grab hold of her, and never let her leave him. She couldn't leave him. They were meant for each other. He was sure of it.

"We do not belong together," she whispered and he shut out the words of the song she had sung to him, the tale of two who didn't belong together, two he was coming to see as he and Aurora, even when he wanted to go against the odds and win her heart forever. "My master is right."

Something in Snow snapped on hearing those words leave her lips. "Screw your master and what he thinks is right. What do you think is right? What feels right to you?"

Aurora glanced at him. "I do not know."

Snow pieced his shattered heart back together, mentally picked himself up off the deck, and took another step towards her, determined not to back down until she had given in to him.

"I know that you fear what is happening between us, Aurora... the Devil knows I do too... and that it is all new to you and may feel wrong, but if you would only give me a chance... I can show you how right we are for each other and that your passion is something to embrace, not deny." He halted in front of her, his entire body shaking and his knees weak, and stared down into her beautiful eyes, catching the spark of warmth that now lit them. A spark that ignited hope within his aching heart.

Snow breathed hard, struggling with himself and the words, trying to get them all to come out right in spite of his nerves. He longed to touch her but he couldn't. He feared he would taint her. God, he wanted to taint her. He had never wanted anything so fiercely.

She looked as though she was going to say something stupid about her master.

Snow's hands trembled, nerves threatening to get the better of him. He wouldn't let her leave him. He lifted his hand, gently slid it along the length of her jaw, and raised her face to his. His gaze fell to her lips.

He pressed his thumb to her jaw, captured her nape with his fingers, and tilted her head, slanting his at the same time.

"I will ruin you."

He leaned in and placed his mouth on hers, cutting off her protest with a kiss. The heat and taste of her struck him hard, and the softness of her lips against his rocked him to his soul.

Snow closed his eyes and gathered her against him with his free arm. The feel of her supple body pressing into his sent him out of his head and it was hard to keep the kiss chaste, giving her time to adjust to it.

His whole body cried out to take things further and kiss her deeper, sliding his tongue between the seam of her lips, ruining her completely.

He gently swept his lips across hers, the feel of her shaking in his arms keeping him grounded, awing him as she mimicked his actions, her soft mouth working against his. Her breath stuttered, moist and sweet on his face, and her palms settled on his bare chest. His heart beat hard against it, hurting his ribs as it attempted to break free of the cage of his body and get to her.

It belonged to her now, no matter what happened between them. In return, he wanted her to belong to him. It was only fair.

He risked it and stroked her lips with his tongue and she clutched his pectorals, her fingertips pressing into his flesh, and her heartbeat went wild.

Snow hadn't kissed in too many centuries, but she had probably never been kissed. He didn't want to overwhelm or scare her, not even when he ached to feel her tongue caressing his, hot against cool.

He reluctantly drew back, releasing her mouth, and looked down at her. She stayed on her toes, her entire body leaning against his and her hands burning into his chest. She looked beautiful with her eyes still closed, head still slanted, and lips parted and rosy from his kiss.

Rain fell softly on her face, drops glistening on her cheeks and brow. A single drop landed on her lower lip, quivering there. He wanted to capture that drop in another kiss.

Her eyes slowly opened. A deep blush crept onto her cheeks.

"Give me a chance," Snow whispered, voice thick and hoarse, tight with the feelings filling his heart and his desire.

She swiped her tongue across her lower lip, catching the raindrop, almost doing him in. He groaned internally, his hunger for her rising, burning away all restraint and goading him into kissing her again, and not relenting until she was completely his.

"I can only give you three days," she said quietly.

It was more than he had dared to hope for and he would be a fool not to take it.

"Snow?" His name trembled on her lips.

He took his hand from her jaw and teased the strands of her damp black hair from her face, clearing it for his heated gaze to devour.

She swallowed and her eyes flickered between his and his lips.

"Kiss me again."

CHAPTER 12

Snow captured Aurora's jaw and drew her back to him, lowering his head at the same time.

He swept his lips across hers, earning a breathy sigh that verged on a moan, and gathered her body closer to his, settling his free hand in the small of her back and then sliding it around to clutch her hip.

The feel of her soft flesh giving beneath his fingers was divine, stoking his desire up another degree. He wanted to run his hands over every supple delicious inch of her but feared it would frighten her away or she would reject him if he tried to slake his need to touch her.

She tasted sweet and addictive, and he knew he would crave her forever.

Aurora responded quicker this time, her small hands sliding up his damp bare chest, teasing him with the warmth of her palms. She clutched his shoulders, fingertips pressing into his flesh in the same hungry way his grasped her side, and tilted her head and kissed him, her actions choppy and a little clumsy, but enchanting all the same.

Rain began to fall in earnest, fat drops that were cold against his bare skin, but he didn't feel them. Didn't notice anything while his lips danced with Aurora's, his heart on fire and his soul filling with light.

He trembled, nerves threatening to get the better of him even when he was battling them, trying to shut them down so Aurora didn't notice them. He didn't want her to think him a weak and inexperienced male, even when he felt like one as he kissed her, drowning in her taste and her heat, afraid he would do something to make her pull away and leave him.

Snow struggled to keep the kiss soft, a tender exploration of her lips and a gentle easing into her first experience. He grew more confident as she kissed him, her mouth working against his, growing bolder with each sweep of her lips.

Her fingertips pressed into his shoulders, clutching him tightly, and she leaned into him, mashing her breasts against his chest. Her heart thundered against his, a frantic rhythm that called to his base hungers, telling him that she wanted more. His body responded in the only way it knew, growing hard for her. Painfully so.

He ached to take things further and he wasn't sure how long he would be able to deny that need, even when he knew he should.

She loosed her first moan and tensed, as though the sound of pleasure emanating from her throat and heart had startled her. He smiled against her lips and deepened the kiss, stroking his tongue over her lips so they parted for him. He teased another moan from her when their tongues touched, causing his to tingle and a shiver to tumble down his spine. He needed more.

Aurora was way ahead of him.

She delved her tongue into his mouth and groaned low in her throat, the sound conveying pure unadulterated bliss. Snow groaned with her and tackled her tongue, taking control of the kiss again, showing her that two could play at her game. She upped the stakes.

Aurora clutched his shoulders, tiptoed and moulded her hot body against his front, her belly pressing into his hard cock and tearing another moan from him. She ran one hand up his neck to his hair and her fingers tangled in it, nails scraping his scalp, driving him out of his mind.

Rain poured down on them and thunder rolled menacingly overhead.

Snow planted his hands against her lower back, gathered her flush against him and leaned over her, kissing her harder and losing himself in sensations that felt foreign to him. It had been that long since he had held a woman like this and kissed one.

He shook that thought away. He had never held a woman like this, clinging to her as though his world would end if she escaped his grasp, and had never kissed like this either, his passion pouring out of him because it was overflowing and he couldn't contain it. A dam had burst and he was powerless to resist the violent flow that swept him along, pulling him under at times until he felt as though he was drowning.

Gasping for more.

Lightning cracked above them, the flash registering even with his eyes closed, and the hairs on the back of his neck prickled. His senses blared a warning he was too far gone to heed.

Unleash

The electricity in the air was nothing compared with the intense energy that blazed between him and Aurora.

Their desire put it to shame, burning at a billion volts, far beyond their control.

Aurora ran her short nails down his arms, clawing at his wet skin, and he growled and gathered her closer.

"Need you," he husked and she didn't deny him. She whimpered in response, kissing him harder, working her body against his in a maddening way.

Snow gathered fistfuls of her white dress, squeezing the water from the saturated layers, and growled as he pulled her closer. She still wasn't close enough to satisfy him, even when there wasn't a trace of air between their bodies. He needed her closer. He needed to be inside her.

He slid his left hand down her exposed thigh and slowly raised it as he devoured her mouth. He hooked his fingers under her knee and held it close to his hip, thrusting against her belly at the same time. She let out another groan and dragged her lips harder across his, kissing him with fierce need that had him rock hard in his underwear. He needed more.

Aurora writhed against him, her actions jerky and tense, her kiss blistering but speaking of her inexperience. She didn't know how to respond to the feelings flooding her, the intense need and hunger. He could feel her desperation and frustration, and he wanted to help her find the satisfaction she needed.

Snow lifted her into his arms, guiding her legs around his waist. She wrapped her arms around his neck and when she rocked her body this time, her core rubbed his hard shaft and she sighed in bliss. It drove him insane.

He couldn't let her go that far with him, not even if she wanted it. He was desperate to feel all of her, to bury himself in her warm body, but he couldn't. She was an innocent.

An angel.

She had never known a man's touch.

Aurora rocked her hips again and threw her head back, her moan of pleasure combating with the thunder rolling overhead. Rain drenched her, the drops splattering on her pale skin, soaking into her dress and making the material transparent.

Ah, Hell.

Snow stared at the taut dusky buds of her nipples, the tight puckered beads clearly visible as they strained against her white dress, calling to him.

God damn him.

He smiled darkly, swearing that higher power already had and now it had sent an angel to tempt him into sinning again, and lowered his head. Aurora cried out when he wrapped his lips around her left nipple, bending over her and holding her bottom with one hand and supporting her back with the other.

He closed his eyes and sucked the sweet bud through her dress, groaning at the feel of her and the cool taste of the rain on her skin. Lightning arced across the clouds, the rain lashing at him, but he didn't care. He would gladly die right now. He had already tasted heaven.

No, not quite. He wanted to taste it before he died.

He wanted to taste Aurora.

Snow fell to his knees, hitting the black tar hard enough to jolt his spine and cause Aurora to shriek. He leaned forwards and laid her down on the wet roof, pinning her beneath him as he continued to tease her nipple with his teeth and tongue. Her legs tightened around him and he took his wicked angel's hint, driving his hips against hers, taking and giving pleasure that had them both moaning and quaking.

Aurora's fingers tangled in his wet hair, clutching the long lengths, holding him to her breasts. He wanted to taste them properly. He pushed himself up on one hand and the sight of her arrested his gaze, stilling his body at the same time. She lay beneath him, her beautiful eyes bright in the darkness and cheeks flushed with desire. The dark passion-filled abyss of her pupils gobbled up her colourful irises, speaking of the needs he could already sense in her and would gladly fulfil. She wanted this too.

"Snow," she whispered, her breath hitching, and he moved above her, rocking between her hips, her hot core burning his cock. He wanted to be inside her as he moved like this, making love to her. Her brow puckered and she tilted her head back into the roof and cried out, clawing his biceps at the same time.

Bright colours filled the corners of his vision and he frowned as he looked down at his arms. A trail blazed across his skin like an aurora borealis.

"What the hell?" He looked back at her, wanting an explanation.

Aurora panted, moaned, and undulated her body against his, almost driving his curiosity to the back of his mind. It darted back to the front when she touched his chest, fingers leaving more bright ribbons of jewel tones on his skin as the ones on his arms faded.

She bit her lip and raised her hips into his, rubbing herself along his hard length, making his eyes roll back in his head. He thrust against her a few times, unable to help himself, tearing more blissful cries from her sweet lips.

Aurora arched her back, caught the cups of her dress, and wantonly pulled the white material down her breasts, exposing them to his eyes.

Now he really couldn't concentrate.

But he did manage to retain enough sense to note she didn't leave colours on her own skin.

He would ask about that later.

Right now, heaven was staring him in the face and he was damned well going there.

He lowered his head and kissed the plush mounds of her breasts, teasing breathless moans from her, causing her to quiver beneath him and claw at his back. Her legs tightened around his hips and her actions turned rougher, harder as she tried to satisfy herself, her inexperience driving her to try anything to reach the pinnacle of her pleasure.

Snow couldn't stop himself. He supported himself with one hand and ran his left one down her soft thigh to her backside. He stroked the curve of her bottom and then over her hip, gently shifting his body to one side, letting her grow accustomed to him touching her. Her movements became more frantic. He laved her right nipple and then sucked it hard, and moaned as his fingers reached the waist of her pale underwear.

He lazily stroked the elastic and then dipped his fingers beneath the barrier, teasing crisp curls. She gasped, arched, and pleaded him in the old language.

Snow did as she bid, easing his fingers downwards to dip into her moist warm petals. His body jerked in response to how good she felt, so damp and ready, eager as she moved her hips and sought his fingers. He ground his teeth and growled, aching to be inside her and ready to spill in his underwear. His cock throbbed against her hip. It was almost impossible to hold himself back but he managed it somehow, his need to make sure she was prepared giving him strength.

He tugged at her underwear, moving it down her hips enough for him to slide his hand lower. Sense told him that touching her wouldn't be enough. He needed to give her pleasure before he took his own, and partly because he was liable to explode the moment he was seated within her.

His performance was not going to be stellar.

She moaned when he broke away from her breasts and then her eyes darkened again and she bit her lip when he shifted down her body. A touch of fear entered her eyes. He chased it away by pressing soft kisses to her thighs and keeping his eyes locked on hers as he lowered her knickers down her legs and drew them off over her bare feet.

Her heart pounded in his head, the beat as quick as his own.

He pulled in a deep breath for control, slid his hands over her knees and gently parted them, revealing her to his hungry eyes. Beautiful.

Aurora lay before him, eyes near black with passion and need, breasts exposed to the rain that continued to fall, her body on display for his eyes. He wanted to worship her. He would worship her.

He lowered his mouth and kissed along the inside of her knee and up her thigh, moving slowly so he didn't startle her. He didn't want her to run away, not now that he was close, could smell her desire and almost taste her sweet nectar.

Snow's broad shoulders forced her to spread herself further to accommodate him, exposing her fully. He groaned and glanced up to meet her eyes. She lay before him, rain bouncing off and glistening on her skin in the low evening light, her chest heaving with each hard breath and her thighs trembling against his arms. She ran her tongue over her kiss-swollen lips and a flicker of nerves filled her colourful enchanting eyes.

"You're beautiful." He didn't just say it to alleviate her nerves so he could continue. He meant it.

He had never seen anything as beautiful as she was.

Snow dipped his head and lightly stroked his tongue along the length of her, from her core to her pert nub. She jolted and gasped, the sound drenched in passion, stoking his own. He wanted to make her scream before he was through with her.

He lavished her with attention, flicking his tongue over her nub and delighting in the taste of her and how responsive she was to each little thing he did. He liked it most when she uttered his name in a dark voice, a commanding snarl that threatened immense pain if he stopped before she was ready.

A slave to her, he swirled his tongue, circling her, monitoring her with his senses so he knew what she needed from him before she was even aware.

Lightning struck close again, charging the air around them, and rain ran in cold rivulets over his body. He didn't care. He would make love to Aurora in the snow if she commanded it and he would always be burning for her.

Snow continued to suckle her aroused nub and stroked her with his fingers at the same time. She rocked her hips and he took it as a sign that she was ready to take the next step. He gently eased a single digit into her.

Aurora gasped and raised her hips, pushing herself against his face and his finger deeper into her sheath. So tight. So wet.

Snow growled into her, his cock pulsing, balls tightening at the thought of his hard shaft being where his finger was.

He gently pumped her with one finger, laving her at the same time, drawing out her pleasure. She clutched his head and rocked her hips in time with his thrusts, uttering things that made his head spin. She wanted him inside her.

"Not yet," Snow muttered darkly, grinding his teeth together. He wanted to plunge his body into hers but he couldn't right now. It would hurt her. "Preparing you."

It was hard to speak. Desire ruled him, driving his actions. He withdrew his finger and eased two back into her. It was a tight fit. He was gentle as he stretched her body, enticing it with scissor motions, working her until her desire drenched his fingers and he ached to replace them with his cock.

He shouldn't.

He had already tainted her enough.

"Snow," Aurora moaned, shattering that last thought, driving it far out of his mind.

He pumped her with two fingers and sucked her nub, focusing on the feel of her, trying to judge whether she was ready for him.

She arched her body, her cries hitting a higher pitch, body tightening around his fingers. He kept his pace, thrusting just enough to keep her spiralling towards bliss, taking her higher. He flicked his tongue over her and swirled it, devouring her.

She was close.

And he was selfish.

He wanted her first climax to be with him inside her. He wanted to feel her quiver and know it was because of him.

Snow withdrew his fingers and she moaned, a frustrated and bitter sound. He shoved his underwear down and she quieted, her eyes on his hard length and her teeth nibbling her lower lip. Her hips shifted again, undulating, tempting him. She tilted her head back, her eyes going hooded. Temptress.

He ran his hand down his length and rubbed his thumb over the crown, groaning at the thought of taking her and how wet he was. He was so hard that it hurt.

"Snow," his temptress whispered, eyes imploring him to take her now, telling him how desperately she needed to climax.

He was damned anyway. May as well enjoy it.

He leaned over her, balancing himself on one arm while his other hand gripped his shaft, and lowered his hips. He moaned as he guided the head to her, rubbing it down the slick length of her. She groaned in response, arching her back again and thrusting her breasts towards him.

He lingered, fearing she still wasn't ready.

He could perhaps make things easier. He released himself and ran his hand over her, gathering her moisture. He smothered his length with it and then gripped it again, close to the base so he didn't rub any of her essence away. He stilled right down to his breathing as the head of his cock breached her core and she tensed.

"Relax," he whispered and she swallowed. Seeing she wouldn't be able to do as he instructed while she was thinking about what he was doing, he settled on his elbows and kissed her. She responded instantly, her mouth devouring his, hot and moist against his.

Snow inched into her, his cock throbbing as her tight sheath gloved him, burning him. He kissed her, keeping her focus on her mouth, and grimaced as she grew tighter, her body grasping his. He wanted to explode. Release climbed to the base of his cock.

He growled when she grew too tight and kissed her harder, thumbing her nipples as best as he could at the same time, trying to arouse her so she wouldn't hurt as much. She was going to hurt regardless. She moaned until he pushed deeper and it turned strangled.

"Steady," he murmured against her lips. "It will sting and then I swear it will feel good."

She froze and he kissed her, caressing her lips with his, coaxing her into relaxing again. The moment she did, getting back into the kiss, he pushed forwards and seated himself as deep as he could go. He swallowed her cry of pain and forced himself to withdraw enough that he could reach between them to fondle her bundle of nerves.

She began to relax then, a moan even leaving her lips as she kissed him. Her body throbbed around his, drawing him deeper, and he took his hand away and eased back in as gently as he could manage. It was killing him. He wanted to pump hard, taking her and making her scream.

He wanted to be gentle too, reverent and tender, making love to her so she would know how much this meant to him. He drew back onto his elbows again and stared down into her eyes.

The storm raged overhead and she didn't seem to notice. Rain spotted her skin and turned her hair into tangled black ribbons even though his body partly shielded hers. Water ran from the ends of his white hair, dripping moisture onto her cheeks, beads that quivered and then rolled down her pale creamy skin.

Her striking eyes locked on his, still dark with desire, and her rosy lips parted on a sigh. She looked as lost in the moment as he felt and her beauty struck him hard, combining with her innocence to fill him with a potent need to savour her and do all in his power to keep her with him.

He gently rocked his hips, shallow at first, moving only a little so she could grow used to having him inside her. She moaned, her cheeks darkening and pupils expanding. Her teeth nibbled her lower lip, reddening it. Snow withdrew further and groaned as he eased into her, feeling all of her. His pelvis brushed her and she groaned and squeezed her eyes shut.

His gaze slid to her throat and his fangs itched to taste her again, to take her blood as he took her body. He shut down that hunger, fearing what would happen if he gave in to it. He had hurt her before. He didn't want to hurt her like that again, no matter how fiercely he craved it.

Her hands sank into his hair and drew him down, and he kissed her again, moving into her with long unhurried thrusts of his hips, teasing her towards her first climax. His wouldn't be far behind. Already his semen was rising and his balls tightening again, signalling an impending release. She felt too good and it had been far too long, and it had never been like this.

He felt deeply connected to her, one with her, lost in her as he made love with her in the rain, uncaring of the world around them or the storm raging above.

She arched into him, her body tightening around his, and he thrust deeper, plunging his cock into her core, giving her what she needed. She moaned, clutched at his shoulders, and kissed him fiercely, biting his lip. The sting of pain made his hips jerk, roughly slamming his erection as deep as it would go inside her, until the head struck her womb.

Aurora shattered, crying out his name in the darkness, her body violently quivering around his, clutching at him and pulling him deeper still. Snow grunted and moved faster, kissing her breathless as he took her, claiming her body completely. She moaned with each thrust, pliant and sated beneath him, her hot sheath grasping him.

He wanted to bring her to climax again but his body had other ideas, the feel of being inside a woman again after countless centuries too much for him to handle.

Snow arched his back and roared as his climax rushed through him, his cock throbbing madly as he pumped his seed into her hot core. He braced himself above her on his hands, fire blazing through his veins, his heart thundering against his chest and his legs shaking.

Aurora lay beneath him, her rapid breathing at odds to his own, and her heart rushing in his ears. Her bliss ran through him, adding to his and combining with it to make him feel as though he was floating, surrounded by heat and light, not cold rain and darkness.

He slowly opened his eyes and looked down to find her smiling lazily, a contented expression on her face that only made her more beautiful. His female.

Snow lowered himself and kissed her, their bodies still intimately entwined, both still quivering with pleasure that he felt sure would rock him for hours to come.

Aurora kissed him softly, murmuring in her throat, her hands playing in his wet hair.

The rain continued to hammer against his back and his legs and his growing awareness of it brought the chill of it to his attention.

As much as he wanted to stay here like this forever, one with Aurora, he would have to move soon for her sake. He brushed his knuckles down her arm, feeling how cold she was already, her skin chilled and gooseflesh forming on it. Could she get sick from exposure to such dire weather? He didn't want to find out.

Snow reluctantly withdrew from her, pulled his underwear up and carefully slipped hers back over her feet and up her thighs.

He stood, took her hand and helped her onto her feet. She stood still as he fixed her dress for her, and then smiled at him when he lifted her into his arms, cradling her under her knees and around her back.

She looped her arms around his neck, brought her lips to his and kissed him.

He paused to savour the softness of it and the reassurance it gave him, chasing the fearful thoughts from the back of his mind. He kissed her briefly and then pulled back. She smiled and settled her head against his shoulder, and didn't ask where he was taking her as he turned. She trusted him and it touched him, but not as much as what they had just done. She had given herself to him, even though he didn't deserve her. She had given him her innocence and he would give her everything in return.

He would take care of her, starting with warming her in the shower and then giving her dry clothes to wear. He would show her that he could be good to her.

Because she belonged to him now.

CHAPTER 13

Aurora lay in Snow's arms, tucked in the midnight covers of his four-poster bed, trying to ignore the feeling gnawing away at her happiness.

She couldn't bring herself to leave, even when she knew that she should. Snow gently stroked her arm, the fingers of his right hand trailing up and down its length. The steady motion soothed her and foolishly made her feel as though everything was right in the world when she knew it was worse than ever, crumbling faster around her now.

The urge to warn him that he had less than three days to prove he was able to live in this realm without endangering innocent lives burned through her again, forcing words to rise to the tip of her tongue. She bit them back, not because she feared her master would believe her compromised but because she feared that Snow would be angry with her if she told him that she would have to judge him soon, and it might end in his death.

He may have embraced that idea once, not so long ago. She had a feeling, a hope, he would despise the thought of going to his death now that he was getting better.

Now that she was in his life.

Snow had taken good care of her after they had made love in the rain on the rooftop, carrying her back into the warmer and certainly drier air of the theatre. Thankfully, no one had seen them as they had made their way back to his apartment. She wasn't sure what someone crossing their path would have made of not only the fact Snow was carrying her, but the fact that they were both soaking wet and Snow was barely dressed.

Whenever she thought of their moment in the storm, her body warmed and trembled, aching to experience it again.

Her legs had still been shaking when Snow had set her down in the black-tiled bathroom and stripped her off, and she had felt disappointed when he had showered with her without intimately touching her again. She had sensed his nerves though and believed them to be a product of doubt. He was back to believing he was able to taint her.

It was too late for that.

With all of her feathers turned black, she was as tainted as they came. All she had to do was lose her soul to complete her fall from grace, and that might be inevitable now that she had given herself to Snow.

After their shower, Snow had carefully dried every inch of her, and had then washed her dress and hung it on the front of his ebony wardrobe to dry. He had led her to the bed and they had been here ever since, bodies bare and pressed against each other.

Aurora caressed his pectorals, busying herself with tracing the contours of his powerful muscles, feeling his heart beating hard beneath her fingers.

"It has been a very long time since you have committed a sin," she said to break the comfortable silence, and because she wanted to hear his deliciously deep voice.

"I sinned no more than a few hours ago, on the roof, with you."

She smiled and playfully slapped his chest. "You know what I meant. Many centuries have passed."

"You sound almost proud of me." He craned his head, as though trying to see her face and gauge whether she was. She stayed where she was, too entranced by the feel of his soft skin and hard muscles to lift her gaze to his. "Was that meant to be praise?"

There was an amused edge to his voice but it had disappeared when he next spoke.

"I went off the idea of wandering around committing sins after I killed my family."

Aurora felt his mood shift, turning towards sombre and angry, two emotions he often seemed to experience together. His heart picked up pace against her ear and she sensed the pain that cut him deeply even after all the years that had passed since that night.

She smoothed her palm over his chest, trying to comfort him and show him that he wasn't alone. She was here with him, and she had told him many times now that she believed in him, and that there was good in him.

"You are a different man now. You are learning to control your bloodlust." She tilted her head back and looked up at him. He averted his frosty blue eyes, fixing them on the ceiling. Couldn't he bring himself to look at her and see her belief in her eyes?

Did he want to cling to feeling wretched about himself that much?

She wanted to point out that constantly punishing himself was probably only making his bloodlust worse but held her tongue, knowing he would retaliate if she raised it and likely kick her out of his bed. She was comfortable here. Too comfortable.

"I am not," he whispered and took his hand away from her arm. He pinched the bridge of his nose and closed his eyes, frowning. The dry lengths of his silver-white hair fanned out across the black pillows. "It still rules me more times than I manage to control it. I think it is your blood that is keeping me sane for so long. Maybe I need to keep you around and drink your blood exclusively, and then I can be my old evil self again."

Aurora saw through the words he had said in jest to the truth beneath.

Snow despised his bloodlust and how it made him feel.

"If you keep fighting, you might perhaps be free of it one day, and able to enjoy life as your brother can," she said and shifted onto her front, so her breasts pressed against the side of his chest.

He heaved a sigh, opened his eyes and lowered his hand to her hair as his gaze met hers. He combed his fingers through the black waves, staring at her with deep tangled emotions in his eyes, ones she wished she could decipher.

She had never felt like an angel until now. The way he looked at her made her feel beautiful and precious, and as though he believed she was pure and good, wonderful because she was here with him and she let him hold her like this.

She wished he would never let go.

A touch of sadness clouded her heart. It wasn't possible.

She was getting in too deep with Snow, and already part of her feared she wouldn't be able to carry out her duty and judge him with clear eyes and heart. Or her master would make a case to their superiors that she couldn't and have her removed from the mission, taking her place so he could finally watch Snow die.

Snow's expression hardened, his pale eyes filling with sorrow and darkness.

"I will never be free of my bloodlust."

Those words hit her hard, forcing her to see that he would never be free of his affliction because he didn't want to be free of it.

Snow still longed for death, and if he couldn't have it, he would have eternal torment.

Aurora hated him for it.

She dropped her gaze, unable to look into his beautiful eyes when all they showed her was a terrible sense of finality, the eyes of a man waiting for his death, shut in a windowless room that felt like a tomb.

She didn't want to lose him. She wanted to save him somehow, even when he didn't want to be saved. The thought that he still desired death even after his impassioned speech on the rooftop and her risking everything by remaining with him was like a knife to her chest, piercing her heart and filling her with pain.

Since the night he had killed his parents, he had constantly sought his death, and had constantly punished himself for living by refusing to fight his bloodlust. He craved the torment as a twisted form of payment for his sins.

"You don't want to save yourself." It left her lips in a whisper before she could contain it.

She felt Snow's glare on her face and refused to let it fluster her. Now that she had started, she needed to continue and let it all pour out of her. She needed to make him see what he was doing to himself.

"You never stopped seeking your death… an easy way out. You would sooner lie down and die than fight to live." Aurora pushed away from him, the feel of his arms around her stifling her now rather than giving her comfort, making it impossible to breathe.

She only made it to the edge of the bed before he gathered her back into his arms, caging her against his powerful body. She tensed, expecting him to be rough with her, angered by her barbs.

Snow gently cleared the hair from her face with one hand and then his large palm cupped her cheek. He stared down at her, lying on his side with her. She couldn't bring herself to look at him, not when nothing she did would change his mind.

He didn't want to save himself. Not even for her sake.

He sighed, curled his fingers under her jaw and tilted her head back. Aurora closed her eyes. It didn't deter him. He found another way to sneak around her defences.

He kissed her, softly and slowly, full of feelings that warmed her body but failed to lift the chill from her heart.

"I could learn to desire to live again in time," he whispered against her lips, "if you stayed with me."

It tore at her heart. "I don't have time. You have less than three days now."

He drew back and she opened her eyes and looked up at him.

"Why do you have to go in three days?" His dark silvery eyebrows knitted into a frown.

"I must report to my master." It wasn't a lie.

"I will take all the time I have with you then, and make the most of every minute." He dipped his head and kissed her again, melting her defences completely and setting her blood on fire.

She responded this time, sweeping her lips over his, savouring his cool taste. He drew her closer, the full length of his bare body against hers beneath the black covers, stirring the fire within her into an inferno that pooled in her belly and at the apex of her thighs. She told herself that she couldn't do this again, couldn't give herself to Snow when all he wanted was death and it would lead to granting that wish.

Her master would kill him without hesitation.

Her body didn't get the message. It burned wherever he touched, achy and hot, shivering with a fierce need to be one with him again, regardless of the consequences.

Aurora slipped one hand around the nape of Snow's neck, burying her fingers in his overlong white hair, and deepened the kiss. Her tongue bravely stroked his and he moaned, the sound wanton and erotic, deep and thrilling, tempting her into doing it again.

A knock sounded.

Snow growled, his hands caught her waist, and he pushed her back, breaking their kiss.

"What?" He twisted at the waist, looking over his shoulder at the panelled mahogany door.

"Let me in, Snow." Antoine, and he sounded very upset about something.

Aurora guessed it was her presence in the theatre, and in particular Snow's room. Antoine didn't trust her. She could never hold that against him. He wanted to protect his older brother and those at the theatre, people he considered his family. She hadn't exactly proven herself worthy of his trust either, sneaking into Snow's room and making herself visible only to him.

"Go away," Snow snarled and rolled back to face her.

Metal scraped on metal.

Antoine would not be denied.

The door opened and Aurora gasped as Antoine burst into the room, his red eyes seeking her. Instinct told her to hide herself from his gaze by shrouding herself but she refused to heed it and instead gathered the black covers to her chest, shielding her nudity. She rose into a sitting position. Snow instantly moved to shield her too. The covers pooled around his waist and his big body blocked her view of Antoine.

"I said, go away." Snow's deep voice was little more than a dark growl. Aurora peeked over his left shoulder.

"Not until I see her." Antoine casually closed the door and leaned against it, folding his arms across his chest, causing the silver-grey shirt he wore to tighten around his muscles. The red in his eyes faded but lingered around the edges of his irises and his pupils returned to normal.

She laid her hand on Snow's shoulder to let him know she was all right with his brother meeting her. She wanted to allay Antoine's fears and didn't want the brothers to argue about her. It had hurt her when Antoine and Snow had come to verbal blows about her at the party. She didn't want it to come to that, or worse, this time.

Snow huffed, the sound feral and menacing, and slipped nude from the bed. Antoine kept his gaze fixed on Snow, tracking him across the room, a wary edge to his ice-blue eyes. Snow swiped a fresh pair of black underwear from the chest of drawers and put them on. Aurora remained where she was, clutching the covers to her, her legs tucked close to her bottom beneath them.

Antoine's pale gaze slid to her. "I take it you have slept with my brother?"

Her cheeks blazed. Snow growled a warning.

"That would be a yes." Antoine's eyes narrowed with his frown, a piercing look she was used to receiving from Snow and one the brothers had practiced to perfection. She had never met brothers who shared such similar facial features and expressions.

Aurora wasn't sure what to say to Antoine to smooth that frown away, and his dark emotions with it. She was tired of lying to everyone, covering her tracks and concealing the real reason she was here.

Or was it the real reason?

Part of her now felt as though the reason she was here with Snow was because she needed to spend time with him, ached to be in his arms and look upon his face, and hear his voice, and breathe in his masculine scent. She hungered for the sweet gentle caress of his touch. She wasn't here to watch him so she could judge him. She was here to satisfy her need to be close to him, because she feared that she was going to lose him.

Sleeping with him had probably only signed his execution order though.

She shoved that thought out of her mind. She could still gather enough evidence to prove that Snow was not a threat to humankind as her superiors believed. She was no longer impartial, but that didn't mean she couldn't make them see the truth about Snow.

They had to look at all the evidence she produced to support her verdict. If she could get enough to prove him capable of functioning safely in society without any danger of his affliction consuming him and causing him to massacre hundreds in a quest for blood, then they would have to accept her decision. Wouldn't they?

She didn't care what happened to her, not anymore, not as long as Snow lived.

She wouldn't falsify her claims though. She needed to do something that would make Snow reveal that he was able to become a part of society again.

He would never do such a thing though. He was too fixated on his past and on punishing himself. He needed to move beyond that before he could begin to recover and gain complete control over his bloodlust. He needed to face his sins and learn to accept them.

"What are you thinking, Angel, to turn your look so dark?" Antoine said and she jerked her head up, her focus zeroing in on him.

Snow stared at her too, his gaze boring into the side of her face, and his curiosity laced the air as thickly as Antoine's did.

"I am thinking on something your brother said to me just a few moments ago." Not a lie. She glanced at Snow, catching his narrowed gaze and the weight of guilt in his pale eyes.

"Will you elaborate?" Antoine said and she looked back at him and shook her head. "Why not?"

"It is not for you to know. If Snow wishes to tell you, then he may." Aurora calmly held his gaze, fighting to contain her fear that he might ask Snow and his brother might answer. That answer would wound Antoine. He fiercely clung to the hope his brother could free himself of bloodlust and lead a normal life, and she admired him for it. She didn't want to deal that hope a blow that might kill it. "This is not the first time you have seen me, is it?"

Antoine didn't answer but she could see in his eyes that her suspicion was correct.

"I had expected you to question me about my lack of wings." She shifted on the bed, bringing her knees in front of her and curling her arms around them. Antoine's eyes darted to her shoulders and back to hers. He quickly masked his curiosity, his expression turning dark again. "I can let them out if you would like to see them for yourself?"

"What I would like is to know why you are here?" Antoine flexed his fingers against his biceps. "Why does my brother suddenly have an angel interested in him? Is it because of what he has done?"

Aurora expected Snow to growl and intervene, angered by his brother's line of questioning. He remained where he was in the middle of the room, between the foot of the bed and the bathroom door, his air relaxed.

"It is not so sudden," Aurora whispered and then tilted her chin up and looked across at Snow. "We have known each other a long time... far longer than you have known your brother, Antoine."

"What?" Antoine barked.

Snow smiled at her and then turned it on his brother. "It is true. Aurora saved my life when I was a boy, barely fifty in age. If it were not for her, you would have no older brother."

Antoine gawked at her.

"So you could say that I am here because of what I have done, not what your brother has done. I felt Snow suffering because of his bloodlust and I desired to soothe him. I did not realise that singing to him had become a way of weakening the hold his bloodlust has over him, not until I sung to him that night, for the first time in two thousand years." Aurora continued to stare at Snow and his gaze drifted back to her, full of warmth and deep emotions, ones she didn't dare to unravel because she still feared what was happening between them.

"She is the reason the females can sing you to sleep and you are much better when you awaken?" Antoine didn't sound as though he believed it.

Snow nodded.

"She is. I remember after she pulled me from the lake... she was singing to me when I came around. It made me feel better. Warm. Safe." Snow chuckled and shook his head. "I suppose it must be the reason why I have more control over my bloodlust whenever a female has sung me to sleep. It subconsciously takes me back to that night and Aurora, and that feeling of calm and safety."

Aurora was glad that she had done something for him all these years without even knowing it. She had given him a way of clawing back control over himself. Could she work on that?

If her blood and her song calmed his demons and turned him into the man standing before her, casual and unaffected by his affliction, as in control of himself as his brother was, could years with her give him back his desire to live and his life? He had said that he could find the hunger to live again if she stayed with him.

An impossible dream.

Her superiors wouldn't accept a verdict on Snow based on theories she had no evidence to substantiate.

Unleash

Antoine raked his gaze over her, assessing her, scrutinising every inch of her. Darkness loomed in his pale eyes again, his expression hardening with each second. He still wasn't convinced. She still admired him for it.

He wanted to protect his brother. Until she proved herself as an ally, and not a threat to Snow, he wouldn't trust her. It would take time to convince Antoine that she had only his brother's best interests at heart. She didn't want to sentence him to death. Her mission now wasn't one to decide whether Snow lived or died.

It was one to prove Snow worthy of a second chance. She would accept no other outcome.

"My brother may have some unfounded faith in you… but I cannot grant you the same." Antoine stepped away from the wall and lowered his arms, straightening to his full impressive height at the same time. He looked down at her, eyes dark and expression fierce. Red ringed his irises. "If you ever harm Snow, you will answer to me… and I will show you no mercy."

"Antoine." Snow was across the room in a flash, his hands clasping his younger brother's shoulders, shoving him against the black wall. "Back down, Brother. I have told you that she is my responsibility, and I will not let you threaten her."

"I hope for your sake you are right about her, and you know what you are doing." Antoine peeled Snow's hands off his shoulders and opened the door. He sighed, turned back into the room and lifted his left hand to cup Snow's cheek, and whispered, "Forgive a man for worrying about his only brother?"

Snow pressed his forehead against Antoine's and closed his eyes. "Always."

Antoine lingered a second longer and then left the room, slowly closing the door behind him. Snow stared at the door, motionless, his muddled feelings flowing across the room to her.

"He is only concerned about your welfare," she said and he looked over his broad bare shoulder at her.

"I know… but I do not like it when he makes out that you are a threat to me." Snow ran his fingers through his hair, tugging the long white lengths back, and clasped the back of his head. "I am more of a threat to you than you are to me."

Possibly. She smiled to alleviate the nervous edge in his eyes. He didn't need to fear that he would hurt her. She was strong enough to handle him even in his darkest rages and she felt certain that she could subdue him now that she knew the power her song held over him.

The fact that he clearly trusted her touched her though. She had watched him for centuries and in that time had come to realise that he had difficulty trusting others because he didn't trust himself.

He also let his guard down around her and the only other person in this world he did that with was his brother.

Both of those things should have pleased her deeply and warmed her heart, but she still couldn't shake the dreadful guilt that dragged her insides down whenever she thought about her mission, even now that she had decided to alter its parameters.

Aurora held her hand out to him and he locked the door and stalked back towards her, the sensual shift of his body with each step rekindling the embers of the fire he had ignited in her veins.

She let the black covers fall away from her and met him at the edge of the bed. There was something she had wanted to do to him ever since he had revealed the full design of his tattoo to her. He stopped before her and she didn't hesitate. She caught the waist of his black trunks above his right hip and pulled the soft material down, exposing the full length of his ink.

Aurora leaned in and ran her tongue over it.

Snow growled, grasped her arms, and pulled her up onto her feet. She wobbled on the mattress. He tugged her closer to him until his body pressed flush against hers and his arms caged her like steel bands, and tilted his head back.

Aurora dipped her head and kissed him. He instantly took control of the kiss, turning it hard and fierce, filled with rough passion that thrilled her.

He had been so gentle with her on the rooftop that she had expected him to be like that again, but this savageness excited her, flooding her mind with exotic possibilities.

She tried to keep up with his kiss and when that failed, she gave herself over to her passion and nipped at his lower lip between kisses, eliciting dark erotic moans from him that rumbled through his big body and into hers.

Her body came alive, belly heating and tightening, desire overwhelming her as her breathing quickened and a need to feel Snow's hands on her, palming and caressing, teasing her to another earth-shattering climax, consumed her. Snow's aggressive kisses, the feel of his body against hers, and his unrelenting grip, wasn't enough to satisfy her dark hungers. She needed more.

Aurora grabbed his shoulders and twisted with him, forcing him down onto the bed. His breath left him on impact and she didn't give him a chance to draw another before she was astride his hips. She braced her hands against his broad chest, moaning at the feel of his hard muscles beneath her fingers, and kissed him again, capturing his mouth with aggression that surprised her.

Snow's big hands caught her bare bottom and he palmed it just as she had desired as he kissed her, taking control of it once more, leading the frenzied dance. Elation swept through her, passion carrying her higher, until she felt dizzy and desperate, lost in her need to feel the pleasure only Snow could give to her.

She moaned into his mouth and shamelessly worked her body against his, rocking her core along his hard length. It felt wickedly good, luring her into surrendering more control, giving in to the decadent desires racing through her blood.

Snow rolled her onto her back and covered her body with his, slowly grinding his cock against her as he kissed her breathless.

It maddened her, tightening her stomach, leading to a strange concoction of bliss and frustration. It wasn't enough.

She ached to have him use his strength on her, to unleash all of his passion and indulge his desires. She wanted to let go too, yearned to let her wildest fantasies rule her in this moment with Snow.

She had dreamed of him seizing command of her, using his powerful muscles to take control of their lovemaking and surrendering to his base instincts to have her. Just the thought of him doing such a thing had her quivering inside, hot and achy, on the verge of moaning breathlessly and begging him to take her.

She ran her hands down his powerful back, delighting in how his muscles shifted beneath her fingers, bunching and stretching, a symphony that made her tremble. She wanted to touch him like this when he was inside her, driving her wild and over the edge. She wanted to feel all that immense power focused on her, and her pleasure.

She nipped at his lower lip, earning a growl and a harder thrust. He rubbed her most sensitive flesh, spreading delicious tingles through her body, and she couldn't stop herself from raising her hips to meet him, forcing him to fight her back into submission. She refused to go quietly, moaning each time his hard cock rubbed her in just the right place to send another blissful wave of shivers tripping along her nerves.

Aurora mastered his mouth with licks and nips, driving him into submission, and rolled them over again.

They fell off the bed and she landed hard on top of Snow on the wooden floor. It didn't stop him. Before she could utter an apology, he had flipped her onto her back on the floor and was fiercely kissing along her jaw and then down her throat.

She tilted her head to one side, sighing with each lick and suck, and playful nip, and tunnelled her hands into his white hair, twisting the ribbons around her fingers and clutching him to her.

Her body rocked involuntarily into his, seeking more pleasure, hunting for another taste of heaven. Snow growled into her throat and devoured it with hungry kisses interspersed with hard sucks on her flesh that she was sure would leave faint marks on her skin. She didn't care. She wanted marks to remember this wild moment by.

Snow froze, his broad body tensed and braced above hers.

"Snow?" Aurora whispered and loosened her grip on his hair. She shifted to one side, enough that she could see his face. His crimson eyes remained rooted on her throat, his pupils thin elliptical slits in the centre of his irises. A new fire burned through her. He wanted to bite her. Part of her thrilled at the thought he might even as the rest of her feared he would go through with it.

She kept still beneath him.

When she realised that wasn't helping him regain control over his darker urges, she gently slid her left hand down to the straight line of his jaw and drew his hungry gaze away from her neck.

His scarlet eyes met hers and narrowed. She gasped when he kissed her again, fiercer than ever, dominating her with the force of it.

His fangs scraped her tongue and her lips, adding a hint of blood to the taste of the kiss. She stroked his cheeks with both hands as she kissed him gently, trying to convince him to do the same. Eventually, his fangs disappeared and his kiss slowed, deepening at the same time. It lightened her insides, stirring different feelings within her, softer and affectionate ones.

Did he feel the same way as she did when he kissed her like this?

Did he feel as though everything was right in the world and nothing terrible would happen to them?

It felt so right as he softly kissed her, his immense body braced above hers and his hips nestled between her thighs. She didn't want him to move or change the tempo again. She wanted to spend the next few hours just kissing him like this, savouring how it made her feel.

Close to him. Cherished.

She sighed against his lips and tangled her fingers in his hair, lazily winding the white silken lengths around them, enjoying this quiet moment with him.

Unleash

Snow gently rocked his hips between hers, reigniting her fire. Hunger for things to remain slow between them gradually shifted back to a need to feel his strength. She worked her body against his, seeking satisfaction as she kissed him.

He leaned down on his left elbow and ran his right hand over her bare thigh, stroking from her bottom to her knee. She wanted him to touch her somewhere else, needed it with an urgency that made her blush, and almost felt brave enough to take hold of the hand that was caressing her thigh and make him touch her where she needed him.

Almost.

Aurora brought her hands between them and pushed, forcing Snow away from her. He frowned down at her and then his look softened, as though he had seen her need and how desperate he was making her.

He moved back to kneel between her thighs and she grew aware of how naked she was, on display for his blue eyes, exposed to him.

They raked hotly over her, his pupils dilating and devouring his irises, his gaze burning her and ratcheting her temperature up to a thousand degrees.

When he looked at her like that, she grew aware of how much he desired her and it thrilled her. She wanted him to see how much she hungered for him too. Her gaze drifted down him, taking all of him in, every delicious millimetre of his beautiful body. Her eyes settled on his underwear and she frowned.

It wasn't fair. She wanted things to be even between them, and that meant she had to get him out of his underwear. She wanted to see every inch of his naked perfection.

She slipped her legs away from either side of his body and moved to kneel before him. He quirked an eyebrow. Aurora grabbed his hands and stood, making him rise with her. He towered over her, presenting her with a view of a wall of honed formidable muscle that shifted sensually, teasingly beneath his pale skin, making her want to run her lips over it and taste every inch of him.

Aurora moved her hands to the waist of his black underwear and pushed it down his hips. She followed it, her gaze roving over him, drinking in the way his torso tensed when she reached his knees with his underwear. He was waiting for her to look elsewhere and she knew where he wanted her gaze.

Aurora lowered it to the impressive rock hard length of his cock. It stood proud from a nest of silvery crisp hairs, eagerly jutting towards her, the crown already exposed and slick with moisture. She nibbled her lower lip, temptation spearing her once more. He lifted his feet for her one by one when she reached his ankles and she pulled his underwear off over them.

Aurora lingered, crouched before him, her eyes glued to his length.

Her teeth worried her lip again, her desire burning at ten thousand degrees now, scorching her.

She leaned forwards, coming to rest on her knees, and hesitantly ran her fingers down the length of him, from the soft tip to his balls, leaving a streak of colour in the wake of her caress. She fondled his balls, feeling their weight and fascinated by the fluid movement of them against her fingers. Snow groaned, his muscles rippling with tension.

Aurora continued her exploration, refusing to rush this first experience of touching him. Her fingertips followed the ridge up the underside of his erection, her touch colouring his skin. She circled the crown and then rubbed the slit with the pad of her thumb. Snow's hips jerked towards her, an animalistic grunt leaving his lips.

She swallowed, licked her lips, and leaned in.

The second her tongue made contact with his flesh, his hand grasped the top of her head, fingers sinking into her dark hair. He clutched her but didn't stop her. His breathing roughened.

She swirled her tongue around the soft head of his cock, tasting a touch of salt on his cool skin, and he groaned again, his fingers tightening in her hair. She liked how he held her, as if he couldn't help himself and was torn between pulling her closer and pushing her away.

Trying to control her actions.

Control this.

She opened her mouth and wrapped her lips around his erection, taking the first few inches of him into her. His hips jerked again, thrusting him deeper, and he muttered dark things under his breath. He had cursed like that before in her presence, but he had aimed it at her like hellfire the first time. This time it sounded more like a plea to her. He wanted her to continue.

So did she.

Aurora sucked as she withdrew, earning a harsh oath and a deep moan from Snow as her reward. She took him back into her mouth and sucked again, enjoying his taste and coolness, and the way Snow bucked and snarled.

His fingers clutched her, guiding her on his cock. She withdrew completely and leaned back in to flutter her tongue around the underside of the head while she played with his balls and stroked the shaft. Snow quivered, his breathing staccato now and his groans coming thick and fast.

He rocked his hips and she took him back into her mouth, sucking him as she continued to toy with his sac. She wrapped her other hand around his shaft and stroked him in time with her movements with her mouth, hoping to heighten his pleasure.

Snow growled and curled his hips, thrusting through the ring of her fingers. His legs trembled against her, body tightening until she was sure he would harm himself. He grunted and tried to push her away.

Aurora didn't let him.

She sucked harder, intent on wringing a climax from him with her mouth, wanting him to taste the pleasure she desired to give to him. She would deny him nothing.

He cried her name and spilled into her mouth, his cock throbbing with each jet of seed. She swallowed around him and continued to stroke him, unsure of the right thing to do. His hands settled more heavily on her, his grip loosening, and he breathed hard above her. She licked him, tasting him on her tongue, and then slowly withdrew and looked up the length of his body.

Snow growled, grabbed her under her arms and dragged her up to him. He kissed her hard, his body quaking under her hands, and laid her on the bed, with her legs dangling over the edge. She moaned when he leaned over her, kissing down her jaw to her breasts.

He lavished them with attention, suckling and rolling her nipples between his teeth, alternating between them. His hand delved between her legs and she gasped at her first taste of pleasure from his touch.

More.

Aurora tried to raise her hips into his fingers, seeking more contact between them, but it was impossible with her legs draped over the edge of the mattress. She lifted one leg, planted her foot on the bed, and rocked into his touch. He circled her clitoris and then dipped lower, teasing her entrance.

"Snow," Aurora moaned, desperate to tell him that she needed him to touch her now, but blushing at the thought of voicing that hunger.

He kissed lower, worshipping every inch of her body with his mouth and hands, and finally reached where she needed him most.

He dropped to his knees before her and took hold of her ankles. The blush on her cheeks burned more fiercely when he draped her legs over his shoulders, caught her backside, and pulled her to the edge of the four-poster bed.

He kissed along the inside of her thigh and Aurora tried to keep still but it was impossible.

She shifted on the mattress, eager for his tongue on her flesh. He didn't keep her waiting. His fingers parted her petals and he delved his wicked tongue between them, teasing her aroused nub. She threw her head back and moaned, shocked by the volume of it.

Snow chuckled and licked her again, adding to her torment by swirling his tongue around this time, circling her and eliciting another groan from her throat. She arched her back and raised her hips into his face, uncaring of how wanton she appeared. She needed this.

She needed him.

She mimicked his earlier behaviour, her hands sinking into his white hair, clutching the lengths of it and clinging to him. He flicked his tongue over her clit, sending sparks shooting down her thighs and turning up the heat pooling in her belly. One finger eased into her core, slowly pumping her, the pace maddening.

"More." She couldn't believe she uttered that aloud but it seemed to work. Her eyes shot wide as Snow withdrew and then slipped two fingers into her, the flats of them rubbing over a spot that made her quiver. "Mercy."

"I have none," Snow whispered and devoured her, the rough sweeps and swirls of his tongue in tandem with the deep thrust of his fingers driving her out of her mind with bliss. She rode his fingers, unable to stop herself from doing it, hungry for that one stroke that would push her tumbling over the edge.

Snow rumbled something about her taste. She was too lost in the incredible sensations overwhelming her to pay attention to him. She clutched his hair in one instant and threw her hands above her head on the mattress in the next, gathering the black sheets into her fists, grasping them as she swirled her hips and forced his fingers deeper into her.

Snow moaned and she followed him, her eyes screwed tightly shut, teeth sinking into her lip so hard that it hurt. He licked her, lapping at her clit as his fingers plundered her. Aurora rocked against his face, her whole body undulating off the bed, fingers tightly holding the sheets, keeping herself anchored.

He sucked her nub and then gently nipped it with blunt teeth as he pushed his fingers deep into her core.

Aurora exploded. The whole world shattered in a million glittering sparks and she lay frozen with her hips high in the air, the sensation overpowering her and carrying her away, stealing her awareness of the world for a brief few seconds.

Snow growled and stood, forcing her backside higher into the air. Her legs slipped down his arms to his elbows but couldn't fall any further while his hands grasped her hips.

Unleash

The head of his cock breached her core and then he thrust in, as deep as he could go, sending more stars exploding across her eyes and ripping a moan from her. He grasped her hips, holding her body at an angle with only her shoulders and head touching the mattress, and pumped her hard. The long deep strokes of his cock pushed her through the haze of her first orgasm and ignited a burning need for a second.

Aurora opened her eyes and groaned as she saw him standing before her, her legs hooked over his arms and her body held immobile by him and completely at his mercy as he took her hard and fast, every muscle on his incredible body rippling with each wicked curl of his hips.

He stared down at her, his blue gaze dark and fierce, possessive as it fixed on her.

The hunger and need in it spoke to her and she gave herself over to him, willingly surrendering to him and letting him have his way with her.

She clutched the blankets above her head and her body shifted with each powerful commanding thrust of his hips, rocking her breasts and sending sparks of bliss exploding outwards from where their bodies joined. His balls slapped her backside, his grunts of pleasure mingling with her own, and she lost herself in him.

This was the side of him she had ached to unleash, this powerful passionate male who was claiming her body, stamping his mark on it and ruining her forever.

Completely claiming her.

He clutched her hips, his fingertips pressing in hard enough that she was sure he would leave marks to remember this wild moment by, just as she had desired. She flexed her body around his, ripping a feral grunt from him, and he pounded harder. The muscles of his arms and torso rippled with strength, power that he now used on her, giving her the ultimate pleasure as the head of his cock struck her womb with each deep thrust and his pelvis slammed against her clitoris, sending sparks of fire blazing over her.

"Snow," she uttered, a plea for more that she couldn't contain.

He grunted again, sneering down at her, his eyes dark with passion, hooded from the same ferocious desire that burned in her.

Aurora tensed around him, milking his shaft with each thrust and withdrawal, seeking more from him. His fingers clenched, pressing harder into her hips and he drove deeper, taking all of her. It pushed her over the edge and her body bowed upwards as she cried out her release.

It flooded her, stealing her senses, making every inch of her tremble and throb, filling her with heat and the sweetest bliss.

Snow growled, his eyes closing and face screwing up, and then panted as his thrusts turned jerky and shallow, his cock pulsing inside her, spilling his seed into her welcoming body. He gave a few more smaller pumps of his hips and then stilled, his broad chest heaving and his trembling hands holding her body off the bed.

She couldn't move as ecstasy flowed through every fibre of her being and it seemed neither could Snow as his orgasm swept through him. He stood before her, holding her body on his, his head bent and chest heaving with his ragged breaths, for what seemed like minutes before he finally opened his eyes and looked down at her.

A beautiful blush coloured his cheeks.

Aurora released the death-grip she had on the black covers and crooked her finger at him. He lowered her hips to the mattress, withdrew from her, and covered her body with his as he settled over her.

She caught him around his nape and lured him down for a soft kiss, wanting to show him that she had enjoyed what they had done and he had no reason to feel embarrassed or ashamed, or at all guilty. She had wanted to feel his strength, his power, and that was exactly what he had given her.

Bliss.

She stroked his cheek as she kissed him, savouring this quieter moment in the aftermath of their lovemaking, enjoying both sides of Snow. She liked his contrasts and how he could go between rough and tender in a heartbeat.

He drew back and stared down into her eyes, and she cursed the sense of dread and urgency that reared its ugly head, reminding her that she didn't have time to savour moments like these with him, not right now. She could savour them after she had saved him. She knew she couldn't leave him now, not ever. She had to find a way to make her superiors believe that Snow wasn't a threat to the world and then she could live with him, just as he wanted her to.

Just as she wanted too.

"Why does your touch leave colour on my skin at times?" he said with a frown, his pale blue eyes dark with curiosity.

She caressed his cheek, a blazing trail of rainbow colours following her fingertips. She had figured he would ask about it sooner rather than later, and was surprised it had taken him this long.

"It happens because I'm experiencing strong emotions." She ran her fingertip over his lower lip, painting it with colour that soon faded.

"Do all angels possess this trait?" He caught her hand and pressed a kiss to her knuckles.

"No." She shook her head. "Many angels can't experience emotion at all. Few of us experience them strongly... I have experienced many that are foreign to all angels... because of you."

He smiled at her, charming and boyish, as though that knowledge pleased him deeply. She glanced away and her cheeks heated. She hoped he wouldn't ask what had prompted her to experience emotions that were foreign to angels. She wasn't sure how he would react if she confessed it was his bite that had awoken them in her.

"I need a shower." Snow pressed a kiss to her lips and slipped from the bed, coming to stand before her.

He wrapped his fingers around her wrist and pulled her up into his arms, holding her by her bottom. Her feet didn't reach the floor. She didn't care, especially when he kissed her again, the softness of it chasing away her dire thoughts.

He set her down and gave her a saucy smile. "Want to join me?"

She did but she shook her head, knowing that if she went to shower with him this time that they would end up making out again. As much as she wanted to make love with him under the warm spray of water, she wanted to figure out a way of saving him even more.

"Next time," she said, hoping there would be one.

He was so handsome as he smiled at her, blue eyes glittering with warmth. He made his way across the room and she allowed herself the time to watch him, gaining pleasure from how sexy his backside was as he walked.

He disappeared into the bathroom and she heard the shower switch on.

Her blood would be almost gone from his system by now and her time was running out.

It was now or never. She had to do something to prove to her master that Snow was worthy of a second chance at life, and after her conversation with him earlier, she knew that first she needed to make him feel and make him learn to accept the things he had done. She had to make him see that it was all in his past now and that he couldn't let it colour his future anymore.

She only knew of one way to do that.

And she knew he would hate her for it.

But it was the only way to save him now.

CHAPTER 14

Snow dressed in a pair of black jeans and a black t-shirt. He tugged a thin black sweater on over the top and was tying his boots when Aurora came out of the bathroom.

He had to stop to watch her.

She was beautiful, radiant with the lingering blush of passion on her cheeks and her white dress clinging to her curves. She paused midway through combing her fingers through her fall of black hair and glanced at him. A touch of nerves coloured her striking eyes, darkening the green and blue, and he frowned. Something was up.

Was she still awkward about the fact she had given herself to him?

Twice.

He grinned at that, finished with his laces, and straightened. She stopped again as he approached her, his long strides eating up the distance between them, and then gasped as he gathered her into his arms and kissed her.

The air turned frigid around him.

Snow frowned and his senses reached out, screaming a warning that they were no longer in his apartment, or anywhere in Vampirerotique. He pulled back and scoured the dark landscape surrounding him. Mountains pierced the sky beyond a stone wall.

A sliver of dread snaked down his spine.

She hadn't.

He swiftly turned to face her and looked beyond her.

Snow clawed his hair back and growled, his heart pounding and vision swimming as he took in the stone chateau with its towers tipped by dark conical roofs.

He stumbled backwards and his knees gave out, the impact with the gravel path jarring his spine. He hunched over, pressing his claws into his scalp, fighting the darkness that descended upon him, throwing terrifying images into his head, ones he didn't have the strength to shut out.

The speed of the assault on him was so swift that he couldn't guard against it. His bloodlust rose in the space of a heartbeat to swamp his mind and drive him right to the edge.

He didn't think he could win his fight against it this time, when he was unprepared and it had come on so strongly and fiercely.

It was only a matter of minutes, if not seconds, before it claimed him completely and seized control. He couldn't let that happen, even when it felt inevitable. He had to fight it somehow.

He tried to claw back some control but it only caused more memories to surface. They played out in his mind and terrorized him.

"No," he muttered and clutched his head, screwing his eyes shut. He rocked, his big body tight with tension, control slipping through his grasp. Blood coloured his vision, staining the memories playing out in his mind, sending him falling deeper into the black abyss. "Didn't. Wasn't. Was. Me."

"Snow?" Her fearful voice called to his darker hungers and he snarled and sprang at her, grabbing her before she could move a muscle. He roared at her, his enormous fangs punching long from his gums, dripping with saliva at the thought of tearing into her soft flesh and tasting her blood.

No. He couldn't do this. He wouldn't do this. Not again.

He threw her aside, turning at the same time, and grappled with himself.

Not again. Please. Not again.

Terrible needs assaulted him, whispering insidious words, taunting him into surrendering to his bloodlust and slaking his wicked thirsts.

He couldn't.

Snow clung to the edge of the abyss, nails digging in, refusing to succumb to it this time. He hated it. He despised how he felt as it seized control of him, trapping him within his own body, leaving him powerless and unable to stop himself from doing the horrific things that forever haunted him.

He roared, dropped back to his knees and slammed his fists against the unyielding ground, bloodying his knuckles, hoping the pain would satisfy his dark needs.

It didn't.

His focus kept reverting to Aurora where she stood only metres away, her eyes on him, drawing his attention to her. He snarled and clawed at his chest.

His blunted nails did nothing, unable to cut through the material and score his flesh, giving him the pain he deserved.

"Snow?"

He snarled at her and held his hand out behind him, trying to warn her to keep her distance, afraid that if she came any closer, he would lose his head. He would kill her.

He would kill himself a heartbeat later, unable to live with himself and unable to keep his promise to Antoine.

Why?

His brow furrowed and tears filled his eyes before he could do anything to hold them back. He clawed at the gravel, bloodying his fingertips, and looked over his shoulder at Aurora. Sharp lances cut his heart to pieces, until he was bleeding inside, feeling the pain he had desired but hating it because it stemmed not from himself but from her. Undeserved.

Why had she done this to him?

She reached out to him and a terrible hunger to destroy her, to spill her blood in retribution and satisfy his need for vengeance by drinking her dry, spiralled through him. Another tattered thread holding his bloodlust at bay twisted and snapped.

Snow growled at her.

She would pay for hurting him like this.

Snow shook his head and rubbed his eyes with the bloodstained heels of his palms, pressing them deep enough to cause pain. She wouldn't. He couldn't hurt her. Not Aurora.

The urge came upon him again, stronger this time, and he almost launched himself back at her.

Snow growled in agony and smashed his head against the ground instead. He had to knock himself out. It was the only way to save her.

"Snow, no!" Aurora raced forwards and he was on her in a split-second, his hand wrapped around her throat and holding her high off the ground.

Sharp splinters ricocheted around his skull, distorting his vision, and darkness encroached, sucking more of his control into the abyss, pulling him down to a place he didn't want to go. Not again.

Aurora grasped his wrist with both hands, her legs flailing and her panic rushing through his body like a sweet intoxicating drug. He began to squeeze.

Snow pushed back against the consuming darkness, clawing his way to the surface and holding on for dear life.

Not his. Hers.

He stared into her eyes, witnessing her emotions. Not only fear. Hope. Affection. Faith. Concern.

Snow closed his eyes, dropped his head and dug the knuckles of his free hand into his left eye. He had to stop this. He wouldn't let it control him, not as it had that terrible night two centuries ago.

He dropped Aurora and loped away from her, desperate for some space. The gravel behind him crunched, warning she intended to follow him, and he roared over his shoulder at her. She froze, her heartbeat off the scale, the wild pounding satisfying his darkest desires.

Snow breathed hard, battling his bloodlust. He forced himself to look at his surroundings, to see the snow-capped mountains that were bright even in the darkness, the full moon illuminating the cragged peaks. He swept his gaze over the plains and down towards the lake in the distance, and then back to the chateau.

The sight of it threatened to send him into another frenzy but he held it together this time, refusing to succumb to the crushing force of his bloodstained memories of this place.

The scene of his worst crime.

He had hoped he would never set eyes on this place again and now Aurora had brought him here, endangering everyone in the area, triggering an onslaught of memories that threatened to send him into his darkest bout of bloodlust yet.

Even darker than the one he had suffered the night he had slaughtered everyone he loved in these grounds and this very mansion.

"Why?" Snow gritted out, barely keeping a leash on his bloodlust, constantly fighting it. He would lose the battle at some point. He had never managed to hold out for long when struggling against a strong attack and they had never come stronger than this.

Aurora stood in the middle of the gravel path down the slope from him, closer to the house, her back to it and her hand wrapped around her throat. He had hurt her. He would do far worse if he lost his head to his affliction.

She didn't answer. Had he damaged her voice box? Could angels heal as rapidly as vampires could?

Concern overshadowed his agony and he ventured a step towards her, needing to see that he hadn't done any permanent damage in the midst of his rage. He couldn't live with himself if he had harmed her.

"Aurora?" he whispered, on the edge again, driven there by the thought that he had hurt her.

He breathed hard, focusing on it just as he had practiced so many times over the years. Antoine had taught him how to breathe through the times when his bloodlust surfaced but it wasn't very strong.

He didn't think he could breathe through this one, not when she wasn't speaking to him, and her backdrop was the place he had lovingly called home until he had butchered most of his family in it and then attempted to kill his only brother.

God help him.

Snow snarled and clawed his hair back, squeezing the sides of his head with his palms, trying to get a grip on himself again as a new wave of darkness threatened to pull him under.

He needed something to focus on, something positive, anything. If he lost it, he would kill Aurora and then rampage through the chateau, no doubt killing its inhabitants, repeating the sins of his past.

He didn't want to go back there. He didn't want to see himself do those terrible things again, witnessing them as though through another's eyes, seeing his familiar claws gouge flesh and hands smash bones to fragments, unable to stop himself even when he desperately wanted it to end.

He hadn't wanted to kill them.

Tears slipped down his cheeks, the frigid air freezing them against his skin. Aurora gave him a pitying look that cut him to his marrow. He looked away from her, not wanting her to see how weak he was, how afraid. He wanted her to think he was strong, just as she desired him to believe she was.

He hated her seeing him like this.

Weak. Pathetic. Scared.

Vulnerable.

Snow focused on the area around him, keeping his field of vision narrowed so he didn't see the house, hoping it would help him regain a sliver of control that he could build on.

The grass around him was long, plants growing in it that resembled weeds, and there were scraggly bushes too, and even trees at the edges of his vision. Patches of grass had swallowed sections of the path.

Snow realised they had never had a path. There had been a drive. It had been wide, at least ten metres across. Nature had reclaimed most of it, leaving only a strip three feet in width visible.

Snow frowned. "Does no one live here now?"

"Antoine never sold it." Relief that she sounded unharmed was overshadowed by what she had revealed.

He could and could not understand why.

He knew his brother loved this place but also knew that Antoine would never return here because it would hurt him too much. He would never be ready to face that night and this place, and neither was Snow.

His brother was clinging to this place because it tied him to the family he had lost. He couldn't let go of the past.

They were the same in that respect.

Aurora turned away, her pale dress bright in the moonlight, and her black wings grew from her back.

Snow hesitated, afraid of following her and hating himself because of it. He was stronger than this. He would discover why she had brought him to this place and then he would force her to take him back to Vampirerotique and never do this to him again.

He swallowed, drew in a deep breath, and took his first step towards the dark chateau, his gaze bravely drifting over the towers that reached up to the sky. His bloodlust began to rise again, gaining ground with each step, and he struggled against it. Aurora was way ahead of him now, close to the doors of the elegant gothic building.

Snow's steps turned laboured, each one a struggle, his legs weakening as he was forced to use all of his strength to keep his bloodlust under control.

Fragmented images assaulted him, causing the mansion to flicker between how it looked now and how it had been that night. Boarded up windows switched back to ones with a warm glow emanating from within.

The chilling silence became laughter and the low hum of chatter as his family went about their business.

He breathed harder, his throat beginning to close, and his heart thundered, sending his blood around his body in a dizzying rush. He dragged himself closer, focusing on Aurora where she stood at the threshold.

For her sake, he couldn't lose control. He didn't want to hurt her. He had already caused her enough pain.

She pushed the ancient double doors open enough that she could enter. The darkness swallowed her.

Snow halted on the path, his bloodlust crippling him, the debilitating pain of his memories stripping the remaining fragments of his strength away. He couldn't go any further.

His legs shook beneath him, threatening to give out and send him crashing to the ground again, and his heart pounded wildly, a sickening rhythm that had his head spinning and his vision blurring. His throat closed next and it became a struggle to breathe. He wheezed with each breath he sucked down into his burning lungs.

He couldn't do this.

Aurora appeared again, concern written across her beautiful face. He spat a vile curse at her and her expression darkened.

"Do not pity me," he snarled and turned his back on her and the building. He clenched his fists, closed his eyes, and focused everything he had on breathing, taking slow unhurried ones that settled his pounding head and gave him back that much-needed sliver of control.

Disjointed memories flashed across the darkness of his closed eyes, torturing him. Silence became laughter and that turned into screams and garbled cries, and the sound of destruction.

Snow buried his fingers in his hair and held his head in his hands, frowning hard. He needed Antoine. He couldn't do this. He couldn't fight an attack this strong. He was going to lose, and then he would destroy Aurora.

He would kill someone he loved again and it would end him.

"Snow?" Aurora whispered, closer behind him than he had expected, and she gently placed her hand on his shoulder. He looked over it at her, his eyebrows furrowed, no longer bothering to hide his pain from her.

"Why?" he croaked, his body already trembling, weakened by the physical and mental assault that gradually stripped his strength away, leaving him more vulnerable than ever to his bloodlust.

"Because you need it."

That wasn't an answer.

He growled at her but she didn't shrink back.

She removed her hand from his shoulder and slipped it into his right one. Her fingers laced between his and she clutched his hand. The comfort and strength such a small gesture gave him shocked him and he stared down at their hands, amazed by the way something so simple could make him feel. Connected to her. Not alone.

She was here with him, even if she was also the reason he was here. She wasn't doing this to hurt him. He could feel that in her and could sense that this pained her too.

Aurora led him to the arched double doors and as she entered ahead of him, candles burst into life, flickering and struggling to chase back the darkness.

Snow wrestled with his bloodlust as it emerged again and fought an urgent desire to flee this place. It took most of his remaining strength but he followed her inside.

He breathed hard, the rough sound filling the vestibule. Candlelight danced from the chandelier hanging perilously by a rusted chain above the centre of the large double-height room. Spider webs covered the cornices and plaster roses on the ceiling, and wove between the banisters of the sweeping mahogany staircase, all of them thick with dust.

The furniture he had broken during his rampage had crumbled to powder, leaving deposits on the marble floor, eaten by insects he could hear scuttling about in the walls and ceilings. He braved another step forwards and regretted it.

The vestibule shifted, the cobwebs sweeping away and the furniture repairing itself, only to end up broken again and as bloodied as his hands. Screams pierced his ears and shattered his heart, and he fought his desire to track them to their sources and rip apart their owners.

He stumbled backwards, losing his grip on Aurora's hand, and hit the wall behind him.

Everything flickered, switching between black and white, to stark crimson. Between present and past. Both of them drenched in blood now.

Snow shut his eyes, trying to hide from the terrible sight, needing the darkness and the emptiness, a moment away from the horrific things he had done.

Aurora's hand came to rest on his cheek, her touch gentle and her heart steady.

"Do you need to rest?" she softly asked, her light voice chasing back some of the darkness in his heart, giving him a momentary respite from the storm of his memories and his bloodlust. He wanted to ask her to sing to him, to make this bearable, whatever this was that she was doing to him. He still didn't understand it.

"No." He forced the word out from between clenched teeth and she moved away, giving him space.

Snow opened his eyes again, took a steadying breath and then looked around the entrance hall, seeing it as it was now, not as it had been.

Aurora moved forwards, leading him onwards down a dark and dangerous path, one he was sure would end in her death.

He was weak now, barely able to retain control even when he desperately wanted to. It was only a matter of time before he saw something that would send him over the edge.

Snow trailed behind Aurora, grimacing whenever he saw the past overlaid onto the present, the blood and the gore, the destruction he had wrought with his bare hands and had watched in abject horror, unable to do anything to stop it.

They entered one of the drawing rooms and he flinched at the sight of a portrait of his parents still hanging above the black marble mantelpiece.

He turned and swiftly walked back out of the room, and leaned against the wall near the door. He laid his palms against the cold plaster beside his hips and pressed the back of his head into it so hard that his entire skull ached. The pain wasn't enough to dull the hollow ache in his heart.

Aurora came back to him, her incredible green-to-blue eyes filled with pity. He didn't bother to curse at her this time. He didn't have the strength to spare. He didn't even have the energy to ask her to let him leave this place of death.

Concern touched her beautiful face and she slipped her fingers into his and squeezed his hand again. It didn't comfort him as much as it had the first time. Each step, each second in this mansion, wore him down and left him weaker than ever, more vulnerable to his bloodlust.

She released his hand and moved off in a different direction, heading under the balcony of the staircase and into a room there. Snow didn't want to go that way, and she had to know it. She had witnessed everything he had done that night.

She glanced back at him over her shoulder, the concern still lingering in her eyes. He trudged behind her, needing to see this through to its terrible conclusion, powerless to stop himself now that he stood on the brink.

The lights came on in the room as she entered, candles throwing what should have been warmth across the tattered furniture and bloodstained floor. Snow saw only a cold, terrible replay of the murders he had committed in this room. His uncle and aunt hadn't stood a chance. He had ripped out their throats before they had even noticed him.

Snow clenched his fists at his sides and Aurora looked back at him again, and it dawned on him why she was doing this.

He had forced her hand.

He had spoken to her of his desire to die and his willingness to accept that fate, and she wanted him to fight to live.

What did she expect from him?

Being here was only hurting him, shredding his control over his darker urges. It took him back to a time he didn't want to remember, a time when his whole world had fallen apart and burned to ashes because of him.

"Take me away from here, Aurora." Snow held her gaze, not concealing any of his suffering or how desperate he was for her to comply with his request. He couldn't face this place, couldn't take being here, and he didn't want to lose himself to bloodlust and see himself murdering his beautiful Aurora.

"I cannot," she said in a low voice laced with regret and a touch of guilt that he could sense in her. She could and she knew it. "Not yet."

Unleash

She took another step towards the arched wooden doors that led onto the patio at the rear of the house.

Not there.

He couldn't go there.

She pushed both doors open, the hinges creaking and shattering the heavy silence.

The overgrown garden flashed into an elegant one with beautiful rose bushes laced with freshly fallen snow. A glittering smooth blanket of powder covered the lawn that stretched down towards the lake too, and twinkling flakes fell in a gentle rhythm from the dark sky.

Snow's breathing accelerated. A cold breeze rushed in through the open doors and he swore he could smell the delicate scent of roses and snow.

And blood.

He took a laboured step forwards and then another, tripping over his feet until he stood at the door with Aurora, seeing the world as it had been that night. He shook his head, fearing what came next. Blood splattered across the white canvas. Screams rent the air. The scent of death filled his lungs.

"Take me away."

He clutched the doorframe as his mother shimmered into being, her long pale hair flowing around her slender shoulders. Blood stained her alabaster skin and her dark dress. She turned to him with fear in her eyes and shook her head. Mama.

Snow ground his teeth and pushed with all his might against the doorframe, trying to stop himself from following a terrible drive to go to her. He wouldn't. The wood crumbled and shattered beneath his hands, and he stumbled out onto the frosty patio.

Snow looked down at his wet hands, horrified by the blood of his relatives that coated them.

His father's blood too.

He advanced on his mother, ignoring her pleas, driven by his thirst for blood and violence, a prisoner within his own body. He tried to stop himself, railed against what he was doing, his soul screaming for him to let her go.

He had vowed that he would never allow anyone to hurt her.

He had to keep that promise.

Snow's hands closed around her throat and no matter how fiercely he tried to convince himself to let her go, to release her, he began to do the opposite. He began to squeeze.

He felt the dreadful crack of her bones as they buckled under the pressure and couldn't tear his eyes away from her pale ones as he dug claws into her flesh, spilling her blood over her body to join that of his father.

She had run so well, fleeing him, as if she could escape. It had only made him chase her, finishing with his father so he could pursue his prey, eager to sink his teeth into her flesh and drink his fill.

None of the others had satisfied his hunger. It gnawed at him, his stomach twisting and turning, calling for more blood.

Affection warmed her eyes together with acceptance.

Snow despised her for it.

Fight.

He wanted her to fight to live.

He wanted her to kill him.

He didn't want to do this.

The light in her eyes faded.

She died too easily and he couldn't bear it. She should have fought him. She shouldn't have accepted her death as punishment for what she and his father and their entire bloodline had brought upon him and Antoine by never muddying their blood.

Snow dropped her and looked back across the lawn towards the woods.

His mother stood there with his father. The world whirled past him and he stood before them, blood rolling down his arms and dripping from his claws, soaking his loose white shirt, the taste of it thick on his tongue. He needed more.

He attacked his father, violently battling the male as he sought to protect his female, shielding her from blows and weakening himself with each heavy strike of claws that cleaved his dark waistcoat and his flesh beneath, turning his white shirt and cravat crimson.

Snow snarled and battered the male, hunger driving him, lost to it as the strong scent of blood filled the air around him.

The male was powerful but distracted, the presence of the female a weakness that Snow exploited. He focused on attempting to reach her, forcing the male to take his blows in order to protect her.

The male fought back though, claws blazing white-hot trails across Snow's body. His blood spilled from him, increasing his thirst and his need for blood. He would drain this male and then devour the female.

Snow shook his head. He couldn't. He loved his father and his mother. He wouldn't kill them too. The male landed a hard blow that sent his mind

Unleash

spinning and he roared and attacked him again, smashing his fist into his jaw, driving him towards a low wall that edged the expansive lawn.

The male said something and the female protested.

Snow tried to stop himself again. Not male and female. Father and mother. Papa and Mama. He couldn't hurt them. Wouldn't. His father was strong. He could stop him if Snow could only control himself for long enough. He could end his suffering by taking his head or his heart.

Snow needed that.

Claws gouged his biceps, ripping through his shirtsleeve, and the lacerations blazed fiercely, the pain obliterating the control he had regained, sending him into a killing rage.

The female ran.

He grinned and launched himself at the male. He would deal with him, drink his fill, and then hunt the female. She would make good sport.

Snow threw his head back and roared.

He collapsed to his knees on the patio, leaned over and clung to it, tears falling onto the flagstones. His entire body quaked as he struggled to breathe, fighting for air and for control.

He wasn't sure how long he had before he went back. His stomach rebelled against the memory of all that blood and the violent deaths he had carried out in pursuit of it.

"Why?" he whispered, voice hoarse as his emotions tightened his throat. He dug his blunt claws into the cold stones beneath him, tears blurring his vision and burning his eyes. "Why bring me here?"

"Because you must think about your sins."

He sat back and looked over his shoulder at her. She stood close to him, her white dress bright in the moonlight that played on her glossy black wings and her dark wavy hair.

"I already have... a million times... each day I close my eyes." He frowned at her, the pain of his memories eclipsed by the pain of her doing this to him, making him suffer like this for no good reason. "I never stop thinking about what I have done."

Her expression remained flat but the concern in her eyes darkened, verging on anger. "You block your memories. You make yourself forget. You think only of death."

He didn't understand. He remembered what he had done. He saw it in his nightmares every day and he despised himself for the things that he had done. He blocked none of it.

"You must face your past if you are to save yourself." She crouched before him and he growled at her.

"I do not want to be saved."

She glanced down at her knees and her black wings drooped. "There are those in this world who wish you to be."

Her solemn tone told him that she wasn't talking only of Antoine, or even those at Vampirerotique. Tears glittered on her long black lashes, in danger of slipping onto her pale cheeks. The sight of them lashed at him, cutting him deep and making him regret his harsh words. She wanted to save him.

Why?

For the past two thousand years, he had caused her nothing but shame and suffering. If anyone wanted him to die for his sins, it should be her. She shouldn't want to save him. She should ask her master to kill him.

"Take me away from here, Aurora." He rose to his feet and towered over her.

She shook her head. "Not until you face your darkest hour."

His spine froze. Dread weighed heavily in his stomach.

"No." He glared at her. She wouldn't. The look in her eyes said that she would.

She meant to keep him here until...

Antoine burst through the doors behind her, dressed in a long winter coat over his black waistcoat and trousers, his expression frantic as his gaze darted around.

The weather turned, white flakes falling thick and fast, driven across the land by a bitter wind.

Snow paused and felt the blood on his hands and his face, chilling his skin. He stared at Antoine.

Blood.

He needed to feed.

The female hadn't satisfied his hunger. He still wanted more.

He dropped her corpse into the rose bushes and advanced on the new male.

CHAPTER 15

Snow tried to stop himself but his body wouldn't listen.

The dark urge to taste the new male's blood consumed him, driving him to stalk towards him where he stood near the chateau, a horrified expression twisting his face and the scent of his fear and anger tainting the freezing night air.

A blizzard swept across the land, thick white flakes obscuring Snow's vision and numbing his wet hands and face.

The male spoke to him, words that swam in his ears and made no sense.

When he was within striking distance, Snow launched himself at the dark-haired male.

The male evaded him, coming around behind him in one fluid motion. Snow turned on the spot and lashed out, claws sharp now and swiping with deadly intent. The male barely avoided them, leaning back and losing his footing. He stumbled off the edge of the snow-covered patio and onto the rose bushes, close to the corpse of the female.

The male looked down at her, tears in his pale blue eyes. His anger called to Snow, a hint of darkness that laced his scent and would taint his blood. Familiar darkness.

Snow shoved away from the calm that tried to overcome him and attacked again, a merciless combination of claws, fists and feet. The male defended well but Snow was stronger, far older, easily able to land some blows, ripping material and cleaving flesh.

Spilling blood.

Blood that smelled so familiar.

He didn't want to do this. He glanced at the dead female, recognising her in the midst of the tempest of his fury and thirst. Mama. What had he done?

He snarled and lashed out at the male, catching him unawares and cutting across his chest.

The male fought back, his attacks increasing in strength and determination.

Snow tried to hold back but couldn't stop himself from throwing all of his power into each blow, beating the male into submission. With each strike that pummelled flesh, each slash that spilled dark blood, his hunger worsened, taking more control, forcing him to watch what he was doing, unable to even attempt to stop himself.

Snow hated himself as he rained fury down upon the male, mindless and vicious, intent on destroying someone he loved with every drop of blood in his body.

The male desperately defended himself but it was no use. He would weaken and then he would die, but at least he was fighting. So many of them hadn't fought him. They had died too easily, failing to satisfy his lust for violence.

He spoke to Snow again, a strange look in his blue eyes, eyes that were so familiar.

Blood that was so familiar.

Darkness tainted it.

Darkness like the beast he had become.

They were one and the same.

"Snow." That word breached the haze in his mind and the scent of his blood cleared more of it, bringing him back to awareness again and giving him the strength to fight.

Antoine.

His beloved brother.

Snow fought his terrible affliction with everything he had, clawing himself to spill his own blood, desperate to stop himself. If he could weaken himself enough, he wouldn't have the strength to fight Antoine. He could save his brother.

Antoine collapsed onto the thick layer of snow on the lawn, blood flowing freely from the deep lacerations across his arms and torso, turning the white into black in the night. He gasped for air, his heartbeat erratic, and Snow roared his agony at the cloud-strewn sky as he realised he had regained control too late to save him. What had he done?

"Antoine." His own voice sounded foreign to him, the taste of blood like bitter ashes in his mouth now. His heart shattered at the sight of his brother laying broken and close to death, fighting for his life even as it seeped out of him.

Snow ran to him and his knees hit the hard ground beside him. He slashed his wrist and held it to his brother's mouth. When he didn't drink, his eyes staring sightlessly at the heavens as his heart gave its last beat, Snow raised his brother's head with one hand and tried again, letting his wretched blood pour into his mouth.

The world faded back to the present and Snow leaned over, pressed his hands into the overgrown grass, and retched. He shook all over, sick to his stomach from the vivid imagery and the things he had done. He had never dreamed of the full brutality of that night. He could see that now.

He had always seen an edited version. The highlights with the worst parts removed.

He had killed everyone he loved. His aunts, uncles and cousins. His mother. His father.

His beloved brother.

He hadn't just savaged Antoine.

He had killed him.

His brother had died and only Snow's tainted blood had given his body the vital energy it needed to kick his heart back into life.

Snow closed his eyes, causing tears to drop, and frowned, grinding his teeth together as the pain of it all overwhelmed him. He couldn't bear it. It was too much, ripping and tearing at him, making him want to throw up again. His limbs trembled and his heart pounded, as erratic as Antoine's pulse had been as he lay dying because of him, bleeding out from wounds that he had never truly healed.

Antoine still bore scars from that night, both emotionally and physically.

Who had suffered more?

Snow, who had committed the atrocities, unable to stop himself even when he desperately wanted to?

Or Antoine, who had come upon the aftermath and witnessed the full horror of what Snow had done, seeing his family torn to pieces, and his parents butchered, and then having his own brother, a male who had acted more like a father to him, try to destroy him too?

Antoine should have killed him that night. He should have taken his life as payment for the brief taste of death that Snow had given him. He had asked it of his brother. His brother had refused, making him swear that he would never take his own life.

Snow had been seeking his death ever since.

Aurora was right about him, but she was wrong to choose this method as a way of making him want to live.

He looked up at her, his dark silvery eyebrows furrowed and his body trembling violently as he struggled with everything he had witnessed and the incredible pain it caused him.

He had killed his brother and he had forgotten all about it, tried to erase it from his memories, pretending it had never happened. Antoine knew though. Antoine would have remembered slipping from this world into the endless dark embrace of death, an embrace his own flesh and blood had delivered him into, together with the rest of their family.

Snow growled and gritted his teeth, tears burning his eyes. How could Antoine look at him with any shred of affection? How could he bear to see his face, knowing what he had done to him and their family? Snow deserved to die for his sins. He felt it now more than ever. He had no right to continue living in this world when he had taken everything from Antoine, replacing a world filled with love and light with one filled with pain and darkness.

He was wretched. Despicable.

Aurora stood over him, compassion in her beautiful eyes, hope and faith that he didn't want to shake, even when he needed to. He couldn't bear her looking at him like that when he felt so vile and disgusting, and deserving of the death she wanted him to forsake in favour of living.

"Showing me death and the horrific things I have done will not give me reason to live."

Sorrow edged her gaze and she eased down into a crouch beside him, leaned in and pressed a kiss to his forehead. Her lips were warm against his clammy cold skin and he closed his eyes as that heat spread through him, erasing some of his pain and giving him a fragment of comfort.

The scents around him swirled and he didn't need to open his eyes to know she had taken him away from the mansion, but he wasn't back at Vampirerotique. The temperature had dropped and snow cushioned his knees and his hands, freezing his skin.

Snow opened his eyes as Aurora drew away from him and rose to her feet. He eased onto his feet as he looked around.

A pristine snowfield stretched around him in the darkness, inky swaths of trees cutting through it in places, and blended seamlessly into the high mountains that reached up into the black sky. The aurora borealis was in full play above him, beautiful and breathtaking as the turquoise, blue and pink ribbons fluttered and danced.

"Where are we?" he whispered, afraid to believe it until she said it.

"You know where we are," she softly said and slipped her hand into his, holding it gently. It comforted him this time, restoring his strength and soothing his weary soul, easing some of the pain in his fractured dark heart. "You said that showing you terrible things wouldn't save you... so I decided I would show you something good... a good memory."

Laughter rang through the silence.

Snow whipped his head around and saw himself as a boy, swathed in pale furs, running circles around his parents near the fire outside the dark stone castle on the hill.

His mother gave chase, her own darker furs shifting with each step and her pale hair fluttering behind her. The boy squealed and erupted into another fit of giggles. His father watched them both with a beautifully indulgent smile as they played together.

It pained Snow to see them again, to see them happy and know what lay in store for them.

He should have died this night. Aurora shouldn't have saved him.

The younger version of himself spotted the owl flying overhead and gave chase, ignoring his mother's warnings. Snow tracked him with his gaze as he struggled through the deep freshly fallen powder, coming towards him, his arms reaching for the bird.

He had wanted to catch it. He had been desperate to kill it and show his father that he was growing up and able to hunt for himself.

He had wanted his father to be proud of him.

Snow lurched forwards when the boy ran onto the lake and stopped himself from calling out in warning. He flinched as the ominous sound of the ice cracking echoed around the mountains. The memory of feeling it give under his feet terrified him even now. He had known what was coming and had known he was powerless to stop it.

The boy went under.

Snow took a laboured step forwards and then held himself back, resisting racing onto the ice to save him. This wasn't real. This wasn't happening now. Nothing he did would change the course of history, no matter how much he desired that.

A beautiful light filled the sky and he froze, his breath leaving him as Aurora descended from the darkness, her small pale wings pinned back and her hair streaming behind her like black ribbons.

Her master called to her, warning her to return, but she ignored him.

She hit the lake with such force that a plume of water shot into the air, spraying chunks of ice onto the frozen surface. A heartbeat later, she broke the surface, wings flapping furiously, and water cascading from her and from the younger version of himself.

She landed heavily on the snowy shore and he saw her fear as she resuscitated him, her shaking hands pumping his chest.

Her mouth moved but no words came out. She hadn't been allowed to speak. It had been her punishment.

Snow moved closer, drawn to her as he had been that night, watching her as she smoothed the wet hair from the boy's brow and stared down at him. Singing to him. He couldn't hear her now but he knew that was what she was doing.

She glowed with light and purity as she watched over him, her expression revealing her agony as she waited for him to wake.

Aurora's hand squeezed his and he looked back at her, his eyes wide, feeling as entranced by her now as he had been back then.

The boy stirred and Snow watched as he communicated with the young Aurora, and then her master appeared. He saw her pain and fear as her master backhanded the boy and she desperately tried to stop him, and tried to go to the boy to help him.

When her master grabbed her and spread his pure white wings, lifting off into the air with her, the scene around Snow shifted. The arctic landscape softened, mountains becoming pale buildings, snow becoming soft cloud.

Snow growled when her master shimmered into being, holding Aurora by her wrist, and chastised her. She didn't deserve punishment for what she had done. If her master was angry over her actions, he should have taken it out on Snow, not on Aurora. The male angel shoved her backwards and released her.

The young girl stood quietly before the adult male, her eyes fixed on his feet, shame written across her petite features. Snow wanted her to rail at the male again, not meekly stand in silence as he berated her.

The dark-haired male struck her hard, bloodying her lips, but the girl didn't break. She took the blows and his harsh words without shedding a single tear. Snow clenched his fists, desire to destroy her master burning in his heart, fiercer than ever now that he knew what the bastard had done to her.

Before he could take a step to intervene, even when he knew it was pointless, the world changed again, revealing Snow's room in the castle.

The young Aurora appeared beside his large bed, watching over him as he slumbered, healing from the blow delivered by the same angel who had struck her and bruised her cheek.

Time skipped forwards and always she was there with him, standing sentinel beside his bed as he recovered, and then throughout other times in his life.

She had always been there with him, sometimes with sorrow in her striking green-to-blue eyes and sometimes with joy.

He saw her maturing at the same rate as he did, becoming more beautiful each time, but her wings becoming darker, more and more of her feathers turning black.

Snow despised himself for what he had done to her and that she had damned herself by saving him that night as a boy.

The world came back and he stared at the frigid dark landscape, standing beside Aurora and not feeling the cold as arctic winds blasted against him, sweeping down from the mountains and stirring the snow so it danced across the valley. He didn't look at her. His gaze remained rooted on the lake.

"Tell me again why you did it," he whispered, the gale catching the words and carrying them away.

She laced her fingers with his and squeezed his hand, her gaze fixed on the distance too. "I did it because I saw a boy with a warm heart, full of joy and happiness, and I wanted to know that boy."

She looked up at him.

"I saw the good in you, Snow, and I believed you deserved a chance at life, and you would bring happiness to others too. I still see the good in you."

Snow sighed, his breath turning to fog in the air before the wind carried it away too. "I brought pain to others, and evil to this world."

Aurora shook her head, raised her other hand, and touched his cheek. "You brought so much happiness. Your parents adored you, and Antoine loves you with all of his heart. You gave them joy and showered them with affection."

Snow knocked her hand away from his face. "And then I killed them."

"No, you did not kill them. The demon that lives within you killed them, not you. I believe you are strong enough to master it and reclaim your life if only you would fight," she whispered gently, the belief in her words touching him even when he tried to deny it.

His strength faded again and his shoulders sagged, and he could no longer resist looking down at her. He needed to see her unwavering faith shining in her eyes, and her affection for him, tenderness he had come to crave.

"I have fought hard for so many years," he said in a tight voice, aching at the thought of everything he had endured and weak from his battle against his bloodlust tonight.

Aurora shook her head, the raven waves of her hair swaying with the motion, caressing shoulders that he wanted to kiss. He wanted to lose himself in her and forget everything he had done, even when he knew that wouldn't change anything. He couldn't go back now that he had remembered the full run of events that had happened that night. He couldn't lie to himself anymore.

"No, you have always sought death, ever since that night." She held his gaze and touched his cheek, softly stroking it, soothing his anger before it could rise again. "You don't think it that way, but it has always been like it. I have watched millions of lives play out in this world and many of them chose the easy way out."

Aurora cupped his cheeks and stared deep into his eyes, tears rising into hers as her eyebrows furrowed and he sensed a hint of her pain through her touch.

"Death is often so much easier than life. Life is difficult... life is a constant struggle... especially when the span of your life is as infinite as ours. Death is simple and easy. In death, you do not need to live with your sins or bear the pain that beats within your heart," she said, her voice growing tighter with each word and tears balancing on her long dark lashes, on the brink of tumbling onto her pale cheeks. He wanted to capture them with his thumbs before they could fall. He didn't want her to cry because of him. He didn't deserve those tears. She sniffed and stroked his cheek. "I know your pain, Snow, and how it makes you suffer... and I know the release death would grant you is temptation incarnate... but it is not the solution. Sometimes the right path is the difficult and treacherous one, the hard one. Do not succumb to the lure of the easy one, for it will not give you the peace you seek."

Snow didn't bother to deny her words. He was too tired from his fight and she was speaking the truth. Ever since that night, part of him had been aching to die, had wanted Antoine to end his life to spare him so he didn't have to suffer. She was right.

He wanted to take a coward's way out.

Rather than mastering his bloodlust, he had given in to the darkness and let it master him.

It had controlled him for so long now that he wasn't sure he had the strength to overcome it or that he had anything left to offer this world.

He felt so weary and hollow, as though he needed to sleep for eternity and only then would he have the energy to go on.

Aurora's hand was warm against his face, erasing the chill from his heart and some of his fatigue, gifting him with the strength to keep standing.

He wished it could give him the strength to keep fighting.

He wasn't sure that was possible.

"I know your thoughts, Snow, and I will do all that I can for you. I will give you a reason to fight, and I am only sorry it took me so long to find the courage to appear before you again." Her eyes searched his and her dark eyebrows furrowed. "I feel I could have averted this if I had only come to you."

Snow raised his hand and covered hers, holding it against his cheek and savouring the sense of connection it awakened in him. "You are here now, and that is enough for me."

He hoped it really was enough. The flicker of fear that crossed Aurora's eyes made him frown. Not just fear. He could sense other emotions in her too. Hope mingled with guilt. Fear with belief. Sorrow with happiness.

He had suffered his darkest bout of bloodlust yet and she had come to him, and her wings had turned completely black. She constantly pressed him to fight, and something told him it wasn't just because she didn't want him to die.

"Why are you really here, Aurora?" It came out harder than he had meant and she glanced away. "I will not be angry with you… but I need to know why. It isn't just because you felt me suffering, is it?"

She shook her head and closed her eyes, and her shoulders sagged. "I did come to you when I felt you suffering, and… you have to understand, everything would have been alright if I hadn't given you my blood."

Snow reeled at that. Antoine had been right and she had committed a sin by giving her blood to him.

"What does your master want you to do?" he snarled, knowing the bastard was behind this, forcing Aurora to do something she clearly didn't want to. "Does he want you to kill me?"

She shook her head again. "I am to watch you and then judge you."

"Judge me how?" The watching part didn't bother him. She had watched him all of his life as far as he knew. He didn't like the sound of the judging part though, and the tears beginning to line Aurora's long dark lashes said she didn't like it either.

"If I can prove you are no longer a threat to humankind, you will be given another chance. If I cannot—" She cut herself off and turned away from him, her shoulders tensing and her pain flowing over him, strong enough that he could sense the depth of the emotions colliding within her.

She didn't want him to die.

She was desperate for him to prove himself worthy of another chance, no longer a danger to this world, and was doing everything in her power to gather the evidence she needed. He had been going against her all this time, proving himself quite the opposite.

"It is ironic that I may have found a reason to live when my time to die has come," Snow mused, more to himself than to her.

Aurora whirled to face him, a scowl darkening her beauty. "Do not think that way!"

She grasped his arms and her fingertips pressed in, tightly clutching him through his thin sweater. He could feel her trembling and it wasn't from cold. He had upset her again by still thinking about death when she was valiantly fighting to give him life.

"You need only prove that you are able to redeem yourself given time. We still have two days in which we can do that. I believe in you, Snow."

He didn't believe in himself, but he was glad that she did.

He had wanted death for so long now that he wasn't sure he knew what it meant to live. Her words haunted him, tumbling together in his mind.

Antoine wanted him to live and be free of his bloodlust, able to control it and keep it at bay. Everyone at Vampirerotique had become like family to him, and he loved to see them change and grow, and enjoyed the time they spent with him, talking to him about their lives and the things they had done, and their plans.

What was it like to make plans?

He couldn't remember.

Snow looked at Aurora, at her beautiful hopeful expression, seeing the tenderness in her eyes that she showed only to him. She was fighting so hard for him. She wanted him to live.

She wanted to live with him.

Hell, he ached for that too. He yearned for the feel of her tucked in his arms each day, warm and soft, sleeping close to him. He longed to hear her laugh and watch her with the others at Vampirerotique. He wanted to walk through life with her at his side, proud that she was his, that he had a female who desired him.

Belonged to him.

His first plan in centuries and it all felt so impossible to achieve.

He stared down into her eyes and his strength left him again, the weight of witnessing his past and the slaughter of his family pressing down on him until he could barely focus. His head swam, the bitter cold stripping away his body heat and leaving him weak and shivering.

He wanted to see his plan come to fruition and wanted Aurora to know about it so she would no longer look at him with despair in her beautiful eyes. He wanted to give her hope, but he couldn't find his voice. It took all of his remaining strength to keep standing.

"Snow?" Aurora stroked his cheek, her expression veering towards concern. "You need to rest."

Unleash

He nodded wearily, fighting to keep himself upright as his bloodlust began to rise again, threatening to overwhelm him in his weakened state. He fought it, not for his sake but for Aurora's. She wanted him to prove himself able to exist in this world without committing another atrocity.

He was beginning to want that too.

She wrapped her slender arms around him and pressed her lips against his, softly kissing him. Warmth cascaded through him, chasing back the cold stealing into his veins and restoring some of his strength. When she drew back, they were at the base of the mountain near the dark pine forest. A small cabin stood nestled amongst the towering snow-laden trees.

Aurora led him towards the wooden building.

She wanted him to live.

He wanted to live too, with her.

CHAPTER 16

Snow prowled around the small dark cabin. A vampire on a mission.

Aurora stood by the door, exactly where he had ordered she remain, and used her perfect night vision to watch him, amused by his very masculine display.

He was checking every inch of the cabin, scouting for danger. His senses would have mapped everything the moment he had set foot in the two room building, but it seemed he wouldn't be satisfied until he had seen with his own eyes that the only threat to them in this place was the frigid cold.

Arctic winds howled through the trees outside and battered the wooden cabin, icy fingers creeping through any gap they could find to clutch at her.

She should have kept her wings out, using them as a barrier around her, but she had wanted them gone. They reminded her of why she was here and she knew the sight of them pained Snow, making him remember the things he had done and that many of her feathers had turned black because of him.

Snow disappeared through the door opposite her, into the other room. There was a bang, a growl, and a muttered curse, and then he reappeared looking too triumphant for a male who had clearly just had a fight with a drawer or possibly a cupboard. He rattled a small box, produced something from within it, and then there was light.

The expression of sheer masculine pride that filled his warmly lit face made her think of a caveman just discovering fire.

He puffed his broad chest out and grinned. Aurora barely resisted her urge to cross the room and pat him on the head as a reward.

She also resisted pointing out that there was a box of matches on the mantelpiece on the wall to her right too, and those had been easy to spot during her first quick glance around the dark room.

"May I move now?" she said with a smile and he frowned, evidently not amused by her tone, or was it the fact that she wasn't preening his feathers for him by saying how charmed she was by his ability to find matches?

Me man. Man make fire.

The man in question tossed her a dirty look, skulked across the room and hunkered down in front of the empty fireplace. He huffed and cast a glance around. There was no wood and if he wanted to be all manly and go back out into the storm to find some, she wasn't going to argue.

And she might actually fake a swoon for him this time.

It was a touch chilly outside. Her bare feet were numb and her fingers were still like icicles. She feared they would snap if she tried to bend them, even though she knew that they were only cold and that she was immune to the true effects of exposure to freezing temperatures.

Snow rose to his full impressive height and stomped across the room to her.

"Stay put." He cut off her protest about his behaviour with a brief, hard kiss that melted her vocal cords and left her nodding dumbly.

The door opened, allowing an icy blast of air to assault her, and then closed again. Aurora rubbed her arms and decided to search the pitch-black room for blankets while Snow tackled the firewood.

The room was sparse, with one rickety wooden chair near the fire, a few wonky shelves in a nook near the door, and one tall cupboard on her left, standing against the wall opposite the fireplace. Her perfect night vision allowed her to see it all as if the fire was already alight. She opened the door and found layers of furs.

Snow cursed outside and barged the door open, letting in another wave of wind that carried white icy flakes across the threshold.

He didn't chastise her for moving. She took some of the furs and laid them down near the fireplace, keeping one in her arms. They would have to do as blankets and she was sure they would be warm. The cabin was basic, the sort of place that had been built to give refuge to anyone caught in a storm.

She felt as though she was caught in a storm herself as she watched Snow.

He crossed the room to her, his arms full of wood, his gaze intent on her and his body shifting sensually with each step. Her heart picked up pace, beating hard against her breast, trying to break free and get to him.

A smile tugged at the corner of his lips, telling her that he had heard her pulse begin to race and could sense her desire.

He dropped the wood beside the fireplace, crouched and moved some of it onto the grate, and set about lighting it, completing her caveman image of him.

He flinched when he struck a match, the light a bright flare in the darkness, and his eyes switched from their true state that allowed him night vision almost as perfect as hers was. His pupils expanded, returning to circles, and the red in his irises quickly faded back to blue.

He seemed better now than he had been at the lake, more in control of himself.

Was having a task to focus on giving him some respite from his bloodlust?

She should have anticipated that taking him to his family's mansion would trigger an episode. It had terrified her when he had clawed at himself, his blunt nails only scoring his black jumper. He had wanted to harm himself.

She had put him through incredible pain tonight and she only hoped that it had some positive effect on him, and he would fight now and desire to live again.

Guilt rode her mercilessly, never letting up, filling her head with a notion that haunted her. If she had simply told Snow why she was here in the first place, would it have had the same effect as forcing him to see that he had never truly fought his bloodlust and the hold it had on him?

He had taken it surprisingly well, but then he had been tired, drained by everything he had experienced when reliving his nightmarish past. He probably hadn't had the energy to lash out at her. He had looked on the verge of collapse at several points, the most recent just before she had decided to bring him here and give him some peace.

Did he hate her for what she had done to him? If he did, then she deserved it. She had been cruel to him and she was beginning to feel she was doing all of this out of some selfish need she had rather than for his benefit.

He didn't want to live.

Was it cruel of her to want to make him live even when he wanted to die?

Snow finished with the fire and looked over his shoulder at her. She hugged one of the furs to her chest, needing the warmth and the soft feel of it. It comforted her.

A frown marred his handsome face, his beautiful blue eyes intense but also laced with fatigue.

He looked lost again, bearing a heart filled with pain and darkness, and a head full of melancholy thoughts. She didn't want to take him back to the theatre yet, even when she knew that she should because Antoine would discover Snow was gone sooner rather than later. His younger brother would be frantic.

She was still feeling a little selfish though and she wanted some time alone with Snow, because she felt that if she spent these two remaining days with him that she would find a way to save him from death. There had to be a way.

"What is it like when the bloodlust takes you?" It was a dangerous question to ask and she feared it would strengthen the hold his affliction had on him and drive him into a rage, but she wanted to understand what he experienced.

She needed to know, because it might offer her valuable insight into his problem and possibly even a way of helping him master it.

Snow frowned and swallowed hard, and red ringed his irises. "I feel caged. When I… back then, two centuries ago… I felt there was nothing I could do to stop myself. I could only watch myself do those things, powerless and pathetic. It destroys part of me every time it takes me, Aurora."

He stared across the room at her, his voice thick with emotion and eyes glittering with pain.

Her heart went out to him again and she stepped closer, driven by a need to comfort him.

He was powerful and a warrior, a strong male, and she knew he hated to feel weak. His bloodlust made him feel trapped in his own body, aware of everything he was doing but unable to control himself. Aurora ached for him, wanting more than ever to find a way to free him from its grip.

Aurora crossed the room to him and he remained kneeling on the furs she had laid on the floor, looking up at her, his soft expression and the need she could feel in him calling out to her. She placed the fur in her arms around his broad shoulders and then wrapped her arms around his head and held it to her stomach.

She looked down at him and ran her fingers through his pale silvery hair.

He was incredibly powerful, yet amazingly tender, and every inch of her warmed as he wrapped his arms around her and held onto her, his breathing slow and steady, his cheek against her belly and his eyes closed.

Calm flowed through him for the first time in hours and she realised that he needed this.

He needed to feel her arms around him. He needed her to show him affection. It wasn't her blood that had helped him maintain better control over his bloodlust these past few days.

It was just her.

Her presence in his life.

She stroked his hair, her gaze locked on him, studying his noble but wild beauty. If it was her affection that gave him reason to fight his bloodlust and perhaps made him dare to dream of overcoming it, then she would give him all of it, and none of it would be a lie.

Did that mean she was falling for him?

She had seen mortals fall in love, and others too, such as the vampires at Snow's theatre.

She had never understood what they were feeling until now though. She felt desperate and scared, happy yet sad at the same time, warm and freezing cold. She had an urge to cling to Snow and keep him here with her forever, hiding from the world, just the two of them.

Whenever Snow spoke of death or looked as though he would still accept that fate, she grew angry and wanted to shout at him and make him take back his words and change his mind.

"What are you thinking, Aurora?" Snow whispered and moved to press a kiss to her stomach. He tipped his head back and she cupped his cheeks and looked down into his eyes. Her noble, beautiful vampire.

Her heart pounded hard.

"I think I am falling in love with you." She spoke those words quietly but they were loud in the room, as if she had shouted them at the top of her lungs.

Snow stared at her, his pale blue eyes wide, filled with the shock she could feel in his trembling body beneath her hands.

"Aurora," Snow whispered and then he was on his feet, drawing her close to him, enfolding her in his strong arms and kissing her so sweetly that it brought tears to her eyes.

She didn't want this to end, and if she had her way, it wouldn't.

She had never feared anything in her life as much as she feared the end of these days with Snow, and she would give anything for just one more day with him, one more day spent in these arms that held her gently and kissing these lips that made her feel alive for the first time in her life.

Tears rose unbidden and she quietly sniffed them back, not wanting to ruin this moment, desperate for it to be a perfect memory for both of them.

They both needed this.

Snow sighed against her lips and pulled away. His large hand cupped her jaw and tilted her head back, so her eyes met his.

"You are not only thinking you are foolishly falling for me… you think sorrowful things too." He stroked her cheek with his thumb, the caress tender and soft, stripping away her defences and leaving her powerless to resist him.

She nodded, needing to confess all because it was the only way she would feel better. She didn't want to hide anything from Snow, not anymore. He deserved to know everything and she would answer any question he posed.

Unleash

Snow brushed a kiss across her brow and lingered there, his lips resting gently against her forehead.

"Aurora… what happens if you judge me wrongly? Will there be a consequence?" The wary edge to his tone told her that he suspected he knew the answer to those questions and feared posing them for that reason.

"I would lose my soul and be cast into Hell, and there I would likely die."

"This is your only chance to redeem yourself?" He drew away and frowned down into her eyes. She nodded and then shook her head, because she honestly wasn't sure whether it would be her final shot at redemption.

"My master gave me this mission as punishment for my sins… but I think perhaps he also did it because he could see I harboured feelings for you."

"He gave it to you because he is a sick individual and he needs to be put down," Snow growled and she placed her hand over his mouth, stopping him from saying more.

She feared that if he spoke foul things about her master that he would come to them to punish Snow and take her away. She didn't want to lose a minute with Snow. Not a second.

"If my verdict is that I believe you able to function in society without endangering anyone because of your bloodlust, and I believe that is the only reason you would prove a danger to a mortal, and I can give evidence to back up my verdict, then my superiors have no reason to harm you or go against my decision."

Snow took her hand away from his mouth. "What if you can't give them solid evidence?"

She swallowed hard. She didn't want to think about that. She didn't want to think about any of this.

"Snow?" she whispered, holding his gaze, hoping he could see in it that this subject pained her and she needed to forget about her mission, her master, and her home.

"Kiss you again?" he said with a wide smile, reading her mind.

She nodded and he gathered her back into his arms and slowly dipped his head towards her. She tiptoed and met him halfway, kissing him softly, drawing out each brush of their lips, savouring the way it lightened her insides and took her pain away.

Aurora didn't stop him when he laid her down on the furs in front of the crackling fire. The heat of it and his touch chased away the last remnants of chill from her heart.

He leaned over her, his body resting half on hers and half on the furs beside her, and continued to slowly kiss her, as if he savoured this moment too. His tongue brushed hers, causing it to tingle and a moan to slip free of her lips.

He did it again, sweeping his tongue along hers, and then kissed her more deeply, fusing their mouths together in a way that stirred the passion that always ran as an undercurrent through her veins whenever she was near him.

He stroked her hair, brushing his fingers through it as he kissed her, the aggressive edge to it at odds with his gentle caress. She melted beneath him, needing more and aching for him to make her forget everything in the heat of the moment. She wanted to lose herself in him and their mutual desire.

She skimmed her hands down his thickly muscled arms.

The soft material of his black jumper clung to the delicious curves, emphasising them and causing a fierce ache to see him nude again. She would never tire of it, not even after a million years with him.

He had a godly form, powerful and masculine, a warrior made flesh.

She ached to lick every inch of him and worship his body as he had worshipped hers.

Snow grunted when she grabbed his shoulder and rolled him onto his back. She shamelessly settled herself astride his hips, feeling him growing hard in his black jeans.

His hands claimed her waist, burning her flesh through her white dress, teasing her with a brief flash of his strength as he ran them upwards. His thumbs and fingers pressed into her stomach and back, and then he brought his hands around and cupped her breasts. She moaned and bit her lower lip, her eyelids falling to half-mast as pleasure ran through her blood, igniting it and making her burn hotter for him.

He thumbed her nipples and she closed her eyes, groaned and thrust her breasts into his palms. She needed him skin-to-skin with her.

He was distracting her, throwing her off her mission to get him naked.

Aurora caught his wrists, leaned forwards, and pinned them above his head on the furs. His breathing quickened and she stared down at him. The sight of him beneath her, held at her mercy, sent a liquid rush of heat through her that pooled in her belly.

The edge of panic in his eyes subsided and he craned his neck and captured her lips, kissing her fiercely.

Each rough meeting of their mouths and the dominant thrust of his tongue sent new heat through her, shooting her temperature up another degree, until she was kissing him as hungrily as he was her, fighting him for control.

Unleash

He moaned and ground his hips, his hard bulge stealing her focus as it rubbed her in just the right place to have tingles arcing down her thighs. He was cheating. She still wasn't used to this and he was using his knowledge of that to his advantage, distracting her with the blissful feel of him between her thighs.

Aurora rocked her hips against him, seeking more pleasure.

Snow rolled her onto her back and had her hands pinned to the furs before she had finished one thrust. He flexed above her, driving his hips against hers and tearing a throaty moan from her. She arched into him, unable to control herself, lost to her desire.

He kissed her even harder than before, stealing her breath away and making her dizzy. The fire crackled, its heat nothing compared to the inferno burning inside her. She rubbed herself against Snow, hungry for more of him.

She was meant to be getting him naked.

Aurora evaded his mouth and twisted free of his grip, surprised by how easy it was to escape him until she caught the warmth shining in his blue eyes.

He didn't want to hurt her.

He cared about her too.

She wasn't the only one falling in love and judging by the nervous shimmer that had been in his eyes almost constantly since he had first seen her several days ago, she wasn't the only one feeling scared by the thought of losing her heart to someone.

She wanted to kiss him again and show him that she was here with him, sharing this moment, experiencing the same confusing combination of fear and happiness. She couldn't afford the distraction though. Not right now. She would kiss him when he was naked.

Aurora caught the hem of his jumper and his t-shirt at the same time, not wanting to waste precious time by removing them one after the other.

She pulled both garments up and sighed as the tightly packed muscles of his stomach came into view. She slowed, filled with a desire to take her time now, inching his tops up and gradually revealing his incredible body to her hungry eyes.

Snow moved to kneel between her thighs and she sat up, unwilling to release his clothing in case he pulled it back down again. The fire was warm enough to keep the chill off his skin. Surely, he wouldn't deny her? If he did, she would fight him on it.

A smile curved his sensual mouth, placing a wicked glint in his eyes.

He grabbed the hem of his jumper and t-shirt and pulled them both up over his chest and then off.

Beautiful.

It was wrong of her to want to run her tongue along the valleys and over the ridges of each honed muscle, delighting in their perfection and power.

He tossed his tops onto the floor on the other side of her to the fire and she barely bit back her sigh as his muscles shifted and bunched, flexing in a way that made her shivery and hot.

He leaned down on all fours, resting on his knuckles, and stalked towards her, crawling up the length of her body and forcing her to lie down on the furs again. Her pulse raced, blood rushing, spreading the achy shivers through her body until it cried out for him to touch it.

He stopped above her, his hands close to her ribs, and stared down at her. Tormenting her.

She wriggled beneath him, rubbing her inner thighs up and down his jeans-clad legs, and stroked her fingertips down his chest. His breathing hitched as she swirled one finger around the hollow of his navel and then continued downwards. Two could play at teasing.

She brushed her palm over the heavy bulge in his jeans and his eyes rolled back, a groan leaving him as a sigh.

Aurora flipped him onto his back again and this time he didn't fight her. He lay beneath her and she seized her chance. She leaned over him and explored his torso with her hands, skimming them over the ridges of his stomach and then his broad pectorals, leaving streaks of dazzling colour on his skin.

His gaze followed her caress, a smile tugging at his lips. He liked it when she left colours on him. He liked to know he was stirring her feelings until they overwhelmed her.

She followed her hands with her mouth, kissing him all over, tasting the masculine spice of his skin. He chuckled when she swirled her tongue around one of his dark pebbled nipples. She didn't react like that when he did the same thing to her. Perhaps it wasn't the same for a male.

She tweaked both of them at the same time and earned a husky growl for her efforts, noted he preferred rough to gentle when it came to his nipples, and kissed down the centre of his torso.

He tensed when she didn't stop at his navel. She ran her tongue around it and tackled his jeans at the same time, undoing his belt and then the buttons, casually grazing her hand over the bulge they encased from time to time to tease him.

He groaned and pushed his hips towards her. Aurora finished with his buttons, caught both his jeans and his underwear, and pulled them down to his knees. Her eyes fixed on his hard cock, her mind leaping back to their last

Unleash

intimate moment when she had kissed and sucked him. She wanted to do that again.

She shuffled back up the length of him and licked him from root to tip.

Snow threw his hands above his head, arched his back, and groaned.

Aurora moaned too.

She had never seen anything as delicious as the sight of Snow bowing off the furs, his face a picture of pleasure, his naked body hard and tensed. A hot flood of arousal pooled in her knickers and she wanted to tear them off and impale herself on him right that moment.

She forced herself to lick him again instead. He jerked in response and his breathing roughened, his arms tensing as he clutched the furs beneath him, his powerful body rippling and delighting her.

"Aurora," he whispered, hoarse and hungry, his passion-drenched voice the most beautiful sound she had ever heard.

She wanted to draw this out but needed him too much and could sense he needed her just as urgently.

Aurora sat back and Snow's eyes flicked open, red ringing them now. They locked on her, dark with the hunger she had heard in his voice, silently commanding her. She obeyed, stripping off her dress and shimmying out of her knickers. She tossed her clothes on top of his jumper and t-shirt, and crawled up the length of him.

He reached for her and she took hold of one of his hands, lacing their fingers together. Snow lowered his other hand between them and positioned his hard length at her entrance.

She moaned as she inched down onto him and he took his hand away, seizing her other one. She grasped his hands and tried to keep her eyes open as she took him into her body, as deep as he could go, stretching and filling her completely.

He moaned and swallowed hard, and stared into her eyes.

Aurora set a slow pace, too lost in his eyes to move faster, absorbing the beautiful look in them. All of his emotions played across his face, none of them hidden from her, and she knew hers were on display too. She rocked against him, long gentle strokes that made her ache and shiver, and heightened everything she was feeling.

Snow began to move beneath her, his thrusts countering hers, taking her higher, until she was soaring and her feelings were running out of control, wild and untamed, like the male inside her.

She stared down into his eyes, feeling the connection blossom between them, awed by the depth of it and the beauty. She shivered, holding onto his hands more tightly now, afraid that she would float away if he let go of her.

He kept their pace unhurried, drawing almost all the way out of her before sinking back in, flooding her body with pleasure more intense than any she had felt before. His hands shook against hers and she arched her back, tightening around his hard length, drawing even more pleasure from the feel of him moving inside her.

Snow's heavy-lidded gaze held hers and she wondered if she looked as satisfied as he did, as though she had found her true heaven and never wanted to leave.

She tried to hold on, wanted to cling to this and make it last forever, even as her body began to tighten around his, clutching him, drawing him deeper into her. His fingers pressed into the backs of her hands and he thrust deeper, as though sensing her need and how close she was to shattering.

It came upon her in a blinding flash that ignited the whole of her body and made her gasp in pleasure, unable to breathe as the intensity of it overwhelmed her and carried her higher.

Fire and lightning spread through her and she trembled, lost in the ecstasy and the feelings that burned in her heart, the bliss and the pleasure, the love and the connection.

Snow pumped her slowly, drawing out her climax, intensifying her pleasure, and then his grip on her tightened and he moved faster, thrusting deeper and harder, losing himself to his own ecstasy. He grunted and jerked his hips up, seating himself as deeply as he could go and spilling himself in her with heavy throbs.

Aurora held onto him, the feel of his climax adding to her pleasure.

He looked up at her, his ice-blue eyes full of affection and other emotions that touched her heart and warmed her. She knew what he needed from her now and she would give it to him, and she would fulfil that desire she could see in his beautiful eyes.

She would never let him go.

CHAPTER 17

It was cold. Aurora huddled into the furs and reached out for Snow, wanting to cuddle into him. Had the fire gone out? She groped around and froze when she realised that Snow wasn't there.

He was gone.

She shot into a sitting position, the furs falling away from her bare body. Snow's jumper and t-shirt were on the floor with her dress, but he was nowhere to be seen.

The door was open a crack, allowing snow to blow in from outside. A steady white streak of it had built up on the wooden floor and was melting further inside the cabin, leaving a wet trail.

Aurora was on her feet in a flash and dressing. She hadn't felt him stir, not since she had woken to find him growling in his sleep, tormented by his past in the form of nightmares. She had soothed him back into a calm state and had tried to stay awake, but must have drifted off again.

Now he was gone and she wasn't sure where, and whether he was lost to his bloodlust.

The fact that he had left half of his clothes behind told her that he was. No sane man would go out into arctic conditions in only jeans and boots.

Vampires didn't feel the cold as keenly as mortals did but they weren't almost immune to it as angels were. She had become chilly while out with Snow by the lake, her bare feet and hands numbed by the cold, but it hadn't pained her. Merely inconvenienced her and slowed her reactions. Snow could freeze to death out there. Could he die of exposure?

She wasn't going to wait around to find out.

She grabbed a large fur from the pile on the floor, wrapped it around herself and headed out into the darkness, closing the door behind her to keep some of the warmth inside.

She scoured the bleak dark landscape for a sign of him and spotted a trail leading down into the valley.

Where had he gone?

There was a settlement near the lake now. Dread chilled her insides as the arctic wind froze her on the outside. She refused to give in to that fear. Snow wouldn't have gone there and he wouldn't harm others. He wouldn't prove her master right about him.

"Snow," she called out to him and struggled against the wind as it howled across the valley between the imposing rugged mountains. She couldn't even fly in these conditions and the gale blew snow into her eyes, stealing her vision. She ran blindly into it, her eyes on the trail Snow had left for her. "Snow!"

The wind cut through her clothes, chilling her skin and stiffening her limbs, making it hard to keep moving. She pushed onwards, determined to find him, her limited senses dulled by the weather. She cursed this cold land and hoped she didn't end up as a meal for a rogue polar bear.

Or Snow.

Aurora shook that fear away and squinted into the wind. She was getting close to the lake now and the trail was heading straight towards it, not veering down the valley to her right, towards the settlement.

A growl cut through the noise of the wind and she pushed on again, doing her best to run in the deep snow.

A shape loomed in the wintry darkness, prowling out of the shadowy trees that edged this section of the concealed lake.

"Snow?" she called out again and halted when he looked over at her. His bloodied lips peeled back off enormous fangs as he snarled at her, a wild and lost male, feral and vicious.

Her heart stopped.

Had he attacked someone?

There was so much dark blood staining his mouth and chin.

Would he attack her next?

He turned and growled at something, and then whirled back again, snarling in the other direction. Could he sense danger? It set her on edge and her heart beat harder, lurching in her chest and crawling up her throat.

She edged a step closer to him and he turned on her again, red eyes burning like hot coals in the darkness, pinned on her.

"Snow?" she whispered, trying not to startle him because she liked her throat as it was. In one piece.

He growled again, low and vicious, gaze scanning the darkness around them.

The wind cutting across the valley buffeted her and caused icy flakes to swirl and dance across the white ground but didn't seem to affect him. He had to be freezing though. He was shirtless as she had expected. She needed to get the fur around him and get him warm before the cold did any permanent damage, or killed him.

She hoped that vampires couldn't die from exposure.

Snow jerked one arm out towards her.

Aurora jumped backwards and almost lost her footing in the slippery snow, and her heart nearly leaped clean out of her throat too.

He showed no sign of attacking her though or lowering his hand.

She looked at it and frowned. He was holding something.

A dead bird.

He huffed and offered it again. He expected her to take it.

Her eyes widened. Mercy, he was re-enacting the night they had first met, only with a difference. He was powerful and experienced enough to capture the owl this time. He unleashed a low feral grunt and glared at her, his crimson eyes narrowing and the pale slashes of his eyebrows coming together.

Aurora took the hint, feeling it was wise not to hurt his feelings and curious about his behaviour. She gingerly walked over to him and took the dead owl, holding it by the very tip of one of its broken wings. Poor thing. She wished she could give it new life but it had been dead too long.

Snow stared at her, red eyes watchful. Waiting.

For praise?

Aurora managed to smile in spite of her nerves, hoping he would think she was proud of him. Very proud. It took a really skilled hunter to kill a defenceless owl. She didn't let her sarcasm taint her smile. If he saw it, he would probably go in search of something bigger to kill in order to impress her, and bigger around here was either humans or bears.

She didn't want Snow fighting either of those things.

Snow rose to his full height and puffed his bare chest out.

She smiled properly now, unable to contain it. Somebody liked to have his ego rubbed.

Aurora studied him as he moved through the snow and beckoned her to follow. Was he lost to his bloodlust or not? It was hard for her to tell. His eyes were red, his claws and fangs extended, and speech seemed beyond him.

Yet he was aware of her and who she was, and he wanted to please her.

The wind howled across the valley and Snow was in front of her in a flash. Her heart shot into her mouth again. He didn't attack her though. In a lightning quick move, his large hand had pressed against her hip and he had guided her behind him. He unleashed a deafening roar into the icy darkness.

He was protecting her.

From what exactly?

He snorted like a beast and sharply turned his head this way and that, scanning the darkness and keeping her behind him the whole time, holding her close to his immense body. She could feel no animals nearby. No threat.

Snow growled, his powerful back and arms rippling with strength and menace. The wind came again, blasting against them, and he tensed and snarled.

Her heart went out to him.

Aurora released the fur she held around her shoulders with one hand and touched his bare back. "It is only the wind, Snow. We are safe."

He perceived even nature as a threat when lost to his bloodlust, unable to distinguish that it was the wind making that terrible howling sound.

"Snow?" she whispered and stroked his freezing skin. He looked over his shoulder at her and then released her hip and turned to face her. She slipped her hand into his. He was trembling and it wasn't only from the cold. He feared. He thought the wind was a beast wanting to harm them.

He wanted to protect her and possibly even felt he might fail. He feared for her safety.

He was incredibly gentle as he held her hand, staring down at it with a blank expression on his face.

She took the lead, luring him back towards the cabin and leaving the fur behind in the snow. She had a feeling that if she discarded either his hand or the owl in favour of the fur that Snow would be upset with her, and she didn't want to push him into a darker rage than the one that gripped him already.

Aurora looked back at him, smiling when he glanced at her and then looked back down at their hands. He blinked, palmed her fingers with his other hand, and frowned.

He wasn't evil or a threat to anyone when he was like this. Not really. Not anymore. He was more of a threat to himself.

He suffered and struggled to comprehend things that were obvious to everyone else. He thought the weather was a danger to himself and to her.

He felt things though, noble feelings that strengthened her belief that he was in there, trying to master the darkness and drive it back. He had hunted for her because he wanted her to be proud of him, not ashamed. He wanted her to believe him strong and capable, because she had seen him weak and vulnerable.

The wind howled across the valley.

Snow twisted her into his arms, shielding her from it, taking the gust against his back. The moment it had passed, he snatched the dead owl from her and bit into it, holding the carcass in his mouth. He scooped her up, cradling her in his strong arms, and carried her through the snow, long strides devouring the distance to the cabin.

Aurora stared up at him, shocked by his behaviour.

The wind blew again, driving snow across their path and against their bodies.

Snow growled and tightened his grip on her, holding her closer. He snarled whenever the gale blasted across them.

The owl dripped blood all over her white dress but she decided it was unwise to ask him to put her down. He clearly felt an intense need to protect her and she didn't want to upset him or make him feel he had done something wrong.

She had never seen this side of his bloodlust before.

She had seen him fight it whenever he felt someone at the theatre was in danger, and had believed that it was because he desired to protect them. Now he was protecting her rather than hurting her.

He was deep in his bloodlust, she no longer doubted that, but he was still extremely aware of her, and wanted to keep her safe. Could she get through to him even when he was in this state?

Was this behaviour the result of his containment at Vampirerotique and his efforts to control his bloodlust by using a strict feeding plan?

It was possible, and it was equally probable that he was unaware of his progress because of the course of action he always took when his bloodlust emerged.

Chaining himself whenever his affliction seized control might have had a negative effect, sending him into a deep rage because he felt vulnerable and felt the need to protect himself from others.

It could have concealed this change in him. Her vampire might have more control over himself than he knew.

Snow shouldered the door open and kicked it closed behind them. He spat the owl onto the floor and gently set her down in the main small room of the cabin, but didn't let her go. He held her at arm's length and thoroughly checked her over from head to toe.

His grip on her tightened and his gaze froze on her left side.

His crimson eyes darkened and he growled, exposing his fangs.

Aurora looked down and saw the blood on her dress.

He thought it was hers. He thought she was hurt.

His expression twisted, rapidly turning as black as his eyes were, and he snarled and flexed his fingers against her arms.

It changed whenever his gaze flicked to her face, a brighter corona of red pushing through the black in his irises. He looked as though he was either going to go back out into the night to find the culprit and destroy it, or mollycoddle her.

Aurora gasped when he grabbed her dress and yanked it up, exposing her lower half to the chilly air.

He dropped to his knees and she shivered when he placed his hands on her. They were freezing. She tried to get away but he growled and held her firm. His handsome face turned dark and deadly as he shoved her dress up further, evidently seeking the wound.

There were a few spots of blood on her stomach above her left hip. It must have soaked through the layers of her dress.

Snow hesitated, gaze flicking between her stomach and his bloodied hands, and then downwards.

What was he thinking?

He startled her by ripping the lower half of his right trouser leg.

It got stuck on his boot when he tried to pull it off and he fell onto his backside, grappling with it. Eventually he realised he had to take his boot off. He shredded the laces, tore the offending boot off and hurled it across the room. It hit the wall with a hard thud and dropped to the floor. He paused and looked up at her, eyes wide.

She held back her smile. It was sweet of him to want to do something and to ruin his clothes to achieve it. She was curious about what he intended to do with the wet material though.

Her heart melted again when he lowered his head and secretly cleaned his bloodied face with it. He didn't want to dirty her. She couldn't contain her smile now. It was more than merely sweet of him to worry about such minor things. It touched her deeply and made her feel loved and precious.

He was gentler this time when he lifted her dress to reveal the spots of blood on her skin. Part of her felt she should tell him that it wasn't her blood and he didn't need to do anything for her, and the rest of her told it to shut up and let him do as he wanted with her because it was incredibly endearing to have this powerful male fussing over her even when in the throes of his bloodlust.

He hesitated again, and then leaned in and licked her skin. My. Oh. My. The way his tongue rasped against her set light to the passion in her veins and she blushed, her temperature soaring. Snow licked harder, making her knees quiver and heart stutter.

Disappointment crushed her desire when he sat back and frowned quizzically at her stomach. His eyebrows shot up. His gaze darted to the dead owl.

Busted.

At least in his current state he couldn't pick her up on it. Speech was definitely beyond him. He knelt before her, his face a picture of innocence, looking up at her. She felt as though he was waiting for her to say something, only she wasn't sure what he wanted to hear.

Aurora stroked his cheek.

He leaned into her touch, his eyes closing, and something like a purr rumbled through his chest. She smiled down at him and sneakily rearranged her dress, covering herself before he could notice. His skin was icy cold beneath her fingers.

"Come to the fire," she said, not holding her breath but hoping he might understand her and do as she bid. "I need to get you warm. Understand?"

He growled when she took her hand away from his face. She smiled at him, hoping to soothe his upset, and held her hands out to him. She backed towards the fireplace.

Snow huffed and effortlessly rose to his feet, the muscles of his bare torso shifting with the action, and obediently followed her. He stopped when she crouched in front of the fire. She placed more logs onto the grate and stoked the flames to get the fire burning hotter. The heat of it warmed her skin and stole the numbness away.

Aurora patted the fur behind her.

Snow plopped himself down.

He didn't growl at her when she placed a fur around his wide shoulders. She took that as a good sign. He was happy for her to touch him.

She made him hold the fur around himself and set about rubbing his chest, trying to warm his skin. He grabbed her, twisted her around and pulled her onto his lap, sitting her with her back against his front and her bottom pressing against his groin. He snaked his arms around her stomach and settled his chin on her shoulder.

The fur slid off his back.

He huffed, released her and pulled it back up. The moment he held her again, it slid off. Aurora sighed as he repeated this process three more times before he realised that he couldn't hold her with both arms and keep the warming fur on his back at the same time.

To his credit, he found a way around the problem.

He held the two ends of the large fur and wrapped it around them both, effectively holding her at the same time. It was warm too, cuddly, and she was loath to mention that they couldn't remain like this. He needed to sleep because she wanted to see if sleeping would help him regain control over his bloodlust.

It was definitely affecting him differently this time.

He knew who she was and was more in control of himself, even though he was still acting more like an animal than a man.

"Snow," she said and feigned a yawn, feeling it would be the only way to get him to rest too. If he thought she needed to sleep, he would likely want to do the same, remaining close to her. She would wait for him to doze off and then do something about the dead owl that was in a heap across the room, disturbing her.

It wasn't the most romantic gift to give a woman, but she did appreciate the cavemanesque gesture.

First he had made fire. Then he had hunted for her.

And then he had worn the sweetest nervous look when he had wanted to clean her wound and had feared sullying her.

She smiled again at that and filed it away for bringing up at a later date, when Snow wasn't in the grip of his bloodlust.

The wind slammed against the cabin. Snow held her closer. She patted his hands to soothe him, glad to feel they were warmer now.

"Will you sleep a while with me?" she said and he grunted and moved just enough that he could lay them down on the furs, proving that he could understand her while lost in his bloodlust. He covered her and pulled her flush against him, his large hand settling over her stomach.

Aurora feigned falling asleep and it wasn't long before Snow had drifted off, his breath cool but steady against her shoulder.

Even in sleep, he didn't lessen his grip on her.

She tucked her arm under her head and kept her focus locked on him, monitoring him for a sign that he was experiencing a nightmare. He slept soundly behind her, his big body pressing against her back with each breath.

The fire popped and flickered, throwing warmth over them. She fought off sleep, wanting to stay awake in case Snow needed her.

When the sun began to rise, she gently removed his hand from her stomach and rolled away from him, intending to return to Vampirerotique and see Antoine. She had to confess what she had done and let him know that his brother was safe and well.

Snow grabbed her and dragged her hard against his body.

"Let me go, Snow," she whispered and it only made him worse. He growled at her, his powerful arms caging her, pinning her back against his front. She wriggled, trying to get him to loosen his hold.

He snarled and sharp pain blazed across her bare right shoulder. Aurora gasped, her breath stolen by the intensity of it. Heat washed through her and fear for Snow followed in its wake as she realised what had happened.

He had bitten her.

Aurora instantly stilled in his tensed arms, expecting him to start feasting on her blood, driven to drink all of her in the midst of his dark lust.

He didn't.

He remained rigid behind her, crushing her against his body, his fangs buried in her flesh.

He hadn't bitten her to drink her blood. He had bitten her to keep her with him and ensure she couldn't try to sneak away from him again. It wasn't an act of aggression. It was an act of possession. And possibly even protection.

It was light outside.

Had Snow feared she would go out into the day and the sunlight would harm her?

Aurora breathed slowly, forcing her fear to settle. His body relaxed a fraction of a degree with each second she lay calmly in his arms and the pain in her shoulder subsided. His breathing slowed again, steady once more, but he showed no sign of releasing her from his hold.

She placed her hands over his to soothe him and show him that she was going to stay. He relaxed further, his body moulding against hers in the most delicious way. His fangs remained buried in her shoulder, holding her still.

Aurora lost track of time, staring at the fire. She tried to stay awake but eventually sleep claimed her.

Something tickled her shoulder. She frowned and focused, clearing the fog of sleep from her mind. Snow had released her and was tenderly licking the spot where he had bitten her, his tongue soft and cool as it rasped over her flesh. His arms still caged her, keeping her flush against his body. He wasn't taking her blood though.

He was healing her.

It surprised her, especially when he allowed her to roll over to face him and she found that his eyes were still blazing crimson. He was deep in his bloodlust even after his rest, but he was affectionate and gentle, two things he had never been before when the darkness had seized him. It gave her hope that she could save him.

She pressed a soft kiss to his lips.

He froze, eyes wide and fixed on her the whole time that she explored his lips. She couldn't resist grazing one of his fangs with her tongue. He purred at that and pressed his palms into the small of her back, tugging her closer. She drew back and stroked his white hair from his brow.

"Rest now," she whispered, her gaze holding his. "I will stay with you. You need not fear, Snow."

To prove it, Aurora settled into his arms, her head against his chest. He tensed at first, then relaxed and rolled onto his back, dragging her with him so she was lying on top of him under the furs.

She dozed off again.

When she woke this time, the sun was close to setting and they weren't alone.

The one she knew as Payne was standing in the middle of the room, shivering despite his thick black jacket and gloves, and looking more than a little annoyed.

"Do you know how big this damned valley is?" he snarled and she gestured for him to lower his voice.

Snow still slumbered, but if he woke, he was bound to attack his friend in order to protect her.

"I have been searching everywhere for you two. I had to hide out in a bloody cave when the sun rose this morning and wait for shade to come to this side of the valley before I could teleport through the forest. Do you have any idea how many trees I crashed into trying to get here and avoid getting fried at the same time?" Payne's eyes darkened. Blue, gold and red mixed together like a tempest.

A very deadly tempest.

It made sense that he would be the one to show up. His incubus side gave him the ability to teleport, but only to places that he knew or could see. He had probably already been to the chateau in Switzerland looking for them and now he was here, in the middle of the arctic, hundreds of miles away from the nearest airport.

He would have had to teleport from there to the furthest point he could see and then repeat the process, risking ending up in a lake or any number of

Unleash

dangerous situations. Judging by his soaked blue jeans, soggy leather boots and damp coat, he had ended up neck deep in snow a few times.

He folded his arms across his chest, causing the sleeves of his thick black wool jacket to stretch tight across his muscular arms, and glared at her.

"Snow needs to come home now," he said and his tone gained an edge she didn't like, one that verged on threatening. He thought she was out to hurt Snow. What had Antoine told him about her? Why did everyone think she wanted to hurt him when all she was trying to do was save him?

Payne's gaze flicked to Snow and then back to her. "Antoine needs him home."

She knew that. She had wanted to go to him but Snow had stopped her.

"When he wakes and darkness has fallen, I will bring him back," she whispered. "I couldn't bring him back any sooner… even though I had wanted to. His bloodlust took over."

Payne took a step back, as though that tiny distance could save him if Snow woke and viewed him as a threat to her.

"Please tell Antoine I am sorry and wanted to go to him and tell him about all of this… Snow would not let me go." She glanced pointedly at Snow's arms around her and the fact they had her pinned against him, trying to make Payne see that she wasn't exactly comfortable sleeping on top of him like this and she certainly wasn't doing it by choice.

Snow growled in his sleep and held her closer.

Payne tensed and crimson shot through his eyes, obliterating the blue and gold.

The growl must have been a threat.

Snow's red eyes flicked open and she pressed her full weight onto his shoulders, cupped both of his cheeks in her palms and kept his gaze on her.

"I am safe," she said and he inhaled, and then his lips peeled back off his fangs and he growled again. He tried to look towards Payne. She stopped him. "Snow, look at me. You know him. He means us no harm. Your brother sent him. Antoine sent him."

Snow frowned at that and huffed as he set about covering more of her body with the furs. He tossed a growl at Payne and rolled her off him in the end, tucking her behind him and shielding her from the male by completely concealing her with his broad body and the furs.

Aurora stroked his bare back, trying to soothe him. She poked her head over Snow's shoulder and caught the flicker of shock in Payne's crimson eyes.

"Why isn't he trying to kill me?"

She kept caressing Snow's back, keeping the motion even and smooth. "He will be if you stick around. I think we had a little breakthrough."

"Snow has claimed you as his female." Payne hit the nail on the head with a resounding bang and looked as though he wanted a prize for it. She was tempted to point out all the evidence that should have made that clear from the moment he had popped into the cabin.

For a start, she had been in bed with Snow, sleeping on top of him.

Payne moved, just enough to undo all of her hard work, causing Snow to tense and toss a dark snarl at him. Snow clutched her closer to his back, his blunt claws digging into her bottom through the furs.

"I'm not interested in her. I'm taken, remember?" Payne said but it didn't stop Snow from growling at him again.

"Perhaps you should leave and return to Antoine. Tell him that as soon as Snow is feeling better, I will bring him home," Aurora said and stroked Snow's hair, desperate to soothe him so he didn't do something he would regret later.

"I'm damned well going to tell him that you fucked Snow some way towards sane." He grinned and disappeared.

Aurora cursed him and was tempted to go after him, catch him before he could say something so vulgar to Antoine, and beat him into a bloody pulp. She should have let Snow have his way with the arrogant perverse male.

She squealed when Snow dragged her over him, caught her before she hit the floor, and kissed her.

Someone was learning fast.

Aurora melted into the furs, letting him have his way for a full minute before she decided that him kissing her senseless while lost to his bloodlust probably wasn't a good thing.

She pushed him back and his eyes flicked open to reveal blue irises.

CHAPTER 18

Snow stroked the tangled waves of Aurora's long black hair from her face, tucking it behind her ear. She stared at him, her beautiful green-to-blue eyes wide and full of the shock he could sense in her. She hadn't expected him to be back. She had expected the red eyes of his bloodlust.

"Payne was here," he murmured, not wanting to break the comfortable quiet that was happening between them. She nodded. Snow frowned. "He was rude to you."

Aurora didn't nod this time. "We should take you back to the theatre."

His frown hardened and he rested his fingers on her warm pale cheek. He remembered her being cold last night, her skin chilled by the wintry weather. He remembered her coming to find him in the darkness, risking her life.

It had angered him, although he wasn't sure why. At the time, he had felt she was in danger and he had been desperate to protect her. The only threat to her in this part of the world was a polar bear and Snow could easily take down such a beast. It wouldn't have laid a paw on Aurora.

"What if I do not want to go back?" Snow said, partly because he didn't want to return to Vampirerotique and partly because he wanted to see how she would react to that question.

"You have to—"

"Yes, I have to," he interjected, disappointed that she was going to take the sensible route of what he must and must not do, rather than allowing her emotions to colour her answer. "But that doesn't mean that I want to go back. If I didn't go back… if I chose to spend the rest of my days in this cabin… would you stay with me?"

She nodded without hesitation.

"Because it is your mission to monitor me and decide my fate?"

She frowned now, the action pinching her black eyebrows together and turning her sensual mouth into a hard line. He had to put it out there. He needed to know that she was here with him because it was what her heart wanted, not because it was her duty.

"No," she whispered and a delicate blush rose onto her cheeks. She glanced down at his chest. Snow stroked two fingers along her jaw, settled them under her chin, and raised her face again, forcing her to look at him. He wanted to see her eyes because he wanted to judge her feelings as she spoke to him and they hid nothing from him.

"But you would not stay for long though… how long do we have?"

She tried to look away again and then met his gaze. "Do not look at me like that."

"Like what?" He wasn't aware he was looking at her any differently from how he normally looked at his female.

"So full of hope… a look I would give anything to keep on your handsome face." Her blush deepened.

She liked how he looked at her as though she was his salvation then, even though she could be his damnation just as easily. Could she read in it that his happiness hinged on remaining here with her?

He desired it more than anything. He needed to stay here, with her in his arms, away from a world that tested them both and pushed them to their limits. He wanted to be with her forever, living peacefully, sharing centuries together.

He ached for that even when his dark heart knew it was impossible and that hoping for such a thing would only lead him to suffer pain a thousand times worse than he had already experienced in his long weary life.

Such good things didn't happen to him. They were the fate of others more deserving. His fate was a dark one, his path fraught with danger and bloodshed.

"How long do we have?" he said and then cleared his throat, attempting to ease the tightness that had built there all of a sudden.

He stared into her eyes, foolishly wishing she had come to him sooner so they could have had longer together. If he could have met her again centuries ago, before or maybe even after he had been drafted into the Preux Chevaliers, he might have been a different man.

He might not have killed his family.

He had witnessed how Sera tempered Antoine's bloodlust, helping him maintain control. He yearned for that with Aurora, that her loving touch and presence at his side would give him back a modicum of control over the darkness that raged within him, and that with her he could come to master it completely in time.

A fool's dream.

"Perhaps a day." Those softly spoken words cut at his dream, tearing it to pieces before his eyes.

Only a day.

Today might be the last day of his life.

How many times had he wished for that?

Now that it was here, he feared what would happen. He feared for himself and for Aurora. The affection she showed to him, the fact she believed herself falling in love with him, wasn't reason enough for her to risk her life by telling her superiors he was no threat to the world. He could never allow it.

He would have to think over everything that had happened to him in the past few decades and see whether there was hope for him, and speak with her about it all. He couldn't do that at Vampirerotique. Antoine would want her away from him. His brother wouldn't understand that they only had a short time in which to decide his fate, and Snow was damned if he was going to tell Antoine that he might die tomorrow. He couldn't inflict that pain upon his beloved brother. Antoine had fought so hard to make him live.

Snow hated himself for deceiving his brother, and himself.

Aurora had made him realise that he had never truly fought his bloodlust. He had always allowed it to steal control over him, desiring the pain and suffering as punishment for his sins.

He would give anything to have a chance to go back and change his past, even if it was only so he could fight his bloodlust in the aftermath of killing his family, and consequently erase the lies he told to Antoine and the black feathers he added to Aurora's wings.

"I think I really should take you back to your brother as soon as I can. Antoine seems a very determined and protective male, and if we do not return, he will make Payne teleport here again."

Snow didn't pay attention to half of what she said. He was too lost in his thoughts, going in circles and feeling increasingly frustrated, unsure whether there was a way to prove himself able to function in the world and whether he believed it possible anyway.

He felt different now that Aurora was in his life, but he had only known her a few days. He couldn't tell her that he was sure he would no longer go on a rampage, slaughtering innocents, when he didn't feel certain.

If she told her superiors that she believed him no longer a threat to the world and then he went and lost his head to bloodlust and killed again, she would lose her wings. They would send her to Hell and he could never live with himself if that happened.

There was no way he could allow that to happen to her. He knew first-hand the horrors of that world and the creatures that roamed within it. Many there would feel drawn to her purity and the remaining shred of good in her, able to sense she was once an angel.

They would torture and abuse her until her body, mind and spirit finally broke and she died in agony. No one there would try to protect her.

Snow swore that if it happened, if something went wrong and she ended up in that domain, he would go there and bring her back. He knew the ways in, the portals that could take him deep into the bowels of Hell. He would find her. He would never let his Aurora suffer.

"Snow?" she whispered, concern lacing her voice. He shook away his dark thoughts and focused on her, catching the worry in her eyes too.

"That could be awkward," he said and she frowned, clearly not following him. "If Payne teleported Antoine here."

"Why?" Some of the concern in her eyes melted under the warmth of curiosity and affection that began to edge them.

"We might be making love." Snow settled his palm in the small of her back and dragged her against him.

He kissed her, needing the connection between them to chase away his dark mood and not wanting to waste a moment he had with her. She surrendered to him, her small hands pressing against his bare chest and a breathy sigh escaping her.

Snow mastered her mouth, keeping the kiss light and soft, savouring her taste and warmth, and how she always responded to him so sweetly.

He had never thought he would find a female like Aurora, one who stood up to him and refused to let him have his way, forcing him to open his eyes and take steps to improve himself.

He wanted to be good for her.

Whenever he was around her, he couldn't stop thinking about what his life would be like with her in it, with her bright smile and tender touch warming his heart, and her soft voice soothing his bloodlust, keeping him calm and keeping the darkness at bay.

He had never dared believe that there could be a female for him out there, someone beautiful and affectionate, and delicate, but strong enough to deal with him even in his darkest moods and in the throes of his bloodlust. He had never dared dream he could have what his friends did.

Someone to love.

Unleash

Someone who loved him.

Aurora knew all of his sins. She bore them all with him. She was his dream made flesh and she had always been with him, watching over him.

"I wish I had met you again sooner," Snow whispered against her lips and she drew back, her brow furrowed and mixed feelings colouring her eyes. He could sense sorrow and hurt in her, and that permanent dash of hope that she refused to let die.

"Do not speak like you are doomed, Snow." She raised her delicate hand and stroked his cheek, her eyes searching his, holding them and entrancing him. "There is still time."

But it was running out.

She got a strange look about her, one he didn't like. She was calculating again.

"Do not even mention returning to my brother." Snow pulled her back to him and started to kiss her again. She pushed against his chest, breaking free of his lips. He sighed and let her have her way, because he would have his soon enough.

"We have a little time before we have to go… but we do have to go, Snow. Antoine will be worried sick and I don't want to come between you. I think he hates me as it is. I don't need to give him more reasons to despise me."

Snow caressed her cheek and cupped it in his palm. He stared into her eyes and ached to erase the hurt growing in them.

"I will speak with Antoine. When he realises my feelings for you, his will change. I promise you, Aurora."

She nodded and then smiled shyly. "Your feelings for me?"

He sighed and brushed his thumb across her cheek. She wanted to hear the words but he couldn't say them, because he feared they would colour her judgement and she would damn herself just to be with him a few more days or years. Her smile faded and she ran her fingers over his bare chest.

"I will not push to know them." Her eyes tracked her fingers as they danced in maddening swirls over his skin, stoking the lust that already burned hotly for her.

Snow tried to kiss her again. She braced her palms against his chest, keeping him at a distance, and frowned up into his eyes.

"What do you remember of last night?"

He groaned. He wanted to kiss her again and make her scream his name in ecstasy before they had to return to Vampirerotique.

He had intended to talk with her later about the past few days, his feelings about his bloodlust, and what he believed her verdict should be. He had hoped to have as long as possible with her without mentioning that he thought she should judge him as a danger, because he couldn't say for certain that he wasn't.

Maybe she could change his mind about it. Maybe she could ask for an extension so she could be sure. Was that possible?

"I remember my bloodlust riding me." And he really didn't want to go back and remember exactly why it had been riding him, because he still hadn't fully forgiven her for pushing him into that situation. She might be strong, but whenever his bloodlust gripped him, he was dangerous and unpredictable. He might have tried to kill her. In fact, he was certain he had at some point. It was fuzzy and he liked it that way. "And then I remember you riding me."

She playfully slapped his chest.

"Then I was damned tired and I fell asleep… and I lost it at some point."

"Because I pushed you too hard. I'm sorry I did that to you, Snow. I have so little time though and you were being stubborn about everything… and I had to do something to make you realise what you were doing to yourself."

He knew that and it was part of the reason he had started to forgive her. She regretted what she had done but she had seen it as necessary. She was trying to save him from death and he had made her desperate.

He smiled inside at that. She fought valiantly for him. No female in his existence had ever fought for him. It touched him and he was feeling foolish enough to admit that when combined with his behaviour around her and that she desired to remain with him, it gave him a sliver of hope.

"You seemed different last night," she whispered, as though afraid to voice those words in case she had read him wrongly.

Snow realised that he had the power to crush all of her hope and her belief in him, and that if he did, he would crush her heart in the process. She suddenly felt so fragile in his arms, her eyes filled with vulnerability that struck him deep and stirred a fierce need to hold her close and say whatever it would take to make her strong again.

He nodded and relief touched her eyes.

"I felt different," he admitted and then bravely took a bigger step. "I felt almost… normal." He grimaced as parts of last night came back to him. "Not quite normal… I gave you an owl."

She stifled a smile. "It was very sweet of you. You took care of me. You protected me."

He had. And then after that he had…

His eyes fell to her right shoulder and the dark puncture marks tainting her pale skin. "I bit you. Did I hurt you?"

"No." She shook her head a fraction. "You were only trying to stop me from leaving. I knew that. You were gentle with me really."

Snow stared at the marks, losing focus as he recalled how sweet her blood tasted. His stomach rumbled, reminding him that it had been too many hours since he had taken a small quantity of blood and he usually needed daily doses to keep his bloodlust at bay. He dragged his gaze up from the marks, over the smooth column of her throat, to her lips.

He smiled wickedly. "You kissed me. I definitely remember that."

Her cheeks blazed. He would never grow tired of making her blush and seeing her innocence shine through.

"I did," she admitted and bravely met his gaze, holding it without trepidation, showing him a flicker of the flipside to her innocence. "Even when you were in the grip of your bloodlust, you still cared for me, and you were still the man I care for."

"Love, you mean." He had issued the challenge and she had to respond. He wanted to hear her say it because he needed it more than air. If she told him a thousand times that she loved him, he might begin to believe himself worthy of those feelings and her.

She nodded awkwardly. "I do love you… and I'm convinced I can help you conquer your affliction now that I have seen you like this. If you want that of course."

"I would like nothing more," he said, keeping his emotions in check so she couldn't detect his uncertainty and the underlying fear that surfaced whenever he thought about what tomorrow might bring.

It felt wrong that he wanted to live now, when doing so would place Aurora at risk.

She was certain that she could help him overcome his bloodlust, and he thanked her for her unwavering faith in him and her devotion, but he still couldn't find any faith in himself.

He would never forgive himself if Aurora managed to get her superiors to grant him a second chance and he ended up doing something terrible and she was cast into Hell. But he couldn't bring himself to tell her to give up and sentence him to death, a fate he surely deserved more than a future with her and had sought for centuries. It would hurt her, and it would hurt his brother too.

Snow closed his eyes and drew in a deep breath to steady himself, his conflicting feelings tearing him apart inside, making it impossible to think straight.

He was going in circles again, lost and confused, unsure what to do. He didn't want to hurt those who loved him, but he couldn't see a path that would lead him to a place where everyone would be happy.

If he chose death, Aurora and Antoine would mourn him, and neither would ever be the same because both would blame themselves for his death. It would destroy Antoine.

It would destroy Aurora.

If Aurora convinced her superiors to grant him a second chance at life, Antoine would be happy, and he was sure Aurora would be too, and so would he, but it would only take one instance of his bloodlust escaping its tethers and him wreaking terror upon innocents for her to lose her soul and then her life.

Snow would die if that happened. She had been through enough because of him. He would go against his promise to Antoine and would end his life. Antoine would be distraught. It would destroy him.

Was there no outcome where they could all be happy?

Did he not deserve some happiness, some good in his life?

Probably not.

"You think dark things," Aurora said, bringing him back to her, the soft melody of her voice causing his heart to tell him to push away from the thoughts she spoke of, closing his eyes to the future and embracing the present. She stroked his cheek, her touch gentle and soothing, bringing light into the darkest corners of his soul.

"So kiss me again and make me forget." Snow leaned in and she met him halfway, her lips brushing softly across his, the taste of her invading his heart and mind, bringing peace to him. Whenever she kissed him, everything felt right and good, as though nothing bad would ever befall them.

She drew back again and sighed. "I wish we could spend longer here."

"Take me to Antoine and I will tell him I am fine, and then we can return." He would like that too. Being here with Aurora, alone in the wilderness, was preferable to being at the theatre while they were still grappling with her mission and what the outcome might be.

"It is daylight though." A beautiful look of concern laced with fear touched her face. "I don't want to risk accidentally exposing you to sunlight. This method of travelling is not the safest. I only used it because it was dark when I brought you to the chateau."

She hesitated, uncertainty filling her eyes and the fear tainting her soft feminine scent increasing, and then she tipped her chin up and her expression turned to one of resolve.

Unleash

"I will go and speak with Antoine…" Her courage faded. "Although I fear he might seek to harm me for what I have done."

Snow frowned. "My brother would never harm you. He would not dare."

Those words bolstered her courage and she nodded, her fear subsiding. He knew Antoine didn't trust her but his brother wasn't crazy, and it would take a crazy person to harm Aurora when they knew Snow had feelings for her. She was his female and he would protect her from anyone, even his brother.

"I won't be long." She pressed a brief kiss to his lips and then she was gone.

He wasn't sure how she did that. Was it a form of teleportation like Payne used?

Snow flopped onto his back on the furs and stared at the wooden beams of the ceiling.

When Aurora returned, he would have to speak with her about her mission and her belief in him. He needed to ensure that she went into this with clear eyes, not clouded by her feelings, but he didn't think that she would be able to manage it.

How could he make her see that it wasn't only his life on the line? It was hers too, and her life was far more important and worthy of saving than his was.

She would never understand that though. From the moment she had appeared back in his life, she had made it clear that she believed him capable of good and redeeming himself. She had shown her faith to him in so many ways that he was beginning to believe it too.

He was beginning to want it.

But not if it placed her at risk.

He would only allow her to judge him as deserving of another chance if he could be sure that together they could master his bloodlust.

Snow closed his eyes and sighed. Antoine had told him not so long ago that finding a female to love could save him. He only hoped his brother was right and that it wasn't about to damn him.

His bloodlust was still strong. It was different now because of his feelings for Aurora and her presence in his life, but it was still unpredictable, liable to surface at any moment.

His stomach growled again and he tried not to think about her sweet blood, or blood in general. He tried not to see it bathing his hands and claws. He tried not to hear the terrified screams of his victims.

They haunted his soul, worse now in the aftermath of returning to the chateau and seeing a full version of events play out and drag him into them, forcing him to relive the terrible things he had done to his family.

Snow swallowed hard and pinched the bridge of his nose, trying to bring his focus back to good things like Aurora singing to him, and her face whenever he did something to boost her hope that she might save him yet. She always looked so happy whenever that happened, as though he had given her a beautiful gift.

Hunger gnawed at his insides and his grip slipped, allowing darker thoughts to penetrate the light, chasing it back. He tried to force them out again but they increased, pushing down on him, his bloodlust rising like an unstoppable tide within him.

Snow clenched his fists and fought the darkness, unwilling to give in to it because if it took control of him, all his hope for a future with Aurora would be gone. He had to master this. He had to prove to himself that he could claw himself back from the brink and didn't have to fear succumbing to its evil.

He didn't have to destroy innocent lives in a quest for blood.

It began to abate again but didn't die completely. It lingered in the depths of his heart, lurking there and waiting for another chance to strike and bring him down.

It would only take his mind turning back to last night at the chateau and the slaughter of his family to unleash it fully. He couldn't think about his past without feeling he was on the brink again, ready to fall.

He was still too unpredictable.

If they had more time, he believed he could find a way to gain more control. Enough to be certain that he wouldn't lose his head and murder innocents, endangering Aurora's soul.

It was too soon after his worst bout of bloodlust in centuries though and he needed to be sure for her sake.

He would sooner die than see her suffer. He had put her through enough already. He couldn't let her wager her soul for him, not even when he desperately wanted to live with her.

He had fallen for her too.

He was in love with her.

And that was just another reason why he couldn't let her make a rash decision about her verdict.

His senses flared and he flung the furs off him and was on his feet a second later, facing the male who had appeared in the small wooden cabin.

The man's amethyst eyes raked over him, his lip curling in disgust, and he folded his large pure white wings against his back.

Unlike Aurora, this male wore white armour that covered much of his body from the neck down. He was dressed for war.

Snow snarled at him, his fangs elongating and eyes switching, their pupils turning elliptical as his vampire nature emerged, enhancing his strength and his senses.

This male had made Aurora suffer as a child and throughout her whole life.

Snow's anger rose, obliterating all sense of calm and positive feelings as he caught flashbacks of the scenes Aurora had shown him. This male had struck her and made her bleed, all because she had chosen to protect Snow.

This male would pay for that.

Snow launched himself at the angel, intent on having his revenge for what the male had done to Aurora and to him. He would break every bone in his body as payment for the blow he had dealt him, shattering his frail body. He would show the angel just how strong he had become.

The male angel disappeared and Snow's senses blared a warning.

He turned on a pinhead, dipping his body at the same time to avoid the blow the angel tried to deal him, and rose again in one fluid motion, throwing all of his strength and bodyweight into his punch. He slammed his fist into the male's stomach, the impact with his white armour barely registering on his knuckles.

The metal gave beneath his blow, indenting violently, causing the angel to unleash an ungodly growl of pain.

Snow ducked beneath another strike and came to his feet again, closer to the angel, and smashed his elbow into the male's face, knocking him off balance.

He quickly came around behind the angel and yanked viciously on his left wing. The angel retaliated then, beating at him with his powerful wings, shattering Snow's hold on him. He tried to evade the angel's next swing but the male was on to him. A feint.

Pain ripped through Snow's chest as the angel landed the blow he hadn't seen coming, sending Snow flying across the room and crashing into the rough log wall. His breath left him on impact and he hit the wooden floor, his knees slamming into it with a force that sent pain ricocheting through his bones.

Snow shook it off and roared as he sprung forwards. The angel would die.

Aurora wouldn't have to judge him then.

He grinned, exposing his fangs, and sprinted across the room at the angel, his mind fixed on murder.

Aurora appeared between them, throwing her arms out at her sides, blocking his way to the male.

Snow skidded to a halt and roared at her, furious that she would protect the angel who had hurt her as a child and punished her for her whole life. She shrank back and then moved forwards again, standing her ground, her eyes gaining a hard dark edge that he didn't like. His senses confirmed the feelings in them.

Anger.

She was angry with him.

Why?

The male behind her wiped his bloodied lip on the back of his hand and stared at Snow, hatred shining in his purple irises, a feeling that was mirrored within Snow.

He wanted to force Aurora to move aside and let him at the angel. She had no right to stand in his way when he was doing this for her sake, and for his. This angel was the source of her suffering.

No. He was the source.

Snow reeled and stepped back. His head pounded, his emotions colliding inside him and creating a maelstrom that threatened to pull him deep into his bloodlust.

He growled and pressed his palms to his temples, trying to get everything straight in his head. This male had hurt her though. He had forced Aurora to watch a young boy die and then he had struck her when she had sought to save him. They had both made her suffer.

Snow looked up at her, battling his darker urges, desperate to deny his desire to tear the male behind her to shreds and bathe in his blood.

"Return now and pass judgement upon this wretched creature." The male's voice was loud in the room, each word falling heavily, shaking Aurora on Snow's senses.

Her heartbeat accelerated and fear washed through the anger in her eyes. She turned on her master.

"We still have a day!" Desperation tightened her voice, flowing from her in tangible waves that curled around Snow and squeezed his heart in his chest.

Snow wanted to go to her and gather her into his arms to comfort her. He equally wanted to rip out the male angel's throat for daring to change the deadline for her mission.

He also wanted to deal himself a pretty hard kick.

Unleash

Her master had come here and Snow had attacked him. He had made the male change the deadline, and he had just done something that the angel could use as proof he was a danger to humankind.

In his rush to avenge Aurora and protect her, he had ruined everything and she knew it, and it was hurting her.

The male stared coldly at Snow, his tone glacial. "You had a day. Now you do not. You will return now and a decision about the soul of this despicable creature will be made."

He disappeared.

Aurora sank to her knees.

Snow stood a few metres behind her, unsure what to do. He could almost feel her hope draining out of her, her pain obliterating it. What had he done?

Her shoulders slumped and her voice was weak and empty as she spoke. "I will speak with him. It will be okay."

She didn't believe that.

Snow wondered if it was for the best. He loved her unwavering faith in him but he had none himself. He gathered his jumper and t-shirt, shoved his feet into his boots, and returned to her.

"Take me home, Aurora," he said, unable to get his voice above a whisper when his conflicting feelings were tearing him in too many directions.

He knew what he had to do.

Aurora stood and brought her hands up to her face before she turned towards him. Her dark lashes were wet with the tears she had tried to hide from him. She knew it was hopeless too, but still she didn't want to admit it. Was she so desperate for him to live that she would lie to herself?

He didn't want that to be the case. He didn't want her to go down that dark path because of him. He had spent centuries lying to himself and knew the consequences. It would ruin her.

He held his hand out to her and she slipped hers into it, stepped into his embrace and stared up into his eyes.

His senses detected the shift of the world around them and the change in scents and sounds. They were back in his room and, thankfully, they were alone.

He didn't want to let Aurora go. He clung to her, keeping her warm soft body against his hard one, holding her and savouring this final moment with her in his arms.

"You have to make the right decision, Aurora," he said and tears filled her beautiful eyes, making him feel like a bastard. "We both know that I am still a danger to this world and I won't let you lose your soul because of me."

He reluctantly took one hand from her back and settled it against her cheek. It was soft beneath his palm, hot and damp with her tears.

He had never hated himself more than he did in this moment, when he could see her heart breaking and knew he was the cause of her pain.

"You've suffered enough, Aurora." He caressed her cheek with his thumb, clearing the diamond drops of her tears away. "I would rather you end my life than suffer any more because of me. My death is long overdue and it is time I paid for my sins."

She shook her head and her brow furrowed. "No."

Snow sighed, cupped both of her cheeks in his hands, and pressed his forehead against hers.

He closed his eyes and wished he knew what to say to make her see that this was killing him too, but that he had to do it even when all he really wanted was to live with her forever.

There was no way she could convince her kind to let him live now though. They would say she was compromised because of her feelings and that he had attacked one of their kind, and they would be right.

Aurora hit his bare chest, her small fists bruising his skin, each strike leaving glittering colours behind that quickly faded, a mark of her strong feelings. "I won't let you die."

He held her, refusing to let her go, weathering her blows and letting her get it all out of her system. Eventually, she would realise that he was right and there was no hope for them, and this was the best path to take.

"Aurora," he whispered and pulled back so he could see her eyes. She swam in his vision and he blinked to clear it, cursing when he realised tears filled his eyes too. He stared down at the face of his female, his salvation, and wished his life could have been different, because he loved her with all of his black heart and he didn't want to let her go. "Thank you for giving me everything I ever desired… for giving me a brief respite from my suffering and making me feel alive for the first time in centuries. Before I met you, my soul felt as though it was on fire, burning with the flames of Hell. Now it feels like cool water, washed of my sins by your love, and my feelings for you."

"Damn you for speaking to me in such a way." She struck him again and he grasped her shoulders, trying to stop her. She struggled against him, her pretty face twisting in grim lines, and her black wings erupted from her back. She hit him with them, tears cutting down her cheeks. "Damn you! You said you would fight."

"I am fighting, Aurora. I am fighting to do what I believe is right… what I must do." He tightened his grip on her shoulders and she stilled, glaring up at

Unleash

him. "Do not let your feelings and desires cloud your heart, Aurora. Not as they have before with me. Judge me how I deserve to be judged. Do that for me and for the world."

She drew in a shaky breath and sniffed back her tears, the fire returning to her eyes again, warning him she was ready to launch another attack because she didn't like what he was telling her.

It wouldn't stop him. She could lay him out cold and he would still say these words to her when he woke. She had to hear them.

"See me as the man I am now, Aurora, not the boy you saw that night. Look upon my history and judge me on the path I trod, the one I chose, and the acts I committed. Do that for me, please, Aurora." He held her face again, gently cradling her jaw with both hands, keeping her eyes on his. "Please. Do that for me."

She was still for long seconds before she finally nodded and resolve coloured her eyes with steel.

"I will," she said in a low whisper and he dared to hope that she would do as he asked.

Snow held it together and stroked her cheeks with his thumbs, unable to bring himself to let her go when all he wanted to do was cling to her and keep her here with him, even when he knew it was impossible.

He realised that the song she had sung to him that fateful night was right and that no matter what they did or what they desired, they would never be together. Destiny would always find a way to tear them apart.

The prince and the angel.

Snow stared down into her striking eyes, memorising them and the love they showed for him, affection he had never thought possible. His female. He had resigned himself to death again to save her, but for the first time in centuries, he didn't want to die.

He wanted to live with Aurora.

He wanted to live.

She threw her arms around him and buried her face against his neck, her tears hot on his skin.

Snow wrapped his arms around her, pinning her against his body, holding her feet off the ground.

The soft feathers of her wings tickled his arms.

He closed his eyes and nuzzled her neck, breathing in her feminine scent of lily of the valley and snow, feeling his heart breaking at the same time as hers was shattering. Her pain became his pain and it was all he could do to keep standing and to stop himself from begging her to run away with him.

They could never outrun fate.

"Don't try to defend me, my love," Snow whispered hoarsely into her fall of dark hair and she shook in his arms, her sobs wracking her. "I don't want them to punish you. Please... tell them what you must and then return to me and take me away from here. I don't want Antoine to see... it would kill him. Promise me... let it be upon my head alone and far away from here."

She nodded and clung to him, her hands twisting in his hair, her breath moist on his neck. She sharply pulled away and kissed him hard, her desperation matching his as he sought to master her, savour her and submit to her all at the same time.

He couldn't take it.

He set her away from him and turned his back, unable to bear the sight of her, knowing her face would be flushed with tears and her eyes filled with pain he had caused.

"Save yourself, Aurora. It is what I want."

She settled her hands against his back and then pressed her cheek to the line of his spine, and he felt her shaking, felt her emotions pouring into him through that touch, and it broke him. He turned on his heel, gathered her back into his arms and held her one last time.

Aurora pushed herself up on her toes and softly kissed him, her lips lingering against his as she spoke. "I will go, and then I will return."

She disappeared.

Snow opened his eyes and stared at his black apartment.

The room that had been his home for a century in the theatre that had become family to him.

He blinked and tears tumbled down his cheeks, cold against his skin, and he clenched his fists, fighting the overwhelming tide of pain tearing through him.

He wanted to live.

He wanted to be here with his brother and Sera, and see them laugh and share in their joy.

He wanted to watch Abby and Alistair grow up, and teach Luca how to drive Payne crazy.

He wanted to bring Aurora here and let the females welcome her into their loving fold. Into his family. A family he didn't want to leave. He didn't want to die. Not anymore. He wanted to live.

Snow sniffed back his tears and scrubbed them from his cheeks.

He needed to see Antoine.

CHAPTER 19

Snow slung on a fresh pair of jeans and headed out. He paused in the black corridor outside Antoine's room.

His brother wasn't there.

He continued to the staircase and had reached the bottom of the theatre before he finally found Antoine.

His brother stood in the double-height black-walled room, talking to Sera and Payne. Snow paused on the bottom step to look at him, his strength failing him as he thought about what he was here to do.

He didn't want to cause his brother any more pain. Like Aurora, he had suffered so much because of the things Snow had done but he retained an unwavering belief that he could fix Snow.

Snow had never wished that were possible more than he did now.

Antoine smiled at Sera, love shining in his pale eyes, the picture of their father with his dark hair and slighter build, and his elegant tailored clothing.

Snow sniffed back the tears that threatened to fill his eyes again and Antoine frowned and looked across the room at him. The happiness in his eyes faded into worry and he moved away from Sera, his expression turning towards a blend of emotions Snow had seen many times on Antoine's face.

He knew why he was here. He knew what Snow needed to tell him. He had always been able to detect when Snow was thinking melancholy thoughts and seeking an end, and today was no different.

"Snow." Antoine halted a few metres from him and tensed, his muscles flexing beneath his charcoal grey shirt.

Snow had felt it too. He growled and his claws extended, his senses sweeping out to map the theatre and pinpoint the intruders.

Payne snarled and disappeared, most likely returning to Elissa and Luca to protect them from the unknown threat they had all sensed.

"Antoine?" Sera started for him and then shrieked when a tall blond male dressed in white armour appeared between her and Antoine, his white wings furled against his back.

Aurora must have made her decision. The angel must have come for him.

Snow wasn't sure how he felt about that. He had wanted her to condemn him to death but there had been a fragment of his heart that had clung to the thought that she wouldn't do it, even when he had made her promise she would.

The angel stared at him, cold malice in his turquoise eyes.

Snow didn't hate her for her decision and he could still appreciate the irony. He had found a woman who had made him feel alive, and made him want to live, and yet she had come to kill him. To save her, he had to die.

He was alright with that. He had been waiting for death to come after all. He just hadn't expected it to be in the guise of an angel.

Snow stepped forwards and Antoine turned to face him.

"What is happening here, Snow?" There were already tears in his brother's eyes. Antoine knew what was happening. He just didn't want to admit it.

Snow clasped his brother's shoulder. "I love you... I always will... but I must do this. Aurora must live. I will not let her die because of me."

Antoine shook his head and opened his mouth to protest.

The angel turned on Sera and drew a white blade from the sheath at his waist.

Snow roared and launched himself past his brother, moving faster than Antoine. He caught the angel just as he raised the blade to cut Sera down, tackling him from behind to the ground. The blade spilled from his grip and clattered across the floor. Antoine grabbed Sera and pulled her into his arms.

The angel beneath Snow struggled and Snow pressed all of his weight down onto his back, using his legs to pin the male's wings.

"She swore it would be on my head alone." Snow gripped the back of the angel's neck, keeping him face down on the ground. "She promised me."

More of his kind materialised and Snow's senses tracked them as they appeared in corridors and rooms all around the theatre, the fury flowing through his veins increasing in intensity as he realised the angel below him was only the vanguard of a larger attack.

They were after everyone in the theatre.

Screams came from upstairs and Snow grabbed the male below him by the back of his head and slammed it hard into the ground.

"What the hell is going on?" Antoine shouted, holding Sera close to him.

"I do not know. She swore she would take only me." Snow bashed the angel's head against the ground again for good measure, wanting to be sure he had knocked him unconscious before he stood.

His hands shook at his sides and he growled as he sensed more angels appearing in the building, and smelled blood. How could she have done this to him?

She knew how much this place meant to him and that everyone here was his family now, people he cared about and loved. She had heard him defend her and swear to take responsibility for her actions. She had betrayed his trust and now his family were under attack because of her.

Because of him.

"She swore it, Brother." Snow snarled the words as his anger took control of him, pain from the thought of dying and leaving those he loved behind turning into rage over the betrayal dealt to him and the danger the angel had placed his family in.

He wouldn't stand for it.

The theatre was his family and he would never fail his family again.

Payne reappeared in the room with Elissa and Luca held close to him, a nasty gash cutting across his right cheek. "The fuckers are everywhere. I need to get Elissa and Luca away from here."

"Worry about Luca. I'm going to kill these bastards." Elissa broke free of Payne's arms and black spirals of magic swirled around her hands and up her arms to caress the straps of her midnight blue halter-top.

Snow looked at Luca and then at Antoine. A shiver bolted down his spine.

"Alistair and Abby." Snow was moving before he finished that sentence, bounding up the stairs to the top of the theatre. Red coated his vision as his rage seized control of him and he embraced it and the strength his bloodlust gave him. He would destroy these angels for daring to bring harm to his family.

He had never had any faith in himself, not where his bloodlust was concerned, but he found belief as he bolted up the stairs.

His bloodlust was rising to the fore, a dark shadow in his mind that ignited a terrible hunger for violence and bloodshed, but he didn't fear for the safety of those he loved or cared about.

He knew deep in his heart that he wouldn't harm his family in the midst of his rage this time. All of his fury would be directed at the angels. He would control it and use it to protect his family.

Snow cut his way through any angel in his path, breaking wings and tearing throats open, desperate to get to the top floor. He had to protect the babies.

Antoine and Sera followed close on his heels.

Payne appeared before him and grabbed him, and tossed the world into a blender.

The black corridor of the top floor greeted him when he dared to open his eyes.

Kristina was in wolf form at the end of it, defending her apartment from a dark-haired angel. Blood stained one of the female angel's white wings and it hung lower than the other, clearly broken and savaged by werewolf fangs.

Kristina snarled, exposing vicious teeth. Her black fur stood on end down her spine and she lowered her head, preparing to attack.

Payne disappeared again and reappeared behind the angel, punching through her back to grip her spine. The angel screamed and then fell silent as Payne sliced across her throat with his claws and snapped her neck in one lightning fast move. He dropped the body to the floor.

Snow raced forwards and Kristina growled at both of them.

"The babes?" Snow said, ignoring her threat, knowing she only meant to protect her young and her instincts were making her view everyone as a danger.

He could relate to that.

The door to their apartment opened and Callum was there, his black shirt unbuttoned and hanging loose from the waist of his trousers, a wild panicked look in his red eyes. The twins wailed in his arms, wriggling in their black romper suits.

The sight of the innocent babies and the thought of them coming to harm sent Snow deep into his bloodlust but this time he retained awareness of those around him, his rage focused on the angels with deadly intent.

"We must move them." They were too vulnerable up here where there wasn't much room to move around. They could easily become pinned into one room, trapped by the sheer number of angels now spread around the theatre.

Kristina snarled again. Snow hunkered down in front of her and stared deep into her eyes.

"We must protect your young. This place is no good," he said in a low calm voice and her growling subsided. He rose and faced Callum and then Antoine.

Payne disappeared again.

Javier came racing along the corridor, a long slash across the right arm of his black suit jacket.

Snow couldn't smell any blood on him. He must have evaded the blow.

He clutched Lilah's hand and she was struggling to keep up with him, her long dark hair falling into her eyes and her short pale blue dress fluttering around her knees. She tried to blow her hair out of her face, unable to sweep it away with her hands because both were occupied. She clutched Chica's hand with her other one, forming a chain with her.

Chica bounded along in her thick knee-high biker boots, her strapless boned purple corset in danger of slipping with each step and exposing her, and her short black skirt equally threatening to flash her knickers as it bounced up and down.

A wicked glint shone in her colourful eyes. She was eager to fight and would be off in search of angels to kill if Lilah released her. Andreu brought up the rear, his suit jacket missing and a tear in his black shirt, wielding a white sword with deadly accuracy.

He chopped the head off an angel and kicked his body back down the stairs. "We need to get our hands on more of these swords."

Snow couldn't agree more. He should have taken the one from the blond angel.

"This have anything to do with your female?" Javier growled as he came to a halt in front of Snow. He released Lilah's hand and huffed as he yanked his ruined black jacket off and dropped it onto the wooden floor, loosened and removed his dark blue tie and dropped that too. His red eyes narrowed on Snow.

Snow registered the threat and rose to his full height, towering over the Spaniard.

"She is no longer my female." Snow hated the sound of those words leaving his lips, even when they were true. He would never forgive her for this. The scent of blood was already thick in the air and he had lost track of a few of the performers, and knew they were dead, killed by Aurora's kind. Snow growled. "Swear to me if you see her among these fiends you will tell me. I want to deal with her personally."

Everyone nodded, even Lilah although she wore a look that cut through him as she hastily tied her chestnut hair up into a ponytail. He never had been able to stand it when a female showed him pity.

He turned away from her, afraid she would try to console him if he remained facing her. He didn't want pity. He wanted revenge. Once Aurora had paid for her betrayal, he would nurse the heart she had broken in the process.

"Our best bet is the theatre. It will give us room to manoeuvre and it has the most escape routes," Antoine said and everyone nodded again. Kristina growled her approval. "Snow, bring up the rear with Andreu and Chica. Javier, Lilah, Sera, with me. Keep Kristina and Callum with the babes between us. We will need to move fast."

Kristina took the lead, snapping at Antoine's heels as she loped past him.

"Fine. Kristina takes point. Callum, keep between us." Antoine began to follow Kristina, Javier at his side and Lilah and Sera behind them.

Sera took a band from Lilah and tied her blonde hair up into a messy knot at the back of her head, tugged her blue t-shirt down and smoothed her palms over her black jeans.

Snow could sense her nerves and Lilah's too. Neither of them had much experience of fighting, and he wanted both of them away from the battle, but he knew their mates wouldn't agree to it and they were right. It was better they remained together, where they could watch each other's backs and fight as a team. They couldn't afford any distractions, and Lilah and Sera being out of their sight would be just that for Antoine and Javier, and Snow.

Snow ignored his brother's order and moved close to Callum, intent on protecting the babies with him. He wouldn't let them come to harm. He would find a way to stop these angels before they could take any more lives.

Chica teleported Andreu behind them and Antoine picked up the pace until they were running along the black corridor and down the stairs.

Callum struggled with the babies and Snow took Abby from him, clutching her close to his chest, keeping one hand over the back of her head to protect it. Callum tried to smile but it faltered when Alistair wriggled, and Snow could sense his fear. It echoed within him.

"I will not allow anything to happen to them. I swear it, Callum." Snow held Abby closer to him, feeling her warmth but also how delicate she was. The babies would make an easy target for the angels, and he didn't dare hope that these males and females were above killing innocents.

"I'm not sure if kissing angels will weaken them but can I give it a shot?" Chica said behind him and Andreu grumbled something dark in response. "I swear I'll make it up to you."

That got a better response from Javier's younger brother.

Snow could understand his reluctance to let his female go around kissing strangers to weaken them, but she was one of the best weapons in their arsenal. Chica had drained the life out of him with just one kiss. If her ability worked on the angels, it could give them the advantage they needed.

They reached the double-height room at the bottom of the building and Kristina growled at the doors that led into the theatre.

Snow had sensed it too.

There were angels in the theatre, but they weren't alone.

Snow passed Abby back to Callum and barrelled through the doors. He ducked as a blade whizzed towards him, grabbed the male's wrist with one hand, and shoved upwards with the flat of his other one, slamming it into the angel's forearm and snapping the bone.

The male bellowed in agony and Snow twisted the sword free of his grip and decapitated him in one fluid motion.

The heads of at least two dozen more angels turned towards him.

Elissa chose that moment to unleash an unholy blast of something black that tore through the angels closest to her and Luca, sending them flying through the air and smashing into the boxes that lined the sides of the theatre. Payne teleported after them, ending their lives with claw and fang.

Snow tossed his sword to Antoine and threw himself into the fight, tearing at the angels' wings to weaken them.

Chica bounced around the room, appearing and disappearing, only remaining in one place long enough to use her wiles on the male angels and kiss them into a stupor. Unfortunately, the effect only lasted a few seconds.

Andreu joined forces with her, together with Javier and Lilah, working as a team to collect weapons from the stunned angels, kill them and then distribute the swords to the others in their group.

Kristina viciously tore through the angels who dared to approach Callum, and Snow stayed close to them, doing his best to protect both the werewolf and the vampire with their young.

More angels appeared to replace the fallen, one shimmering into existence right next to Snow.

Snow growled and attacked, not giving the brunet angel a chance to get his bearings or draw his weapon.

The angel defended, blocking every punch or kick that Snow levelled at him. The male's fist smashed into Snow's cheek and blood flooded his mouth, his teeth aching from the blow. He followed up with a second strike to the same place, knocking Snow off balance, and then caught him with a powerful uppercut.

Snow stumbled backwards into the first row of red-velvet seats and caught Payne's worried look as he battled another of the new angels.

They were stronger than the others.

The brunet angel drew a white short blade from his waist and slashed at Snow with it, his cold blue eyes void of emotion as he fought.

Snow blocked the blade with his left forearm, the metal slicing into his flesh, and swung a right hook, landing it hard on the angel's jaw.

Bone gave and shattered under the force of the blow but it didn't slow the angel down. He attacked again, faster this time, and Snow had difficulty keeping up. He ducked, dodged, and did his best to evade each swing of the knife, but several attacks caught him, lacerating his bare chest and arms.

Antoine appeared behind the angel, his white blade cutting upwards through the air in a swift arc, and slashed through the angel's pale wings, turning them crimson. The angel howled in pain and turned on Antoine. Victor came out of nowhere, landing a solid punch on the angel's already broken jaw, sending him crashing backwards into Snow.

Snow grabbed him from behind, wrestling with him. It was going to take all of them fighting together to defeat these angels. They were powerful and this one alone had dealt Snow some serious injuries. He couldn't afford to grow weak. People were depending on him and he would protect them.

He managed to snap the angel's white wings and got his arm across the male's throat, locking it in place by grasping his wrist with his other hand.

Snow ignored the burning cut on his forearm and pulled back, straining against the angel as he fought his hold, struggling to keep him contained. Antoine and Victor fought to keep the other angels at bay, buying him time to question the male.

"Why are you here?" Snow dreaded the answer to that question, part of him still clinging to the sliver of hope that Aurora wasn't responsible for this attack on the theatre.

"It is justice," the angel said, his voice cold. "We are saving human lives by doing this. To save the mortals... you all must die."

Snow growled into his ear, his anger rising like a tide, consuming him and driving him deeper into his rage. "Don't you care that there are babies here and you are taking so many of our lives? Are those lives not worth anything?"

"No." The angel struggled again and elbowed Snow in the ribs, and Snow tightened his grip, cutting off the male's air supply and choking him. When he began to weaken, Snow eased off so he could speak again. "You will all die. It has been decided."

By Aurora. She had sentenced them all to death, not just him.

"No humans die in our shows... not for decades!" Antoine slashed at another angel with his blade, cutting across the female's white armour, driving her back as she attempted to reach her comrade. "You have no good reason for doing this. We draw blood but we do not kill."

"It is true," Victor weighed in and ducked the wild swing of the male angel he was fighting. He kicked the male between the legs and he crumpled into a heap on the black stage floor. "We use human performers who do this sort of thing for a living. We meet them and they form a natural connection to us, and then we place them under thrall and perform."

"But they fear," the angel in Snow's grip said and Snow growled when he tried to struggle again.

"Only because the vampire makes the audience feel that emotion, a flicker they sense and then the thrall feels pleasure again," Antoine growled and thrust his blade through the female angel, skewering her on it, straight through her chest. She clutched the blade, her eyes wide, and then slumped and slid off the sword, leaving blood streaking the white surface.

"We have orders. We will eliminate you for killing humans." The angel was grasping at straws now and it only served to piss Snow off even more. They wanted to kill them and it seemed that no matter what evidence his family gave them, the angels weren't going to stop until they were all dead, the babies included.

"You want us dead for doing what comes naturally to us?" Antoine sounded as incredulous as he looked as he turned on the angel, his blue eyes veering towards crimson. He tossed a dark look at Snow. "Kill the bastard."

"It would be my pleasure." Snow snapped the angel's neck, feeling a little better as bone crunched and the male fell lifeless to the floor.

Antoine scooped up a sword and tossed it to him. He caught it and fell back towards Callum with Antoine, ushering them onto the black stage where they had more room to fight. Sera joined them, helping Kristina deal with any angel who tried to get to her babies and their father.

Payne and Elissa fought across the stage, combining their attacks to dispose of as many of the weaker angels as they could, leaving only the stronger ones behind. Luca remained close to them at all times, the scruffy sandy-haired boy's eyes shining vivid blue and gold, a sign of his incubus nature. He grasped a small white blade in his hand and was attacking the legs and hips of any angel who dared to come near his makeshift parents.

Lilah and Javier fell back, edging towards Snow and the others. He moved forwards to help them when he saw the gash on Lilah's upper arm and smelled the blood on her. Javier flicked him a grateful look and fought harder, keeping the attacking angels away from his mate.

Snow fought a fair-haired female, his sword clashing with hers, searching for a weakness he could exploit. Another shiver bolted down his spine, warning him that more angels had arrived.

Among them was a familiar scent.

Snow's lips peeled back off his fangs and he pinned the black-haired male with a murderous glare at the same time as he cut the female angel down, driving the blade into her shoulder and diagonally across her chest, straight through her heart.

Aurora's master stood on the stage ahead of him, dressed in his white armour, a long blade gripped in his hand. His cold amethyst eyes met Snow's blazing crimson ones.

Snow roared and attacked.

CHAPTER 20

Aurora fidgeted on her seat in the waiting room, growing more impatient with each minute that ticked past without anyone calling her in. She stroked the longest feathers of her black wings, preening them and making them glossy.

Other angels milled around the pale room, discussing matters that ranged from the current wars that ravaged the mortal world, and the uprising of demons in one of the smaller realms in Hell against one of the larger ones, to more mundane things like what stupid thing one of their human wards had done.

She tapped her fingers against her knees. What was taking them so long? They had demanded she returned immediately and gave her verdict, and now they were keeping her waiting.

Her thoughts drifted away from the angels around her to Snow. He would be surprised when she returned to him.

She wanted to see him again and missed him already. This time when she returned to him, she was going to stay in his world, with him. They would never part again.

Aurora couldn't wait any longer. She turned her gaze inwards and towards Snow.

The theatre shimmered into existence before her and then her vision swept through the layers of the building, seeking her target. Her eyes slowly widened as she saw blood in the hallway on the level where the owners' quarters were and her heartbeat accelerated.

She dove faster towards Snow, panic making the world blur past in streaks of white, black and red.

So much blood.

Her vision halted when she could see into the main theatre and horror crashed through her, threatening to still her heart in her chest.

Angels were at war in Vampirerotique.

Aurora shut down the connection, the sudden switch between the mortal world and her angelic one jarring her senses and sending a sharp spike of pain through her mind. She burst from her seat and shouldered open the door to her superiors' office.

The four male angels turned from their perusal of a set of maps spread over a circular white desk and faced her, surprise in their multi-hued eyes.

"Is there a reason for this intrusion?" The tallest of the angels frowned at her, his black hair drawn back into a tight ponytail and his purple-to-blue eyes narrowing.

Unlike the other angels in her realm, these four wore golden armour and had beautiful golden wings furled against their backs. They were the elite of the angelic realm and barging in on them had probably sentenced her to a few weeks in captivity as punishment for disrespecting them, but she didn't care.

"I was told you wanted to meet with me and I came back to file my verdict... and was kept waiting... and now I turn my gaze upon my ward and he is... angels are attacking him." She still couldn't believe that, and saying the words aloud made her heart thump harder, pumping fury like acid through her veins, making her want to disappear from this world and go straight to Vampirerotique to aid Snow and his family. She needed to know what was happening though, and why.

The male exchanged a glance with the other three and then turned his gaze back on her. "Your master came to us and said he had spoken with you, and you had declared all at the theatre must die. He offered to lead the team in your stead, carrying out your execution order."

Her knees weakened, shaking beneath her and threatening to give out. Her ears rang and she felt as though someone had just punched the wind out of her lungs and rattled her senseless.

He had done what?

Aurora trembled, her head spinning, unable to comprehend everything her superior had just told her and fighting to find her voice.

"I gave no such order." She forced the words out and frowned at the four males. Her panic overwhelmed her and she couldn't hold back the tide of her emotions. "I didn't order any damn execution!"

The male tensed and his eyes darkened. The other three looked equally as horrified by her outburst.

"You desired the vampire to live?" The blond short-haired one at the back raised an eyebrow, as if he couldn't believe her. The brunet and silver-haired males on either side of him looked equally confused by her decision.

"I have seen the good in him." Aurora stepped forwards, gathering her courage, intent on issuing the verdict she had come here to give them. "He is capable of redeeming himself given time. My verdict is that Snow can be saved and he is not a threat to humankind."

The black-haired male closest to her folded his arms across his chest, his handsome face turning pensive. "Then we have a problem. Your master believes you said otherwise."

She knew why the bastard was doing it too. "I admit that he had an altercation with the vampire, but Snow only sought to avenge acts committed by my master that he believed were wrong. It has to be the reason my master came to you and lied about my decision."

Aurora drew in a shaky breath to steady herself. Everything rested on her keeping her head and convincing these angels to assist her. She could save everyone at Vampirerotique if she could make them listen to reason.

"Please. Call off the team."

They exchanged another look and the blond male spoke. "We will consider it."

Aurora growled in frustration, her temper and fear getting the better of her. Consider it? How dare they. She needed to get to Snow before it was too late and her master killed him.

"Why has he done this?" She turned on the black-haired one again.

It was the silver-haired one who responded. "I admit… it is a clever trick. I had not anticipated he would find this loophole."

"Loophole?" She didn't know what the hell they were talking about and she didn't have time for them to send her in circles.

"We shall have to congratulate him upon his return," the brunet said, his deep voice laced with amusement.

It dawned on her that they were stalling her.

They had no intention of calling off the team. They wanted Snow to die and her master to succeed.

"Damn you all to—" Aurora cried out as sharp white-hot pain blazed across her side.

She pressed her hand to it, struggling for air, the unexpected pain making stars wink across her vision. Her hand became wet and she pulled it away from her body and shook at the sight of the blood coating her fingers.

Her head shot up and she stared at the males.

"What is this?" she gasped, her side burning and blood saturating her dress, sticking the white material to her skin.

The blond at the back smiled coldly and viciously. "You are bound to the loathsome creature. Your master's sword will carry out the duty given to him millennia ago."

Aurora swallowed reflexively, her ears ringing again as those words swam around her mind, cutting through the debilitating pain.

She was bound in more than one way to Snow. Not only destined to bear his sins.

If he died, she would too.

She couldn't believe it.

The black-haired angel leaned his backside against the edge of the white desk, his golden wings curling around his shoulders, the tips of them grazing his boots. "You should have died the night you allowed the vampire to live. You were supposed to take his place as an equivalent exchange to maintain the balance."

What the hell?

She stared at him in disbelief.

The silver-haired male behind him folded his arms across his chest, his expression turning stern and dark. "We tasked your master with carrying out your execution, but we did not give him a deadline, and he abused that."

"And now he has found a loophole." The blond smirked.

She hated them all. Her master and these males. Her master had wanted her to judge Snow as beyond salvation, sentencing Snow to the death he so desperately sought, unaware that she would also die. Why?

She was damn well going to beat the reason out of him.

She wouldn't let Snow die.

"If you don't call off your men, I will kill them all," she snarled and disappeared, willing herself back to the London theatre.

Aurora appeared in the thick of the battle between the angels and the residents of Vampirerotique.

She grabbed one of the fallen white blades and shoved her way through the fight, defending herself against any vampire who tried to harm her and attacking any angel who dared to get in her way. Her side blazed, stealing her focus as her blood continued to leak from the vicious wound, slowly weakening her. She had to find Snow.

An unholy roar shook the theatre and a wave of anger swept over her.

Snow.

Unleash

She fought to reach him and broke through the throng of angels and vampires, into an open space on the strip of red carpet between the stalls and the stage. She immediately wished she hadn't.

Snow slashed at her with the sword clenched in his hand and she fumbled with her own, blocking his strike. His blade hit hers with force that sent her stumbling backwards into another vampire.

"You," Snow snarled and her eyes widened when she felt the pain in him and saw the hurt in his eyes.

He thought she had ordered this.

"Snow, wait," she said but he struck again and she barely managed to block this time. Her side ached, the pain blistering her skin, stealing her strength and making her dizzy. She was no match for him when she was bleeding out.

Aurora desperately kept blocking him. He was bleeding from several cuts on his bare torso and his arms, but none of them was as deep as the gash in his side. In the exact same spot as the wound on her body. A wound created by the heavenly sword of her master. It was proof that their lives were linked and it scared her.

"I didn't do this," she shouted over the din of battle and he snarled at her, exposing bloodied fangs.

He had been drinking from the angels, keeping his strength up so he could continue to fight despite his wounds.

His crimson eyes pinned her with a deadly glare, his elliptical pupils little more than thin slits in the centre of his irises. She could feel his pain and the turbulent emotions that ruled him, and she ached to make him see that he was wrong about her. She hadn't turned against him and those he loved.

She would never do such a thing to him. She loved him too much to ever hurt him.

"I cannot believe I trusted you." Snow stalked away from her, his shoulders hunched and tight, speaking of his agitation. She went to follow him, desperate to explain and make him see reason, and he turned on her with a dark snarl, his pale blade nothing more than a blur as it cut through the air in her direction.

Aurora leaped backwards, using a fast beat of her wings to help her barely avoid his attack, and brought her sword up, knocking his away from her.

"Please, Snow." She tried again, not only to save herself from his wrath now. She had to ease his hurt somehow. She knew how hard he found it to trust people because he didn't trust himself, and she wanted him to know that he hadn't been wrong to trust her. She hadn't betrayed him.

He stormed away from her, attacking any angel who foolishly placed themselves in his path, slaughtering them in the midst of his rage.

Antoine and another male vampire fought closer to the double doors at the side of the theatre, doing their best to defeat the angels attacking them and protecting Sera at the same time.

Aurora couldn't allow Snow to reach his brother. Antoine would surely attack her and she wasn't strong enough to withstand a full strength attack.

Snow was mad at her but he was pulling his punches too, not putting all of his power into each blow.

It had to mean he still felt something for her and it gave her hope that she could get through to him and make him listen.

"I would have accepted death to defend you and give you the happiness and life you deserved, Aurora, and you did this!" He turned and attacked her again, forcing her backwards towards a group of vampires and angels where they battled behind her.

She defended as best she could, afraid that one of his blows would make it past her sword and cut her down. If that happened, he might die too. She didn't know whose sword he possessed and she didn't want him to die, so she fought harder, desperate to live so he would too.

His face contorted in anger and agony. "This I will not accept. I cannot accept! I will never allow harm to come to those I love... to my family... to innocent children!"

Aurora reeled from the verbal blow. How low he thought her. He truly believed she had ordered this. He believed she would send angels to kill the babies and those he loved.

Snow leaped up onto the black stage, grabbed an angel by his throat, and hurled him at Aurora.

The blond male hit her and knocked her down, and she cried out when the pain in her side worsened, stealing her breath, and her wings ended up twisted at awkward angles beneath her.

Snow glanced back at her, a flicker of remorse in his eyes before he turned away and attacked another angel, dealing vicious blows with his sword, cutting a path across the stage.

He was heading for Callum and Kristina at the back of the stage, fighting to reach them so he could shield their babies. The werewolf was in her animal form, snarling savagely at the angels as she attacked them, protecting her young.

The witch was with her, together with the young incubus. Payne formed an impenetrable wall with Kristina, fighting to protect his female and the boy.

Aurora grasped her blade in both hands, rolled the male angel off her and plunged it into his heart, killing him. She shoved to her feet and gave one powerful beat of her aching wings, flying up onto the black stage, unwilling to give up her fight to make Snow see the truth.

She swung hard and cut down another injured angel, doing her best to give him a painless death, feeling remorse over how things had turned out. She had never wanted this. She had dragged these angels into her master's personal vendetta because she had wanted to save Snow.

She had wanted to be with the man she loved.

That man turned on her, wild and savage, an immense warrior with only violence in his dark heart.

Aurora swiftly blocked his sword and had to use her other hand to cradle the flat of her blade as he pressed down on it, forcing his closer to her. Her bare feet slipped on a slick patch of blood-drenched black floorboards and she almost lost her footing. She shoved with all of her might and rolled to one side as he struck again, coming to her feet further away from him.

Her side burned from the action and she pressed her hand to it, her other one trembling, barely able to keep hold of the grip of the sword. The point of her blade hit the black wooden stage floor and she leaned on the weapon, using it to support her shaking body and keep her upright.

"This is not my doing, Snow. I swear it." She breathed hard through the pain, trying to subdue it. Snow decapitated another angel, sending the female's head toppling to the ground. Aurora looked at the pandemonium surrounding her, a battle between life and death. Her superiors would keep sending more angels to their deaths, an endless wave of them, intent on killing everyone here, including her. They couldn't win this. "They kept me waiting. I never passed judgement on you!"

That got Snow's attention. His head whipped around, the bloodied threads of his overlong white hair spraying outwards before coming to settle around his noble features. Red eyes held hers, intense and penetrating, looking straight through her for a sign she was lying.

"If I had been able to voice my verdict about you… it would have been to say that you did not deserve death… that I had never met anyone so selfless and loving, so protective and strong… so beautiful." Aurora wavered, the pain becoming too great to bear, and came close to collapse. Darkness encroached and then drifted away, and when she could focus on Snow again, he was closer to her, confusion and concern in his dazzling crimson eyes.

He frowned at her side. Blood pumped from between her fingers and she winced, fighting to retain consciousness.

"What is this?" he whispered and darkness threatened to drag her under again. His hand caught her wrist, steadying her.

Tears filled her eyes but she blinked them away, feeling stronger as he held her, both in body and in soul. "I did want the happiness and life I deserved, and that was why I came back. I came back to tell you that I love you, and I was giving up my wings to be with you. You are my happiness."

Snow's frown hardened and he gathered her closer, shielding her in his arms as he weathered an attack by another angel. Antoine appeared from nowhere, assisting him. Aurora clung to Snow, fighting the darkness, glad to be back in his arms and hoping he believed her now and wouldn't turn on her again.

Snow shifted his attention back to her. "What happened to you?"

She smiled sadly. "You are not the only one who feels betrayed… but I am the only one who has been betrayed. I am bound to you in more ways than one. My life is bound to yours."

She raised her bloodstained hand and his eyes darkened, flooded with the rage she could feel burning inside him.

"You also bear the wound your master dealt me." Snow slipped one arm around her back to support her. His handsome bloodstained face blackened into a scowl. "Your master meant for you to judge me poorly… he sought to end your life too."

Aurora nodded weakly, anger over her master's actions rushing through her, giving her the strength to stand and fight.

She had trusted everyone she had grown up with, everyone she had spent thousands of years with, and this was how they repaid her? Had this been her master's intention all this time?

He had wanted her to suffer Snow's sins and pay for the pain he caused, and then die with him as punishment for everything Snow had done and everything she had unleashed on the world by saving him that night.

Snow roared, his rage pouring over her, anger that she knew was directed towards her master.

"Antoine," Snow said and his younger brother finished the angel and returned to him.

There were multiple lacerations in his clothing, blood staining it and his face in places. Everyone was suffering because of what she had done and her wretched master. She wanted him to pay for hurting these vampires and their loved ones. She wanted him to pay for hurting Snow.

And for hurting her.

Antoine cast her a dark look that promised pain. Snow gathered her closer, his thickly muscled arms banding around her like a shield.

"She is not to be harmed," Snow growled.

"She did this." Antoine glared at her.

"No, it was her master's doing. Aurora's life is bound to mine."

The darkness evaporated from Antoine's expression, replaced by shock. "You mean if she dies…"

Snow nodded. "We must protect her and find her master. He will pay for this."

A vampire behind Antoine cried out, the tip of a sword appearing in the centre of his chest. The body fell and revealed her master, and Aurora straightened in Snow's arms, glaring at him. Antoine whirled on the spot to face him, his sword at the ready.

Aurora pushed free of Snow's arms and picked up the blade she had dropped at some point, too weak to hold it then. She found the strength to wield it in the face of death, determined not to succumb to her master's plan for her and Snow.

Snow readied his own blade, standing beside her.

Payne, Kristina, and Elissa continued to fight off to their right, battling to protect Callum and their young.

Sera, the male vampire, and Javier and Lilah fought below them on the red carpet. Across the room, Chica and Andreu fought bravely, the female succubus whizzing between the angels, sucking out their energy through deadly kisses, weakening them for her male to finish.

Aurora faced her master.

"Why did you do this? Because you knew I had gone to judge Snow well, giving him a chance to redeem himself? Because you blamed him for all the suffering and darkness that would consume me if my faith in him was proven wrong?"

He smiled darkly and preened a few unruly strands of his long black hair from his amethyst eyes. "You have too much faith in me. I came here to kill the vampire because he deserves to die… and so do you."

Snow growled at him, exposing his fangs at the same time. It warmed her heart. He wanted to protect her from the angels and save her from her master. He still loved her.

Antoine shifted beside them, engaging a brunette female angel who dared to step into the firing line between them and her master. Another vampire joined in, battling beside him to bring the female down, tearing through her wings with claw and blade before decapitating her.

Aurora stared coldly at her master. He showed no sign of remorse or any flicker of emotion as the angel fell, exhaling her last breath. He didn't care how many died here tonight and it sickened Aurora.

"They ordered you to execute me but gave you no deadline... so you drew it out as long as you could. You're exploiting a loophole." She wasn't sure what that meant exactly but if she pretended that she did, she might get him to reveal the truth about it to her. "Our superiors are amused by that. I am not."

His smile gained a proud edge.

"You were ordered to kill me with your own sword but you couldn't bring yourself to do it. I hate you for that. I hate you for trying to trick me into committing suicide in order to spare yourself." Aurora spat the words at him and took a step forwards, only for Snow to catch her arm and hold her back.

She looked over her shoulder at him and he shook his head. She knew that fighting her master would be committing the suicide she just spoke of, but she wanted to drive her sword right through his black dead heart.

Her master preened his white bloodstained feathers in the way she had witnessed him do a million times and something dawned on her.

"You shallow bastard!" She hurled herself forwards, raising her sword at the same time, but Snow held her firm, refusing to let her attack her master. Aurora tried to break free but Snow pulled her back to him, his grip on her unrelenting. "You would have been following orders if you had struck me down that day but you also would have gained a single black feather for the sin of killing a fellow angel."

A look of sheer disgust crossed her master's face. "I had kept them perfect for thousands of years before you were dumped on me as my ward. In only a handful of years, you threatened to undo all of my hard work."

Aurora spluttered, unable to believe what she was hearing. He valued the purity of his feathers over her life and the life of these people around her.

"Our superiors felt it was what I deserved for not teaching you well enough as a child and allowing you to commit your first sin the night you saved this despicable creature." Her master tossed Snow a black look and Antoine snarled beside her, his back tensing as his fingers flexed around the hilt of his bloodied white sword.

Snow moved forwards, angling his body slightly in front of hers, shielding her again. It irked her this time. She wanted to be the one to end her master. She wanted to make him pay for what he had done to her.

"You wanted me to suffer," she said, enraged by that and the thought that he had masqueraded as her companion for all these years, pretending to care about her when really he had been biding his time, waiting for Snow to commit enough sins. "You watched me as I bore Snow's sins, my feathers turning black one by one, and then Snow went two centuries without committing another. Oh, how that must have annoyed you!"

Unleash

Her master scowled at her, and she hated him more than ever. She had thought he had been happy when Snow had stopped sinning, driven into isolation by his bloodlust, taken away from the world by his brother. In reality, it had annoyed her master, forcing him to bide his time, waiting for Snow to sin again.

And when that had failed, and Snow hadn't sinned, he had changed his plans.

"You waited until I gave in to the temptation to visit Snow again, knowing that when I did you could punish me, turning my final feather black. You could make me judge him." Aurora readied her sword. "You son of a bitch!"

She broke free of Snow's grasp and attacked her master, catching him unawares with a direct strike across his upper arm, slicing deep into his white armour. Her sword came away bloodied and her master's purple eyes flashed with fury.

He attacked but Snow was there, blocking his blade, driving it away from her. Antoine joined forces with the other vampires, keeping the other angels at bay, out of their fight with her master.

If she could kill her master, then it would send a message to her superiors, a warning that she would come good on her threat to destroy every angel they sent to Vampirerotique if they didn't withdraw the troops. She was sure they would choose the sensible course of action and recall them, and she would have spared Snow and his friends.

If only.

Her master was ancient, almost as old as their superiors were and almost as powerful. No one had defeated him or even come close, and he had battled the strongest demons in the realms of Hell, surviving each battle without a single wound.

She had wounded him though, and he couldn't kill her directly without committing the sin of killing a fellow angel. He needed to kill Snow and have her die because of her link to him, leaving him untainted because he had only killed a demon. She could take advantage of that if Snow would only let her. The trouble was, she knew he wouldn't want her to fight her master alone. He would fight to protect her, placing himself between her and her master, even when it made sense for her to be the one to fight him.

Aurora timed her attacks with Snow's, slashing at her master whenever he blocked Snow's blade, leaving himself open.

The angel was too fast.

He easily countered her, quickly switching between blocking Snow and blocking her. She tried to come around behind him but he shifted, nimbly moving so he continued to face them both.

An angel broke through the ranks to help him, forcing her to break away to attack him instead. Her master lured Snow further away and, although Snow fought viciously, he landed blows, slicing Snow's arms and his chest. Each cut on his body appeared on hers and she grew weaker, the pain stealing her strength and her focus.

It was her master's sword that could give them simultaneous injuries, and possibly that weapon alone. If she could get it away from him, she could perhaps give them a chance to defeat him.

Antoine came up behind the angel attacking her, savagely slicing down his back, scoring his white armour and bloodying his wings. She used it as a chance to attack the angel.

Her sword cut through his middle, spilling his entrails across his front. Antoine was gone in a flash, moving so swiftly she could barely keep up, and someone cried out behind her.

She wheeled around to face them and found Antoine there, his sword buried deep in the gut of a female angel who stood with her sword still raised above her head, ready to strike Aurora down.

Aurora's heart skipped a beat at the thought she might not have sensed the attack before it was too late. Even though she was sure Antoine had only saved her because the blow may have killed his brother too, she still thanked him with a brief smile before launching herself back into the fight.

Snow and her master had moved further away, a swath of angels blocking her path to them now. Snow had landed several blows but the cuts on her body said that he had taken more.

Crimson soaked her dress, turning it almost completely red, but she wouldn't stop fighting.

She struggled to battle her way through the angels with Antoine's assistance and her head spun when her master slammed his fist and the hilt of his sword into Snow's temple. She staggered backwards at the same time as Snow and then screamed in agony when a sharp pain pierced her shoulder, echoing Snow's bellow as the sword stabbed into his flesh.

Her master grinned and kicked Snow in the stomach, sending him falling backwards. The sword fell from Snow's bloodstained fingers and clattered across the stage, and a look she didn't like crossed his face when his gaze sought hers.

A dreadful sense of finality pressed down on her and she shook her head.

Unleash

She redoubled her effort to get through the angels to him, clawing and shrieking like a wild thing, desperate to reach Snow before he did something crazy. He wanted to protect her and end her master, and she had seen him fight enough times to know he was going to go all out and lay everything on the line in order to defeat the angel.

Antoine must have sensed her desperation to reach Snow and seen the look on his brother's face, because he hacked at the angels, using all of his strength to cleave through their armour, killing them with a single blow.

Snow found his feet, stared at her a moment, and smiled. "Forgive me."

He launched himself at her master. Barehanded. Her master grinned and thrust forwards with his blade, a direct hit that skewered Snow's broad chest close to his heart, and speared hers too, chasing her breath away.

It didn't stop her vampire.

He ploughed into her master, wrapped his right arm around the front of his throat, locked his other hand around his wrist behind her master's head, and dropped to one knee, bringing her master down backwards over his outstretched thigh.

The crunch of the bones in his neck snapping was loud in the theatre, silencing the battle as all heads turned towards the two males.

Snow followed through, landing on his front on the stage floor next to her master's body.

Aurora pushed through the stricken angels, rushing to him in spite of the fierce debilitating pain emanating from her chest, throbbing in every inch of her. She couldn't breathe. Blood drenched the front of her dress and pooled beneath Snow too. He wasn't moving but he couldn't be dead. He couldn't be. She was still alive. Barely.

She crashed to her knees beside him and tried to pull him over onto his back. He cried out when the sword's blade dug into the stage floor and tears filled her eyes. She had to pull it out. She grasped the hilt and tugged. The wet sucking noise and the feel of his bones scraping along the blade turned her stomach.

Antoine was at her side in a heartbeat, helping her pull the sword free of his brother's chest, his gaze locked on Snow's face. "Don't you dare give up."

She wanted to say those words to him too but couldn't speak through the blood steadily choking her. She coughed, trying to clear her throat and lungs, desperate to tell Snow not to leave her. She wanted him to live.

She glanced up at Antoine as they finally pulled the blade out and Snow slumped onto his back, his head on her knees. Tears streaked Antoine's face and Sera looked as though her whole world was falling apart as she came to a halt behind him and saw Snow.

The angels around them disappeared, revealing Snow to everyone in the theatre.

Aurora couldn't take the oppressive wave of sorrow that flowed through them and crashed over her, or the grief that shone in their eyes and beat in their hearts.

She stroked Snow's cheeks, her own tears blurring her vision, willing him to come around.

He couldn't be dead.

She had fought so hard for him.

He had fought so hard to live and to protect those he loved, her included.

Her pain faded as she stared down at him, her touch leaving sombre streaks of dark colours on his skin. Her only comfort was that if he was to die from this terrible wound he had taken to save everyone he loved, that she would soon follow him.

Her pain would be short lived. She wouldn't suffer as his brother would, or anyone else here who cared about her beautiful warrior.

She hoped that wherever their journey led them, they would see each other again.

What if they didn't though? That thought gripped her heart with icy sharp claws, spilling fear into her veins.

She was heavenly and he was classed as demonic.

What if she was taken to Heaven and he was taken to where the dead resided in Hell?

There was only one way to make sure that didn't happen. She wanted to be with him in the afterlife. She wanted to live with him, just as he had desired, even if their home was the dark bowels of the underworld.

Aurora clung to Snow and didn't hesitate, her love for him giving her the strength to do what she had to do in order to be with him no matter what happened.

She tipped her head back and stared up at the lights rigged above the stage.

"I renounce my duty," she said, her voice firm and level, showing none of the pain crushing her heart to pieces.

She dropped her head, bent over Snow and cried for him, shedding heavenly tears for the last time as her wings began to fall apart feather by feather.

The pain of falling was nothing compared with the pain of losing Snow.

She couldn't lose him. Blood bubbled up her throat, choking her, and she tried to swallow it back down, hating the acrid taste of death in her mouth. Her eyes widened.

Blood.

Snow had saved Antoine from the grip of death by giving him blood. If she did the same for Snow, would it work? His injuries were severe and he was losing blood at an alarming rate. Antoine had been in death's embrace when Snow had brought him back though.

There was only one way to find out if she could do the same for Snow and, right now, she was willing to give anything a shot.

Aurora shifted forwards, tipped Snow's head back in her lap, and brought her lips to his. She opened his mouth and kissed him, allowing her life force to flow into him, desperate that it would kick-start his healing process and save her beautiful noble vampire, and grant them a second chance to have the life they both desired.

Together.

Tears slipped down her cheeks and she kept kissing Snow, stroking his cheeks at the same time, silently begging the higher power to give them the chance at happiness that they deserved after enduring so much darkness and pain for two thousand years.

Aurora tried to reassure herself that no matter what happened, they would be together, whether it was in the realm of the dead or in this world of the living.

They would be together now.

The prince and the angel.

CHAPTER 21

Warm hands drew Snow up from the darkness. His head was foggy. His body burned. His chest was damn near killing him.

He couldn't remember what had happened but he felt as though someone had put him through several rounds of torture for fun, cutting him to ribbons.

The pain buzzing in his skull and chest faded enough for him to regain control of his body, and he weakly opened his eyes. Aurora shimmered into view above him, colourful tears streaking her flushed cheeks, slipping in a steady stream from her closed eyes and cutting through the dirt and blood on her face.

It was her hands on his cheeks, stroking them softly.

It was her blood on his lips and tongue.

Her sweet intoxicating blood flowed in his veins, warming him from his very core and soothing his pain, stealing it away piece by piece and gradually restoring his strength.

His Aurora was the reason he was alive.

She had saved him from the brink of death.

A black feather floated over her shoulder and brushed his arm before landing on the floor beside him. It wasn't alone. Her wings were falling apart. He looked out of the corner of his eye and saw hundreds of feathers scattered across the stage, the blood of battle soaking into them.

"Are you crying because of your wings?" he whispered, feeling sorry for her and filled with the need to comfort her and take her pain away. He was in so much pain that he probably wouldn't notice if hers was added on top of it. He would gladly bear it for her.

She started and her eyes opened wide, her caresses ceasing. She stared down at him and the shock in her beautiful colourful eyes became relief.

"I wasn't crying for them... I was crying for you." More tears came, slipping down her bloodstained and bruised cheeks to land on his forehead, and then she moved so fast that she startled him and kissed his brow, her hands clutching his cheeks.

"For me?" he whispered, incredulous. She nodded, her lips shifting against his skin. He had never felt so blessed, so loved. So needed.

"I thought you were dead." When she drew back, she glanced around her. His senses were functional enough to tell him that they weren't alone, and she wasn't the only one feeling relieved but sorrowful. Or the only one who had thought he was dead.

They also told him that the angels were gone.

His pain subsided until the buzzing in his skull ceased and he could recall what he had done.

Snow tried to smile but it came out as a grimace when his chest blazed anew, the pain in it threatening to steal his senses and render him unconscious again.

"I'm not that easy to kill. Have a little faith in me." He looked up at his upside down Aurora and she smiled shakily at him. "Were you worried your number was up?"

She shook her head. "I took measures to make sure we would be together."

"Your wings?" he said and she nodded. "You didn't have to do that."

Pain lashed at his chest again and he gritted his teeth. Aurora grimaced too, reminding him that he had a lot of apologising to do and needed to find a way to make things up to her. He could smell her blood, knew she had the same injuries as he bore, and was suffering again because of him.

Aurora drew in an unsteady breath and swallowed hard, and then tried to smile at him again. He had to admire her courage and was grateful she had a leash on her temper and wasn't beating the hell out of him for getting her skewered through the chest too. Yet.

"I did. I wanted to do it because I would like to be with you... if your offer to live with you still stands?" She looked beautifully hopeful and fearful at the same time, as if he would turn away the most wonderful thing that had ever happened in all his dark existence.

He managed to smile properly. "It might have been made two thousand years ago, but it still stands."

Snow slid his gaze away from Aurora's and bravely met Antoine's. His younger brother stared at him, his ice-blue eyes red from the tears that cut pale lines through the bloodstains on his face.

"What the hell did you think you were doing?" Antoine snapped and Snow let him off for his outburst, knowing that it was relief making him raise his voice and not anger. It was just the depth of his brother's love for him.

"It was the only way of killing him." A crazy way, but at the time, he had seen Aurora growing weaker, bleeding badly from wounds her master was inflicting upon him, and he had lost his head.

"Killing yourself more like," Antoine grumbled and looked as though he was considering throttling him.

Snow suspected he might limit his punishment to long term verbal aggravation and constant reminders that he had almost got himself and Aurora killed.

"But I did kill him... I presume I did." Snow could still smell the bastard angel. He tried to sit up to check the male was dead but it hurt too much. He seized up halfway and collapsed back onto Aurora's knees.

She nodded and stroked his cheeks. "He is dead."

Snow hoped that didn't mean they would be receiving a visit from other angels looking to carry out vengeance killings. If they were wise, they would see tonight as a sign not to mess with him. He had taken down one of their strongest, proving himself stronger.

He didn't feel particularly strong right now though.

Aurora offered her wrist to him. As much as he hurt and needed more blood to begin healing his wounds, he needed to see her healing more. Only then would he feel better.

Snow shook his head and stared up at her. "You are injured and must conserve your strength."

"I have a theory... the quicker you heal, the faster I will feel better." She offered her wrist again and he wanted to shoot her theory down, but didn't have the heart. He would take another sip from her if it would alleviate her fear and make her believe he was on the mend.

Snow allowed his fangs to extend. Aurora brought her wrist to his lips and he closed his eyes and eased his fangs into it, not wanting to hurt her. She gasped and her heart missed a beat, but it was pleasure that he felt in her this time. He closed his mouth around her arm and suckled softly, controlling himself so her pleasure didn't become pain.

The taste of her was still divine and he could feel her blood mingling with his, renewing his strength and accelerating the rate of his healing. He stopped himself from taking more than a sip of her delicious blood and licked her wrist, sealing the twin puncture marks, feeling her shiver under his tongue.

He opened his eyes and looked up at her. Her cheeks were pink and there was more colour in her ashen lips now. Perhaps she was right and the bond between them linked her physical strength to his, meaning that the faster he healed from his wounds, the quicker her strength returned and she healed hers.

Snow pressed one hand to the wound on his chest and sat up with Antoine's help. He froze when he saw all the blood on his brother's shirt and all the injuries beneath. He braced himself on instinct, waiting for his bloodlust to seize him, roused by dark memories of the night he had attacked his brother.

For the first time since that night, the sight of his brother bleeding didn't send him into a fit of bloodlust.

Antoine's shoulders relaxed. He had braced himself too, expecting an attack to happen. His blue eyes darted to Aurora behind him and then back to Snow.

"It seems the latest addition to the Vampirerotique family has absolute power over you."

Snow smiled and looked over his shoulder at her, his heart warmed by the coded welcome his brother had just issued to his female and the truth in his words.

"She does."

Aurora blushed a pretty shade of pink that made him ache to kiss her.

"We should get you tended to," Antoine said, a pointed reminder that he was in no condition to be getting physical with his female, no matter how badly he wanted her.

Payne moved forwards with Elissa at his side and Luca tucked between them. Snow looked up at the part-incubus vampire.

Payne offered his hand to him. "Express ride to your room, limited time offer."

"Take Aurora," Snow said, not wanting her to be left behind, even for a second. Payne glanced at her.

"I've got the girly." Chica appeared behind Aurora, causing her to jump, and Aurora opened her mouth to speak but only a squeak came out before Chica caught her arm and they disappeared.

Snow growled and turned to warn Andreu that his female needed to learn manners around his woman.

Payne took that moment to grab Snow's arm and teleport him, landing him square on his four-poster bed with him on his back and Payne standing on the mattress. The young elite vampire wobbled as he gingerly walked to the edge of the bed and hopped down onto the floor.

"Not my best landing, but at least I didn't land on top of you." He awkwardly ran his fingers through his dirty blond spiked hair, flashing the lines of fae markings that tracked up the underside of his forearm and causing the rolled up sleeves of his dark blue pinstriped shirt to tighten around his muscles.

"I win that one, Incupire." Chica looked far too full of energy as she bounded away from Aurora, leaving her in the middle of his black apartment. Chica's knee-high biker boots banged heavily on his wooden floor and her black skirt and jaw-length hair bounced with each leaping step. She twirled when she reached Payne and poked a finger against his chest. "Try to keep up. I'm streaking way ahead of you."

Payne growled at her. "Just because you're all hopped up on kisses. Some of us don't flaunt it, Sweetheart."

Chica's brown-to-blue eyes widened in horror and she planted one hand on her hip, fingertips pressing hard into her purple strapless corset. "Are you calling me a hussy?"

Payne knocked her other hand away from him and rubbed a dark patch on his blue shirt, over the left side of his chest. Blood. Payne bore wounds from protecting his female and their youngling.

"No one is calling you a hussy," Andreu said as he entered the room, his Spanish accent thickly lacing his English, a sign of his anger. His black shirt had more slashes in it now and there were some in his trousers too, and a long gash across his left cheek that had bled down to his jaw. He shot Payne a glare. "Were they?"

Payne shrugged nonchalantly and then rushed to Elissa and Luca as they entered behind Andreu. "You both okay?"

Elissa smiled and nodded. "Perfect, although Luca wants to keep the sword."

"Just in case," the young boy said, his grey eyes bright with enthusiasm. Payne ruffled his messy hair.

"Sounds like a good idea, Kiddo." Payne gathered Luca up into his arms, winced and set him back down again.

"Let me take a look," Elissa said and Snow was awestruck when she raised her hand and colourful swirls of light danced around her fingers. He had never expected magic could be so pretty. Or beneficial.

The wounds visible through the tears in Payne's shirt healed before his eyes.

Antoine entered with Sera. Sera immediately broke away from her mate and crossed the room to Aurora, wiping her bloodied hands on her t-shirt as she walked. Lilah joined her the moment she entered in front of Javier, and the two females helped Aurora into the bathroom, shutting the door behind them.

Snow closed his eyes, taking a moment to steel himself, glad that those closest to him had survived the battle, and grateful that Lilah and Sera were helping Aurora with her wounds.

He sensed Antoine halt beside the bed.

"Come on. Up," Antoine commanded, caught Snow's hand and pulled him slowly into a sitting position.

Snow flicked his eyes open and bit back a groan. He hated it when Antoine fussed over him, but he obediently sat at the edge of the four-poster bed, letting his brother have his way because he knew it would make him feel better.

Andreu and Javier moved into the corner, both males leaning against the wall beyond Payne, their black shirts and trousers causing them to blend into it.

Javier sighed, tipped his head back and closed his eyes. Andreu flicked him a look of concern. Javier had taken some serious blows but he would live. Andreu didn't need to worry about him.

Snow could sense that it was fatigue causing his brother to look as though he was about to fall asleep on his feet. Both males had battled valiantly to protect their females. There had been only a few patches of blood on Lilah's pale blue summer dress and her bare arms. Javier must have fought like a wild thing to protect her.

Snow smiled across at them. Javier opened his eyes, met Snow's gaze, and then smiled too. He yawned, scrubbed a hand over his face and talked to Andreu about the fight, discussing how many angels they had taken down. Chica fussed over Andreu, muttering about all the cuts on him and that she liked scars but she preferred his sexy body perfect and lickable.

Snow tuned them out before he retched from the information overload and switched his focus back to Antoine, tempted to tell him that Aurora's blood was already healing him from the inside and that he didn't need to worry or fuss over him. He didn't have the heart when he saw the tears shining in Antoine's eyes and felt the underlying current of hurt and fear that ran through his blood. Antoine needed to feel he was helping him mend and Snow would happily go along with it to make him feel better and alleviate his fears.

Antoine gathered bandages, cotton wool, antiseptic and various other medical supplies from the cupboard near Snow's bed and set them out on his ebony nightstand. Snow winced when his brother tore open a pack containing a surgical needle and took up some thread. He hated needles. He steeled himself and focused on everyone else in the room as Antoine began to sew the wound on his chest, trying not to tense too much.

Elissa finished with Payne and moved straight to Callum and Kristina as they entered. Kristina was wearing Callum's shirt, her legs bare beneath it. Blood covered most of her skin and it was hard to tell how badly she was injured.

Werewolves fought violently and their methods meant they often ended up bathed in the blood of their foes. Snow hoped she looked worse than she was. Elissa healed her first and then rubbed the back of her hand across her brow, fatigue beginning to shine in her silver-grey eyes.

The witch stepped away from Kristina and Payne moved over to her, his arm settling around her waist, slipping beneath the hem of her midnight blue halter-top to rest on the belt of her black jeans.

Elissa leaned against his chest, closing her eyes, and remained there for long minutes while Payne tenderly caressed her long silver-streaked dark hair. When she emerged and nodded, he brushed a kiss across her brow and then released her, concern in his dark grey eyes. She smiled, touched his hand and then turned to Callum.

Payne took the twins from Callum and the black-haired elite male slumped into the nearest chair, the life draining out of him.

Snow could sense it was relief draining him rather than any injury. With the exception of Chica, who had been healing her wounds on the fly by kissing and stealing energy, he was the least injured. There wasn't a scratch on his bare chest. Not even a bruise.

The babies wriggled in Payne's arms, giving him hell.

Snow amended his observation. With the exception of Chica, Alistair and Abby. The twins were in perfect health, not a scratch on either of them. Even Luca had picked up a cut or two.

Callum and Kristina were perfect parents. They had protected their young.

Everyone had protected them.

Snow wriggled his fingers at Abby when she looked across at him, her big baby blues filled with tears. She giggled.

Luca joined Payne and peered up at the babies. Payne crouched so the young incubus boy could see them and they squirmed harder, writhing in his arms.

"Be nice to your godfather," Payne muttered and frowned as he struggled to keep hold of the twins.

Luca petted Alistair on the head very carefully. "I want a baby."

Payne swallowed hard, his grey eyes wide and full of alarm. "Careful what you wish for, Kiddo. Wait until you're a few centuries old, okay? They're a lot of responsibility and with an incubus's appetite… well… you might want to find your mate first and settle down."

Luca smiled up at him. "Like you did with Elissa."

Payne nodded and glanced at her, affection warming his eyes. She smiled down at him and then focused on checking over Callum.

"Make me a sister or a brother then."

Payne choked this time and Callum yelped as Elissa tensed. A black scorch mark on his shoulder told Snow that demand leaving Luca's lips had shocked her as much as it had her mate.

"Sorry," Elissa muttered and used her magic to heal the wound.

"Er… um…" Payne glanced at Elissa again, looking like a man desperate for a lifeline.

Elissa finished with Callum, squatted next to Luca, and brushed his wild hair from his brow. "Maybe when you're older."

Luca looked as though he might demand they make him a brother or sister right that minute but then he looked back at the twins, and then up at Callum and Kristina. "Can I be their big brother?"

Kristina smiled and settled her hand on Callum's shoulder. "Of course. You did a wonderful job protecting them today. You have to keep them safe with the rest of us. That's what big brothers do. They make sure their siblings are protected and safe."

Snow looked away from them, his gaze falling on his younger brother.

Antoine smiled at him before he could say anything and gently squeezed his shoulder, showing him that he knew what was on his mind and it was all in the past now.

Snow would make it up to him. He would be the big brother he always should have been, had always tried to be for Antoine. He would protect him and ensure he was safe, and would never allow anyone to harm him or those he cared about.

His gaze drifted across the black apartment to the bathroom door, his senses reaching for Aurora, needing to feel her and feel she was safe. He felt terrible for doubting her and believing she would want to harm those at the theatre. He wanted to see her again and apologise, and tell her that he would make it up to her somehow.

Antoine finished with the deepest wounds on his chest and back, and then stitched the already healing stab wounds in his side. He cut the thread, set the infernal needle down and picked up cotton wool and antiseptic, and cleaned all of the lacerations.

Snow bit his tongue to stop himself from wincing as each cut stung.

Antoine's pale eyes kept flickering to Snow's face, the guilt surfacing in them telling Snow that Antoine could sense his pain.

Snow gave him a tight smile that grew even tighter when his younger brother wrapped enough bandages around his chest and stomach to make several mummies in Ancient Egyptian times. Antoine pulled them so tightly that Snow could barely breathe.

Snow tried to take it as a sign of Antoine's deep love for him and his need to ensure he recovered quickly.

He would slightly amend the bandages later when his brother had gone, removing half of them so his ribs no longer felt as though they were being mercilessly shoved inwards.

Antoine cupped his cheek and Snow looked at him, and caught the deep pain in his pale blue eyes before he masked it. He had scared his brother again. Snow caught him around the nape of his neck and pulled his brother down into a brief embrace.

"Oh, are you two going to start kissing or something... because I think that's illegal... but kinky." Chica sounded far too interested in seeing him kiss Antoine.

"Not going to happen." Andreu steered her away from them. "Like you haven't fed enough already tonight anyway."

Elissa finished with Callum and came to Andreu, healing the few cuts he had picked up, and then healed Javier. She took another break before approaching Antoine, and Snow was grateful for her distracting his brother.

He didn't think he could take much more of Antoine's mollycoddling and there would be a world shortage of bandages if his brother continued, wrapping them around even the most minor of Snow's wounds.

Sera and Lilah came out of the bathroom, followed by Aurora, and Snow's gaze instantly sought her.

She wore his black silk robe around her slender frame and it pooled around her feet, far too long for her. Someone had tied her beautiful hair back and it was damp. The females must have washed her too, cleaning all the blood away. She looked pale still.

Elissa healed Sera and then Lilah, and then came to Snow. She looked tired, dark crescents beneath her sparkling silver eyes.

Snow held his hands up and smiled at her. "Call it a day. Payne looks itchy to get you back to your apartment and I don't want to see what happens to a hungry incubus when he watches his mate lay her hands on a man ten times better-looking than he is."

Payne shot him a dour look. "Very fucking funny."

"Thank you." Elissa shakily smiled, the twinkle in her silver-grey eyes backing up her words and letting him know that she truly appreciated him letting her rest now.

Payne handed the babies back to Callum, took Luca's hand and walked across the room to Elissa. The moment she was within his reach, he grabbed her, tugged her against him, gathered Luca closer and teleported.

Chica nibbled her lower lip, looking as though she really wanted to follow Payne's lead and get her mate back to bed so she could have some dessert. Snow shot her a smile and she winked at him, a blush staining her cheeks, and kissed Andreu as they both disappeared.

Javier rolled his eyes. He stood near the door with Lilah tucked against his side, his arm around her. "There is far too much victory sex happening in this place tonight."

Lilah pouted and looked up at her lover. "I'll just have to shower alone to get all this blood off me then."

Javier's dark brown gaze slid to her, lighting up with interest. Snow couldn't blame the elite male when he turned, released Lilah's shoulder and grabbed her hand, and pulled her from the room. It seemed Javier was no longer feeling tired.

Snow glanced at Aurora, catching the flush of colour on her cheeks as she watched the couple leave, sensing that her thoughts were following the same lines as his were. He wanted to kiss her and hold her in his arms. He wanted to make love with her.

He was beginning to regret not letting Elissa heal him now.

He ran his gaze over her and frowned at the bandages that poked out above the robe, wrapping around her chest. He should have told Elissa to heal Aurora at the very least.

He wasn't used to having to worry about another like this and it was going to take some getting used to. Aurora was his to take care of and protect. He would do better next time and would place her first. Not that he would ever let her end up injured like this again.

Antoine sighed as Callum and Kristina left the room too, leaving them alone with their females. "My money is on Lilah becoming pregnant next. Having the apartment next to Javier's is becoming a nightmare. I swear they never sleep."

Sera looped her arm around Antoine's and smiled sweetly at him. "This from the man who puts his brother's spare restraints to use each morning?"

Snow grimaced.

"I am in enough pain without that image branded on my mind." He flicked a serious look at his younger brother, ignoring Sera's scowl. "I want new restraints. I am not being chained by ones that have been used in sex play."

Sera reached over and patted Snow's cheek as she leaned down, bringing her mouth close to his ear.

"I guess you'll need new restraints for your bed every day then… if you don't want to use ones someone has used during sex?" she whispered and his cheeks heated, the thought of being chained to his bed gaining appeal for the first time in his life.

Sera laughed and led his brother towards the door. Antoine paused there and let her go on ahead. He looked back at Snow.

"You will be alright?" Antoine said, concern in his voice and his pale blue eyes.

Snow nodded to reassure him.

Antoine smiled. "Try to get some rest."

He closed the door behind him. Snow felt suddenly very aware of Aurora where she stood near the bathroom, her wickedly curvy body wrapped in his black robe. He rose to his feet and faltered, unsure what to say to her. He had so much he needed to tell her, but he wasn't sure where to begin.

"How are you doing?" Nothing had ever sounded as lame to his ears as those words leaving his lips. He clenched his fists but the action caused the cuts on his arms to sting. His fingers fell open again.

Aurora nibbled her lip and slowly approached him, the blush still burning her cheeks. Her scent of lilies and snow wrapped around him, comforting him. She settled against the thick steel post at the foot of his double bed, leaning the front of her right shoulder against it and holding onto it with both hands. Her gaze tentatively met his.

"Much better already… really," she said, her soft voice warming him right down to his bones, soothing his tension away.

Snow sat back down on the bed and glanced at her, hoping she would join him. She shuffled away from the post and sat close to him, her thigh brushing his, burning him through his jeans. He ached to feel her hands on him again. Her lips on his.

"I am sorry I doubted you." It was a weak apology and he knew it, and he would find a thousand ways to apologise to her until she forgave him for believing she had betrayed him.

Unleash

She shrugged and leaned her head on his shoulder, and the feel of her there was bliss, reassuring him and calming his ragged feelings.

Snow looked down at the bandages around his chest and then at her. The sight of her bleeding, sharing the terrible wounds on his body, had driven him crazy with a need to protect her. It had torn him in two, pulling him between a need to fight to keep her safe and a need to stay his blade so he wouldn't pick up another injury that she would share.

"I shouldn't have done that." He reached over and parted the top of the black robe she wore, his fingers shaking. The bandages around her chest had spots of blood marring the pale fabric already. "I am sorry, Aurora."

"You scared me," she whispered and then pulled away and stared up at him, her green-to-blue eyes overflowing with her fear and with tender affection. He stroked her chest and could feel her pain in the blood flowing in his veins. She caught his hand and squeezed it, clutching it tightly. "Why did you do that? I thought I had lost you."

"You sound like Antoine. I was almost certain I would survive. It takes more than a few stab wounds to kill a two thousand year old vampire." His words didn't seem to reassure her. If anything, they only served to increase the hurt in her heart, until it showed in her beautiful eyes and hit him hard. He gathered her into his arms, gritting his teeth against the pain moving so swiftly caused him. "I didn't mean to hurt you."

She nestled close to him, her hands pressing against his chest, her cheek resting on his shoulder.

He leaned his cheek against her other one, savouring the feel of her in his arms, the knowledge she was safe now stripping away his strength. He had feared he would lose her too, had been bombarded by one emotion after another tonight, and all of them conspired to leave him shaken, desperately clinging to his female, needing to feel her in his arms.

Aurora drew out of those arms and surprised him by standing. She held her hand out to him and he slipped his into it, curious as to what she was up to. She made him stand and he raised an eyebrow when she stripped him down to his underwear and then removed her robe.

"Come," she said and tugged the black covers on his bed back. She crawled onto it, took hold of his hand again, and lured him onto the bed with her. "You need to rest."

He wanted to mention that she needed to rest too. She turned her back again as she moved across the bed to make room for him and he frowned at the thick twin vertical scars on her back, visible above the top of her bandages.

She had forsaken her wings for him, because she had feared they would end up separated in the afterlife. It touched him deeply. She had made a great sacrifice for his sake, proving her love for him. She turned to face him and settled down in his bed.

Their bed.

Snow clambered onto it, lay beside her on his back, carefully coaxed her into his arms so he didn't aggravate her injuries or his and drew the covers up over them both. Aurora settled her head on his shoulder and her hand on his chest, and then pushed herself up and looked down at him.

She smiled and it hit him hard in the chest, and he wondered if her smile would ever stop doing that, or if there would ever come a day when he couldn't help but stop and stare whenever she entered a room and he realised all over again just how beautiful his female was.

His female.

She leaned down and softly kissed him, showing him that their thoughts had been running along similar lines earlier and she wanted to indulge in victory sex too. It would have to wait, but he could definitely spend the time it took them both to heal doing this. He would never grow tired of kissing her.

Snow held her close to him, her soft body pressing into his and warming him, her lips dancing across his, teasing him. He kissed her until he felt as though he was floating, light enough inside that he might drift away, a feeling he had never experienced before he had met Aurora again and fallen in love with her.

She settled against him and he closed his eyes and held her, and found a new bliss in the act of falling asleep with her nestled against him, tucked safely in his arms where she belonged.

His beautiful angel.

He felt whole again, the empty space behind his sternum filled with light not darkness, with love not rage.

He felt normal.

And for the first time in forever, he couldn't wait for tomorrow to come.

He was looking forwards, towards a future filled with hope and a new beginning, and he would never look backwards again.

CHAPTER 22

∽∞∽

Snow leaned against the wall of the theatre, lurking in the shadows, watching the finale of the first show of the season and keeping an eye on the audience as they enjoyed the acts playing out on the stage. He barely paid attention to the performance, just enough to know what had happened and that everything was running like clockwork. The shows were mundane to him, designed to titillate.

They didn't thrill him as being with Aurora did.

Just the thought of the beautiful female awaiting him in their quarters had him growing hard in his jeans and aching to return to her. He tamped that feeling down and scanned the audience again, folding his arms across his chest and stretching the material of his black shirt across his muscles. A few females glanced his way and he paid them no heed.

He was spoken for.

He smiled at that.

A beautiful angel had not only fallen in love with him, but she had remained with him, and had even helped him through an attack whenever one happened. He felt blessed to have her in his life, a woman strong enough to deal with him even when he was in a black mood and lost his mind to bloodlust.

He dragged his attention back to the show and shook his head when the audience gasped in unison, not understanding what they found so appealing about the acts on the stage. He didn't need to understand it though. He just needed them to behave and enjoy it.

Life at Vampirerotique had been quiet over the past few months, blissfully uneventful. Payne and Andreu had remained, working with Callum and Javier on new shows and helping them run the theatre. Everyone had welcomed Aurora into the family, and even Antoine had admitted that he liked her.

It hadn't surprised Snow. Antoine liked anyone who could help Snow through a bout of bloodlust or even keep one at bay. Aurora was exceptionally skilled at both of those things.

His mind drifted back to her until his senses sparked. A ripple of discord went through the theatre.

Snow smiled and shook his head when his hearing caught a muffled curse and then the audience settled, becoming unaware of their non-vampire member again. Snow could still sense her, even with her best veil in place.

He was tempted to call Chica on it but decided to let her have her way and leave her to watch the remains of the show in peace, thinking she was deceiving everyone in the theatre.

He tried to focus on the show again, knowing Antoine would expect a full report when he returned.

Snow still couldn't believe that he was covering for his brother. He had never thought he would live to see the day that his brother missed a show or the day when he was an active member of management at Vampirerotique.

It still felt strange and it was definitely going to take more than a few weeks to get used to it and having to do mundane things like attend meetings and talks about what to add to the shows to make them new and exciting for the audience.

Part of him was actually hoping for a relapse. A break from work would be nice. Or at least easing him into a daily work schedule. Antoine and Aurora both thought that throwing him into full-time work was good for him though, and all attempts he had made to make them change their minds had failed.

He couldn't even tempt Aurora with the promise of more time spent in bed.

She did look torn whenever he mentioned it, but then she got that steely look in her beautiful eyes and stuck to her guns.

Snow cocked his head and smiled.

Antoine had returned, and his brother's feelings were all over the place.

Snow slipped out the double doors and into the high-ceilinged black room beyond to wait for Antoine.

He leaned his back against the wall, folded his arms across his chest and crossed his legs at the ankle. He tracked his brother's swift approach. Snow looked across to his right as he appeared along the black corridor. He looked more than on edge, far worse than Snow had anticipated, and he pushed away from the wall, concerned now.

He frowned at Antoine. "Well?"

Antoine looked agitated, swallowed a few times, and began to pace, shoving his fingers through his dark brown hair. It set Snow on edge too.

Sera came up behind Antoine, looped her arm around his and smiled, and Snow had never felt so relieved. It couldn't be bad news if she was smiling so brightly, buzzing with joy.

"He's going to be a daddy." She grinned, her dark green eyes overflowing with the happiness he could feel in her.

Antoine looked ready to pass out.

"I hope you have a firm hold on him, because he might go at any second." Snow moved closer, afraid that his brother was going to faint. He was getting paler.

Sera laughed, the sound musical and full of excitement. She flicked her long fair hair over her shoulder with one hand and squeezed Antoine's arm with the other.

"He did go. He hit the desk and the floor in the doctor's office pretty hard too." She reached up and brushed Antoine's dark hair back from his forehead, revealing a nasty gash near his hairline.

Snow laughed, earning a growl from his brother. He couldn't help it, not when he could easily picture Antoine's reaction to the news they were going to become parents.

Light footsteps sounded on the stairs behind him and then Aurora was rushing up to him, her short cream dress fluttering with each long stride. Her green-to-blue eyes shone brightly and he could feel her excitement flowing through her, and her nerves too.

"Good news I take it?" She halted beside him, her gaze darting between Antoine and Sera, and him.

"What gave it away?" Snow looked down at her and she scolded him with a frown.

"You never laugh unless something good has happened… or Alistair is throwing toys at Callum's head." Her frown deepened. "I think his parents are wrong about you and you're a bad influence on him. You're teaching him to be mischievous like you were as a child."

Snow couldn't deny that. She was right, but she was also hardly one to talk. She took immense joy from Alistair's well-aimed attacks on his father too, but mostly because they made Snow laugh. It seemed to make her happy whenever she saw him smiling.

Aurora looked back at Antoine and Sera, her expression expectant.

Antoine mumbled, "Baby."

Aurora clapped her hands and was pulling Sera into a hug, tugging her away from Antoine, before Snow could warn her that his brother needed the support. Snow caught Antoine before he could make a fool of himself, tightly clutching his left arm through his shirt.

"Easy, Brother," Snow whispered, unable to keep the amusement out of his voice.

Antoine scowled at him. "Wait until it is your turn."

Snow began walking with him towards the stairs, feeling his brother needed the assistance all the way to his apartment and a good lie down to recover from the shock of discovering he was about to become a father.

A father.

Snow couldn't imagine what that must feel like. He didn't think it was possible to get a fallen angel pregnant, but he didn't mention it. Antoine looked as though he needed to feel that Snow might have to go through this with Aurora one day so he could be there to laugh when Snow had a heart attack, and then watch him suffer as he spent months panicking about babies.

What Antoine didn't know was that he didn't have to wait.

Snow felt as weak-kneed and out of sorts as Antoine, and he was already sharing his brother's panic that something might happen to the baby before it was born or the birth might end up happening in daylight, with no doctor around to assist with it, and a million other terrifying scenarios.

He shuddered at the thought of any of them coming to pass.

"You are not alone in this, Brother," Snow said with feeling and Antoine gave him a grateful and relieved look. "You may have to think about opening a crèche at the theatre though."

"What a fantastic idea," Sera piped up from behind them.

Antoine's expression turned dour, showing Snow how little that amused him.

"We already have one," Antoine said sullenly and glanced over his shoulder at his mate. "Don't you spend every performance and most days with Kristina and Elissa, and the children?"

"I suppose so. We'll just formalise it then and maybe take one of the spare rooms and turn it into a playroom." Sera smiled at him.

Antoine sighed. At least he was beginning to regain his colour and was walking more steadily as they neared the floor where their quarters were located. In time, his brother would grow comfortable with the idea of having a baby of his own, and then it would be born and Snow would teach the child to throw toys at their father's head.

Aurora parted ways with them at Antoine and Sera's door, hugging and congratulating Sera one more time. Snow helped Antoine into their dark green apartment and settled him on the four-poster double bed. Once his brother was comfortable and looking more at ease and himself again, Snow couldn't hold his tongue any longer.

"I should have taken that bet you made about Lilah and Javier being the next ones to bring a baby into the world." He grinned at Antoine, who groaned and flopped back onto the bed. Sera laughed and Snow looked across at her. "I swear, he will find this something to be excited about once the initial shock wears off."

Sera smiled at him, sat down beside Antoine, and patted his black-clad thigh. "I know my mate is excited about this somewhere beneath his terrified exterior."

Snow could understand some of that fear. Antoine had bloodlust too, and bloodlust was genetic. But Sera was elite, and a turned human herself. There was a high chance that their baby wouldn't be born with the same affliction he and Antoine had gained from their pureblood lineage.

He would have to remember to keep reassuring Antoine about that over the coming months and even after the baby had been born. He would be there for him, taking care of him and helping him raise his child, just as he had helped his father raise Antoine. Snow sighed, his heart filled with warmth and light, glad that he would be there to witness a new generation of their family, one hopefully free of bloodlust.

He pulled Antoine up into a sitting position, clutched him by his nape and pressed a kiss to his brow.

"Congratulations, Brother."

Antoine drew back and looked up at him, and the look that normally would have been in his eyes in this sort of situation, the need to reassure him that he was still loved and needed in this world, and that he couldn't live without him, wasn't there. Snow wouldn't miss that pained look and the knowledge he was hurting his brother.

Only love and happiness filled his brother's eyes now, and Snow was glad, although he still felt he had a long way to go before he made things up to Antoine. If he ever could.

He would keep doing his best though, fighting his bloodlust and working to master it. For Antoine's sake. For Aurora's sake. And for his own sake. He had wanted just one thing to live for in the million reasons to die and now he had many.

He bent down and pressed a kiss to Sera's cheek. "Congratulations."

She kissed his cheek and smiled when he pulled away from her.

Snow let himself out of their room, crossed the hall to his, and pushed the panelled mahogany door open.

He froze on the threshold.

Aurora had lit every candle in the room and they cast a warm glow over his ebony furniture and the black walls. He stepped into the apartment and closed the door behind him, curious as to why. He was even more curious when his fallen angel came out of the bathroom to his right dressed in a sexy little white number.

"What is this all about?" He couldn't take his eyes off her as she twirled her raven hair up and pinned it at the back of her head, the action of raising her arms squashing her breasts together to form enticing cleavage in her white satin and lace bodice.

His mouth turned dry and he swallowed, unable to stop his gaze from raking over her dangerous curves to the matching white knickers and then her sheer stockings.

His body put in that it knew what this was all about, growing hard at the sight of her, hungry to peel away the layers of her beautiful underwear and reveal her inch-by-inch to his eyes.

Snow had the feeling his little angel was out to seduce him.

No complaints there.

She pointed to the bed. "Those."

Snow dragged his eyes away from her long enough to see what she was pointing at, and his gaze darted back to her, his right eyebrow cocking at the same time.

"The restraints?"

Aurora nodded and his heart pumped harder, slamming against his chest, driving all his blood to his already hard and aching cock.

"It has been one month to the day since you had to shackle yourself." She advanced on him, each measured step making her hips sway enticingly and making his heart beat faster.

She was right too. It had been a month since he had last suffered an attack of bloodlust.

A whole month.

It stunned him.

They'd had ups and downs. Sometimes he had been doing well until an attack had come out of nowhere, crippling him swiftly and taking him down. Other times, it had come on because he had felt Aurora was in danger, normally because he dreamed of the battle at Vampirerotique and saw her bleeding again. Just thinking about that night stirred darkness in his veins.

"I heard Sera that night." Aurora's soft voice filled his heart with light that chased the darkness back.

Snow frowned, not following her. She blushed. Hard.

"Oh." Snow grinned as it hit him. "Scratch Sera... you're the dark little thing. You want to tie me up."

A beautiful look of panic crossed her face and then she recovered, tipping her chin up and meeting his eyes. "I do. I have been thinking about it since that night and... well, I have never been brave enough to do it because I know you don't like being restrained."

True. He hated it, but she wasn't the only one who had been thinking about it since Sera had put it out there. It was always on his mind.

Snow took a step closer to her, his gaze drifting over her again, lingering on all the spots he had discovered made her crazed with desire. She knew all his spots too, knew precisely where to lick and nip, or swirl her tongue to drive him out of his head with the need to have her.

The thought of her doing that to him while he was tied up and at her mercy, while she was completely in control, set his blood on fire and had his cock harder than steel.

"I have a feeling I might come to like it," he whispered, his voice thick with his desire, a bare growl that brought a beautiful flush of colour to her cheeks. He locked gazes with her, his mind already ten moves ahead, imagining her astride him, riding him while he was restrained, mastering his body and bringing him to a scorching climax.

He breathed hard, closed the distance between them, and grasped the nape of her neck in one hand.

He tilted her head back and stared down into her eyes, lost in their beauty and the desire that shone in them. Passion that ran in her blood too and coursed through his veins. "I will always gladly submit to you. You mastered my heart the first time you looked at me and I have been your willing slave ever since."

She blushed again, pressed her hands against his chest and tiptoed, bringing her mouth to his. Snow growled and claimed her mouth with a feral kiss, bending her to his will, needing a moment in control before he passed it to her.

Aurora kept kissing him as she backed him towards the bed. She broke away when they reached it and slowly unbuttoned his dark shirt, her eyes gradually filling with hunger at the same time, passion that flowed in his veins too. He groaned when she stroked her fingers over his chest, teasing him, leaving streaks of colour on his skin.

She had been surprised when she had discovered she still had that trait about her, and others too. She could teleport as easily as she had been able to before falling from grace, and had taken him to the chateau near Lausanne several times over the few months they had been together, helping him deal with his past and lay it to rest.

She always rewarded him afterwards by taking him to the cabin in the far northern reaches of Norway and spending a few days with him there, erasing his pain with incredible pleasure.

She slipped her hands over his chest and up to his shoulders, and eased his black shirt down his arms.

Panic spiked his blood when she tossed the shirt onto the floor and stepped aside, clearing the way to the bed, but he held it together, breathing through it. Aurora would make it feel good and he wanted to see if he was strong enough to do this now. He was curious about this sort of sex.

Snow clambered onto the black covers of the double bed, coming to settle with his head on the pillows.

He studied her face as she locked his right wrist first. The cuff felt alien to him now, strange. He had worn them every day for as long as he could remember, but had been free of them for a whole month. The marks on his wrists had completely faded in that time and he hadn't thought about the fact that he hadn't needed to be restrained for over thirty days, not until Aurora had mentioned it.

And now she was rewarding him again, turning his experience of restraints into something positive, changing his perception of them and his expectation too. He no longer expected to feel weak and vulnerable, crazed by his bloodlust, a danger to everyone he loved, when the cuffs closed around his limbs.

He expected to feel pleasure, bliss, and his female worshipping his body, and making love with him.

She closed the cuff around his other wrist.

Snow exhaled slowly and was glad that Aurora gave him a moment to grow used to being shackled again. She moved to the foot of the bed and crawled onto it, drawing his attention away from the restraints and to her.

Her white lingerie pressed her breasts together, forming a tempting display as she slowly prowled up the bed towards him. He swallowed and frowned, his nostrils flaring as he caught the heavy scent of her arousal. He bucked his hips, hungry for her touch, for her to slake her desire on him and not stop until she was sated.

She halted with her knees between his spread thighs and grazed her fingertips across his stomach, the caress feather light and teasing.

Streaks of rainbow colours glowed on his skin, a sign of her heightened emotions.

Unleash

He would never tire of that trait. It gave away her feelings, letting him know her mood even when she tried to conceal it from him. If she was upset or hurt, she left darker shades in the wake of her touch, and he knew to do something to make her feel better.

Aurora leaned over him and pressed kisses to his stomach, her breasts brushing his caged erection. He groaned and tipped his head back into the pillows, and grasped the chains of his restraints, pulling them taut.

She licked the top of his tattoo, something she always did when they were making love, and then swirled her tongue around his navel. She always did that too. She had told him once that she couldn't resist it.

They had been skinny-dipping in a lake at the time.

He grinned.

"What are you thinking?" she whispered against his skin, curiosity battling the desire in her eyes.

"The lake." The two words brought a fierce blush to her cheeks and his smile widened.

They hadn't been together for more than two weeks when Aurora had confessed she had watched him swimming in lakes throughout his life, always curious about it. They had used her ability to take them to a warm one and they had swum a while before Aurora had pounced on him.

It had been the first time she had taken the lead, rough in her passion and need for him, dominant as she took him on the sandy shore beneath the moon, her body glistening with moisture.

She blushed whenever he mentioned a lake now, even when he did it casually in conversation.

Of course, he had skilfully worked the word into several conversations with Antoine and everyone else at the theatre. Aurora pinched him whenever he did it, but she hadn't stopped blushing yet.

"After tonight, I might add restraints to my list of words that make my angel blush." He grinned at her and she sat back, folded her arms across her chest, and glared at him.

"I might leave." She fixed him with a look that said she would too.

Snow tugged at his restraints and growled at the thought of her leaving him like this, locked up and unable to get at her. The wicked glint in her eyes said she wouldn't stop at that and would parade around the room in her sexy lingerie too, driving him wild with need for her.

He smiled sweetly.

Aurora relaxed and ran her fingers in patterns across his lower stomach, idly teasing him. "Swear you won't."

"Swear it." He didn't even wait for her to finish before he said it, hungry for her to continue. He could still make her blush with the word lake.

She palmed his erection through his jeans and he rolled his eyes back and groaned, thrusting against her. She undid his belt and jeans, and he watched her as she shimmied backwards, pulling them down his legs. She frowned at his boots and moved off the end of the bed.

Snow toed them off and kicked his feet, tossing each one across the room. His left one slammed into the chest of drawers and almost toppled several of the pillar candles on top of it.

"Eager," Aurora said with a wicked smile.

"Always," Snow countered and she proved he wasn't the only eager one by hastily pulling his jeans off and crawling back up him to tackle his underwear.

She caught the waistband of his black boxers and eased them down, her actions slower now, her expression telling him she was savouring this moment. She always savoured it. He had the feeling that she would never tire of stripping him, revealing his body to her eyes. It made him feel beautiful and deeply desired by his female.

Aurora stopped when his boxers were around his thighs, leaned over him, and looked up into his eyes as she licked the hard length of his shaft.

He groaned and struggled to hold her gaze, his eyes going hooded, pleasure rippling through him. She bent her head and swept her tongue over him again, swirling it around the soft crown this time, a quiet moan leaving her lips. She briefly teased his balls, cradling them and rolling her fingers, and then she was moving again, pulling his underwear down to his feet and off.

She tossed them over her shoulder, her smile wicked again, and surveyed him. He burned wherever her gaze fell, that part of him desperate to feel her touch or her kiss.

She glided her hands over his feet and spread them, and his breathing quickened. He had forgotten this was all about chaining him, had even forgotten the cuffs that held his wrists. She made it all go away whenever she touched him, driving it to the back of his mind, the pleasure she gave him overwhelming any trace of fear or vulnerability.

Her eyes met his again, seeking his approval. He nodded, silently letting her know he was ready for her to restrain his ankles, leaving him completely at her mercy.

She closed the first cuff around his right ankle and carefully secured it, and then dealt with the left one.

Snow held his breath, waiting for a negative reaction.

Nothing.

Just an undeniable need to have her clamber over him, take him into her sweet body, and ride him.

Aurora shimmied out of her knickers, revealing her neat thatch of dark curls, tearing a growl from his throat. He wanted to delve his tongue between those plush petals to drink her nectar. He ached to hear her moan his name in a voice drenched with pleasure and need.

She crawled back on the bed, kissing her way up his legs and then across his hips. She swept her tongue over his tattoo again, pulling another moan from him, and stroked his rigid shaft, leaving streaks of colour down its length. He bucked his hips, rubbing himself against her palm, and bit his lip. He needed more.

She moved on, denying him, her hands skimming over his stomach and fingers tracing the ridges of his tensed muscles. She swept her leg over him, straddling his body, and kept advancing. Her hands rested against his chest and she looked down at him, her mouth tantalisingly close to his. He craned his neck, eager to feel her lips on his, wanting to kiss her.

Aurora lowered herself to almost within his reach and then drew back again, a smile curving her lips.

He growled and pulled on his restraints as he planted his elbows on the mattress and tried again to reach her.

Tried and failed. She kissed over his jaw, his chin, down his neck, always evading his mouth. Tease. She knew what he wanted most and she was going to deny him until he was crazed with a need to kiss her, straining against his bonds and desperate for relief.

"Kiss me," he husked, pleading her to put him out of his misery and give him the pleasure he needed.

She stroked his cheek, her gaze holding his, the green-to-blue of her irises dark with passion.

Her lips descended on his and he didn't need to take the lead to get what he wanted. She kissed him fiercely, dominating his mouth, flooding him with pleasure that melted his bones.

He relaxed into the bed beneath her, lost in the feel of her mastering him, her soft warm tongue stroking and teasing his. She flicked it over his left canine and he groaned as his fangs extended, drawn out by her teasing.

It didn't stop her.

She caressed his fangs, sending hot shivers running through his blood, adding a new level of pleasure that he couldn't take. He rocked his hips, thrusting against nothing but air, unable to control himself.

Damn, but he could climax from just this.

She moaned and her hands shook against his chest, her need echoing through him, telling him that her thoughts had taken a dark and tempting path.

Aurora shot back, suddenly pushing herself up, and stared at his mouth, her gaze near-black with desire and her rosy lips parted. She frowned, licked her lips, and pressed her short nails into his chest.

"Bite me," she uttered, completely undoing him, pushing him to the edge of control.

So much want in her voice. So much need. He knew he should deny her in case this was just the heat of the moment talking, but he couldn't.

She pulled all the strands of her black hair from the smooth unmarked left side of her throat and continued to stare at his mouth.

"Please?" She lowered herself and undulated her hips, rubbing her naked core against him. If she meant to convince him to go through with it, she was wasting her time. He didn't need convincing.

"Later," he pushed the word out, not wanting to bite her while restrained. He wanted to bite her when he was the one in control.

She mewled, the sound deliciously erotic, and rotated her hips against him, her wet heat slipping over his length, making it throb and ache.

If she kept doing that, he would be climaxing before he was even inside her. Her face twisted in frustration and he could sense her desire taking control of her, driving her to seek her satisfaction. She bit her lip and then swallowed hard, her eyes falling to his mouth again. What was she thinking to turn her eyes so dark, flooded with hunger?

Snow found out when she bravely rose off him and crawled further up his body. She ran her hands along his tensed arms, moaning as her fingers traced the contours of his muscles, and then swept them back towards him.

Her teeth worried her lower lip again and she tangled her fingers in his white hair, forcing his head back and his chin up. She kissed him, nipping his lip with her teeth, driving him right to the edge, and then pulled back, leaving him panting for more.

He wanted to taste her again.

She intoxicated him.

Made him drunk with need.

Aurora moved again and he groaned when he realised her intention. She gripped the headboard and pressed her knees into the pillows above his shoulders, positioning her core above his face. Snow craned his neck and flicked his tongue over her inner thigh, ripping a moan from her. She trembled as she lowered herself, and he delved his tongue into her moist folds.

A gasp escaped her and then she settled more firmly, pressing herself to his mouth. He laved her with his tongue, a groan rumbling through his chest at the first sweet taste of her flesh. She tensed and he worshipped every inch of her that he could reach, teasing her nub and then spearing her core with his tongue, driving her to the same edge where he hovered.

She rocked her hips, riding his face, her breathless moans cranking him tighter, until he couldn't stop himself from bucking his hips too, aching to feel her riding him hard.

She tensed, going rigid, and lifted off him, placing herself beyond his reach.

"Aurora," he whispered, wanting her to come back, needing more of her. He wanted to push her over the edge.

She had other plans.

She was going to push him over first. He groaned as she shimmied down the length of him, sweeping her lips over his body, and her hand wrapped around his length. She stroked him up and down, propelling him back to the edge, her wicked smile saying she wouldn't stop this time.

Snow bucked his hips and pulled at his restraints, moaning with each glide of her hand over his hard flesh.

"Aurora." It came out as a groan this time, filled with hunger, an overwhelming need to be inside her.

She moved astride him and gripped his cock, poising it beneath her. Snow stared at his erection, couldn't drag his gaze away as she eased the head into her hot sheath and took her hand away, pressing both of them against his hips. She eased down onto him, her pace torturous, taking him into her inch-by-agonizing-inch.

He gripped the restraints, clutching the thick chains, trying to resist the need to thrust into her. She pressed down on his hips, her strength ensuring he couldn't move and was completely at her mercy. Snow stared, breathing hard, watching her body envelop him and join them as one.

The tip of him reached the deepest point within her and she rose off him again, withdrawing all the way before taking him back inside.

He tipped his head back and stared down at her, lost in the pleasure fluttering across her face as she rode him with long strokes that gradually quickened.

Her breasts bounced in her white satin and lace bodice top, her eyes turning hooded, her bliss flowing over him. She clutched his hips as tightly as he clutched the chains, using them as an anchor as the incredible sensation of her hot tight body gloving his, the feel of her riding him, and the sight of her lost to desire, combined and began to overwhelm him.

"Snow." She rode him harder, shorter bursts that pushed him deeper inside her, as far as he could go, and rotated her hips. Her teeth sank into her lower lip.

Snow groaned and rocked against her, curling his hips and thrusting his cock hard into her core, taking them both higher. Release crept up his shaft but he focused on giving her pleasure, wanting to bring her to a shattering climax before his own took him.

Aurora opened her eyes and locked gazes with him, frowning as he countered each of her movements, driving into her as she bore down and pulling away when she rose up. She breathed harder, panting as pleasure tightened her frown and drew his own eyebrows together. More. She was close, her body tightening around his, tugging at his shaft, telling him she would shatter soon.

He pumped her harder and she arched her back in response, almost undoing him. She was so tight around him, so hot and wet. He grunted and tipped his head back, arching off the bed as she pressed his hips down and quickened her pace, seizing control once more.

"Snow," she uttered in passion-drenched bliss and jerked forwards. Her hands trembled against his hips, her thighs quivered and her core milked him as her orgasm crashed over her.

Snow growled. He wanted out. Now. He pulled on the restraints, fighting them even as she continued to ride him, driving him towards bliss. Not yet.

"Aurora," he said and her eyes slowly opened and the haze cleared from them. "Unleash me."

She dazedly looked at the cuffs and then back at him.

"Want to bite you." It was all he needed to say to have her lifting off him and shakily clambering over the bed, tackling his restraints with trembling fingers.

The moment Snow was free, he dragged her to him and kissed her hard, clasping her against him with one hand against the nape of her neck and the other on her hip.

He delved that hand between her thighs, tearing a moan from her as he plunged his fingers into her body, feeling her still quivering from her climax. He wanted back inside her, in more ways than one this time.

Snow rose to kneel in the middle of the bed and came around behind her. He grasped her nape and pushed her forwards, and she gripped the steel headboard with both hands, bending over.

He kneed her legs apart and teased her towards another climax with swirls of his fingers around her pert nub, until she was moaning and writhing, and begging him for more.

He took his hand away, positioned his cock at her entrance, and then gripped her hip with one hand and her neck with the other and growled as he thrust deep into her.

She rocked forwards and cried out, but quickly pushed against the steel bars of the headboard, holding herself steady.

Snow curled his hips and grunted with each deep plunge of his body into hers, grinding his teeth together as she clenched him in her core, gripping him hard. He grasped her neck harder, forcing her to remain bending forwards as he took her hard and fast, dominating her. His hips pistoned, wild and relentless, driven by a hunger to possess her. All of her.

She arched forwards, pressing back against him, forcing him to take her harder, pulling him in deeper.

His cock ached, his balls tightening as release climbed again. He growled and tightened his grip on her neck and pulled her away from the headboard, bringing her back flush against his front. He lowered himself so he could keep pounding into her, needing to be the one in control now.

Aurora seized his hand on her hip and brought it to her mound. She guided him to her and touched herself with him.

He had never experienced anything as erotic as touching her together, her hand guiding his, showing him what she needed.

He released her neck and clasped her breast, tearing the soft material of her corset down and thumbing her nipple as he drove into her, as deep as he could go. She tensed around him, on the precipice of another release, and slung her free arm over her shoulder and buried her fingers in his hair, clutching him to her.

"Snow. Now," she uttered, a breathless command he immediately obeyed.

He grabbed her chin, yanked her head to one side, and struck hard, sinking his fangs into her throat.

She screamed his name as her body seized and then shattered around his. Her bliss flowed into him with her sweet blood, sending him over the edge with her, and he growled into her throat as he thrust his cock into her and spilled himself, throbbing discordantly to her.

Heat blazed through him like wildfire, the combination of their dual ecstasy and her blood, and the feel of her shaking in his arms wringing another release from him. His knees weakened in the wake of it, bones turning soft and useless, and he sank back with his body still impaling hers, ending up with her on his lap.

Snow drank slowly, lost in the sensations rushing through him, easing himself down. Aurora breathed hard in his arms, trembling against him, her hand still clutching his hair and quiet moans still escaping her lips.

"Well..." she whispered, her voice hoarse and tight. "I definitely... want to do... that again."

Snow released her throat and licked the puncture marks, a chuckle rumbling in his chest at the same time. He pressed a kiss to the marks and lingered there, savouring the feel of his female shaking in his arms, sated because of him.

His female.

She bore more than one set of his marks and he was old-fashioned like Antoine. Those marks announced her as his, telling the world that she belonged to him.

"I almost wish we hadn't waited so long to try it out." She giggled and leaned back into him, her hand slipping from his hair to caress his shoulder and then fall onto her lap.

"Me too." Snow pressed another kiss to her throat and then eased her off him and gathered her into his arms. He shoved the wrinkled black covers down with his legs, laid her down on the bed and then joined her.

She pulled the covers over them both and curled up beside him, her head on his chest and her heart beating rapidly against his side. Snow wrapped his arms around her and held her against him, still slowly coming down from one hell of a high. Aurora kissed his chest and he angled his head, pressed his lips to her brow and closed his eyes.

He was blessed.

He had felt cursed for most of his life and now he felt blessed.

He was blessed to have Aurora, and his new family, and he couldn't wait to see what his future would bring. His family was growing, Vampirerotique was going strong, and he had an angel in his arms.

A woman who knew all of him, had seen him at his best and at his worst, and still wanted to be with him.

A female who had given him a reason to fight and to live, and who constantly watched over him, keeping him on track and moving forwards towards overcoming his bloodlust.

He would be forever grateful to her.

Unleash

"Aurora?" he whispered, hoping she hadn't fallen asleep already because he had something he needed to tell her, something he thought he would never feel and never say to a female, and had never said to her.

"Mmm?" she murmured sleepily. That wouldn't do.

Snow cupped her cheek and drew away from her, and she lifted her eyelids and looked up at him, her beautiful green-to-blue eyes striking him right down to his heart as they shone at him with affection.

He smoothed his palm over her cheek and dragged his courage up, assured by the tenderness in her gaze that what he had to say would only please her.

"I love you, Aurora."

Her rosy lips curled into a wide smile and her eyes twinkled at him, the colours shimmering like the aurora borealis he had named her for the night they had met two thousand years ago.

She pulled herself up his body and kissed him briefly, softly, before drawing back and brushing her thumbs across his cheeks as she stared down into his eyes.

"I love you too."

Snow lured her down and kissed her again, showing her how much that meant to him and how much he adored her.

His beautiful female.

Two worlds had collided.

Two hearts had become one.

This prince had finally caught his angel.

And he would never let her go.

The End

ABOUT THE AUTHOR

Felicity Heaton is a New York Times and USA Today best-selling author who writes passionate paranormal romance books. In her books she creates detailed worlds, twisting plots, mind-blowing action, intense emotion and heart-stopping romances with leading men that vary from dark deadly vampires to sexy shape-shifters and wicked werewolves, to sinful angels and hot demons!

If you're a fan of paranormal romance authors Lara Adrian, J R Ward, Sherrilyn Kenyon, Kresley Cole, Gena Showalter, Larissa Ione and Christine Feehan then you will enjoy her books too.

If you love your angels a little dark and wicked, her best-selling Her Angel romance series is for you. If you like strong, powerful, and dark vampires then try the Vampires Realm romance series or any of her stand alone vampire romance books. If you're looking for vampire romances that are sinful, passionate and erotic then try her London Vampires romance series. Or if you like hot-blooded alpha heroes who will let nothing stand in the way of them claiming their destined woman then try her Eternal Mates series. It's packed with sexy heroes in a world populated by elves, vampires, fae, demons, shifters, and more. If sexy Greek gods with incredible powers battling to save our world and their home in the Underworld are more your thing, then be sure to step into the world of Guardians of Hades.

If you have enjoyed this story, please take a moment to contact the author at **author@felicityheaton.com** or to post a review of the book online

Connect with Felicity:
Website – http://www.felicityheaton.com
Blog – http://www.felicityheaton.com/blog/
Twitter – http://twitter.com/felicityheaton
Facebook – http://www.facebook.com/felicityheaton
Goodreads – http://www.goodreads.com/felicityheaton
Mailing List – http://www.felicityheaton.com/newsletter.php

FIND OUT MORE ABOUT HER BOOKS AT:
http://www.felicityheaton.com

Printed in Great Britain
by Amazon